201.7

Scribe Publications
INSIDE TRADER

Dear Noriko

I hope I can MAKE
You Laugh
AND ALSO Shed
A Little Tear
with a big HUG

From

J. Trader

This book is dedicated, in the hope that it might be of value, to my family: Sasha, Jim, Quinn, Eliza, and Jamie. And to Bobo, without whom there would have been no family. With much love.

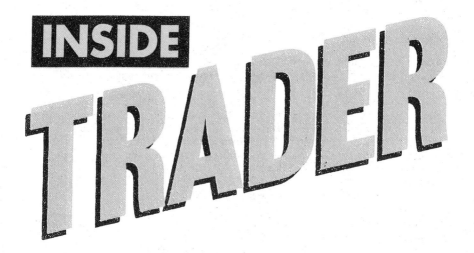

TRADER FAULKNER

SCRIBE

Melbourne • London

Scribe Publications Pty Ltd
18–20 Edward St, Brunswick, Victoria 3056, Australia
50A Kingsway Place, Sans Walk, London, EC1R 0LU, United Kingdom

Published by Scribe 2014

This edition published by arrangement with Quartet Books Limited,
a member of the Namara Group, London

Printed and bound in China by 1010 Printing

National Library of Australia
Cataloguing-in-Publication data

Faulkner, Trader, 1927- (author).

Inside Trader / Trader Faulkner.

9781922070852 (paperback)

1. Faulkner, Trader, 1927-. 2. Actors–England–Biography.
3. Australians–England–Biography.

792.0280924

scribepublications.com.au
scribepublications.co.uk

CONTENTS

PREFACE

IT WAS ON a chilly morning, 1 May 1950, when I first set foot on English soil at Southampton after a month's voyage from my home in Sydney, Australia. Stepping down the gangplank with my dad's old battered suitcase, I caught a train for Waterloo and took a room at a hotel in Victoria.

I'd been invited to London some months before by the great British theatre director Tyrone Guthrie, who had seen me as Dr Caius in *The Merry Wives of Windsor* in a Sydney theatre and offered me the juvenile lead in *Top of the Ladder*, a play that was to star John Mills in London that summer. All I had to do was get myself there and I was promised a job.

And there I was — a twenty-two-year-old fledgling actor from down under with very little money in my pockets, but filled with excited expectations of finding the glorious theatrical career in London that my good friend and mentor Peter Finch had assured me would be mine if only I made the effort.

As soon as I could, I telephoned Guthrie at the number he had given me — only to be told that the play he had spoken of had been postponed, and that at the moment he had nothing to offer me. Full of apologies, he assured me that he would sort something out, and rang off.

Two months went by. In the meantime, I found digs and, desperate for an income, took a menial job at a Lyons Corner House while I made the rounds looking for an agent to take me on — without success.

Then one morning the phone rang. It was the H.M. Tennent office in Shaftesbury Avenue offering me an audition. A replacement was required for Richard Burton in John Gielgud's production of Christopher Fry's *The Lady's Not for Burning*. Burton was off to

Stratford to play *Henry V* and Gielgud — who was also starring in the play, along with Burton and Pamela Brown — wanted to take his successful West End production on to Broadway. Apparently, Tyrone Guthrie had contacted H.M. Tennent (the producers of *The Lady's Not for Burning*) and suggested that I should be seen.

After attending a general audition, at which the playwright Christopher Fry weeded out all unsuitable applicants, I was surprisingly called back to read again — this time for the director himself. On the appointed day, when I had finished my reading, a tall, elegant man with a very large nose sauntered down the aisle and addressed me from the stalls.

'A very interesting reading.'

'Thank you, sir.'

'I'm John Gielgud. What's your name?'

'Ronald Faulkner, sir.'

'Ronald! Oh, God! What a dreary name!'

'Well, sir,' I said, 'down under I'm known by my nickname, Trader.'

'Trader! What a wonderful name! We'll bill you on Broadway as Trader. Welcome to the company.'

And that's how it all began.

How did I get that nickname? Well, that's another story.

PART ONE

AUSTRALIA

CHAPTER ONE

UNWANTED BUT UNSTOPPABLE

MY FATHER AND MY MOTHER always maintained that I should never have been born, because they were both incapable of dealing with a screaming baby.

'Your father and I did everything possible to get rid of you,' my mother claimed, 'but you were obviously perverse from the moment of conception.'

'What a beautiful little boy,' my parents' friends said. 'But he's so quiet. He never makes a sound!'

I defy anyone to make a sound when they're fed on nothing but dill water! My granny, Mum's mother, with her corseted Victorian ideas, had told her: 'Breast-feeding is disgusting, Sheila. You must take something to dry up your milk.'

I think my mother took belladonna, which soon resulted in a drought on the nipple. For weeks on end, poor infant Ronald was given dill water and nothing else. That, on Granny's advice, would 'keep the wee baby quiet.'

One day my granny's brother's wife, Aunt Lily MacDonald, arrived.

'Sheila,' she said, 'your wee boy seems to sleep a lot.'

'Yes, thank God!' replied Mum. 'He never stops howling when he's awake.'

'What do you give him to eat?'

Apparently, I was shortly thereafter taken to the doctor, who diagnosed me as undernourished and sent me to the Tressilian

1

Children's Hospital in Sydney where I remained for six months. When I eventually came home, my parents decided I was to be adopted. Dad, a film actor, was then an ageing fifty-five through drink and wild living. My mother, a former ballerina, was thirty-five and they were definitely not parental material. They simply didn't know what to do with a squealing baby. So my Aunt Lil said: 'I'd be delighted to take the wee child.'

But 'that natural charm, and those gorgeous blue eyes' — obviously not my quote — finally won Dad and Mum over and they decided to keep their 'infuriating little liability'.

Next whooping cough set in and I kept the poor parents awake night and day with a retching cough. In spite of everything, I recovered, and slowly grew, to quote Mum, 'uglier and wickeder with every month'.

My father adored me and, being handsome and very well-built, was always a presence of protective strength to me. My mother, who also adored me, used to tease me, called me 'Diddle' (which I detested), and smacked me at every provocation.

We lived in Sydney's surfing paradise, Manly, on the northern side of Sydney harbour, and the storms that came unbridled across the sea from New Zealand and beyond were ferocious. Along the shoreline from South Steyne to Queenscliff there was, and still is, an avenue of very tall Norfolk pine trees. The prevailing north-easterly wind would sough through those pine fronds like the exhalations of evil demons. That was what I thought as a child of two, lying terrified in my cot. I remember hiding under the bedclothes as the wind howled at the doors and windows.

My very earliest memory is of standing in my wooden-slatted cot, listening to a raging wind from across the sitting room where I had been wheeled to give my exhausted parents a quiet night's sleep. Suddenly, the sitting-room window flew open and the veranda door banged with such violence that I screamed. To the child that I was, the fury of the wind roaring off the Pacific was terrifying. It is my first recollection of the threatening power of the elements. Within seconds, both parents came in and I was rescued. But what remains so vividly in my memory is the way that angry wind slammed the door.

Ours was the top flat of a duplex block called Ceramic, built in 1906 and locally famous because the bus conductors always used to call out 'Any Ceramic?' midway along North Steyne. Invariably, hands would go up and the local Manly to Queenscliff bus would stop right outside the door.

The stories of my colourful father make me wish I'd been old enough to really know him before he was taken from me.

The veranda of our top-floor flat, number six, was separated from the neighbour's by a wooden partition. There was also a concrete balustrade that you could lean on and look out across the road to the beach and the rolling breakers beyond. My father would often stand there smoking his pipe and gazing at the sea. For a time, a nurse lived next door at number five with her patient, Ceessi. Ceessi had been a violent lunatic and was on remand from the asylum. As Mum told the story many years later, the nurse must have had him tethered because they used to hear chains rattling in the night.

One evening, Dad was calmly smoking his pipe, deep in thought, when suddenly round the panelled partition an ape-like man loomed into prominence, laughing manically. Dad immediately rocketed backwards at breakneck speed.

'Get back onto your own veranda, you witless bastard!'

Dad apparently nearly choked on his pipe. (Mum had witnessed this exchange through the sitting room window.)

The outcome was that the nurse and Ceessi had to vacate five, and I think Ceessi was returned to Callan Park loony bin.

One other bizarre event happened just before I was born. The wooden panelling had blown down in a storm so there was no divide between the verandas of five and six. According to Mum, she was heavily pregnant with me and needed constantly to lie down. The occupants of five at this time were a genteel elderly couple, Judge Backhouse and his wife Fanny. The judge had fallen on hard times and they had been threatened with the bailiffs. Dad had got wind of this and warned my mother on no account to encourage any social contact with Fanny. Mum was soon to learn why.

Dad was away filming that day at Cinesound Studios in Sydney. About two in the afternoon, while Mum was resting, there was a knock at the back door.

'Coooeee!'

'Yes, Mrs Backhouse. What is it?'

'Mrs Faulkner, we have a slight problem. We're expecting a call from the bailiffs. Would you mind terribly if one or two small items crept onto your veranda, well out of sight?'

Mum felt too ill to raise objections.

'All right, but get them back before John comes home or God help you!'

Fanny reassured her. Mum went back to bed and fell into a deep sleep.

She was woken suddenly later by an almighty crash and Dad's voice booming from the darkness.

'Sheila! Where in God's name am I?'

Mum turned on the light to find Dad in the narrow inner hallway, his bulky figure wedged tightly into a hipbath and the hall stacked high with crockery and other odds and ends.

'That old bitch!' Dad raged. 'We've got the entire Backhouse domestic movables in here!'

Apparently, the panic-stricken Fanny had transferred the entire contents of her kitchen and bathroom into our kitchen and hallway. Some time later the bailiffs had arrived and Fanny could now be seen through her sitting room window entertaining them with glasses of gin. So Dad — having finally been prised out of Fanny's hipbath — simply took everything and hurled the lot back onto the Backhouse's veranda.

Prawns were one of Dad's many gastronomical weaknesses — preferably washed down with glasses of whisky. A gentleman normally of impeccable manners, Dad, who was leaning on the balustrade to enjoy his plate of crustaceans, was on this occasion too fortified with booze to realise that the husks he was throwing onto the newspaper at his feet were being blown in the strong wind down onto the veranda of the Miss Fenwicks, three maiden ladies living in four directly below. Dad's name for them was the 'Daisybells'. He had apparently finished his lunch and was sleeping it off when the front doorbell rang. Dad opened the door to a distraught Daisybell.

'Mr Faulkner! Prawn husks have been raining down on our veranda smelling the place out! Do you know anything about this?'

'Dear Miss Fenwick, how disgusting! No! I never touch prawns. Doctor's orders. But I'll come down at once and sweep them up for you. Prawns all over your veranda — how disgusting!'

As Mum used to say, 'John could have charmed his own executioner, but when in the wrong he did have the decency to try and put things right.'

From as far back as I can remember until the day she died my relationship with my mother always involved large amounts of rage, laughter, and love. From my infancy, she would tease me and I would lash out and try to strike her in retaliation. In the early years Dad had two walking sticks that hung from a shelf. I would grab one and try to whack Mum either on her bottom or her legs. My lithe mother would quickly grab the other stick and set to raining thumps on my bottom or the calves of my legs. With her longer arms she invariably won. Dad would always come in sooner or later and peace would ensue.

My mother didn't have the temperament to control me subtly and her reasoning with me was ineffectual. Left alone with her so much I quickly learned how to manipulate her.

One day, walking along the street with her, I was apparently in a great sulk. I think I wanted a penny for a Nestlé chocolate and Mum had refused to let me have one. So I crossed a dangerous road and sat down on the beach. My poor mother, in a hurry, grabbed me by the collar and propelled me back along the road. I started howling. I'd seen a man approaching from the other direction and must have decided to play this moment for all it was worth, crying and yelping. Mum started laying into me — always the legs, never my head or face — and was achieving some very stinging direct hits. Suddenly, the man rushed forward.

'Madam, if you hit that child once more I'll report you to the police!'

'He's my child and I'll do what I like with him,' Mum replied.

Little Ronald threw himself towards the man and wrapped himself round his trouser leg.

'Thank you so much, Mister. Me mum's very cruel.'

Oh, Mum. Wherever you may be, please forgive that little monster!

An unforgettable incident occurred around this time: little Ronald got himself well and truly constipated. Eight or nine days went by with no deliveries. Day after day, 'Have you been, darling?' Granny would ask.

'No. I'll die soon if I don't go, Granny! Why can't I? What's happening?'

There's no terror like a child's over the simplest things.

Well, castor oil had no effect and they finally decided to call in Nurse Cuneen. This ferocious-looking lady arrived at the door carrying a doctor's bag from which she produced a white can with a hosepipe attached to it and a nozzle at the end. There were whispers, and I made for the door. Too late! Nurse Cuneen, Dad, Mum, Granny and Grandfather grabbed me and held me face down on the bed.

Without going into detail, to violently pin down a five-year-old child and subject him to such humiliation was parental folly. Had it been explained to me beforehand what was about to happen, and why, I might have accepted the inevitable; but to take me by surprise, and with force, was well-intentioned stupidity.

I can only say that as a result of the events of that day I've gone through my life with a most irrational loathing for the physical practices of homosexuality.

For the brief time I knew my father, I always felt absolutely safe when he was nearby. One day he took me for a walk down Ceramic Lane. Suddenly, from round the corner came a horse and milkcart, careering towards us. Dad threw himself on top of me to protect me. At the last minute the cart swerved, and as Dad let fly in rage at the departing cart I had my first lesson on how and when to use foul language.

One Halloween night, however, he was away and I was staying with my grandparents at The Orchard, Manly Vale, which was for me a place of total enchantment — with a magnificent garden filled with fruit trees and beautiful flowers, the domain of birds and insects in which I could amuse myself endlessly.

That summer evening my grandfather — whom I called 'Ganfie' — had decided to give me a magical surprise. Inside a glass-panelled lantern he placed a little doll in a white gown. In the four corners he had placed four lit candles. He hung this lantern on the branch of a tree where it swung very gently in the breeze.

Meanwhile, I was kept inside with Granny and my mother, squirming with excitement as we awaited my grandfather's call to come out.

It must have been a moonless night, because I remember pitch darkness. When the call came I was told to close my eyes and was led into the garden between Mum and Granny. Off we went down the familiar stone steps and across the large lawn. Finally we stopped.

'Now, open your eyes, Ronald, and see the dancing fairy.'

I did. But the vision of the tiny revolving figure in her glass prison absolutely terrified me. It was as though my fear of the dark was personified in this minute creature, trapped within the lighted box. If she escaped I was sure that she would fly through the darkness and bewitch me — just as had happened in all the stories of fairies, goblins and witches that my mother regularly read to me.

I screamed and ran for my life. The light was on in the sitting room. I remember hiding under a chair but very little else. All that remains is a recollection of the blackest fear and a sense of helpless desperation.

My father was usually in the fortunate position of being able to leave the domestic responsibility of childcare to my mother. But whenever Mum's temper was fraying, Dad would suggest I be given a treat — which meant getting us both away to avoid any further confrontations. This invariably meant some exciting excursion for me.

In March 1932, the Sydney Harbour Bridge had finally been finished. A few days after its official opening Dad decided to give me such a treat — an occasion that turned out to be terrifying and unforgettable.

We arrived at Wynyard Station to catch the tram across the bridge to Manly, which you could do in those days. We entered what seemed to be an underground cavern smelling of fresh concrete where we boarded a tram called a 'Jumping Jack' — two small highly-sprung carriages linked together. We sat outside. The noise of this tram in the pitch-dark tunnel was deafening, and the tram itself seemed to hop along like a kangaroo.

Suddenly, we emerged into dazzling sunshine. In a short while we approached the southern entrance of the great cantilevered bridge. Huge steel supporting girders seemed to soar upwards above me as we started across. I looked down at rippling, green water hundreds of feet below, and those old, coal-burning Sydney ferries belching black smoke as they passed slowly beneath us. Absolutely petrified, I buried my face in Dad's waistcoat. The height, the vastness, and the howling wind up there on that brilliantly sunny afternoon is an indelible memory for me. I must have clung like a leech to my father and we had gone a long way beyond the bridge before I dared look up again.

CHAPTER TWO

MY PARENTS

MY MOTHER WAS BORN at West Hall in Suffolk in 1892, the only child of Scottish, upperclass, and very conservative, parents. She adored her father, William Whytock, who as a young man had sold out his share in Whytock and Reid, a well-known carpet shop in Edinburgh, to farm in South America. With the sudden death of his father, his South American stay was cut short and he returned to Scotland to look after his four sisters, finding work as a factor to Lord Wemyss at Gullane, near Edinburgh. During this period he met and married my grandmother, Mary. Shortly after the wedding, they moved to Suffolk, where William found work as factor for Lord Stradbrook. Reared in the Suffolk countryside, my mother grew up a wild little tomboy, and was always fighting with the village lads — several of whom she left with a bloody nose. I know little else about her youth except that she drove her mother to despair because she simply despised the bourgeois respectability that Granny championed.

Still driven by the urge to find his fortune elsewhere, my grandfather left his Suffolk employment in 1898 and took his small family to Pietermaritzberg in South Africa — arriving just in time for the commencement of the Boer War. He then hastily booked return passage to Britain, where he settled the family first at Exmouth in Dorset, then at Wimbledon, after which he found work with the Foreign Office, remaining there until the Great War.

From an early age my mother was obsessed with dance and dancing, and after the family had settled near London she was able to train under Edouard Espinosa, one of the British patriarchs of the dance, who later founded the British Ballet Organisation.

My mother's dancing career was an exotic one. For his first London season in 1911, the great Russian impresario Sergei Diaghilev took on six English girls to join his *Ballets Russes* company. His remark, after my nineteen-year-old mother had danced for him, was: 'I'll take the little English girl who smiles as she moves. Her technique is limited, but she dances with her soul!' Diaghilev's *Ballets Russes* had taken Paris by storm in 1909, so expectation was electric. Mother spent the entire London season dancing with his company, which included the great Nijinsky as its principal dancer, and was able years later to tell some wonderful stories about her experiences.

It seems that the lesbians in the company found the slender new English girls very attractive, and when Mum and her friend Pica de Valera were lining up with the others to dip their toe shoes in the resin box, or bending over in their dressing room, they would often be 'touched up' by their Russian colleagues. Having had enough of these indecent fondlings, Mum went to Diaghilev himself about it. The great man roared with laughter. Apparently, the situation appealed to his sense of fun.

The following evening there was a little screened-off section of the dressing room with a notice attached: *For les demoiselles Sheilova and Pica. STRICTLY PRIVATE!* Beneath the notice was Diaghilev's signature.

Needless to say, there were no problems thereafter.

My mother's account of the first night of *Spectre of the Rose* in London gives a wonderful idea of Diaghilev's unique talent.

At the final dress rehearsal, Nijinsky — standing on a raised platform offstage — was to fly into view through an open window and land beside his partner, Karsavina, asleep in her chair. As they rehearsed this moment, Diaghilev suddenly ordered the orchestra and dancers to stop.

'This moment is not working for you, Vaslav,' he said. 'You *must* symbolise the spirit of the rose, but at the moment you are simply a wonderful dancer with a spectacular elevation. Wait a minute! I think I might have the answer.'

He sent for Nijinsky's dresser, gave her sixpence, and told her to go next door to the Covent Garden flower market and buy a dozen pink roses. When she returned with them he then sent her off to fetch a needle and a reel of pink cotton. He also asked for several tins of talcum powder. Nijinsky was called and Diaghilev set to work lightly sewing pink rose petals onto his flimsy, diaphanous costume — enough to cover it entirely. Finally he sent for three flymen and gave each a tin of talcum powder. They were to take their positions up in the flies and when they received the signal they were to sprinkle the powder down onto the stage below. Everything, according to the Maestro, had to be timed to the split-second.

Before curtain-up that evening everyone took their positions, with Nijinsky on his elevated rostrum offstage and Karsarvina asleep in her chair. High above the stage, the three flymen prepared themselves and the houselights dimmed. Diaghilev had wanted to achieve a pale green effect, using what were called 'limes' for the lighting. The music and the lighting began softly; then, as the curtain rose on the scene, what seemed like a very fine, shimmering mist settled slowly over the stage. Finally a lithe figure flew upwards and outwards through the open window and onto the stage. As he descended, dozens of pale pink rose petals floated from the ethereal form of Nijinsky — who had now truly become the very spirit of a rose.

That is how my mother conjured up that moment for me as a child years later. She absolutely worshipped Diaghilev, and begged her straitlaced parents to see the shows. I know little of their response except that Granny Whytock felt that Nijinsky's rose was 'rather indecently clad'.

My grandfather's introduction to Diaghilev is worth describing.

One afternoon, my mother stood at the stagedoor with her father, waiting for Diaghilev to emerge. When he finally appeared, Mum seized Ganfie's arm and drew him over to introduce them. The Maestro, she said, was aloof but utterly charming. Mum told me that he always used a favourite eau de cologne by Guerlain called 'Mitsouko'.

'Well, Daddy,' she asked Ganfie when the great man had departed, 'what did you think of Diaghilev?"

'My God, what a cad! And what an odour!'

★   ★   ★

In 1912 my mother was back with Diaghilev's company, dancing in *Les Sylphides*. Then, in 1913, the *Ballets Russes* returned several times and she was gaining priceless experience either watching or participating in such ballets as *Thamar*, *Petrouchka*, *Les Sylphides*, and *Le Carnival*, all of which were now in the repertoire.

In July 1913 the Diaghilev company appeared at the Drury Lane Theatre for four performances of *Le Sacre de Printemps*, which had been premiered in Paris the previous May to a rowdy, riotous audience. According to my mother (as one of the dancers involved), this ballet with Stravinsky's complex rhythms offered an unprecedented challenge to Nijinsky's choreography.

Nevertheless, *Le Sacre de Printemps* took London by storm.

At about this time my mother's mother, Mary, sailed from England to visit her brother Jim MacDonald in Sydney, and was very favourably impressed with the country and its climate. She returned with glowing stories of her stay and, in 1917, after my grandfather had become sickened by the patriotic fervour in Britain that had caused so many young men to be sacrificed in the trenches, he decided to heed his wife's positive reports about her visit 'down under' and to emigrate there with his family. They left England for Australia aboard the SS *Suevic*, and as they steamed through the Channel in the night the SS *Athenic*, immediately ahead of them in the shipping lanes, was torpedoed by a German U-boat.

'After that, we ran "dark" to Free Town in Sierra Leone,' my mother told me, 'and then safely round the Cape of Good Hope to Sydney.'

Once there, grandfather Whytock bought property in Manly Vale, across the harbour from Sydney, at number 1 Lovett Street — a weatherboard cottage (The Orchard), and an acre of ground, where later I was to spend many happy days as a boy.

No sooner had they arrived than Mum was off on tour, dancing her way through Java and the East Indies. I remember as a child hearing her description of the golden-domed Swaidagong Pagoda in Rangoon.

She told me that she became gravely ill in Java. While dancing one evening, she drank a bit of the local water and typhoid fever was the outcome. The company must have embarked the next day because her fever broke out on the voyage. Fortunately, a kind mixed-race Malay girl nursed her and she recovered.

When Mum disembarked at Karachi she was met by a British Indian Army officer, a friend of her father. She and the girl who had nursed her came down the gangway together, arm in arm. The officer greeted my mother warmly, then took her aside.

'Where is your friend going to stay while you are here?'

'With me, of course.'

'Out of the question,' replied the officer. 'She's a half-caste!'

'That girl saved my life. Wherever I go I shall look after her as best I can.'

I don't know the outcome of this story, but I trust Mum was as good as her word and made sure the girl had some money when they parted company. All I do know is that my mother went on to tour India dancing and that, at one point, accepting the invitation of an army officer, she rode pillion on his motorbike up through the Khyber Pass that links Afghanistan to modern Pakistan.

'We sped like a shooting star through that mountain pass,' she told me. 'And at times I felt it was going to be my last journey on Earth!'

Not long after my mother's return to Australia, she happened to meet my father in Sydney. John Faulkner soon fell in love with the pretty ballerina and asked her to marry him. Apparently, however, he was still involved with another woman. My mother, who had fallen for the dashing Jack, was tempted by his proposal. But she had already accepted the offer to be a part of Anna Pavlova's ballet company for its upcoming tour of South and Central America, and would soon have to set off to join them. So, telling him to 'get himself sorted out', she left the door open for a possible future liaison and departed for South America.

Her months spent with the Pavlova company were filled with adventures she was never to forget. Apparently, Pavlova had a sadistic streak; when the girls had to rehearse those cat-like leaps called *entrechats* she would sweep a cane across the floor and if the girls didn't elevate absolutely on the right note they'd receive a crack across the ankles. Nevertheless, my mother adored her. 'When madam danced, she was possessed with a force I can only describe as superhuman — or even divine! It wasn't so much what she did, which was often very simple, but the way she did it. She spent hours studying swans until, as she danced, she virtually became a swan in human form.'

In Mexico City they were performing in the bullring to cater for the size of the audience when all the lighting suddenly fused. Pavlova was in the middle of an excerpt from *Swan Lake* when the huge arena was plunged into darkness. Pavlova and her husband Victor Dandré soon hit on a solution. She made an announcement to the audience, declaring that she was sure the Mexican *caballeros* could rescue the spectacle if all who possessed motorcars would drive them into the arena and shine their headlights onto the outdoor stage. Then all would be able to see *Swan Lake* — and her dying swan — as expected. Her suggestion was taken up and the performance continued — though, according to Mum, the *corps de ballet* swans were blinded trying to dance faced with such a barrage of dazzling headlights. Pavlova's performance was a triumph — but there must have been an army of drivers with flat batteries.

Determined that every theatre in South America would see her *Dying Swan*, Pavlova drove her company to physical and mental exhaustion. My mother had even suffered severe nosebleeds, dancing in the high altitudes of the Andes. Then, on a train journey down from La Paz, Bolivia to Callao in Peru, and travelling third class in a box carriage little better than a cattle truck (Pavlova herself always travelled first class), the train was stopped on a mountain pass by the police, and the engine driver forcibly removed. It appeared that the driver had murdered his mother-in-law and the police had finally caught up with him. The passengers were told to wait; another driver would arrive shortly. The time was 1 a.m. The mountain pass was freezing. Eventually, at 9 a.m. the next morning, the train moved off with its load of frozen passengers.

'If you could survive the rigours of a Pavlova tour,' my mother said, 'life was certainly neither dull nor predictable.'

Pavlova kept her girls on a very tight financial rein. At the end of the tour she sent Mum 'steerage' to New York out of the port of Callao on an old tramp steamer, the SS *Lobus*, which was carrying 'white cargo' (a gaggle of Peruvian prostitutes) bound for Panama. My mother used to chat and laugh with them and one evening they asked her to dance for them. Typical of Mum, she obliged.

'Poor things, why not?'

They were so delighted that in return they gave her a little silver dagger similar to those they wore in their knickers. A few weeks later, Mum was to find the little dagger very useful for self-protection when she arrived penniless in New York and had to spend a night on a bench at Pennsylvania Station (known today as Penn Station). Awakened from a sound sleep she realised she was being groped. Quick as a flash, the little dagger found its way to discourage nimble fingers!

The next morning my mother was able to ring Kay Swift, my father's niece, to whom he had given her an introduction. Kay was married to the wealthy banker Jimmy Warburg. A few years later, in 1926, George Gershwin — with whom Kay had a long affair and collaborative working relationship (Kay had studied piano in Paris and had a background in classical music that she was able to draw on to make suggestions to him for his compositions) — wrote his musical *Oh, Kay!* and dedicated it to her. The musical, which starred Gertrude Lawrence and the Hollywood comedian Victor Moore, was a great success.

After her night in Penn Station, my mother was able to stay with Kay, who lent her money to buy clothes so that she could audition for the Metropolitan Opera House. She auditioned for the ballet mistress Madam Galli, and ended up as principal *coryphée* there for the next four years. These were vintage years at the Met, with Gatti Casazza, as impresario, booking Enrico Caruso, Feodor Chaliapin, Amelita Galli-Curci, Maria Jaritza, and Beniamino Gigli.

My mother always said that Caruso had a voice of gold and Gigli a voice of silver. According to Mother, Caruso was full of humour and a great practical joker. He was also talented in drawing sketches, and, with an eye for a pretty girl, was always sketching the ballerinas in the wings. One night he did one of my mother as she was preparing to make her entrance. As she stepped into the resin box and raised her arms, preparing to glide onstage, Caruso deftly popped his folded sketch into her cleavage. Onto the stage Sheilova floated, but as she took her place with the others the sketch suddenly dropped from her bosom onto the floorboards. At the interval she rushed to retrieve it, but it was gone. How precious that little sketch would have been, had she been able to keep it.

At Christmas the generous tenor gave my mother a ten-dollar piece, as he did to all the ballerinas. To the singers he gave a five-dollar piece. The chorus got to know of this and several confronted him, wanting to know why they should receive less than the dancers.

'Because there are far fewer of them,' was his reply. 'Also because those ballerinas have such beautiful legs — therein lies my weakness!'

The chorus apparently forgave him because of his golden voice and good-natured charm. He was very much loved by everyone at the Met.

According to Mum, it was during his performance in the opera *Le Juif* by Halévy that Caruso hit a high note and burst a blood vessel. He was helped to his dressing room and sang no more that night. Soon after, Caruso returned to Italy and died, and Gigli replaced him at the Met. Mother told me that the morning Caruso's death was announced there was a black crepe band placed right round the old Met building.

Another awesome performer during my mother's years at the Met was Feodor Chaliapin. Gatti Casazza, the impresario, had gone to Russia, had seen him as Boris Godunov, and booked him on the spot. Because Chaliapin had made a brief visit to New York in 1907, wherein his revolutionary 'naturalistic' acting was seen to undermine the effect of his singing, Gatti's New York backers insisted that he give an audition, but Gatti knew that to ask the Russian idol to come to New York to audition would be an insult. Thinking he would cross that bridge when he had to, Gatti arranged the great man's passage. When Chaliapin arrived at the Met, believing he had been firmly booked for *Mefistofele* by Boito and *Boris Godunov* by Mussorgsky, Gatti told him the situation.

Amused, Chaliapin agreed to give the sceptical backers their required audition.

At Chaliapin's suggestion, the entire company was called to observe. All arrived at the scheduled time. The backers lit their cigars and waited. Finally Chaliapin appeared, strode down to the footlights, and nodded to the accompanist. When the renowned Russian opened his mouth, however, a pitiful *basso profundo* voice emerged — the sound of a man suffering the worst effects of flu. The backers believed Gatti must have lost his wits. Shaking their heads, they refused to finance him and made their departure. To the impresario's amazement, Chaliapin roared with laughter.

'Raise the money yourself,' he told him, 'and you'll laugh all the way to the bank!'

Taking a huge risk, Gatti set about finding the money.

On the opening night of *Mefistofele*, the house was packed. My mother told me that the dancers were allowed to watch the maestro from the wings. The orchestra began, up went the curtain and when Chaliapin's voice rang out — smooth and deep, with his characteristic richness of tone — Gatti's trust was vindicated. And from that performance on he was indeed laughing all the way to the bank.

'What luck to have witnessed these unforgettable years!' Mum would often tell me.

My mother's abundant writings — now in the Australian National Archives in Canberra — may well contain descriptions of these events and others. Perhaps someday someone will properly research her papers. In any case, these stories are offered exactly as my mother told them.

My father was much older than my mother — almost old enough to have been my grandfather. Born in 1872 at Ashby de la Zouche in Leicestershire, he was one of fourteen children. Four of his siblings died in childbirth, and my poor paternal grandmother herself expired bearing the fourteenth. Born, according to his youngest sister Kathryn (my Aunt Kitty), with a flair for sartorial style, the village kids at Ashby would yell at him 'bloody snowdrop!' as he glided by on his bicycle. According to Kit, the village mothers always kept their daughters indoors whenever Jack Faulkner was cycling about on the prowl.

Of the ten surviving children, the eldest, Percy, became an officer in the Royal Navy. In 1900, while serving in India, he committed suicide by jumping from the crow's nest onto the deck of his ship.

From what I've heard, their father — my grandfather Edwin — was apparently a martinet; he gave the orders and God help the children if they didn't obey. After his first wife Lucy died of exhaustion, he then remarried, taking as his second wife a large, formidable woman called Louie (nicknamed by the kids 'Diamond Louie'). Unlike her predecessor, Louie hated children, so they were all put out to fend for themselves as quickly as possible. The eldest girls, Frances and Margaret, went to the USA. In 1888 my father was sent to work on a pig farm in Canada, where he arrived wearing an English blazer, white ducks, smart shoes and a straw boater.

'Poor Jack, the Victorian dandy out to make an impression,' said my Aunt Kit.

In his late teens, Jack managed to escape from the pig farm and went to work in a bank in Montreal. I know nothing of his movements thereafter, except that he managed to reach Sydney by 1909. It is quite possible that in the years before that he had spent time with his sisters in New York, where they had settled. When war erupted in 1914, varicose veins luckily made him a reject for active service.

In 1922, during her tenure as principle *coryphée* at the Metropolitan Opera House in New York, my mother received a telegram from him.

Am Free To Marry. Come To London At The End Of Your Met Season. John.

Madam Galli must have thought a lot of my mother as apparently she gave her permission for her to travel to London to marry, with the proviso that she return on the date specified in a telegram that would later be sent to her. All of this must have been agreed with the Met impresario, Gatti Casazza. The story, as my mother told me, was that she then took the boat to Liverpool and was met by my father. They soon arranged a civil marriage in London, and afterwards went to live in a flat at Castelaine Mansions, Maida Vale.

As the weeks passed, my mother was eagerly awaiting the promised telegram from New York inviting her to return. Why didn't it come? Captivated by her new husband's charm and the distractions of married life in London, her mind was partly diverted. But after months had passed, and the telegram had still not arrived, she resigned herself to the fact that it would never come. Then my father owned up. The telegram had in fact turned up and, not wanting his new wife to leave his side, he had read it and destroyed it. Much as my mother loved him she never forgave him for that.

In 1924, my parents left London and returned to Sydney, where they took a flat in a building facing Queenscliff beach in Manly (Ceramic). Over the next two years, my mother was able to find work as a choreographer of floorshows at Sydney's fashionable Ambassadors nightclub. My father, being a handsome, middle-aged and very English gentleman about town, had found work during his first antipodean stay in the Australian silent movie industry, where he rapidly became a featured screen 'heavy'. On his return to Sydney, he continued that career. His films, made between 1918 and 1930, include: *The Enemy Within*, *£500 Reward*, *The Lure of the Bush*, *The Man from Snowy River*, *Silks and Saddles*, *Far Paradise*, *Tanami*, and *The Blue Mountains Mystery*. His final film, for the MacDonagh sisters in 1929, was *The Cheaters*, which I believe was the last silent film to be made in Australia. In 1930, the cast was called back to add a limited soundtrack.

Some years ago, the Australian Film Archives kindly sent me several VHS copies of his silent films. Then in 2006 a package arrived containing a print of *The Cheaters*, with the compliments of the Film Archives in Canberra and a note saying: *Your father's voice is on the print*. I poured myself a stiff whisky and, sitting alone, played it. For the first time in seventy-one years, I heard Dad's voice again. It was an eerie experience as so many memories came flooding back — including one I had forgotten. In the late 1920s my father received an offer to do a screen test in Hollywood. He turned it down. His reason?

'Why should I go to a country where a man can't buy a drink?'

This was, of course, during Prohibition.

As for the rest of my father's brothers and sisters — Nell, Ada, Bill, Ronnie, Kitty, and Bard — I met three of them (Bill, Kitty, and Bard) when I came to England in 1950.

Bill and Bard I only met once. Bill was very old and, like my father, showed the effect of having had more than his fill. Bard was a very sad little man who had been put inside for fiddling the books in the bank for which he worked. I remember that a feeling of profound melancholy seemed to emanate from him. He had my father's eyes, but Bard's were haunted. His was the blank gaze of a broken man.

Aunt Kitty lived in Dorset and was wonderful to me in my early years in the UK. She had an enormous sense of humour. It was Kitty who was able to fill me in on so much of our family background.

According to Aunt Kitty, the illustrious Warren Hastings (1732–1818), the former and first ever Governor General of India (later involved in a corruption scandal, but acquitted of wrongdoing and subsequently appointed Privy Councillor), is said to have begot my great-grandfather by the woman who was nursing him, and whom he secretly married shortly before he died. The birth was recorded in the parish register at Ashby de la Zouche, but shortly afterwards the entry was expunged. Apparently, the marriage (if it was formally undertaken) was disallowed or ignored, and the nurse and her child given a house for their pains — Warren House — where my grandfather Edwin's father, was raised. Edwin later became the manager of the colliery at Ashby called Moira, which closed down in the fifties.

While I was staying with my Aunt Kitty in Dorset in the 1950s she drove me to Birmingham to meet Bard, and then onward to Ashby de la Zouche to see Warren House. One extraordinary incident has remained in my memory from that visit. I was standing in front of the house, trying to picture the young Victorian family who had lived there in the 1870s and 1880s, when a very, very old lady came up and seized my arm.

'Jack! You've come back! Oh, I remember you, Jack!'

Kitty was awaiting me further down the road. When I got into the car and we drove off I told her what had happened. She laughed.

'Oh yes! You're very like your father. You've got his eyes and his smile.'

Was the old lady one of the local girls he had known? Probably.

One anecdote Kitty assured me was gospel. After Uncle Percy's death my aunts Ada and Nell, who had an enormous idea of their own social importance, pleaded with my father to set about claiming the Hastings estate. His response, which both my mother and Kitty verified, was: 'Why should I claim the bloody title? I know who and what I am without recourse to a title. Who would be fool enough to claim the title and inherit all their unpaid bills? I'll stay who and what I am!'

There is one other story my mother later told me that occurred before I was born. Apparently, one night there was a frantic ringing of the bell at 6 Ceramic Flats. My mother opened the door to a distraught woman holding a baby in her arms.

'Is Mr Faulkner at home?' asked the woman.

'No, why?'

'Because this is his child.'

'Well,' said Mum, 'that's his affair. He'll be home in about an hour. You'd better come back then and tell him because it's absolutely nothing to do with me.'

When my father came home Mum apparently confronted him, and all he said was: 'I don't know the bitch. Anyway, I'll deal with her when she arrives.'

She did come back, and according to my mother there was a flaming row outside the door and he sent her packing.

God only knows what else in my father's life was kept secret.

CHAPTER THREE

LOSING MY MARBLES

ALWAYS A HARD-DRINKING, gregarious womaniser, my father was known by his barroom cronies as 'Jack the Rattler' — a reference to his overactive one-eyed trouser snake. But by 1933 the Great Depression had really set in. Dad was on the skids, and his career had collapsed. He was drinking so much and his blood pressure was so high that every time the arc lamps were focused on him his nose poured blood because of the heat. He was fast becoming unemployable in the film industry.

At an early age, Dad had learnt to fend for himself and to survive come what may. When working for Bass's Ales in the first decade of the twentieth century, he had learnt a recipe for whisky that was lethal but of prime quality. So when the Depression hit Australia and he was out of work as a film actor, he turned his hand to distilling whisky in the bath, and kept us off poverty row by flogging his creation to his freemason colleagues. He called it 'Rattler's Whisky' and, if any of this hooch remained in the bath after the old alchemist had bottled what he needed, the bathroom door was always kept locked awaiting his return.

My first school was the local state school at Manly, where I started at age six and remained for eighteen months. The school was known as the Manly Public School — the 'Manly Pubic' to us scruffy youth. It was there that I had my initiation into the obscenities of Australiana. In my class were Billy Barber, Ray Harney, Alec Lecky, Mike Hunt (try saying that quickly), Poofta Sykes (very effeminate with adenoids) and Tusker Mackintosh, a freckle-faced kid minus his front teeth and with a crew-cut hairstyle on a head that resembled a mallee root.

The Manly girls were just as wicked: Lorna Wunderlich, Stella Godbolt, Emma Hazel Royds ('Emmeroids' to us), and a hot little sheila called Norma Tryke. Norma was dead wicked. Chalked up on the wall of the boys dunny was: 'Norma Tryke is the town bike. Who's for a niked roide?'

Now marbles were all the rage at that school. You had to knock out of a circle drawn in the dirt as many as possible of your opponent's marbles, or goolies, which you could then keep. You did this by flicking in one of your own.

Dad bought me a hundred goolies. I soon lost the lot. Far worse, I lost face.

'No uthe thtanden there loike a one-legged man at an arthe-kicking contetht!' yelled Tusker. 'Gow howm and git th'more goolieth!'

Home I ran. But nothing could induce Dad to invest further. My dad was never a soft touch.

That afternoon he had left the dregs of a batch of his gut-rot in the bottom of the bath. My lucky day! A builder's ladder had been left propped up against the outside wall of Ceramic flats. Why couldn't I just nip up through our bathroom window and fill some empty ginger beer bottles with Rattler's? These I could then trade at school for my lost goolies.

Up I scuttled like a rat up a drainpipe, my satchel full of empty bottles. In no time I was down again with five of them filled to the brim. At twenty goolies a bottle, I'd be sure to regain my one hundred goolies — and my lost pride.

Next morning Tusker waylaid me.

'Gotcha goolieth, thport?'

'Got better than that. I've got five bottles of Dad's best whisky. Couple of swigs of that and yer nuts'll drop. It's twenty goolies a bottle, five goolies a snort and one goolie a sniff.'

Ray Harney parted with one goolie and took a sniff.

'Strewth!'

Poofta Sykes took a mega snort and had to cough up two goolies.

'Jeez, what a stink! Lay ya flat like a lizard drinkin'!'

'G'is a swig, Rono!' (Rono was the Aussie abbreviation of my name, Ronald.)

Quick as a flash, I got back my hundred goolies and we weaved our way back to our desks like a swarm of swatted flies.

Rodney Bottomley was to read to the class 'How Horatius Held the Bridge.' But we never discovered how he managed that because midway through his reading Rodney lurched to his feet, turned cholera yellow and did a technicolour yawn all over his desk. The heavy guzzlers now started crashing like skittles in a bowling alley. Those too drunk to stay vertical were rushed to the Manly District Hospital to be stomach-pumped. Dad was summoned to remove me and was told I'd traded his precious Rattler's for marbles.

Puce with rage, he marched me home where I was walloped with his razor strap. Needless to say the school expelled me for a time.

'The only possible school for you, my lad,' growled dad, 'is the reformatory.' Adding, 'I seem to have spawned a right little trader!'

The name stuck.

My father, in his declining years, would often come home paralytically drunk and penniless. Usually he would be paid in cash for his whisky, or for any filming work he did. He would spend it at the Hotel Pacific on Manly's oceanfront, or simply lose it.

These early years were very traumatic, with my mother trying to cope financially by teaching ballet. Of one thing I am certain: in spite of everything, they adored each other. But my father was much the weaker character.

At that age, I was absolutely 'pro' my father. He used to take me with him for holidays to Newport Beach, where a lot of his rich friends had weekend cottages, or to Bon Accord luxury guesthouse at Springwood, in the Blue Mountains.

One night in 1933 we stayed at Bon Accord so that he could attend a party thrown by the owner, Hugh D. MacIntosh, who was his friend. Though I had been put to bed early and was fast asleep, apparently the party became a drunken orgy, and a number of the maids also got very drunk. The following morning they were all lined up in the vestibule dressed in their black skirts, white aprons and little white housemaids' caps, about to be sacked and sent back to Sydney. One of them, an extremely pretty girl, had completely captivated me. I begged Dad to use his friendship with the owner to spare the girl, but he wouldn't raise a finger to help her. I wonder now what part he had played in all that revelry? Nothing would really surprise me.

Of those early formative years at Bon Accord, one memory is indelible. A kindly boy a few years my elder, Kevin Parker — a fellow guest — had an air rifle that shot tiny lead pellets. The Bon Accord guesthouse was surrounded by bush and scrubland, a haven for birds and Aussie animals of many varieties. Early one beautiful spring morning, Kevin invited me to go shooting with him. We set off towards Valley Heights — the town down the railway line that passed through Springwood. In those days the steam locomotives from Sydney would take on a second engine at Valley Heights for the long steep climb up to Mount Victoria. I always remember as a child the mournful shriek from the two engines as they set off for the steep climb.

We were making our way through a lovely wood of gumtrees, which in the early morning sunshine was redolent with the sound of hundreds of birds.

'Look Ron, up in that branch!' Kevin said suddenly. 'It's a robin red breast.'

'Shoot it, can you?' I said impulsively. 'I want to see it close up.'

He took careful aim and fired, and down it came. I rushed over, picked it up and gazed at the little wounded creature. It shivered and died in the palm of my hand. As I looked down at the little dead robin I could hear the mournful shriek of the twin locomotives in the distance as they set off from Valley Heights.

I have never forgotten the lesson that childish act of foolish curiosity taught me. Later I had my own air gun, but I couldn't ever bring myself to shoot at any living creature.

Another vivid memory. I was about seven years old, it was the May school holidays and I was again staying at Bon Accord with my father. There was also a girl staying there called Marilese Simpson.

I can see her now as I write this — brown eyes, black hair, and a gaze at young Ronnie that was riveting. There was always a group of children staying at the guesthouse, where we could enjoy large gardens, endless games, and organised treasure hunts. On one such treasure hunt, Marilese and I worked out where the treasure was and arrived at the final staging point well ahead of the others.

'Look!' she said. 'It's a key. Now we can get the treasure!'

While we had been scrabbling over the hillside searching for the hunt waypoints I had caught frequent tantalising glimpses of her upper legs and knickers (known as 'bloomers' in our day), and I'm afraid that by that time she and I were thinking about two different treasures. Oh, how I wanted to explore her secrets! But before I could voice my desires, Marilese ran off with the key to claim our reward.

Minutes later we had collected our prize — a large box of Nestlé chocolates — and were sitting together in the empty ballroom at Bon Accord to share out our win. Looking up at one point, I found myself gazing into a pair of very knowing, very naughty dark eyes. It was too much. I gave her a tentative kiss. Immediately Marilese responded, and forcefully. It was like being kissed by a human vacuum cleaner.

Unfortunately, before we could explore these sensations further we were disturbed and our moment ended.

Soon afterward a group of us were sitting at the end of a long, well-kept garden, talking about where babies came from. Marilese, who was a year or two older than me, said, 'Would you like me to show you where we come from?'

There was something so sexy about her manner that, child though I was, she made me want to rip her skirt off myself right then and there. But Mrs Simpson, who obviously knew a thing or two about her daughter, suddenly appeared in the archway behind us and broke the spell.

'Marilise! Come here at once!'

Sadly, I never saw her again.

Marilese Simpson awoke in me an impulse so strong (the first of its kind) that I have never forgotten it — the start of that long, agonising, treacherous voyage of sexual awakening.

Bon Accord guesthouse was burnt to the ground in 1936 in a

fire that consumed the huge weatherboard building in a matter of minutes. But the escapades I engaged in there are still, all these years later, clear in my mind.

These kaleidoscopic events ended quite suddenly for me six days after my seventh birthday.

My father had a film projector. On the wall opposite our front door he'd hang a white sheet and with curtains drawn we would all settle to watch the flickering images on the improvised screen.

By this time Dad was in rapid decline. He couldn't stop drinking. And there was now a girlfriend, a wealthy Jewish lady past her prime but still rather beautiful called Mrs Florence Cohen. Dad had once taken me to afternoon tea with her in her large mansion in the up-market suburb of Cremorne, and she had been very kind to me.

What's more, by that time Dad had twice been rushed to hospital with strokes. The first time he was paralysed temporarily down his left side, and with the second, shortly after, he lost the sight of his left eye.

Thursday 13th September 1934 is a date I will never forget.

Early that morning I sat with my father and watched him getting dressed up in his very best to go into town. Dad always believed that even with little money, one should buy expensive clothes — good shirts, the best shoes, and tailor-made suits. His wardrobe was sparse but he always wore quality. I watched him put on his elegant Windsor check suit. His socks, I remember, were in blue and white horizontal stripes. On his feet were immaculate, narrow brown shoes and spats, which made his feet look like penguins. Then there was the starched collar, a pale cream bowtie, and a stylish satin waistcoat to match the suit.

Father was going to meet Florence, and soon he set off, dressed to kill, strutting along the pavement and swinging his cane. I remember running beside him to the bus stop, on his way to catch the ferry from Manly to Sydney.

This was to be a very special day. Dad and Mrs Cohen would have their lunch, then he had promised to return for my birthday treat, which had been delayed.

The birthday treat was to be the showing of one of his films, *The Blue Mountains Mystery*, made in 1921 and directed by Raymond Longford, in which they used the then-innovative double-exposure technique, as my father played identical twin brothers. He had in the past shown us cartoons — *Mickey Mouse*, *Popeye* etc. — but never one of his films, so this was to be a very special treat indeed.

Apparently, no trace of the film now remains. Ironically, when I was preparing to leave Australia in March 1950 cans of that film were in a cupboard in our hallway. No one at that time wanted them. Because of the inflammability of nitrate film, I was advised to bury them outside. This I did the day before I left for London. Acting on Mother's instructions, I buried them — together with my father's ashes — in the garden of my grandparents' house, The Orchard. But there's no chance of finding them again now, because in the mid-sixties The Orchard was torn down and replaced by an apartment building. In any case, the nitrate film would have disintegrated long ago. So that was the end of *The Blue Mountains Mystery*, of which my mother always said: 'Of the fourteen films he made, that film was John's finest work.'

In those days 13th September was part of the school holidays, so in the early spring sunshine our gang was down on the beach building sand castles or crawling over the rocks of Queenscliff headland. By the early afternoon we were playing rounders, a game that was popular among Australian kids in those days. They had all been invited to watch the film with me, so everyone was very excited as Dad would soon return to set up the projector and screen. But there was no sign of him. At 5pm an ambulance drove up and parked outside Ceramic Flats. All I saw when the back doors opened was a recumbent form under a blanket on a stretcher...and the striped socks. I remember yelling 'Dad!' and starting to run. My playmates grabbed me.

'No, Ronnie! You mustn't!'

Quickly sussing the situation, they crowded round and held me firmly.

I saw the stretcher being pulled out and the attendants disappeared with it through the building's front door. Eventually, I managed to break free and raced across the road, through the door and up the stairs with the mob of kids behind me.

They'd just got Dad into the bedroom. The door was shut. I opened it to find a crowd of people surrounding the bed. I couldn't see my father. All I can remember is several people holding me back.

'No, Ron! You mustn't go near your father. He's very ill.'

I caught another glimpse of those striped socks. I remember wrestling frantically to get free from my grapplers and pushing through to the bed.

Dad was completely paralysed. Only his eyes moved. Ever since that day I've wondered: was he trying to say something? Then I was lifted bodily and carried out of the room. Someone drove me in a car to my Aunt Lil's.

Dad died shortly afterward.

I was told that he'd 'gone for a holiday' — a fatal error to lie to a child, albeit with the best intentions. For weeks they carried on this charade. Of course I was well aware of what was going on.

'When's Dad coming back?' I asked. 'Why can't we go and see him?'

Six weeks later there was a family gathering and I was finally told the truth.

'Your dad will never come back, darling. He's dead.'

CHAPTER FOUR

LIFE WITH A SINGLE PARENT

WHAT SADNESS FOR A BOY to lose his father so early in his life.

And what a challenge for the single parent left to rear a difficult, lonely child.

When Dad went, Mum was left holding a stack of unpaid bills. Despite this, her ballet school was flourishing. It exhausted her, but gave us something to survive on.

When my mother started her dancing classes, she had rented a large room above the junk shop of an old ex-salvage tug captain named Emmanuel Garscadden. In his spare time Emmanuel was involved with a circle of spiritualists.

Mum had always known she had a gift for clairvoyance, though she was reluctant to use it. But Garscadden persuaded her that it would be useful for her to exploit her special gift to earn a bit more money and she finally agreed to try it. In addition to her dancing classes, she went into business as an astrologer and clairvoyant, and was uncannily successful at it. But she soon began to hate the dangerous game she was playing.

One day a beautiful young woman, Anna Philomena Morgan, came to see her. I clearly remember Mum's description of what happened.

'We sat down,' she later told me, 'and after analysing the details of her birth, I began to experience an awful sense of foreboding. Anna told me she had a lover with whom she was living.

'You have Saturn very badly aspected, I told her. That's a warning sign. You must leave him. He's no good.

'And if I can't? Anna asked.

'Then there will be a disaster of some kind. Don't chance it, I told her. For God's sake, leave him!'

Anna left, deeply troubled by Mum's words.

Several months later Mum bought an evening paper. Splashed across the frontpage was the headline: *Girl Brutally Murdered by Lover*, with a photograph underneath.

It was Anna.

From that point on, Mum never did another professional reading.

In December 1935, Mum was putting on her end-of-year concert with all her pupils at the old Olympic Theatre in Sydney Road, long since vanished. To keep me out of mischief, I was roped in to play a silvery fish. Of course, I loathed the whole idea. A wooden toadstool was made, onto which my Mum's beautiful sixteen-year-old star pupil Gwenda Hall ('Gwenny' to me) would lift me as she kissed me (that kiss was the only reason I agreed to do it). Worse still, I had to recite a poem.

If I were a fish, a silvery fish,
What do you think I would do?
I'd swim all day in a silvery pool...

Of course, I was a laughing stock among my mates. The comments from the elder pupils and their mothers didn't help.

'Dear little Ronnie, isn't he sweet?'

In spite of my embarrassment, the concert was a sell-out.

Shortly after the show had finished, Mum was called to the phone. 'Ganfie' was very ill. Could she take a taxi to Manly Vale at once?

We found Ganfie at The Orchard, lying pale and unmoving on the bed.

All his life, Willie Whytock had been a devoted golfer. During his last years his skills were called on for designing new golf links, and the previous afternoon he had been laying out the new greens and fairways at Deewhy in sweltering heat when he'd suffered a massive heart attack.

'Go on,' Mum told me. 'He won't be with us long. Say goodbye to him.'

Tentatively I approached the bed and was about to speak when all of a sudden Ganfie rolled towards me, vomited directly over my legs and feet, and fell back dead on the pillow.

So now my grandfather was gone as well.

With the death of my grandfather, my granny became helpless. Mum took us out of Ceramic to stay with her, a decision I bitterly resented. On Queenscliff beach I was at least able to work out some of my rebellious frustrations struggling against the rolling breakers of the Pacific Ocean. At The Orchard I felt completely stifled, literally and figuratively. The January heat that summer of 1935 was over thirty-seven degrees. Stuck in a weatherboard cottage with a corrugated iron roof, I felt I had been confined to hell. Unable to bear it, I fled back to 'Queensie.' Distraught, Mum called the police. I was found and escorted back to The Orchard. Mum walloped me, Granny wept. I swore; Granny shrieked. As soon as I could, I ran straight back to Ceramic (no one bothered about a key in those days). Finally I won. Mum and I returned to Ceramic, leaving Granny to cope on her own. And there we stayed till 1941.

From the age of seven I had been more than curious as to what lay under a girl's skirt, but you weren't supposed to think about that, let alone do anything about it. I might have approached my father about it had he been alive, but he was gone.

I used to have to go every Saturday morning from nine until one to watch what to me were my mother's unutterably dreary ballet classes — all these little girls cavorting round to Bucalossi's *Grasshoppers' Dance* or to excerpts from the *Ballet of the Hours*. There was no money for comics to entertain me — only these nubile babes leaping before me in short skirts with bare legs and their knickers showing most of the time. Needless to say, I soon felt some very strong urges.

Mum's ballet school in Manly was now located at a place called the Palais Hall in Whistler Street. The space was owned by a tailor, Mr Machon — a kindly man who had cut off from the premises a modest space sufficient for his tailoring business and left Mum the rest, generously installing a large mirror and practice barres. Off the ballroom was a little changing room.

The girls were all very pretty, aged from six to sixteen. Ronnie, with his innocent blue eyes, didn't arouse any embarrassment when the girls came in to change. But by this time, thanks to Marilese Simpson, the 'innocent blue eyes' were darting about like piranhas in a fish tank.

I decided to try a bit of seduction. It didn't take me long to pluck up the courage, so to my favourite girl, Gwenda Hall, I said, 'Gwennie, can I see what you've got?'

'What do you mean?'

'Pull down your panties,' I said. 'I wanna have a gandah.'

She blushed and ignored me.

'Come on, Gwennie. Give us a squiz. If you show me yours, I'll show you mine.'

Still blushing fiercely, Gwenda rushed from the dressing room to join her class.

I propositioned girl after girl without any success. They simply looked appalled and ran off. It wasn't until my mother, a week or two later, mentioned that the classes were falling off that I realised the consequences of what I had done. So I confessed and the balloon went up.

In desperation, Mum went to her bosom friend, our downstairs neighbour, Mrs Betty Flook. What was to be done with her larrikin' son?

'Send Ron to the Jesuits,' Mrs Flook said. 'They'll straighten him out very quickly.'

And that's exactly what happened, but not for another two years. Before then I was kept on watch, given a chance to sort myself out. Did I? Did I hell.

Still, there were mitigating circumstances. My dad had died the previous year, my grandfather shortly after, so I felt the whole world was against me.

In the mid-1930s, the draconian respectability of the Australian middle class was a slavish copy of the English. My grandmother was sweet and well-intentioned, but her cloying Victorian hypocrisy was anathema to me.

'Nice people mustn't offend social etiquette,' she would say.

Of course, that simply brought out in me a compelling urge to be an Aussie larrikin. To infuriate Granny, I'd suck peas off my knife, and 'make an odour' as loudly as I could when in her presence.

By 1936, having still not mended my ways, Mum decided that I needed a complete change to shock me into behaving more responsibly. Desperate to get me away from the 'Manly Pubic', she went to see the Rhodes scholar and Oxford University Fellow Ian Edwards, who was about to open a new private school for boys in Manly — St Andrews Presbyterian College — and was able to wangle me a place there (she was making just enough with her dancing classes to make that possible). At St Andrews I had to wear a uniform; but far worse, a straw boater, which my surfing companions soon called 'Faulkidge's dog biscuit' ('Faulkidge' being a typical Aussie schoolboy bastardisation of my surname). I loathed the school, but I worshipped Ian Edwards, who always treated me with respect. I was at St Andrews for two years.

For the most part, those two years were good for me. I was popular with my classmates, and though I never excelled either academically or at sport, I did well enough to earn their respect and acceptance. Then, in December of 1937, Ian Edwards was sacked by the school governors, who considered his ideas too progressive for their conservative mentality. This was particularly painful for me as the following year I was due to be taught by him, something I had greatly looked forward to. My mother, who'd become close friends with both Ian and his wife, was furious at the injustice shown to him, and removed me from St Andrews forthwith. Immediately I started to play up.

Looking back now, Ian's dismissal must have seemed like yet another betrayal to me. I took out my frustrations on my poor mother, and on my Aunt Lily and Granny, who showed me nothing but unselfish love.

One day I was at my Aunt Lily's. Uncle Jim had disappeared off to his club, and Lily had gone off somewhere with my mother. My cousin Rosemary, Lily and Jim's adopted daughter, was a few years younger than me. Left alone with her, and still hankering to get my revenge on all the women who controlled my life, I persuaded Rosemary to doff her pants and show me what she had. While it was a thrill that I will never forget, as I write this now I'm overwhelmed with shame for what I did. Aunt Lil had always shown me nothing but love and kindness, and here I was taking advantage of her adored wee Rose. Fortunately, Rose pimped on me, and I was made to see how deeply I had wronged her, Aunt Lily and my mother through my actions.

Mother had had enough. It was time to take up Betty Flook's suggestion.

In 1938, I was enrolled as a dayboy in St Aloysius Jesuit College at Milson's Point, North Sydney.

Shortly after my arrival at St Aloysius one of the masters, Father Hessian SJ, called me into his office. As soon as I was seated before him, he got straight to the point.

He leant forward on his desk, clasping his hands.

'You probably know your mother's at her wits' end over your behaviour with girls. You really fancy them, don't you? I suppose you call them *sheilas*.'

'Yes, sir, I do fancy girls. Is there anything wrong with that? Is it a sin?'

'Not at all,' said the shrewd Jesuit, 'but like most of the good things in life — sweets, a new bike, good friends — it depends on how you treat them. Do you know what a fuschia is?'

'Yes,' I said. 'They grow in my grandmother's orchard at Manly Vale.'

'Have you ever tried to open the white petals of a fuschia blossom before they spread themselves naturally?'

'Yes, Father, I have. You pull open the little petals and you can see the beautiful red centre of the flower.'

'Exactly,' he replied. 'But after you tore open the petals, did the blossom flower properly?'

'No, sir. It withered.'

'Well, there you are. You see, in forcing it open you destroyed that bloom, didn't you? If you tamper with a flower before it opens of its own accord you do the flower irreparable damage. Now Ron, you must think of a girl's body as if she were a fuschia. Of course, you want to explore her secrets, but in doing so before she's ready you'll damage her. My advice to you is wait.'

'How long?'

'Till you're eighteen or nineteen, at least. Will you shake on that?'

He extended his hand and I shook it. He sat back. 'The tragedy is that you have no man in your life to explain these things to you. The best thing would be to talk it over with your friends. But I will say something to you now, which as you grow older I hope will mean a lot to you.'

He stared straight into my eyes, and I could sense the importance of what he was about to say.

'A woman's body is like a temple, Ronnie,' he told me. 'It must be treated with respect and honour, not used as a plaything to satisfy your appetites. Learn that lesson and you will never trouble your mother, or any other woman, again.'

Though it didn't stop me from lusting after girls, that conversation did at least make me aware of what was at stake. I like to think from that point on I was somewhat more conscious of the damage I could do if I was not careful to control my selfish natural urges.

CHAPTER FIVE

FACING THE UNFACEABLE

THERE'S A SHORT STORY by Guy de Maupassant called 'La Peur'. Passengers sitting on deck on an ocean liner one evening each recount a moment of unforgettable terror in their lives. I believe most of us have experienced — or will experience — such moments at some point in our existence, when imminent death is a distinct possibility that is only just, and miraculously, avoided. I have had it on several occasions, and it has made me realise that perhaps for each of us there is a moment when we are predestined to die.

One overcast day shortly after my father's death, I was standing at the water's edge on Queenscliff Beach at Manly watching a surf race. *BANG!* went the starting pistol, and some forty bronzed men raced down to the water. There was a channel about sixty metres wide and ten metres deep, across which the competitors had to swim. Reaching the sandbank on the far side, they sprinted across that and plunged into the surf beyond. They then had to swim out to a row of marker buoys, swim round them and return to the beach. The channel ran for several hundred metres parallel to the beach, then veered at right angles out to the open sea.

As the competitors rounded the buoys and swam back towards the sandbank it was obvious that curly-headed Colin Grant was well in the lead. Reaching the sandbank, he sprinted across it to the cheers of the watching crowd and plunged into the channel for the last lap to the beach. The other competitors had themselves by then reached the sandbank and were running across it in hot pursuit. Suddenly, the water where Colin had dived in turned crimson.

'Something's got hold of the calf of my leg!' he shouted, as his head broke the surface.

The competitors behind him halted, transfixed at the edge of the sandbank.

In those days the captain of the Queenscliff Surf Club was a tall, hefty policeman called Lofty Sharp. Standing at the water's edge, Lofty cupped his hands and shouted.

'Colin, don't struggle! If you do, whatever's there will tear your flesh. Just breaststroke very gently towards us. Come as close as you can to the shore, and when whatever it is lets go we'll grab you!'

As a seven-year-old, I was watching this horror between the legs of the bystanders now crowding round Lofty. Several of the surf lifesavers were standing beside him, ready to seize Colin when he came within reach.

Looking back, it was reminiscent of the Israelites on the shore of the Red Sea, praying the waters would divide so that they could get to safety. Only in this instance, it was us that represented safety and poor Colin who needed to get to us.

Painfully and slowly, Colin breaststroked towards the shore. It was impossible to see what was happening beneath the surface because the water had turned murky red. Closer and closer he moved, until finally he was within reach of Lofty.

'The bloody thing's let go!' Colin yelled.

Lofty Sharp and the brothers Keith and Dudley Parkhill (Dudley was later to become Captain of Queenscliff Surf Club) seized him under the armpits and hoisted him out of the water. I shall never forget — from knee to ankle were large bloodied teeth marks. Carrying him shoulder high, the three men raced across the beach to the clubhouse. Soon after the ambulance arrived and he was rushed to the Manly District Hospital. We learnt later that the surgeon had had to amputate his leg just below the knee.

A surfboat brought the other competitors back across the channel, but the shark, thought to have been a hammerhead, had by then disappeared.

Gradually, and with the advent of war in 1939, the memory faded.

However, being a morbid child I would sometimes wander across the beach on grey, windy days to gaze at the bloodstained steps of the old clubhouse, up which Colin Grant had been carried.

The event had one positive outcome: after the attack, patrolling aircraft always flew along the Sydney beaches at weekends from Cronulla in the south to Palm Beach in the north, on shark patrol. If the surf was safe they fired a long green streamer; but if there was a shark in the area, a red rocket was fired. Later, I believe, nets were laid that were supposed to keep the beaches reasonably safe. But experience has taught me that you are the trespasser in the shark's territory, as subsequent fatalities have proved.

Ten years later I had joined Queenscliff Surf Club. The old weatherboard clubhouse had in the interim been demolished and a new brick building with modern facilities built nearby. The central room of the new building featured a large, elegant wooden floor often used for club dances on Saturday nights. A door from the ballroom opened onto a flight of steps leading down to a courtyard where we all sunbathed. One Sunday a large crowd of us were lying prostrate in the courtyard, enjoying the midday sun. Presently we heard, crossing the ballroom floor, what sounded like someone with a walking stick. The sound stopped. There was a moment's silence, then:

'God Almighty, it's Colin Grant! You've come back!'

We all turned to look. Smiling down at us from the doorway was a man with a wooden leg — the man I'd seen hoisted, bleeding, onto the shoulders of Lofty Sharp and the Parkhill brothers ten years before. The older members who had witnessed the shark attack — some now servicemen on leave from the war — were gathering round him. Colin told them he wanted to exorcise the spectre that had haunted him all these years. Would we come into the surf with him to still his 'demon of fear'? We did. I've always remembered his words when we escorted him back to the clubhouse at the end of our swim.

'Thanks, boys. With your help, I've laid my nightmare ghost to rest. Now I can live with myself.'

As far as I know, he never returned to Queenscliff.

★ ★ ★

At this time, surfboard riding was all the rage, and every summer the Queenscliff Surf Club held its annual surfboard race.

One summer Sunday in 1944, on the day scheduled for the race, I was cycling towards the Club when walking towards me came several of the boys who had entered for the race.

'G'day, young Ron. Seen the surf?'

'No.'

'Well, go take a gander. We'll come with you.'

All the previous week tempestuous storms had whipped up colossal waves along the east coast, and even now it was like watching a succession of mini tsunamis thundering onto the beach.

'Well Ron, still game to join the boys? Or are you a bloody chicken?'

That was blackmail: risk drowning, or be forever remembered by 'the boys' as a coward. There was no choice for me.

We all changed into our bathing trunks and I went off to the boatshed to collect my board. Just as I was taking the weighty board off my shoulders, who should come up but the man who had sponsored me as a junior club member: Lofty Sharp.

'Hello there, young Ron. You're not entering that race, are you?'

'I've got to,' I said. 'All the others have signed up.'

'Don't be a bloody fool. That surf will drown you. I defy anyone to get out through those breakers.'

'Well, what about the others? If they're game, I can't chicken out.'

'Ron, you're a featherweight. If those fellows are stupid enough to try, that's their funeral. But you're too slight, and as a surf club official I feel responsible for you.'

Despite being scared witless, there was no way I could back out, so Lofty took me down to the water's edge.

At the northern end of Queenscliff beach there is an entrance through floodgates and a tunnel to the lagoon behind. After heavy storms, like those of the previous week, these floodgates are opened and hundreds of tons of trapped water rush out into the surf alongside Queenscliff headland. Lofty showed me that by skimming my board along the water's edge until I hit that outflow I could race out on the surge of released water from the lagoon.

'Once you're beyond the line of breakers you'll be OK,' Lofty told me. 'Head southeast for Shelley Beach and we'll pick you up in the lorry in a couple hours' time. Don't try to make it back to the beach. If you get on one of those waves, you'll be dumped and drowned in seconds.'

By now, the other competitors were lining up on the sand. That Sunday was chilly and grey, with a biting northeasterly wind. In spite of that, a large crowd had gathered because the Open Surfboard Race was a popular event.

Terrified, I waited at the starting line. The pistol cracked and off I sped along the water's edge until I hit the channel where the water from the floodgates surged out into the sea. Lying on the board I paddled furiously, gliding out along the channel very quickly, and soon I was well clear of the breakers. I had paddled thus far without looking right or left. I now took stock of my position. I was well beyond Queenscliff headland in a mountainous swell, with the wave crests rising precipitously ahead of and behind me. I glanced back to see who had followed. I was the only one in the water! All the other competitors were watching from the beach. Apparently — as I was later to discover — at the pistol shot they had all taken a look at the monstrous size of the breakers, given up the challenge and sat down on the beach to watch me instead.

Suddenly, I heard a sound that struck fear in anybody surfing at Queenscliff: the hand-rung shark bell on Queenscliff headland. Remembering what had happened to Colin Grant, I have never before or since known such terror.

Making sure my hands and feet didn't touch the water, I could only wait, lying on my board in that mountainous swell, to see if the shark's fin would appear.

Suddenly, a grey knife-edged triangle broke the surface about one hundred metres off, between Shelley Beach and me. In a second it had vanished. I waited. When it resurfaced it was somewhat closer, between me and Queenscliff Beach. It disappeared and I waited again. When it reappeared nearby I realised it had picked up my scent and was circling me. It would now swim in ever decreasing circles until it found me.

I had only one option, to swing my board towards the beach and try to take a wave on my body. With those monstrous breakers, I knew I wouldn't stand Buckley's chance on my board. All surfers know that amid the myriad waves that billow in from the open sea there is always a smaller one that can be taken on the body. My only hope now was to catch one that would give me a reasonable chance of being carried to the beach. I prayed and waited. The waves were rolling in like thundering dinosaurs. Then I saw a wave that I could catch on the body. But I had to be nearer the shore than I was to take it on its crest. I paddled the board as fast as I could towards the beach, which was easy because the swell was giving me impetus. Where the shark was, I didn't want to know. Then the moment of truth: I had to leap off the board and just go for it.

'Down the mine, Daddy!' (Aussie slang for catching a huge wave.)

At the top of what looked like a water precipice I rolled off the board and down I plummeted, riding the wave with my body — when suddenly from the left I was walloped very hard.

'Bloody board!' I thought. 'I hope it doesn't hit me on the head and knock me out.'

I remember little of what happened next, except that I seemed to rush like a flying fish through the water. The next moment — agony! I could feel my solar plexus grazing the beach at the water's edge. Very dazed, I stood up, suddenly aware that I was bleeding profusely. It was as though someone had run a piece of coarse sandpaper viciously down my body.

By now, Lofty Sharp and a large crowd had gathered around me. I felt a surge of triumph and arrogance.

'Did you see that wave?' I yelled. 'Did you see what happened?'

Lofty Sharp gripped me round the waist.

'Ron, we're taking you straight to the clubhouse casualty room. We've got to stop the bleeding.'

'But did ya see what happened?' I persisted. 'My board nearly killed me!'

'That was no board, mate,' said Lofty. 'As you came down the wave what looked like a twelve-foot bull shark cut across, grazed you, and veered off to your left out to sea. Luck was with you today, boy.'

For the first and only time in my life, I fainted.

A searing pain along the length of my body brought me to on the operating table in the casualty room. Lofty was applying Friar's Balsam with cotton wool. They then gave me a small glass of brandy and told me to drink it down. I did. I found it revolting. (I've long since acquired good taste.)

'Righto, mate,' said Ray Bathgate. 'You're coming straight back in the surf with us.'

'No bloody way!' I argued. 'I'll never go near that surf again.'

'No argument.'

Three of them hoisted me up — as they had Colin Grant all those years before — and carried me, protesting wildly, down to the surf. All I remember now is a crowd of people and being forced out into the water twenty yards or so from the beach. It was perfectly safe, as nothing could have come closer in that surf.

Ten minutes later I was back in the casualty room, where I was again dabbed with Friar's Balsam and finally released. Aching all over, I got dressed and rode my bike home to Manly Vale, thinking what I would tell my mother. No way could I tell her what had really happened.

'Trader! What on earth have you done to yourself?' she demanded when she saw my wounds.

'Came off my bike on the road, Mum. But I'm OK. Don't worry.'

Fortunately, she accepted the story without further questions. But in bed that night my imagination ran riot as I thought back over the morning's events.

Clearly, it had simply not been my time to go.

When I returned to Australia fifty-nine years later with my friend Kathryn Park, I took her to Queenscliff to show her where it had all happened and to exorcise that dark spectre of terror that had haunted me intermittently over the years.

Kathryn, unused to the surf, refused to go very far out. I swam out to where it had happened. Then I turned and caught the crest of an incoming roller, finding that even after so many years I could still maintain that sensation of coming down the unbroken wave.

Levelling out in the foam, I shot forward and the wave carried me right to the beach. Kathryn said nothing, but the egoist in me hoped she'd been impressed.

At last I had stilled my own memory of terror, as Colin Grant had done so many years before.

CHAPTER SIX

WAR AND CATHOLICISM

IN 1939, about to turn twelve, I was staying with our friend Lieutenant Commander Alan 'Squeak' Mather and his family in their flat overlooking Sydney Harbour at Watson's Bay.

Squeak had got his nickname at naval college. He was the bugler, and for an early-morning parade his fellow cadets decided to queer his pitch by stuffing lavatory paper up his horn. At the great ceremonial moment, with the Admiral present, Alan blew what sounded, to quote him, 'like a high-pitched fart.' The nickname commemorated that event.

During the time I was staying with him, he was serving in HMAS *Canberra*, Australia's heavy cruiser, and, if my memory serves, the RAN flagship at that time. (She was sunk a few years later by the Japanese. Luckily, Squeak had left the *Canberra* by then.)

On this bright Monday morning, Squeak woke me with the news that we were at war with Germany. He took me to the window and showed me five old First World War destroyers being towed from their berth at the Garden Island naval base to buoys in the harbour where the 'old ladies', as they were regarded, would be prepared for battle.

I remember Squeak saying, 'Take a good look, Trader. Some of them may not come back.'

He was right. Three of them were later sunk by the Japanese.

In May 1939 the Nossal family — Rudi, Renée, and their three sons, Peter, Fred, and Gus — arrived in Sydney as refugees from Vienna, which they'd had to leave in a hurry as Rudi was Jewish. They landed in Australia with very little money, but with most of their valuable furniture and a wealth of genuine charm. The Nossal brood had the brains to master English in a matter of months and to triumph all round academically. Apparently, the papal Nuncio, Archbishop Panico, used his influence and the Jesuits at St Aloysius College took the three boys for the price of one. That paid dividends as all three went on to carve out brilliant careers.

I was in my second year at St Aloysius College. When the three Nossal boys arrived at the school that May, three of us students of different ages were selected to host the young Austrians and to make them feel welcome. My charge was Fred Nossal, who was my age. Hosting Fred implied making him *au fait* with what was expected of him outside the classroom, introducing him to the boys in my class, and simply letting him take it from there. By September, when war with Germany was declared, they had already settled in and were accepted.

As a very uncultured, surf-addicted Aussie, my friendship with Fred and his family was to have a far-reaching influence. This was my first close contact with Europe and European culture.

The Nossal family lived in a large house in Buena Vista Avenue, Clifton Gardens. To enter that home with its Biedermeier furniture, and the grand piano on which Fred used to practice, was to sense the unmistakeable atmosphere of Vienna, which I was to experience personally some forty years later. Arriving there after school, afternoon tea with 'Auntie' Renée in her sitting room was magic. Coffee (never tea) was served with *kugelhupf* — a sponge cake with a fluted hole in its centre. Mahler's Symphony No 2 conducted by Furtwängler would be played on 'Uncle' Rudi's wind-up gramophone. (Mahler, I remember, was his musical addiction.) Being so far from his native Austria, Uncle Rudi was desperately homesick, but he was determined to make Australia work for his family and himself. This determination he also instilled into his three sons.

'Always remember,' he told them, 'we're lucky to be here, and we owe this country a debt of gratitude.'

Fred Nossal became my closest friend.

By 1940, preparations for Australia's participation in the war had accelerated.

During those years I was a frequent visitor to Aunt Lil, Uncle Jim, and my cousin Rosemary's house at Balmoral (Mosman), where I was born. The house, Fairyknow, is on a hill with a magnificent view of the entrance to Sydney Harbour.

On his front veranda, Uncle Jim had a large telescope on a tripod. Hours of my youth were spent gazing through this at the daily traffic of the great ships, so I soon knew the details of many of the vessels passing to and fro.

The ships I knew intimately from boyhood were the ferries that went between Sydney and Manly: SS *Barrenjoey* and *Balgowlah* and the MV *Bellubera*, on the former two of which the captain would occasionally allow me up on the bridge to take the helm. I'm proud to say that under his guidance I steered the five-hundred-ton *Barrenjoey* or the *Balgowlah* safely across Sydney Harbour on some very stormy crossings. To have control of such vessels in a heavy swell, albeit with the captain at my side, taught me that however scared you may be of whatever challenge that confronts you, you have to go for it.

One wartime Saturday morning, I was at Fairyknow swotting maths for my last exam before the summer holidays. Drifting into a daydream I heard, or thought I heard, a distant band playing what I now know was Verdi's 'Grand March' from *Aida*.

An urgent voice outside my door brought me back to reality.

'Ronnie, come quickly! You'll never see anything like this again.'

I rushed out. Everyone was heading for the veranda. From there, we saw a tremendous, unforgettable spectacle.

All painted battleship grey were the *Queen Mary*, the P&O liners *Mooltan*, *Narkunda*, *Chitral*, *Comorin*, *Strathmore*, and *Strathnaver* and the Orient liners *Orion*, *Orcades*, *Ormonde*, and *Oronsay*. They steamed very slowly in a single line as they came into our view off Middle Head. Then, gradually gathering speed, they sailed out between North and South Head, the entrance to Sydney Harbour.

With them as escorts, led by the cruiser *Australia*, were the cruisers *Canberra* and *Adelaide*, and the sloops *Swan* and *Yarra*. Even the five 'old ladies' had been invited: the destroyers, *Waterhen*, *Voyager*, *Vampire* and *Vendetta*, with their flotilla leader *Stuart*.

The crews of these ten warships, in dazzling white, stood motionless on deck in the blazing sunshine. On the quarterdeck of the *Australia* a band was playing the music that had entered my daydream.

On the troopships, thousands of Australian and New Zealand diggers were packed not only on the decks but also on the funnel ladders, the davits, the ratlines, the taffrails, and up in the crowsnests — countless cheering men, dressed in khaki, waving their familiar slouch hats.

This vast armada, we learned later, was taking two divisions to Tobruk and the North African desert to fight against Rommel.

All over the wide expanse of Sydney Harbour, looking like toys in comparison, floated every imaginable small craft from ferry steamers to canoes — family members and sweethearts who had taken to the water to wave goodbye.

A brisk wind carried across to us the sound of countless ships' horns blowing their farewells. All this was awesome and glorious. I was just a kid, but I knew many of these boys would never come back.

It was my first awareness of what the war — until then so very far away — was really about.

By 1941, I was still near the bottom of my class at St Aloysius. My mother decided that I needed a more disciplined academic environment and sent me to board with the Jesuits at St Ignatius College, Riverview. I loathed it, and suffered continual pangs of homesickness. At St Aloysius I had felt free. Here, the Jesuits forced me to work, and there were no distractions of surf and mates for me to escape to at the end of the day. However, there was a rule established by the Jesuits at St Ignatius that gave me a very strong incentive to do well. The rule was that if you got A-grades in every subject, you were allowed to return home for the weekend. Given that dangled carrot, I soon amazed myself by coming top of my class in all my academic subjects. What a surprise! I wasn't such a dunderhead after all.

★   ★   ★

One weekend in July 1941, I arrived home from St Ignatius to be told that Granny, relieving herself in her outside 'dunny' lavatory at The Orchard, had been bitten on the finger by a Redback spider. As a Rabelaisian mate of mine later joked (referring to the lethal 'funnel web' spider): 'Your granny was lucky she wasn't bitten on her funnel by a Finger Web.' Typical raunchy Aussie humour.

In reality it was the beginning of a long and tragic end for my grandmother. The bite became septic and took a long time to heal. Eventually, she got better, but then depression, to which she was subject, set in with a vengeance.

During my early years living in Ceramic, when I was six or seven, I had noticed that hardly any of my young mates were on the beach on Sunday mornings, and could not be found in any of our usual haunts. One day I challenged them.

'Why aren't you ever around on Sunday mornings? Where do you go?'

'We go to Mass,' I was told.

That was my first awareness that most of my crowd were Catholics, and that intrigued me.

'Why do you go?'

'To say thanks,' they told me.

Even though I couldn't quite understand what it was they were offering their 'thanks' for, I think it was the example of their obvious belief that must have sowed the seed that was later to grow into my unswerving Catholic faith.

The Jesuits at St Aloysius and St Ignatius influenced me further, helping me to understand the need for a balance between spiritual knowledge and enlightenment, and the academic knowledge that I was receiving in my classes. Taking Descartes' famous *cogito ergo sum* ('I think, therefore I am') as a point of departure, they taught me that if it is true that I 'am' because I 'think', then it is also true that the 'am' can be directly influenced by the quality and the depth of the 'thinking' that takes place. In other words, the more you think good, quality thoughts, the more you will become a fully developed and serene person. It's important to remember that at that point in my life — having lost my father, and living with a mother working hard to keep us in food and shelter — I felt like a rudderless ship, without direction or real guidance. Taking all these factors into account, it is understandable why, in my twelfth year, I decided to become a Catholic myself, and made my conversion under the guidance of my Jesuit guardians.

Do I still hold the same faith I embraced so willingly when I was young? Basically, yes — and will continue to do so, until someone convinces me to the contrary. In a long life of ups and downs, my Jesuit teaching and my Catholic faith have held me in good stead, and given me a priceless gift: peace of mind.

One day, not many months into my stay at St Ignatius, a rugby match was played by our boys against the boys of my old school, St Aloysius. I was part of the St Ignatius team, and when at one point I found myself with the ball, instead of passing it out to a fellow player, I clung onto it and scored, later adding two more tries. It was a rout, and I was enormously proud to have played so major a part in that victory. But my selfish hogging of the ball was not appreciated by all — a fact made clear to me when I was called over by the Jesuit master James McInerney after I'd scored my last try.

'I'll see you at 4pm in the classroom,' he told me, frowning.

This meant I was to get six of the best on the palm of my hand with his leather strap.

On the stroke of four, I confronted McInerney in the empty classroom and held out my hand for the expected punishment. But he waved my hand aside.

'Come and sit on my knee,' he said instead.

At thirteen I thought that a strange request, but complied all the same. He proceeded to lecture me for behaving so selfishly on the pitch. All the time he spoke, the palm of his hand was moving up and down my bare leg (I was, of course, wearing shorts) from my knee to my upper thigh. Paralyzed with fear, I could smell his stale nicotine breath and sensed his breathing growing heavier. When his hand moved to my groin I jumped up and away from him.

'Give me the strap, sir, or I'm off!'

McInerney sat up straight and gave me a sheepish look.

'Go on,' he said. 'I'll see you another time.'

I fled, running immediately to my mates in the playground to tell them what had happened.

'McInerney's a poof, mate,' they said. 'You'd better tell your mum when you get home.'

'What's a poof?' I asked in my innocence.

'Faulkige doesn't know what a poof is!' they cried, roaring with laughter.

The following weekend was my escape home, by which time I had been told exactly what it meant. Still, at the Sunday lunch with Uncle Jim, Aunt Lily, Granny, little Rosemary and my mother in attendance, I couldn't resist raising the subject.

'Mum,' I said, 'What's a poofter?'

Immediately, several knives and forks clattered onto plates.

'Trader!' barked Uncle Jim, choking on his roast. 'You're not to use that *wurrd* in this house!'

Highly amused, Mum asked where I had heard it. I told them the whole story.

'Roman Catholic priests!' sputtered Uncle Jim. 'Fancy letting the wee chap loose among that lot!'

'I'll see the rector first thing Monday morning,' said my mother. And she did.

'Father,' she told him, 'you've got one bad prawn among a box of good ones. I'd advise you to sort it out. I'm sending Trader back to St Aloysius!'

A schoolmate later told me that shortly after I'd left a number of the boys had been sneaking out after 'lights out' and had passed a curtained window. Through a tiny gap they saw McInerney stripped to the waist and being flogged. Apparently, the Jesuits had their own ways of dealing with that kind of perversion.

By Christmas of 1941, it was decided that my mother and I had to leave Ceramic and live permanently with Granny at The Orchard in Manly Vale to look after her.

Back at St Aloysius, I tried to get on with my schooling, escaping whenever possible down to the surf at Queenscliff. I hated my new home with silent, depressed, sedentary Granny.

In 1942, I decided I wanted to join the Royal Australian Navy, which meant I had to pass my Matriculation examination at seventeen, so my mother sent me to J. W. Cornforth's crammer academy in Mosman.

Meanwhile, Granny simply existed, wandering aimlessly about the house.

To pick up my spirits, I was given a fox terrier puppy we called 'Boy'. He didn't like Granny and from the start the feeling was mutual. The dog became my comfort and distraction and I loved it. Granny continued with her sulks. Then, far worse, dementia began to set in. One morning during classes at J.W. Cornforth's I received a phone call from Aunt Lil.

'Trader, darling, your wee dog's been run over.'

It had been killed instantly.

CHAPTER SEVEN

THE NIGHT ALL HELL BROKE LOOSE

IN 1942, THE CITY of Sydney was considered well clear of the war with Japan. A line had been drawn westwards from near Noosa, north of Brisbane. If the Japanese ever did land in Australia, we were told, our troops would hold them at that line.

On the night of 31st May 1942, I caught the ferry *Bellubera* home from Circular Quay to Manly at about 9 p.m.

In those war years there was a boom (defensive anti-submarine net) stretching across Sydney Harbour from Watson's Bay to Clifton Gardens. This had two gates to allow shipping to pass through; one at Watson's Bay, the other at the western side. This latter gate was usually kept tightly closed, except to let the giants through: the *Queen Mary*, *Queen Elizabeth* and *Mauretania*, which by this time had all been converted into troop ships. Due to their immense size, they would never have sailed comfortably through the eastern gate.

On this particular night, the *Bellubera* approached the eastern gate at Watson's Bay and went through. As we approached the gate we had reduced speed. After clearing the gate we increased speed again and on we sailed across Sydney Harbour to Manly. I went home and was in bed sound asleep when all hell broke loose.

Three Japanese midget submarines, each with a crew of two and armed with a pair of torpedoes, had entered Sydney Harbour. Two of these had managed to pass unchallenged through the boom gates, but the third got tangled in the net. The two successful submarines had entered by following the Manly ferries at periscope depth.

History shows that several Japanese ships had brought the midget submarines to a position seven miles outside Sydney Harbour. One of the ships had launched a small seaplane a few hours before dawn, which had flown low over the harbour, noting the ship and torpedo net positions.

The three midget subs planned to enter Sydney harbour at twenty-minute intervals after moonrise that night, around 8 p.m. They were to wait to enter the inner harbour via the boom gates, positioning themselves close behind one of the scheduled ferries.

At around 9 p.m., the first got fouled up in the boom net near Clifton Gardens. The two-man Japanese crew committed suicide after setting the charge that some hours later scuttled it. The other two subs got in cleanly, but one of them was soon spotted, attacked, and damaged with depth charges. Its crew also committed suicide around 5 a.m.

The last midget submarine managed to penetrate the harbour defences as far as Pinchgut (Fort Denison), the tiny, fortress island east of the Harbour Bridge. The heavy cruiser USS *Chicago*, in panic, bounced some shells off the fort that ended up ricocheting into the northern suburbs. Luckily, the sub ignored the nearby HMAS *Canberra* and turned back to line up her torpedoes on the *Chicago*, anchored east of Garden Island.

She fired twice at the *Chicago*. The first torpedo passed in front of it and hit the harbour floor beneath the old ferry *Kuttabul*, which was then being used to accommodate sailors. The blast apparently lifted the old ferry clean out of the water and immediately sank her. Twenty-one men sleeping on board were killed; three were saved. The second torpedo ran aground on rocks at Garden Island just ahead of the *Kuttabul* and didn't explode.

All this while I was at home in Manly Vale, blissfully unaware of the horror unfolding only a few miles away.

That third midget sub was thought to have escaped Sydney Harbour around 2 a.m., but she didn't return to her mothership. The favoured theory is that she turned north to draw attention away from her compatriots.

A few years ago, amateur scuba divers discovered a midget submarine partly buried in the seabed five kilometres out from

Bungan Head, just north of Newport Beach. Her upper deck had been pierced by shells (probably those fired from the USS *Chicago*). The Australian Naval authorities don't want the exact location of the sub known as she has been designated a war grave.

Later the hulls of the two mutilated, recovered submarines were joined into a single, intact one, which toured southern Australia to help raise morale and funds. It's still on display in Canberra.

So ended the only episode of World War II with which I might have had some indirect involvement.

When I turned sixteen, my cousin Rosemary, with her own pocket money, bought me a blue tweed sportscoat to impress the girls. At the height of the war dances were held at Mosman Town Hall every Friday night. All the young teenagers from Mosman would attend Miss Bullough's ballroom dance evenings. Her sister, sitting at a table, would collect two shillings each from the randy, brilliantine-creamed lads and would-be sophisticated virgins and we would line up at each end of the ballroom — boys at one end and girls at the other. Miss Bullough would play 'I'm a Little on the Lonely Side' and when the music started the boys would advance down the room like a small army, each of us having eyed the little 'sheila' we fancied dancing with. If permission were granted, away we'd go, dancing the foxtrot, quickstep, waltz, or the maxina, with our sheilas gripped tightly to our hipbones.

One night a beautiful redhead arrived at the Town Hall. It took me two weeks to pluck up the courage to ask her to dance. We danced the maxina, I remember, but her eyes were fixed on a tall, good-looking fella called Bill Buckle and I was given to understand that he was my redhead's choice. Eventually, I learnt that her name was Paula Moccatta, and she and her family had arrived in Sydney in 1941 from Rabaul (one of the New Britain Islands, northeast of New Guinea). In school at that time we were studying the short stories of Joseph Conrad, among which is one called 'Freya of the Seven Isles'. For me, Paula personified Freya as I merged fiction with reality. Paula's father had owned a copra plantation at Rabaul. When the Japanese attacked Pearl Harbour in 1941 the family had fled with only what they stood up in. Paula held a unique mystique for me. She was also a very generous girl and always favoured me with a dance — then off she would go back to the arms of Bill Buckle for the rest of the evening. After the war ended, I thought I would never see her again. But I always remembered Paula, 'the gorgeous Joseph Conrad redhead from the Pacific Islands'.

In 1979, when I was leaving Sydney after promoting my Peter Finch biography, I looked in the phone directory and found one Moccatta listed. When I got back to London, I wrote to Paula at the address given. Several months later I received a reply:

Dear Trader, are you really the boy with the beautiful blue eyes who used to look at me so forlornly at Miss Bullough's hops at the Mosman Town Hall? If you are, then of course I remember you. You were so very sweet.

Yes, I thought. That's why I never used to get anywhere with any of the girls!

When I returned to Australia the following year, I met up with Paula. She was married with three sons and we became close friends. She was still the most generous girl and very sweetly lent me her car, which enabled me to travel to see other friends while in Sydney. I invited her to London a year later and showed her some of the art treasures here, as she was a painter.

Sadly, Paula died in 1989. Still, what a wonderful thing it is to be able to re-connect like that with people from the past.

Meanwhile, as the war continued, Granny continued to decline. Even though the strain was enormous, Mum refused to put her in a home and was still looking after her.

One night in July of 1943, Mum — alone with Granny at The Orchard (I was staying with Aunt Lil so that I could concentrate on my studies) — had fallen asleep in the sitting room in an armchair. Granny was in another armchair opposite.

After some time, Mum woke to find the front door open and Granny gone. She rushed out. It was pitch dark and freezing. Frantic,

Mum raced along the road, but there was no sign of Granny so she returned and rang the police. They came at once and a search began. At around two in the morning they found Granny's frozen little body about a quarter of a mile away near the golf links, curled up in some bushes.

At the time I was thankful I wasn't there, but now I feel ashamed I wasn't able to support my mother during all that. She told me long after that she knew her mother's days were numbered, but no one could have foreseen the sad way she was to go.

Mum told me that Granny often used to murmur, 'Willie! Willie! Where are you?'

I'm quite sure my grandmother had simply gone out to find him.

By 1945, the Second World War was coming to an end. After the period spent at J. W. Cornforth's crammer, I passed my matriculation examinations at a modest level and set off to realise my life's ambition of joining the Royal Australian Navy — only to be failed because I was underweight. Three weeks previously, the atom bombs had devastated Hiroshima and Nagasaki. Now, at the end of the war, they could afford to be choosier in their selection criteria.

A week or two later I had a second go, this time with lead balls in my trouser pockets. That put my weight up a stone.

'But you're as thin as a Hong Kong chopstick,' said the Navy medico. 'And what's that bulge in your trousers? It can't be your manhood. Get back on the scales — stripped!'

I was exposed, in all senses.

Left without any firm ideas of what to do with my life, for a time I drifted, taking one job after another. The influence of my Uncle Jim got me into Lever Brothers to be groomed for executive status. I lasted a week. Next I was employed by a labouring gang, clearing scrubland for building sites at £9 a week. I was rich! Then I worked in a factory assembling and painting toys.

Through Bob Strong, a next-door neighbour who ran the record library at the Australian Broadcasting Commission, I was offered a job as a junior assistant in the record library. I was allowed, occasionally, to choose records for off-peak programmes, so I was able early on to learn a little about music, its composers, and interpreters.

At the record library, Bob Strong had three women working under him to whom I was answerable: Daphne Taylor, Ray Threlfo, and a third whose name I can't remember. To me they were Macbeth's three witches. I was as green as new-mown grass and they nicknamed me 'the cretin'. All three had an inspired talent to make me look a fool. In those days the studios were in Forbes Street, round the corner and up a steep hill from the record library in William Street. The sadistic trio would select seventy-eight rpm records for the two stations — 2FC and 2BL — and lay them out in piles. I would then fill two strong Globite suitcases with the records and await my orders.

'Right, Ron,' Daphne Taylor would say. 'Go for your life. 2BL are running low on music.'

Out I'd run and up the hill. Sometimes I'd creep into a studio with a distraught female announcer halfway through her last seventy-eight (the announcers were then all elderly ladies with lovely voices). I could never understand in retrospect why there wasn't a stack of records in a bin nearby for an emergency.

The crunch finally came one blistering summer day when I returned from my exhausting climb up Forbes Street with two suitcases full of records to find the record library as hot as a tramp steamer's engine room.

'Why lug two heavy cases up there at once, Ron?' said Daphne. 'Why not make two trips with less weight?' She sighed, crossing her arms. 'Ronnie Faulkner, if only you'd been given brains as well as beauty!'

Daphne's remark was ill-timed. Fed up, I picked up a large pile of records and dropped them onto the floor at her feet.

'I'm taking permanent leave, girls. The next haul up Forbes Street is all yours!'

That was the end of my stint at the record library.

One day in 1945, shortly after Japan had surrendered, I got word from a close friend in the Navy that the hospital ship SS *Centaur* was due to berth at Woolloomooloo docks the following morning. She was bringing back former prisoners of war from New Guinea.

At seventeen, having missed the chance to join up to fight the Japanese by three weeks, I was determined to see this.

At the docks in those days there was a space with railings through which one could watch the passengers disembark. My memory of the details of the scene is vague, but what does remain clear is the image of the seemingly endless stream of wounded and disabled coming off that ship — soldiers and civilians (men and women alike) who had been taken prisoner and suffered in the camps. I shall never forget their emaciated, crippled state — some on stretchers, some minus arms and legs, others with their faces concealed by bandages — as they slowly filed past. This macabre spectacle has haunted me ever since, and has served for me as an unforgettable demonstration of the horrors of war.

In 1951, in London, when I read that we were at war again (this time in Korea), I felt such a loathing for the politicians who could choose to set in motion once more these dark forces of our destructive human nature. Then, of course, came Vietnam, Iraq, and later Afghanistan. It seems we never want to learn. That to me is the eternal sadness of the human condition.

CHAPTER EIGHT

PETER FINCH AND FIRST PROFESSIONAL STEPS

ONE NIGHT EARLY in 1946, shortly after my departure from the ABC Record Library, my mother and I attended a performance at the old Theatre Royal of Noel Coward's *Tonight at Eight-Thirty*, which starred the celebrated Australian husband and wife team Cyril Ritchard and Madge Elliott. A packed house had applauded the actors and Mum and I were making our way out of the auditorium when suddenly she tapped me on the arm.

'Come and meet Tamara Tchinarova,' she said.

Tamara had come to Australia in 1939 with the Colonel de Basil Monte Carlo *Ballets Russes*, and somewhere along the line my mother had met her. We arrived where she was standing and I was introduced. Then Tamara introduced us to the handsome young man standing at her side who she told us was her husband, the actor Peter Finch.

As it happened, a few days before I had been held spellbound by a performance Finch had given on radio as the mad Russian Tsar Paul the First, in a play by Ashley Dukes called *Such Men Are Dangerous* — a performance for which he received a Macquarie radio award. I was, of course, delighted to meet him.

My first impression of Peter was of a withdrawn though self-confident man some eleven years my senior. He was extremely thin and not very tall, with brown wavy hair, fine prominent cheekbones, a high intelligent forehead, and wonderful magnetic eyes that seemed to change constantly from hazel to greenish-blue. But the feature that made me realise he'd have enormous appeal for women was his full sensual mouth. I remember thinking, 'You look just like one of those characters from the eastern Mediterranean.'

Little was said at our first introduction, but he invited me to meet him a few days later at Repin's Coffee Shop in King Street, near the ABC studios. I arrived at Repin's to see Peter seated in one of the booths, waving a pair of very expressive hands at his young actor audience, who were all helpless with laughter. 'Finchie', as he was known to all his friends, was doing his impersonation of the perpetual 'whinge' — Australian slang for a moaning, complaining pessimist who never knows when he is lucky. It was an impersonation I was often to hear subsequently, given new inventive touches.

I was welcomed, and soon joined in the general laughter. Hour after hour passed while he held us enthralled with his comic turns and his thoughts on life and love and theatre. I'd arrived at about 4 p.m. By nine we were still there, discussing films — particularly the work of the French screen stars of the 1930s and 1940s. His ambition, he told us, was to go to France to work in the company of the great Louis Jouvet (Peter had been partly raised in France and was a fluent French speaker). What he admired about French actors was the total professionalism they brought to their craft, crystallised for him in two great films: *La Kermesse Heroique* and *Les Enfants du Paradis*. Subsequently, he took me to see both films at a remote cinema in Narrabeen, and I realised at once the style and standard for which he as an actor and director was striving. Suddenly, this form of working life seemed hugely attractive to me.

'Look,' Peter said, 'your father was a successful film actor. Why not give acting a try? I've just started an acting school. Why not join us?'

The die was cast. I joined Finchie's gypsy caravan and entered into the no-man's-land of the actor's world.

That is how my career began, with classes with Peter Finch and others at the Mercury Theatre School. I have never regretted my decision. Peter widened my artistic horizon, and became a mentor and an elder brother figure.

The first thing I had to deal with was my broad loutish accent. Peter had a suggestion.

'If anyone can remedy the syphilitic vowels you sometimes emit,' he told me, 'Bryson will.'

Bryson Taylor — a portly, jovial, retired ABC radio announcer — had the most beautiful, unaffected speaking voice. My lessons with this avuncular fellow are one of the happiest memories of my early acting career. Bryson ('the Bison', as I called him, as that was exactly what he looked like) had great patience and took care to eliminate my slovenly diction.

'Come on, dear Ron,' he'd say as I laboured with a passage from Shakespeare.

'But soff, what loit threw yonda window brikes? It is the yeast an Jewliut is the Sun. Aroise fair sun … '

'Less through your nose, dear Ron,' the old fellow would say. 'Try to open your throat. Come on, try it again.'

Looking back now, I realise how lucky I was that Bryson Taylor took me on. He worked with me to remove all the Australian flat vowel sounds. The initial stages were humiliating. Bryson — the kindliest, most gentle and patient teacher — used to say, 'Nevermind, young Ron. You'll get there, and the knocks you experience on the way will be the making of you.'

How lucky to have had such a guiding influence at the start of my career.

While continuing my work with Bryson, I began to take part in radio dramas for the Australian Broadcasting Commission.

My first radio job as an eighteen-year-old actor was in a children's serial called *Five Weeks in a Balloon*. Full of arrogant confidence, I found the producer, Dion Wheeler, a carping nit-picker. Everything I said seemed to him flat and lifeless.

'What a cretin!' I thought. 'Why does he constantly pick on me?'

When the serial was broadcast, I listened to it.

'Mum!' I yelled. 'That bastard Wheeler has replaced me! They've got some other kid to do my part and he stinks!'

'No,' said Mum, 'that's you all right. And you certainly do stink. Now perhaps you'll listen when I tell you to speak the King's English!'

What I had heard out of that radio speaker was so awful. Later I asked Bryson, 'Was that really me?'

'I'm afraid so, Ron. But I know you'll work to improve.'

Somehow, between Bryson and Finchie, I was slowly dragged up to an acceptable vocal quality.

I was learning my acting skills in Sydney radio, where the standard was world class. Sydney radio was a superb training ground for voice and characterisation because the script writing was so good. We played English classics with the George Edwards Production Company, broadcast through station 2UW. You picked up your scripts the night before, or they were posted to you. On several occasions the scripts hadn't been finished and you didn't get one until you turned up at the studio. You went into the Homebush Studios at 9 a.m. and worked through till 1 p.m. The scripts were brilliantly adapted from Dickens, Wilkie Collins, Somerset Maugham, and Edward Bulwer Lytton, and were recorded onto the old seventy-eight rpm wax discs. If we were running overtime, George Edwards or his wife, Nell Stirling, would give a signal from the control booth to 'cut'. This was indicated with the index and middle finger miming scissors, and referred to passages of the script already marked as potential cuts. On the other hand, if time needed to be filled, another gesture of stretching something between the hands meant to slow down — in other words, to tease it out. It was a hair-raising way of working, but, if you worked for George Edwards, you learnt from a very skilled company of radio actors.

Theirs was a brilliant system, but required technique, nerves of steel, and the ability to think fast and to characterise quickly. The responsibility was enormous. You couldn't afford to fluff or falter on a line because you'd spoil the recording and they'd have to begin all over again on a fresh disc. I don't remember this ever happening as a result of an artist faltering on their lines — which indicates the high standard of the actors in the George Edwards Group.

Another thing I learnt from these early years in Sydney radio was the necessity to develop a bawdy sense of humour.

In my time there, there was an actor named Cecil Perry who was considered almost unemployable. In his youth, he had been strikingly handsome, with a beautiful voice, but by the time I knew him he was in decline — a heavy drinker. On one occasion Finchie and I and a number of other actors were rehearsing a jungle scene and the producer wanted the sound of a muffled distant drum. A large kettledrum was erected near the FX microphone, but when struck with the padded stick this drum didn't make the muffled throbbing the producer wanted. We were all at the second microphone with our backs to the drum. Suddenly, there came the sound of a soft throbbing.

'That's it!' called the producer from the control booth. 'You've got it! That's exactly the sound we want.'

He hadn't looked up to see who had made the drumming, and we were too focused on our scripts to see what had made that perfect sound. Suddenly, Cecil Perry roared with laughter. We turned round to see what he had found so amusing.

Very well-endowed, Cecil had taken out his large member and was banging it gently on the drumhead to create the desired muffled effect. Unfortunately, they hadn't recorded it — which was a shame, since whatever we ended up using didn't sound anything like as effective.

Over coffee, after the recording finished, Finchie said: 'Had I been producing, I'd have sent the girls out, used Cyril's honourable member, and recorded that ideal sound!'

I don't believe Cecil ever worked again. I will always remember him as a wonderful actor of enormous charm, humour, and presence.

Starting my apprenticeship as an actor under Peter Finch's tutelage, I was totally susceptible to any suggestions he made as to how I could improve my technique.

'If you want to be the best as an actor, young Ron,' he said to me one day, 'you'll have to rid yourself of inhibition. An actor must feel totally free to express what's within him. Will you be my guinea pig?"

Back in 1935, the then nineteen-year-old Peter Finch had played the juvenile in the drama company of a travelling circus run by the British-born and Jamaican-descended impresario George Sorlie, which had toured the Australian Outback. Among his mates in the circus were the Flying Ardinis, a married couple of trapeze artists. A decade later, Ted Ardini had opened an acrobatic school in Sydney.

Finchie had decided that I was the ideal candidate on whom to try out one of his theories.

'You have to learn how to act with your body as well as with your voice,' he told me. 'To do that, you need to have the physical flexibility of an acrobat. So, I'm taking you over to Marrickville to my friend Ted Ardini's gym. He'll teach you the backflip.'

'Oh, yeah!' I enthused. 'That'd be terrific!'

'Yes,' Finchie added, 'but when you do the backflip you'd better be careful. Mis-time that move and you'll end up blowing your nose through your bum!'

Ted Ardini taught all his pupils, all of them twelve years of age and under, to do the backflip. He would support them in a harness attached by ropes through pulleys to the ceiling and ask them to do a back somersault. On my first day, after an agonising warm-up, Ted strapped me into the harness. Ted's wife Jean stood ready to pull on the rope. 'Hooo-huuup!' yelled Ted. The palm of his hand was in the small of my back to support me. Up I sprang and backwards, banana-shaped, onto the palms of my outstretched hands, the pulley taking my full weight. Then I was over and back on my feet, earning a round of applause from Ted's young students, and a pat on the back from Finchie.

'I'll be back in a month to see you fly solo, mate, so go to it. If you're successful, I'll cast you as an acrobatic Puck in *A Midsummer Night's Dream*, or, better still, as a flying Ariel in *The Tempest*.'

After a couple of weeks in the harness, thanks to the physical input from Ted and Jean, I was beautifully air-borne, the harness always taking my weight.

Then came the day Finchie arrived to see my progress.

'Tonight,' he said, 'this emu will fly!'

Ted fitted the harness. The emu preened his plumage.

'Ho-hup!'

Ted jerked the harness. I was over and back on my feet before Finchie could blink.

'OK,' said Finchie, 'now take off the harness.'

The harness was removed and I took up my position on the mat and flung my arms downwards, ready to leap. There I remained, rooted to the spot.

'Go for it, Trade!' shouted Ted. 'You can do it, lad,'

The emu stood there, stricken. The crowd of students started barracking,

'Go for it mate!'

'You can do it!'

'Have a go, sport!'

Abject funk rooted me to the spot.

Finchie got angry.

'For God's sake, Ronnie! Do you expect to play Ariel in a harness with someone pulling the bloody strings every time you make an entrance?'

Humiliated and losing my temper, I lashed out.

'You try this, Finchie, and I'll pull the bloody strings!'

Finchie went off into a huddle with Ted. Then he came over and told me Ted had a plan. Ted had disappeared for a moment and returned with his hands behind his back. He then explained that he and Peter would stand on either side of me, and when Ted said 'go!' I was to throw myself backwards with all the strength I could muster.

'If you're in trouble, Finchie and I'll catch you,' said Ted. 'But for God's sake GO, man, or we'll be here all bloody night!'

Panicked thoughts raced through my mind. The floor? Concrete! The crash mat? Thin rubber.

They moved in.

'Shut your eyes, Trade,' said Ted, 'and when I say "Ho-hup!" reach for heaven!'

I took up my position, got the signal and — feeling like Sputnik — lifted off. But just before I heard the 'Ho-hup' I felt an excruciating pain across the calves of my legs, as though I'd been flicked with a red-hot wire. Up and backwards I sprang, and my palms hardly seemed to touch the floor before I was back on my feet, light as a feather, to a round of applause. Ted and Finchie hadn't touched me. But Ted had used an old circus trick, flicking me across my calves with a thin cane-like whip to make the emu fly.

'Is that what you did to Finchie to get him to lift off, back in the Sorlie days?' I asked Ted.

'Oh, I've never tried it,' said Finchie. 'But you were brilliant. I was right. You're my successful experiment.'

'Then I hold you to your promise about Puck and Ariel,' I told him.

We shook on it. But Finchie left for England eighteen months later without my having played either part.

Ted Ardini knew exactly what he was doing. The whiplash stung for a while, but my fear of making the leap had gone. From then on, week after week, Ardini's acrobatic classes were exhilarating. The whole experience symbolised a small victory in my life's constant conflict against fear and self-doubt.

Although, it would be forty years before I'd try to do the backflip again.

One day in the summer of 1946, Peter approached me at the end of one of his classes.

'The Independent Theatre in North Sydney is mounting a production of *Hamlet* and they're looking for a young actor. The part's only a few lines, but it'll get you in front of an audience. You won't be paid but it's a start. How about it?"

My first role in the theatre! I was thrilled. I would play The Messenger, who delivers letters from Hamlet to Claudius.

Before curtain up on opening night I was struggling into a pair of black tights a size too big that concertinaed from thigh to ankle. To brace them up I was given a long length of tape and several large penny coins.

Having put the tights on, I placed the pennies inside the tops as makeshift buttons — an old actors' trick — securing the tape to the pennies, winding it several times over my shoulders, round and round my waist, and endlessly under my crotch. By the time the tape had been fully extended, I'd trussed myself up like Tutankhamun.

Now alarm bells were ringing: I was busting for a leak. My back teeth were already awash. The play by now was well under way and my cue not far off.

'I've got to get to the dunny,' I told Johnny Craig, who like me was awaiting his cue.

'Then you'd better put your skates on, sport,' said Johnny.

Seizing my prop letters, I raced to the lavatory, directly below the stage and as cold and dark as Fingal's Cave. Dropping Hamlet's letters to the floor, I frantically unwound the tapes and with enormous relief let Nature take its course. Above me the play droned on. How near was my cue? I listened. Laertes was whingeing on about Hamlet killing his old man.

And so have I a noble father lost ...

'Oh shit!' I thought. 'I'm on!'

Heaving up my tights, I wrestled frantically to rewind the tapes, gave up halfway, groped and grabbed Hamlet's letters from the floor, and stuffed them into my doublet. Forgetting it was strictly forbidden to pull the chain during performance because of the noise, I flushed the ancient dunny — rightly called Volcania. Loud guffaws came down to me from the audience.

Up the stairs I stumbled, my cue now missed, and saw that Johnny Craig wasn't in the wings waiting to go on as Osric. Johnny, who was a wizard at improvising Shakespearean doggerel, was onstage bowing to Claudius.

The messenger, my liege, was taken short.
And thus delayed in making his report.

I hobbled on, my tights sagging to my ankles, penny coins rolling under the seats of the audience, and landed prostrate at the King's feet.

'Letters, my Lord, from Hamlet,' I gasped. And withdrew from my doublet a wadge of lavatory paper. In my panic I'd snatched it from the dunny floor instead of Hamlet's letters!

Wild ribald laughter from the audience encouraged me to tear off a sheet from the crumpled roll and hand it to the King.

'This to your Majesty!' I declaimed.

Claudius, gobsmacked, grasped the proffered sheet with his fingertips.

'This ... ... from Hamlet?'

We were no longer in a play. This was vaudeville. Johnny Craig, now well in his stride, let his inspiration flow.

My Lord, these strange events take not amiss,
For when your bladder's full you've got to piss.
And if you, too, need urgently to go,
Volcania's throne awaits you down below!

That was it. Down came the curtain. Johnny and I were sacked on the spot.

Soon after, the Minerva, one of two professional theatres in Sydney, sent out word it was looking for a versatile young actor. I auditioned and was cast in Warren Chetham-Strode's *The Guinea Pig*, which was based on the Fleming Report of 1944 that recommended that selected grammar school boys be sent to English public schools. The character Jack Reid was a gift of a part for me — a cockney boy from Walthamstow who ends up speaking and behaving exactly as an English public school product. The play was my first big chance in the theatre, and luckily I scored with it, getting all the notices — one of the papers declaring in their review headline, 'Boy Outstanding!'

Several months later, I played Richard Miller, 'love's young dream', in Eugene O'Neill's domestic comedy *Ah, Wilderness!* — and then enjoyed a run in Max Catto's *They Walk Alone*. My character in the play is seduced by a notorious killer called Emmy Baudine — a story apparently based on fact. Towards the end of the play, Emmy says to my character: 'Larry, come into the barn and I will teach you about love.' Larry is thereafter discovered unspeakably murdered. Anxious to know how he was murdered, I eventually learned that the real Emmy had, in her moment of ecstasy, bitten off her poor victim's testicles!

The play became a talking point, and in the entertainment sections of one of the tabloids mention was made of me and of my character's sad and painful demise — 'an unusual, but very effective way to gain notoriety as an actor.'

CHAPTER NINE

DR CAIUS, FIRST LOVE, AND TYRONE GUTHRIE

DURING THIS PERIOD, around 1948, Fred Nossal and I were into nightclubs and women — all very innocent, believe it or not. But we still knew how to enjoy ourselves.

There was a nightclub called Carl Thomas in those days at Sydney's Circular Quay. So sophisticated we felt ourselves to be there, as we spooned away at our avocados and sipped our chilled Anjou rosé wine in the upstairs balcony restaurant that overlooked the dancefloor and the ferries coming and going from the nearby dock. On one occasion Fred was escorting Ruth Lawrie, a young journalist who worked on the *Sun* newspaper on which Fred was a cadet reporter. I immediately felt violently attracted to Ruth. We all drank and danced away the night.

'There's nothing between Ruth and me, Trade, if you're interested,' said Fred, a few days later. 'She's just a colleague.'

I couldn't believe it. I rang Ruth and we spent some time together, but I never felt that I was getting anywhere with her, even though I became ever more enamoured.

Around this time I was cast as Claudio in a production of *Measure for Measure* and gave what must have been a disastrous performance — playing the part with a broad Australian accent. A few weeks later, and completely unexpectedly, the same director (John Alden, who was making some waves with his Australian Shakespeare productions) came to me.

'We're doing Shakespeare's *Merry Wives of Windsor* next. You have a good ear. Do you think you could do a French accent?'

'Of course I could,' I rashly replied.

Accordingly, I was cast as Dr Caius, and decided to play him as an outrageous eccentric. I fashioned a mini Cyrano de Bergerac false nose using plasticine. When I'd finished my make-up for the dress rehearsal, Alden turned to me and said: 'My God, Trader, that's a transmogrification!'

On the opening night, I got raucous rounds of applause on every exit. I also received rave press notices. My success as Dr Caius gave me enormous confidence both as man and actor. This confidence was increased when my paramour Ruth suddenly avowed her love for me. It was my public success with Dr Caius, I reckoned, that had won her over.

At that time, Tyrone Guthrie was visiting Australia to advise on the possibility of forming an Australian National Theatre. In Britain, Guthrie had directed all the greats — Olivier, Guinness, Gielgud, and Richardson — in some of the most famous productions of the 1930s and 40s. In Australia, however, he was intensely disliked for having candidly told his hosts, 'Well, ladies and gentlemen, as regards an Australian national theatre, you're simply not yet ready. So you'd better put that idea down the lavatory and pull the chain.'

This was said at a reception in his honour, after his having seen what Australia had to offer theatrically. However, Guthrie had agreed during his visit to interview actors, directors and designers to advise them, so I thought, 'What have I got to lose?' and put my name down to see him.

Guthrie was a huge man, well over six-feet tall.

'Well, young man,' he said, 'what can I do for you?'

'I'd like to know what my chances would be as an actor in England ... '

'With that accent you wouldn't have a hope in hell,' he said. 'But tell me what you've done.'

I reeled off a list of radio productions — which meant nothing to him — and my recent theatre work.

'At the moment,' I said, 'I'm playing in *The Merry Wives of Windsor* at the Independent Theatre.'

'I saw that last night,' said the great man, 'but I certainly didn't see you.'

'I was there,' I said, continuing in my broad Australian accent. (I had decided to play a game with Mr Guthrie because I knew I was unrecognisable in my elaborate Dr Caius make-up.)

'Well,' he went on, 'if you were there, it must've been in a non-speaking part because I certainly didn't see you.'

'Oh, yeah,' I replied. 'Ya did see me all right. I'd take an oath on it.'

'Then what did you play?'

'Dr Caius, the French physician.'

'No,' scoffed Guthrie. 'You certainly weren't Caius.'

'Oh, but I was,' I protested. 'And I've got me photos here ta prove ut.'

I pulled out a folder of Caius photographs and handed them to him. He looked at them, then looked at me, then looked at the photos again.

'You bloody rascal!' he said. 'So you can speak properly, after all.'

I did my posh English voice from *The Guinea Pig*. He roared with laughter.

'I don't believe this!' he said. 'How old are you?'

'Tweni-one, sir.'

Silence. Then: 'Well, you were the best thing in it.'

I remember feeling a huge surge of pride. I only knew Guthrie by reputation, but I had just been paid an extraordinary compliment by a man not known to give praise freely.

'Next year I'm doing a play called *Top of the Ladder* with John Mills,' he went on. 'There's a juvenile part in it. It's yours if you can get to London by next May.'

He gave me his card. 'This is my address and telephone number. If you get there, ring me up. Goodbye, good luck, and congratulations on Caius.'

An acceptance by Guthrie and a beautiful girl in love with me. For the first time in my life, I thought I was quite irresistible.

Not long after my success with Dr Caius I was hired to appear in *Fly Away Peter* by A.P. Dearsley for the producer J.C. Williamson, with performances in Melbourne and Sydney. In the cast was a feisty young English actress whom I immediately fell for, in spite of my recent conquest of Ruthie's affections. I shall call her 'Trixie'. Unfortunately, being away in Melbourne for some weeks without Ruthie, my casual flirtations with Trixie evolved into something decidedly stronger. Trixie was ripe, luscious, and 'experienced', and I — still a virgin — was determined that she would be my first bite at the forbidden apple.

Accordingly, when the end of the Melbourne run came I callously broke off with Ruthie — causing her great hurt and distress and myself, eventually, a lifetime of richly-deserved guilt. Ruth Lawrie was the sweetest girl, but I was selfish and immature and indifferent to her pain. The years that followed taught me that sooner or later what we do to others is reflected right back at us. That was a lesson I was to learn only too late.

In any case, I invited Trixie to spend a weekend at The Orchard. To my delight she was quick to say 'yes'.

The first hurdle I had to pass, however, was to equip myself against any unwanted consequences — occasioning a visit to a chemist that threw me into a state of catatonic embarrassment. Eventually, the purchase was completed and I beat a hasty retreat, thinking that now there was nothing standing between me and the culmination of my lustful desires. When we arrived at The Orchard, however, things began to look not so easy.

For a start, Mum obviously saw Trix as ninety miles of bad road.

From the moment Trix walked in the door (looking like Mata Hari), Mum — clearly aware of my intentions — laid a cunning plan. She invited two friends to stay: Sybil, and Sybil's odious lover Ray. Egged on by Mum, these two never left us alone for one second.

Mutual passion finally drove us to seek what we both desperately wanted in the great outdoors. We planned our romantic tryst for that night, but dinner that evening was endless.

Afterwards there was the washing up. Then a game of cards. It was nearly 1 a.m. before anyone made a move towards bed.

In my room I waited. Outside there was bright moonlight and silence, except for the buzz of cicadas. Inside, a mixed chorus of nasal road-drilling from the sleeping jailers eventually told me that I was clear for take-off.

Into the garden I sped and round to Trix's window — a screwdriver in one hand, and a ladder under my arm. Up I climbed and scratched ever so delicately on the wire fly-screen.

Trix, appearing in a flimsy nightie, was obviously hot to trot.

'When I've got these bloody screws out, give the fly screen a shove,' I hissed.

But the wooden frame holding it wouldn't budge. Trixie, frantic, tried to kiss me through the wire.

'Oh, darling! My lovely beetle! For God's sake get it out!' she whispered.

'I can't get a grip on it,' I moaned back.

Suddenly, the screen gave. Out shot Trix like an intoxicatingly perfumed missile. I grabbed her, and CRASH! Down went the ladder and us with it, arse over turkey, giggling and rolling over each other in the soft grass.

'Who's that?' bawled Ray, who was at his window. He soon spied the ladder and the fly-screen on the grass.

'Sheila!' he yelled. 'It's those bloody kids!'

We shot out of that garden like a fart from a racehorse.

My choice for our love-tryst was a low-lying jungle of clover on the ninth fairway of the Manly golf course. When at last we reached the chosen spot, Trix tore off her nightie and flung herself down naked into the clover — which was soaking wet.

'Shit!' she screamed.

'Don't worry, darl,' I whispered. 'I'll soon make you forget the dew.'

I plunged my hand into my trouser pocket for the most embarrassing purchase I'd ever made. But looking at it in the bright moonlight, I suddenly froze.

'Trix, it's got a hole in it.'

'What!' she yelled. 'A hole? You're an arsehole!'

Slapping me an almighty wallop across the face, she snatched up her nightie, leapt to her feet, and vanished into the night.

The next day Trix and I finally managed to find a moment together alone.

'Listen,' she said to me, 'why don't you come to London with me? You could try your luck there.'

Trix had decided to return to London to work first in rep, and then to try for the West End.

Smiling, she laid a hand on my arm. 'We could travel together.'

My mind boggled with the propects that might bring. That evening, during dinner, I told my mother that at twenty-two years of age now was the time for me to leave Australia and try my luck as an actor in London.

There was a moment of gob-smacked silence.

'I've saved enough money to survive for a year,' I continued. 'I'll take on any sort of job to get started. I've done as well as I can as an actor here — *and* I've got Tyrone Guthrie's offer of work in the play with John Mills, so what have I got to lose?'

'He'll be most welcome to visit my parents in Hampshire,' added Trix. 'My father has a farm there.'

Trix's theatrical contract had expired so, we rashly announced, we'd travel together. This is when I began to realise what an ace player my mother was in life's game of chess.

'Fine,' she said, 'because then I can come with you and follow my life's ambition to go to North Africa, where I can study the ceremonial dancing of the Algerian berbers.'

Over coffee, she outlined her plan in more detail. Determined that I should be undistracted in London while attempting to make good as an aspiring actor, she was dead against the idea of Trix and I travelling together. Her proposal was that we should not see each other for twelve months. Trix would sail home to London. I would travel to London on a different ship with my mother, who would disembark at Malta and make her way to North Africa to study and to write about the *Ouled Nails*, as they were called. She would then travel to Spain, where she intended to live for a while in Seville.

Much as Trix and I loved each other (we thought), we did pledge not to see one another for a year.

On 31st March 1950, our tearful farewells were made and Trix, with Sybil and Ray, saw Mum and me off from Woolloomooloo on the SS *Moreton Bay*. Trix would sail four days later on the MV

Empire Star for London via South Africa.

Held up by a strike in Melbourne dock, the *Moreton Bay* arrived several days later in Port Adelaide at midnight. In the morning the ship I could see berthed ahead of us was the *Empire Star*. Due to the strike, both ships would now be delayed even longer. Amid gales of laughter, Trix and I embraced passionately at the foot of the *Empire Star*'s gangway. (Luckily we'd both risen early and so were alone.) Obviously we were not meant to undergo the year-long sentence of separation.

Needless to say, when Mum surfaced the excrement hit the fan. I can't remember the intervening days till we sailed except for two memorable incidents.

The first was that Ray and Sybil suddenly arrived from Manly. But this time our prison warders were outmanoeuvred. Trixie and I were free agents, and we seized our opportunity, made up a picnic hamper with several bottles of Seppelts' best South Australia wine, and escaped for the day to the Adelaide Hills.

Boozed up on a mountaintop with the woman you love ... what a way to lose one's virginity!

The last days in Adelaide were very strained. Together with mother, Ray and Sybil, we visited vineyards and drove to beauty spots. Then there were more tearful farewells as the *Moreton Bay*, with mother and I on board, left several hours before Trix and the *Empire Star*.

The sad lovers were parted once again.

PART
TWO

LONDON –
THE EARLY YEARS

CHAPTER TEN

LONDON AND NEW YORK

AFTER STOPOVERS AT Colombo, Aden, Suez, and Malta (where Mother disembarked for North Africa), the SS *Moreton Bay* finally docked at Southampton on 1 May 1950.

Very early that morning, I caught the train for Waterloo. My first hotel was the Eccleston in Victoria — at a cost of £1 per night in bleak, desolate, post-war London. What a godforsaken place it seemed, so far from home and the sunshine that was the essence of life to me. Everywhere were the scars of bomb damage, a full five years after the war had ended.

As soon as I could, I telephoned Tyrone Guthrie, who told me that the play in which he had offered me a part had been postponed — leaving me high and dry in a new country halfway round the world from my home, with no job and no friends.

With very little money I had to move quickly. I wandered round the neighbourhood into Ebury Street. Outside a door hung a card with large printed letters: VACANCY. I knocked.

The squeaking door opened a fraction. A high-pitched voice, in very refined English: 'Yis?'

'I'm looking for lodgings.' (How lucky that I was wearing my best suit and tie!)

'Well, it's £2 a week. And you must love my pussy!'

At that moment, from under her ankle-length skirt emerged a very thin, mangy, grey cat.

'Oh, I'm sure your pussy and I will become very well acquainted, madam,' I told her.

'I hope so. I'm Winifred Bamborough. This is a very respectable area — we're a SLOANE telephone exchange.'

My room on the first floor overlooked Ebury Street. It was 'bed and breakfast', but as there was no dining room every morning Winifred brought breakfast up to me on a tray. Of course Pussy had to come too; that was part of the deal. My 'breakfast' was a congealed fried egg peppered with Pussy fur and a slice of shrivelled bacon.

Now I had to find a job and quickly. In this, Winifred came up trumps.

'I must find work Miss Bamborough, but where? Do you have any ideas?'

'Try any Lyons Corner House. They're always looking for casuals.'

She suggested the one in the Strand. I went along and, after a brief interview, I was employed in the kitchen, washing and rinsing Knickerbocker Glory glasses. These tall flutes resembled the receptacles doctors provided for urine samples.

At Lyons these came to me on a conveyor belt. On my left was a sink into which I had to plunge two glasses at once into hot soapy water to remove the remains of the Knickerbocker — jelly, meringue, custard, and ice cream. I was then supposed to dip them into the sink of hot water on my right to rinse before putting both cleaned goblets back onto the moving conveyor belt for drying and redelivery to the front. All superbly timed — if you weren't conscientious. My first two glasses arrived, but I wasn't satisfied that one plunge was enough and plunged them a second time. Fatal! The goblets started to pile up. Soon a mountain of them crashed to the floor.

I was demoted to boiling the potatoes. But at least I had an income.

London — one of the busiest, most vibrant, and exciting cities in the world — answers Dr Johnson's description absolutely: 'When a man is tired of London, he is tired of life.' But being twelve thousand miles from home, and alone, took all the determination I could muster at the time. London on a Sunday could be as lonely an experience as I've ever known. But I was young and full of energy, so I began to explore the city and to mine its cultural and historic riches. The challenge was to keep depression at bay at any cost. It was seeing others in a bad way — some indeed in a truly deplorable state — that provided the incentive for me to put aside any thoughts of home and self-pity. I knew my future would be what I would make of it, so I set about going to museums and art galleries. I also began making the rounds, trying to get an agent to represent me and to find a job somewhere in the business.

Given my experience with Australian radio drama, I applied for and was auditioned by BBC Radio. An elderly Englishman with impeccable manners and a twinkle in his eye named Martyn C. Webster called me into his office and told me that the panel weren't very taken with what I'd done. But what had been my radio experience in Sydney? In the ensuing conversation it came up that, among other things, I had played the cockney boy Reid in Warren Chetham-Strode's *The Guinea Pig* onstage. Immediately Martyn brightened.

'I'll shortly be doing that very play for the Home Service. Can you really do an impeccable public school accent?'

'Oh yes, sir. *Rahther!* And I'm confident I shan't let you down. Please, sir! Do let me try.'

He took a chance and my fifty years in BBC Radio began. Over the years Martyn gave me loads of varied radio work, and remained a true friend.

A month or so after my arrival, walking up Shaftesbury Avenue one dreary, wet afternoon, I stopped outside the Globe Theatre (now renamed the Gielgud) to gaze enviously at the playbill and photos of Paul Scofield in Jean Anouilh's *Ring Round the Moon*, directed by Peter Brook. (Little did I realise then that in only a few years I'd be working with Scofield and Brook myself.)

Just inside the theatre door I noticed a girl who was also examining the show photos. She turned.

'No!' we both shrieked. 'It can't be! It is!'

It was Trixie — the one person I'd been determined *not* to see in England until I had my first job. We roared with laughter, and off we went — to Fortnum and Mason for a cuppa and a bite of *cike*. Why not? Here I was, my unvarnished Aussie self again, suddenly and happily reunited with my lost 'sheila'.

Once again my mother's determination to break up the relationship had been foiled. Needless to say, we decided to see one another regularly. This million-to-one encounter seemed to me heaven sent. Over the following weeks we lived, shared, loved and laughed. I also met her delightful family, and spent occasional weekends with them in Hampshire. Then, in July, came a call inviting me for an audition that changed my life and put our relationship on hold.

The call came from Hugh 'Binkie' Beaumont at the H.M. Tennent office in Shaftesbury Avenue. Richard Burton was leaving John Gielgud's successful West End production of Christopher Fry's *The Lady's Not for Burning* to play *Henry V* at Stratford. Gielgud wanted to take his production to Broadway and needed a replacement.

As I have said, Tyrone Guthrie, with whom I had hoped to find employment after my arrival in London, had been unable to offer me anything, as his play had been postponed. Embarrassed, he had contacted H.M. Tennent, the producers of *The Lady's Not for Burning*, suggesting that I should be auditioned.

The playwright Christopher Fry was hearing the first of the thirty-odd applicants for the part when I arrived to join the end of the queue. After I had read my piece I heard a light voice from the darkened auditorium.

'When did you see this show in London, Mr Faulkner?' asked Fry.

'I haven't,' I replied.

'Oh?' he said. 'Well, you gave an interesting reading.'

I didn't tell him that I had spent the previous day hunting for a copy of the play, finally finding one at a railway station bookstall late in the evening — after which I spent half the night studying the part I would have to read.

A few days later I was contacted again and told to attend a second audition, this time with the director — John Gielgud himself. When I had finished giving my reading, as I have described, he asked my name, recoiled in horror at my given-name Ronald, then brightened when I told him of my nickname, Trader — telling me that that would be how I would be billed on Broadway. I had the job!

Once I was set to go to America I again approached the agent Peter Eade, who had told me earlier when I had met him: 'Get a job and I'll come and see you. Then we'll talk.' Hearing the news of my casting, he was only too delighted to take me on. With the prospect of replacing Richard Burton on Broadway, I was suddenly hot property.

One morning a letter arrived for me from my father's youngest sister, Kathryn Lynn, my Aunt Kitty — who was, as I soon discovered, a very reserved English lady. The letter informed me that if I wished to contact relatives of my father I was to reply and send my details. I wrote and Kitty came to vet me in London.

'My God!' she said, when she first saw me. 'You're Jack's issue all right — you have his silly look.' Then she raised an eyebrow. 'Are you also partial to drink and girls?'

I'd better play my cards carefully, I thought.

'In moderation, Aunt. But at the moment it's my career that takes precedence.'

'You humbug!' she said. 'You certainly have John's charm. Watch out it doesn't do for you as it did for him!'

I was more or less free until starting rehearsals for *The Lady's Not for Burning*, so Aunt Kit drove me to Birmingham to meet more relatives. These were Dad's younger brothers, Bill and Bard. Kit then drove me up to Ashby de la Zouche in Leicestershire, where they were all born. The place, and what I knew of the family history, gave me the shudders. 'Was my dad's forebear truly an issue of Warren Hastings?' I wondered, as I looked up at Warren House, imagining all those Victorian children growing up there.

The rehearsals of *The Lady's Not for Burning* were to take place at the Shakespeare Memorial Theatre at Stratford-upon-Avon, where Gielgud was playing *King Lear* (with Alan Badel as The Fool), Angelo in *Measure for Measure*, and Cassius in *Julius Caesar*.

Those three productions, and the performances by Gielgud and his supporting cast, were memorable by any standards. To me, fresh from Australia, I saw what seemed to me the summit of brilliant acting. But my most unforgettable memory is of the actor George Rose, playing the Porter in *Macbeth* and Pompey Bum (the Hogarthian procurer for Mistress Overdone's brothel) in Peter Brook's production of *Measure for Measure*, pulling calling cards out of his bulbous codpiece. George quickly became a loyal and trusted friend.

I also met Richard Burton while we were rehearsing. Initially, Richard and all the rest of the cast were very aloof. Who was this unknown Australian given the enormous privilege of replacing Britain's most promising young actor on Broadway?

The plan was that Burton would open the show on Broadway, get the press notices, and then return to Stratford to play Prince Hal and Henry V, at which point I would take over.

During our rehearsals Gielgud was uncompromising as he relentlessly bullied me to rid my voice of any trace of 'Australiana'. John was a very impulsive man and, at times, had a barbed wit, of which I was often the victim. Whenever a flat Australian vowel crept into my dialogue, a yell came from Gielgud in the stalls.

'Oh, Trader, for God's sake! Take that compost out of your vowel sounds!'

Then he would send me round the block, reciting a sequence of dreary vowel exercises, such as: 'Brown's cows go round and round the townhouse.'

One day I finally did something that pleased him.

'Yes, dear Trader, yes!' said Gielgud, and he rushed over and ran his hand through my thick head of hair. Having realised what he'd done, he immediately recoiled. 'Oh! Forgive me. I mustn't do that. I'm a poof!'

The vulgar Aussie in me sprang to the surface.

'That's all right, John. You can grope my thatch as often as you like, but never below the navel!'

John could always take as good as he gave, and he was such a gentleman of the old school that no one could take offence.

At Christmas 1950, Gielgud gave every member of the company a gift. His gift to every male was a fur-lined, rhinestone-studded jock strap. Instead, I received a pair of silver cuff links. As the new boy he obviously did not want to offend me.

When we travelled to America, we took the show first to Boston, where it ran for a week or two at the Shubert Theatre with Richard Burton in the cast. Then the company was moved into New York to begin rehearsals prior to our opening.

As a member of *The Lady's Not for Burning* company I was given a list of New York City digs and was expected to arrange my own accommodation. As I was then on a minimal salary I chose the Sherman Square Hotel on the West Side — a long way uptown — at only eight dollars a week. When I gave the address to the taxi driver, his laconic 'rather you than me, buddy' should have told me I was in for trouble.

By the look of it, the hotel had been fashionable back in the Victorian era. Now the foyer was dark and sinister.

My bedroom door didn't lock, and the large central heating radiator gurgled incessantly. My immediate thought was: if I'm still alive by morning, I'll be out of here fast. The sheets, at least, were clean and as I began to doze off there was a gentle but persistent knocking on my door. When I finally opened it, before me stood an enormous matronly black woman in a dark dress, clutching a bottle of gin.

On her face was a smile that matched her size.

'Hello, honey,' she cooed. 'I'se Marigold, and I'se included in da tariff!'

'Well, Marigold,' I told her, 'come on in — I'd love to share a nipple of that gin.'

My mind was in a whirl, but I felt it was best to play along. We sat on the bed, I remember, and while we sipped her gin this black angel warned me to leave the place the next morning and to take a hotel she recommended down on 45th Street, where I'd be safe. Then she stood up, gave me a peck on the cheek and was gone. The address to which she sent me was a block away from the Royale Theatre where we were soon to open.

I shall never forget her. What a gift of good advice for eight dollars!

The next day I was called for a costume fitting with the play's designer, Oliver Messel. The fitting was at Messel's apartment, which he shared with his giant of a Swedish boyfriend, Lars. On my arrival, they both insisted that my 'member' must be smaller than Richard Burton's, and that therefore wearing his tights with codpiece attached would make me look rather like a genital Cyrano de Bergerac. When they made as if to take a measurement, I drew the line firmly.

'Come on, darling. The theatre's no place for shyness,' said Lars. 'Don't be unprofessional.'

'As far as taking any measurement,' I retorted angrily, 'you'll have to use your imagination.'

As I turned to go, the Swede pinned my arms from behind. Messel made a playful attempt to grope me, but I managed to back-hoof the Swede, who let me go, and I ran for it.

Consequently, my Broadway codpiece remained 'size Burton'.

Shortly after the show had opened on Broadway and secured its good reviews, Richard departed for London and I took over his role. There is a line in the play that describes the character we played as 'Richard, son of Nobody'. On my first night I received a telegram from Burton, which I still have. It reads: *Best of luck tonight from 'Richard, former son of Nobody'*.

I didn't see Burton again until the mid-fifties, when he visited me on my houseboat, the *Stella Maris*.

At an early period in the New York run, Gielgud took me to one side.

'Dear Trader, Richard had such a beautiful smile. You have those unfortunate crooked teeth. You really should do something about them.'

I went to Dr Pfeiffer, a top New York orthodontist, who said he'd straighten them with a special appliance.

Two small wire grids were made; one to go under my tongue, the other in the roof of my mouth. These grids were attached to hooks soldered onto metal bands. When Dr Pfeiffer finally fitted the bands, he hammered them down and cemented them onto my molars.

'Alrighty, Mr Faulkner. How does that feel?'

'I car spee properly. My outh's ired uh ike a unky caye.'

'Say for me, "She sells sea shells on the seashore."'

'Shee shells heshells o' the heehore.'

'Mr Faulkner, you have to wait an hour or so to allow for subsidence. After that, your articulation will sound just beautiful. Mr Gielgud will love it.'

I reeled onto Fifth Avenue, knowing I'd be speaking Christopher Fry's complicated verse to a packed house in two hours' time.

As the curtain rose there I was, onstage as usual, writing at a medieval lectern. Gielgud appeared, framed in a large Gothic window. He paused on the ledge and called my name.

'Soul!'

At this juncture I was supposed to say, with my back to him: 'And the plasterer ... that's fifteen groats for stopping up the draught in the privy.'

What came out was: 'An er hasterer ... ash heheen gwots hor opping he dra' i er hrivvy.'

From the Gothic window came an anguished 'Oh!' The rest of the act was a nightmare. At the interval, as I bolted distraught from the stage, Gielgud called:

'Trader! Are you drunk?'

He saw my eyes fill with tears.

'Dear boy, for God's sake. Just tell me. I won't be angry.'

'Ish an affiance to shatan my hore hee.'

'Oh my God! We've got to get this frightful thing out quickly.'

Rushing me to his dressing room, he called for Harry the stage carpenter and told him to bring his toolbag.

'I've only got these,' said Harry, and out of his bag came a hammer, chisel, pliers, and a screwdriver.

'Use them!' cried Gielgud. 'Use any tool you've got. But for heaven's sake get that revolting contraption out before the audience ask for their money back.'

Harry managed to remove the lower brace with pliers and a screwdriver. He had succeeded in loosening the top brace when the bell rang for Act II. Luckily in this act I simply had to wash the floor, with very little to say, while Gielgud and Pamela Brown romanticised at the Gothic window.

By the second interval, Gielgud was distraught. Harry had

managed to lower — but not remove — the top appliance. I was now able to speak intelligibly, but with a pronounced 'lithp'. Gielgud panicked.

'We must get the curtain up. Trader, be sure you articulate, and for God's sake see your dentist first thing tomorrow morning!'

Harry having managed to remove the bottom appliance gave me confidence that I was all clear for take off.

Then out of the blue, over the tannoy in my dressing room during the call for Act III beginners, came: 'Miss Penny Munday has unfortunately become too ill with flu to continue. Her understudy will take over for the rest of the performance.'

Penny, playing the *ingénue* Alizon Eliot — my romantic partner in the play — was petite. The understudy, Hazel Terry, was all of 6' to my 5'10". She also had a drink problem.

Act III was our love scene. Up went the curtain with me onstage. As Penny's replacement made her entrance, she seemed very unsteady on her feet. My first line, 'The crickets are singing well with their legs tonight,' sounded to me reasonably intelligible. But she fixed me with a stare of glazed amazement and started to giggle. To shut her up I planted a smacking kiss on her mouth. Whew! Whisky! Light a match and we'd both have gone up in flames.

On my next line — 'Oh Alizon, I so love you. Are you afraid to come away?' — she was supposed to bend down and lift up the back of her overskirt to make a hood, ready to elope. On this occasion, up went her underskirt as well! Over her head went both skirts, blinding her, and revealing a shapely bottom clad in a pair of sexy red knickers.

A galvanised audience rippled with laughter.

Hazel had had that fatal double whisky to get her onstage. From my bride-to-be (enveloped in her skirts, with legs apart and looking like a photographer with a tripod about to take a flash) burst an anguished whisper that carried to the back of the dress circle:

'Where the hell am I? Why's everybody laughing? I'm blind as a fucking bat!'

At that moment one of Dr Pfeiffer's fittings sprang out and zapped itself onto my upper lip. And there it stayed.

For the rest of the play I was not only a man with a cleft palate; I was also a man with a harelip.

My months in New York left me with a wealth of memories and images. I shall never forget walking along Broadway and into teeming Times Square, strolling past music shops with snatches of Chopin mixed with bursts of loud, brassy jazz filling the air. Then there were the streetside vendors of doughnuts and hamburgers, the hooting of car horns, and the muffled roar of the New York subway as it shook the pavement. At night in 42nd Street the neon signs blazed, flashing every colour of the rainbow.

As I said, in the early days in New York most of the London cast were very aloof and I felt very isolated at times. However, one member of the cast did befriend me — the kind and very elderly Esme Percy. He had acted with Sarah Bernhardt, and through his demonstrations I came to know just how Bernhardt must have acted, sounded, and moved.

Esme was minus one eye because his faithful dog had one day jumped up to lick his nose and accidentally removed his eye instead. But he assured me they were still the best of friends. Consequently Esme — who stood all of five-feet tall in high-heel boots, and whose pate was covered with strands of what had once been a fine head of reddish hair — wore a black eye-patch and looked exactly like Rumplestiltskin. He sported a cane with an ivory handle — a gift from the 'Divine Sarah' — and often wore a red cloak.

One evening he invited me to accompany him to dinner in a smart New York restaurant. 'Rumpledforeskin' told me he was madly in love, absolutely revitalised at eighty-seven by having met a very shy lady called Dolores, and asked if I would come along as a third party.

'You, darling heart, will, I know, charm her and make it a most memorable occasion.'

Esme had booked a table for three at an expensive restaurant in Greenwich Village. His paramour should have been waiting for us there, but she wasn't. As the minutes ticked by I kept wondering with whom this old fellow could possibly be in love. Was it some elderly fan from his early days? Some besotted geriatric who had seen him in his glorious 'Sarah Bernhardt' youth and was making a date to see him again after God knows how many years? That was the impression I had gleaned from Esme's extravagant innuendoes. I was expecting at any moment to see an antiquated version of Isadora Duncan totter through the door.

Our table was in the centre of this vast barn of a room. Esme ordered champagne. I sipped. He quaffed in large gulps. Still no sign of his date. A second bottle was ordered. I couldn't help remembering a Bing Crosby song we used to hear on the wireless in the 1940s.

I like the kisses of Dolores...
Aye yi yi, Dolores...

I began to believe that he'd been stood up. How wrong I was. Rising to his feet, he began to declaim: 'Who has known love? Love that can begin as a tiny bud ... the flicker of an eye lid ... a shy glance.'

At tables all around us people began to fall silent. Like a racehorse, Esme was beginning to find his pace and stride.

'Who has known the ecstasy of love's first awakening? Ahh ... the sweetness of that first reciprocal glance. The shy smile ... the intimate knowledge that your love is mutual. Ahh ... '

It was like an aria. By now the entire dining room was staring at him in amazement. I was in two minds: do I pull him down and try to shut him up (how I wish I had), or do I let him continue this extraordinary evocation of Sarah Bernhardt? Finally, he took up his refilled glass of champagne and concluded:

'Love ... that spiritual flowering of the human soul. Oh, what it is to feel love's passion in my decline! And the object of my passion, the flower of my ecstasy about to bloom, my darling is ... you!'

And toasting *me* — swallowing the entire glassful — he collapsed onto his chair.

Suddenly, the restaurant was bedlam. A waiter came over and shouted at me.

'You goddamn fairy! Get out of here, and take that decrepit faggot with you!'

I remember lowering my voice an octave as I bellowed, 'I am not a poofter!'

'Then what're you doing with that senile faggot? This is a respectable eating house. Get out of here, goddamn you!'

By now there was a chorus of diners shouting.

'Goddamn fairy! Get the hell out of here!'

I remember dragging the poor, very drunk old man out and into a taxi.

'Driver!' he yelled. 'Take us to the Hudson River Bridge. I'm going to throw myself off it! My love is destroying me!'

'Driver,' I said, 'my friend is very drunk. Please take us to Park Chambers.'

We got to Park Chambers and I handed him over to the concierge, who agreed to see he got safely to his room.

At the next evening's performance Esme wouldn't speak to me and I felt it would be tactful to leave him alone. A week later he seemed to have embroiled himself thoroughly in the New York gay scene. In any case, his new American lover was a most obnoxious parasite who seemed to be taking him for all he was worth. I met them once on Fifth Avenue and Esme proudly introduced me to this creature.

'We're going to Italy!' he announced, with a look that implied: 'Look what you have missed!'

I never saw Esme again, but I shall always remember him as a kind, ultra-sensitive, extravagant theatrical personality from an age that is long gone. He was one of the gentlest, kindest men I ever had the good fortune to know. Part of his tragedy was living in an age of sexual intolerance. In his defence I can say he would never have been a threat to anyone, even a child. Thinking back now, that is exactly what he was: childlike.

CHAPTER ELEVEN

FILMS, FLAMENCO, AND DOROTHY TUTIN

HAVING ACQUITTED MYSELF successfully in the role Richard Burton had triumphed in the year before gave me one great satisfaction — making the break with Australia had obviously been the right decision.

New York liked *The Lady's Not for Burning*. I remember a stream of celebrities trooping backstage after the performances to congratulate Gielgud — Danny Kaye, Charlie Chaplin, Claude Rains, and Spencer Tracy. Marlene Dietrich was there once, in glittering golden shoes, a gold hat, and something white and body-hugging in between.

One night when I came offstage towards the end of the run Gielgud collared me.

'Well done, Trader. You were every bit as good as Richard in the play tonight.'

Those words gave me enormous self-confidence. His persistent criticism of my performance, I now realised, was for a very constructive purpose — helping me to realise my own acting potential.

From New York the play moved to Washington DC, and six months after opening on Broadway we gave our last performances to packed houses in Philadelphia. Then I went back to New York alone and spent two weeks seeing Broadway shows and visiting Harlem nightclubs.

After our run in New York finished, Claude Rains followed us into the Royale Theatre in *Darkness at Noon*, by Arthur Koestler. My cousin Lucy Faulkner Bryan (who had put me up for most of the run of *The Lady's Not for Burning*) knew Claude and took me backstage to meet him. He and John Barrymore were the two actors I admired the most of any I'd seen on film. His dressing room was packed, but he gave me a few minutes. He agreed about John Barrymore being one of the greatest and advised me: 'Work in English theatre before you make films, which you could well do with your looks. Go for quality in your work and success should follow. I'm coming to London shortly and staying at the Connaught. Look me up.'

I did. Unfortunately, my underground train was held up and I was ten minutes late. A busy man, he was cross but forgiving. He told me he'd been a stage manager for a show playing in Sydney in 1910, and believed the way to learn to act is by first working backstage in the theatre. He told me he'd been taught one golden rule:

'Never lose your sense of humour. Also, remember young man, you're only as good as your last success — if you're lucky enough to have one!'

He confessed that his greatest love was his home and family life, and his privacy.

He offered me a lift in his taxi. I told him I'd walk to the tube as I needed time to digest his words. We shook hands and he was gone. I never saw him again.

I'd been away for nine months with *The Lady's Not for Burning*. On my return to London in May 1951, thrilled to see Trixie again, we resumed where we had left off.

During this period I was getting regular work with BBC Radio. Then I discovered that John Mills was to star in the forthcoming *Mr Denning Drives North*, for London Films, a script adapted from a bestseller that was to be produced by Alexander Korda and directed by Anthony Kimmins. They were looking for a young actor to play a gypsy. I decided to have a go. I went to see Anthony Kimmins who said I looked right, but asked if I could sound like an itinerant gypsy. I read a few lines in cockney. My Australian radio training must have stood me in good stead.

'The part's yours,' said Kimmins.

I was to be paid £25 per day — quite a reasonable fee in those days. To research the part I went to Chertsey, south of London, where I was told I'd find a gypsy encampment. There I watched gypsies bargaining over horse-sales and lounging against bars. I studied their movements, their hands, their eyes, and listened to their talk and laughter.

I mingled with a group who were cordial but initially suspicious. Eventually, I was invited into a caravan to share some muddy-looking soup, with fiery homemade alcohol to wash it down. When I finally told them the truth — that I was researching for a part in my first film — they seemed genuinely interested. In a short while I got what I needed for my character. Confirmation came when I was told that the first rushes of my scenes were excellent.

To play opposite a seasoned veteran like John Mills was like walking a tightrope. At one point we had to fight, and on the day that scene was filmed he couldn't have been more helpful and supportive. As we parted he said, 'Trader, if ever I can help you in any way, let me know.' I never did seek his help, a mistake that I have always regretted. On the other hand, I felt it an imposition to approach Mills without a specific reason.

During our lunch breaks at Shepperton Studios, I dined daily with glamour girls, stars, and extras in the studio cafeteria. There was a long table. At one end sat the VIPs, paying a full five shillings for their meal. In the middle section sat the established but not famous actors, where three shillings was paid. At the far end of the table (where I took my lunches) sat the extras and newcomers, who were expected to sit as far away as possible from the stars and producers and chief cameramen. The upside was that we only had to pay one shilling and sixpence for our meal. All I can remember now is that it was hard for me to concentrate on my food because of all the beautiful females around me. (Trix meanwhile was away working in rep.)

As a result of *Mr Denning*, Peter Eade rang me again.

'The director Richard Vernon, who's just seen you in *Denning*, wants you to test for a film he's about to make with Laurence Harvey and Susan Shaw called *Gathering Storm*.'

I went to Vernon's home and read for the part. The script, a strong melodrama, was the story of two brothers. The elder, Ned (to be played by Laurence Harvey), is in love with Joan Grey (Susan Shaw), a good-time girl, and plans the death of his grandmother (Ethel Edwards) in order to inherit the family farm — putting the blame for her death on his younger, slightly retarded brother, Frankie (me).

'I've seen you on screen so we don't need to test you. You're ideal casting for the younger brother,' Vernon told me.

Mine was a gift of a part and Ethel Edwards, as the granny, was warm and responsive to work with.

Richard Vernon had seen Robert Wise's 1949 boxing ring masterpiece *The Set Up*, which starred Robert Ryan as a washed-up boxer, and was so impressed by the film that it inspired him to make *Gathering Storm* along similar lines. Vernon knew exactly what he wanted, and the whole project seemed set fair. The ninety-minute film was shot in four weeks, as planned. One evening I was sitting with Peter Eade and my mother, watching rushes at Shepperton Studios. Directly behind us were Laurence Harvey and John Woolf of Romulus films. I heard Larry whisper to Woolf:

'Hey! The kid's getting all the gravy!' (Larry Harvey always addressed and referred to me as Kid.)

'Don't worry,' muttered Woolf. 'We'll cut him.'

The last scene of the film was a fight between Harvey and me that had to be vicious and violent. It was. It had been carefully choreographed. We started off, but instead of pretending to hit me Larry actually connected. It was clearly deliberate. We fought on a landing, down a flight of stairs, then back up again, hitting each other the whole time. The camera rolled and we fought on. Finally, Larry punched me so hard I fell against the railing and the whole thing gave way. I landed on the floor, luckily still on my feet. I was a bit bruised, but no bones were broken.

'Cut!' shouted Vernon. 'It's a wrap! Boys, I think we've got a movie.'

Before I'd overheard Larry's remarks in the screening room, I was convinced I was on the way to screen stardom. But Woolf was as good as his word and most of my work apparently ended up on the cutting room floor. (I never saw the film.)

The director also ended up unhappy. Richard Vernon later told me that he had withdrawn his name from the credits because his film had been hacked to pieces. He was broken-hearted when I went to lunch with him. Apparently, John Woolf was grooming Laurence Harvey for stardom. (I'd even heard that he and Harvey were lovers.) The records show the film titled finally as *A Killer Walks*, and directed by 'Ronald Drake'.

Richard Vernon was a wonderful director to work with. Sadly, I lost touch with him. I have tried to find a copy of the film through the British Film Institute, without success. The records show that the finished film ran for approximately one hundred minutes; when released it ran for fifty-seven.

Laurence Harvey's career was soon made with memorable appearances in such successful films as *Room at the Top*, *I Am a Camera*, *The Alamo*, and *Butterfield 8*. Sadly, he died of cancer in 1973, visited and comforted in his last days by his close friend Elizabeth Taylor. Larry was a fine, powerful actor, and challenging to work with, and I've always regretted the tacit friction in our scenes together.

I believe the whole episode broke Richard Vernon, who was a deeply sensitive man — perhaps too sensitive for the film industry.

I, on the other hand, was lucky. Within a month I was offered the role of Joan Dowling's husband in *Twenty-four Hours in a Woman's Life*, adapted for the screen by Stefan Zweig from his novel *Beware of Pity* (*An Affair In Monte Carlo* was the film's US title).

I remember little about the filming except that Victor Saville directed very capably and that Joan Dowling was a giggler — and fun to act with. I was totally shocked when she committed suicide soon after.

Merle Oberon — who was also in the cast, and whom I'd idolised after seeing *Wuthering Heights* — was very aloof. Years later, at a dinner party given by Laurence Olivier and Vivien Leigh for Alexander Korda, his wife Merle Oberon and I were seated together at the table. I tried to make conversation, reminding her of the film we'd made together, but she refused to communicate. It was quite extraordinary — like trying to talk to a wax image. She had been very beautiful, and was still well-preserved, but I sensed she felt herself to be a social outsider.

I was lucky enough to have the qualities needed to make a success in film — good looks and natural charm — but I lacked confidence. Success seemed to be coming too quickly and too easily.

Immediately after my work on *Twenty-four Hours in a Woman's Life*, John Redway — a powerful London agent — called me in for an interview.

'ABPC [Associated British Picture Corporation] want to offer you a five-year contract,' he told me. 'If you accept you will belong exclusively to us, but it will give you great scope for realising your potential. We've signed up Richard Todd, Dirk Bogarde, Richard Attenborough, Anthony Steel, and several others.'

This was a tantalising temptation. Should I accept the security of a regular income, or should I stick to my intended career plan, which was to gain more theatre experience? Accepting Redway's offer would also mean betraying my current agent, Peter Eade, who had negotiated my contract for *The Lady's Not for Burning*, as well as for my films, and all of my BBC Radio work. He had also just negotiated the terms of my contract for a new theatre job. Not long before, and thanks to John Gielgud, H.M. Tennent had offered me the very small part of The Messenger in their forthcoming production of *Much Ado About Nothing*. It would star Gielgud and Diana Winyard as Benedict and Beatrice, with a wonderful supporting cast that was to include Paul Scofield, Sir Lewis Casson, my old friend George Rose, and several other West End luminaries.

I rang Gielgud to ask him if he thought I should take the offered film contract.

'Oh, dear Trader! Yes, take it! It will make you an international star. Don't worry, we'll find a replacement for you in the play. You can't refuse such an offer; it's your chance of a lifetime!'

I remember telling him that I felt I lacked the essential grounding that could make me the actor I aspired to be. He agreed with me, but stressed that this was a gilt-edged offer that shouldn't be ignored.

The outcome? I went back to the Redway office.

'I've decided against accepting your offer, sir,' I told him. 'I need time to mature as an actor. Before I do more films I must first get the experience that only the English repertory system can give me. That will build my confidence.'

I shall always remember Redway's reaction of utter disbelief.

'You're mad! Don't you realise what we're offering you? Have you any idea of the opportunity you're throwing away?'

I didn't care. I was an inexperienced twenty-four-year-old, finding this sudden rush of success and popularity hard to comprehend, let alone handle.

I shook hands with John Redway, thanked him and told him I was well aware of the value of his offer, but that I had to follow my intuition.

'No actor has ever turned us down,' he told me, shaking his head. 'I hope you know what you're doing.'

Have I ever regretted that decision? Not for an instant. Whatever I sacrificed in terms of security and potential celebrity I gained in having the freedom to live, love, and work exactly as I have wished. Above all, I have always been my own master, and that is a prize well worth preserving, whatever the cost.

One afternoon between jobs during the summer of 1951, I was walking up Shaftesbury Avenue when I noticed a large hoarding: *ROSARIO and ANTONIO, Internationally Acclaimed Spanish Flamenco Dancers at the Cambridge Theatre, presented by Peter Daubeny.* Curious as to what 'flamenco' could be (I had an idea it might have something to do with flamingos), I bought the last available ticket up in the gods (this was the Festival of Britain year, and quality novelty was in vogue). The lights dimmed and two pianos played Granados' 'Dance No 10'. Up went the curtain and that packed theatre sat riveted for an hour as the two young figures performed regional dances of Spain and South America — some of the tunes very familiar to me.

At the interval the bars were packed. The second half would be flamenco — with three guitars and two singers. I shall always remember as the interval bell rang there was an excited buzz as people left drinks unfinished to hurry back to their seats. Three guitars began to strum and the two figures in black started to complement each other in counter-time. For the next hour, Rosario and Antonio held us spellbound with the various forms of flamenco — dancing together *Siguirya* and *Soleares*, then Antonio's solo tour de force, *Zapateádo*. The effect of the dynamic, fast footwork was electric — a form of theatre entirely new to post-war London.

My mother had often tried to describe for me the effect Nijinsky and Diaghilev's ballet had had on London audiences in 1911. Antonio's solo *Zapateádo* must have been something similar, for when he'd finished he got an ovation the likes of which I've rarely heard. It was a first for me, a performance of unforgettable magic.

Excited, I read the programme notes.

Antonio — reputed to be the greatest dancer that Spain had produced in the twentieth century — had been born in Seville, and had danced with his cousin Rosario from early childhood. At the outbreak of the Spanish Civil War they had left Spain and settled in New York — appearing in several Hollywood films, and mounting their cabaret show in New York's famous Sert room at the Waldorf Astoria Hotel. Their rise to fame from then on was meteoric.

That afternoon watching Antonio and his cousin dance changed the course of my life. I suddenly knew that I wanted to master this dance form if it took me a lifetime — not to become a flamenco dancer myself, but simply through its study to become a better actor, free of the cancer of inhibition that prevailed in the profession at that time. But where to begin in London?

Elsa Brunelleschi, an Argentinian, had founded a dancing academy in Westbourne Grove some years before the war that was known as *the* school of Spanish dance in London. She was also a regular newspaper critic for Spanish dance. Along I went and met this witch-like woman. Then in her early sixties, Elsa had an incomparable sense of humour, coupled with the ability, if provoked, to be a copper-bottomed bitch. She soon discovered — and made it public to the rest of the class — that I had two left feet. As she had no male pupils (until Robert Helpmann arrived some time later), the style

I was learning was very effeminate. Also I was learning Spanish folk dances, not the flamenco I craved. When I complained, I was told I had to learn the basics before I could begin anything as difficult as flamenco. Finally a brilliant flamenco dancer from Capetown, a hefty redhead named Cora Martell, took me in hand. For the next eighteen months, whenever I was not working, we passed day after day together pounding the floors in the basement of the old Chelsea Community Centre.

One day quite by chance, walking along Piccadilly, I met Fred Nossal and his wife Audrey. They had just arrived in London from Sydney and Fred had taken a job with Reuters. They were living at 110 Walton Street in Chelsea and had a spare attic room. Would I like to move in?

I would.

The Nossels had the entire house. I lived in a charming attic room on the fourth floor. Life with Fred and Audrey was very cosy, but Audrey — though a loving wife to Fred — was the epitome of 'respectability', with no sense of humour. Also, she was very easily shocked. Fred had a bawdy sense of humour, so between the two of us behaving together with outrageous ribaldry poor Audrey was on the rack. I'd hang my washed underpants over the window ledge. Sometimes I'd play my flamenco records very loudly, making the old house shudder as I practised the steps I was learning from Cora. Looking back, my pranks were adolescent and ridiculous, but Audrey got her revenge.

My main meal would always be left for me when I came back late from work. It was usually cold and sometimes inedible (one of her favourite dishes was cold pig's trotters and boiled potatoes). Spoilt by a doting mother (who was still living in Spain), I was relying on Audrey to look after me. To supplement my lack of nourishment, I used to drink the cream off the top of the gold top milk bottles in their fridge — until Audrey out-played me and left mine in a jug.

The balloon went up when my mother arrived to join me. Audrey very kindly offered her my room and I moved into a room in the basement.

I had gone down to Tilbury by train to meet Mother off the

Mooltan. On her voyage, Mother had become close friends with a well-known Australian medic, Pat Penfold. As we stood on the quayside, Ms Penfold said to me:

'Trader, you are not a good colour. Have you had a medical check-up recently?'

I hadn't, and promised that I would.

It transpired I had malnutrition. Whose fault was that? Mine. I obviously should have looked after my own well-being. But on learning what my diet had been, Mum went for Audrey one evening in a memorable verbal set-to. Sheila Faulkner's one and only had been virtually starved of nourishing food. Audrey retorted that Trader was surely old enough to look after himself. But Sheila was more than a match for poor Audrey. Within seconds she had reduced her to helpless weeping.

It was obviously time to leave.

We moved out and found a wonderful maisonette in Knightsbridge at 32 Beauchamp Place for seven guineas a week. That was in 1952. I had been apart from my mother since she had left the SS *Moreton Bay* in Malta for her trip to North Africa. The last thing I wanted was to live with her in London, but financially there was no other option.

During my run in *Much Ado About Nothing* at the Phoenix Theatre I developed friendships with two people who were to become hugely important in my life. The first of these was the bewitching and highly talented new ingénue in the company, Dorothy Tutin, with whom I was to become embroiled in a stormy romantic relationship for the next seven years. (By that time, alas, Trix and I had drifted apart — in one of my many absences she had taken up with an old boyfriend — but we remained the best of friends for years.) The second friendship was with Paul Scofield and his wife Joy, with whom I remained close until his death in 2008.

Occasionally several of us from the *Much Ado* cast would go round the corner, between the matinee and evening performances, to a little café called Velotti's. There Paul would have us hysterical with laughter with his theatrical anecdotes and his inspired impersonations of fellow actors.

Halfway through the run of *Much Ado* — by now totally obsessed with Dorothy Tutin — I asked her to Beauchamp Place for lunch and she accepted.

During these years Dorothy suffered with some internal problem that caused her to throw up. It could happen anywhere, at any time. She was a tragic little figure with enormous talent and absolutely magic to watch — she had London at her feet — but this medical problem was always threatening. Her mother, very possessive and domineering, had rung to ask my mother what she proposed to give 'Dottie' for lunch.

'What would she like?' replied Mum.

'The ideal would be a soft-boiled egg, bread and butter, and a little salad,' said Adie.

Mum went to Harrods, and bought six of the best.

Dorothy arrived looking angelic in the style of the early 1950s — *broderie Anglaise* white blouse, grey-green tweed skirt, and soft brown moccasins. To use that maternal catchphrase of the time, she looked 'so fetching'.

It was Mum's first meeting with Dorothy, though she had long known of my obsession. I thought she couldn't help but be impressed. Later I quizzed her.

'Well, Mum?'

'Yes, she's very sweet. A little mousy, perhaps.'

Never underestimate that maternal sting.

So, lunch was served and we waited for 'Dottie' to spoon tap her egg. She did and it virtually exploded. What a stink! It was as rotten as a nine-day-old corpse.

Dottie leapt to her feet and dashed for the bathroom. A taxi was summoned and my paramour departed, prone on the back seat. Mum rang Adie to tell her the news.

'Oh dear! I should never have let her come. What on earth did you give her?'

Mum couldn't resist.

'A very expensive egg from Harrods.'

Well, this was one of those occasions when truth belies fiction. Mum then raced up to the Harrods egg counter and thrust the remains of Dorothy's lunch at the supercilious gentleman from whom she had earlier bought it. There was a commotion behind her and a woman poked my mother in the shoulder.

'Excuse me! The lady with me takes precedence. She is before you.'

'Not today she isn't!' replied Mum.

'Do you realise who it is?' snapped the woman.

My mother looked.

'Yes. Well, I'm sure you'll agree that the sooner we get this stinking matter sorted out, the better it will be for everyone.'

I was standing behind my mother, thinking what a film clip this would make for a news slot. Mum got her fresh eggs and an apology and we quickly left.

I hoped Princess Margaret's eggs were fresh, too, but couldn't help thinking what a very unlikely place to confront her.

CHAPTER TWELVE

BERMUDA AND THE STELLA MARIS

IN THE AUTUMN of 1952, after the run of *Much Ado* had finished, I was invited to join a company of actors to perform five plays at the Bermuda Arts Festival, where I was cast as the young male lead, appearing in plum roles in Jean Anouilh's *Ring Round the Moon*, *Traveller's Joy* by Arthur MacRae, *Family Reunion* by T.S. Eliot, *The Magistrate* by Arthur Wing Pinero, and *Miranda* by Peter Blackmore.

Leading the company was the by then virtually sightless actor Esmond Knight. He had been a Lieutenant Commander on the bridge of HMS *Prince of Wales* when she'd suffered a direct hit from the German battleship *Bismarck* off the coast of Iceland in 1941. Shrapnel had pierced Esmond's eyes and sent him all but blind. Invalided out of the war, he had resumed his pre-war acting career — thanks to his wife, the actress Nora Swinburn, who taught him how to memorise his moves as well as his lines. Through her guidance and patience he was able to use the stage in such a cunning way that the audience never realised he was blind.

The Bermuda Festival was a two-month arts festival of music and drama. One unforgettable performance that year, I remember, was the pianist Cyril Smith playing Chopin.

In those days I sported a rather trim body and had a compulsion to show it off. This I did often and outrageously by dancing my rudimentary flamenco at parties for the amusement of the rest of the festival company and our Bermudian guests.

During our weeks on this island paradise we were often invited to parties and barbecues after the show. The highlight of these evening fiestas, I remember, was a late-night celebration on board HMS *Superb*, which had just arrived in Bermuda as the British flagship on the West Indies station. A member of our cast, Doreen Alexander, was married to a young officer serving on that ship. Doreen had obviously told her husband that Esmond Knight had served on HMS *Prince of Wales*. There was great excitement in the company when we received an invitation from the Commander-in-Chief of the Royal Navy, West Indies Station, to attend the party celebrating the *Superb*'s arrival.

The dress was to be smart-casual. I went in all-whites: shirt, shorts, and socks. Luckily, I also had a pair of white shoes. We were to meet by the jetty in the harbour in front of the Bermudiana Hotel (where we were playing our repertoire) after the performance. Very excited, we all assembled and waited for the transport that was to take us to the ship.

It was a beautiful tropical night, and presently up the harbour came a launch. As it swung alongside we realised it was the pinnace, sent by the Admiral himself. As it berthed, a sailor began to pipe us aboard. Ex-Lieutenant Commander Esmond Knight was escorted down the steps and onto the launch by two sailors, and we followed after. Steaming up the harbour and round a headland, we saw the cruiser ahead of us, her decks ablaze with light. At the steps leading up to the cruiser's quarterdeck, Esmond was again piped aboard, with us in trail, where we were all welcomed by the Admiral.

Many island civilians had been invited to this fiesta, which was to prove fateful for me. We were feted, given champagne, and told to mix with the other guests. Somebody had told the Admiral that I danced flamenco. He came over to me and with true naval charm asked if I would give them a brief demonstration. I agreed, did a few minutes of my limited flamenco, and got a cheering reception. As the evening progressed we were given a magnificent banquet and lots more champagne. Then we were taken by launch back to our hotel.

Some days later I received an invitation written on an elegant card. I and (I wrongly assumed) other company members were invited to a late-night reception at the Belmont Manor Hotel by a gentleman I shall call 'Leslie Horniker'.

On the night indicated, after the show, and dressed all in white as before, I bicycled towards the Belmont Manor Hotel, which I knew lay on a lonely headland some two miles south of the Bermudiana. When I reached the gates of the hotel, to my surprise they were locked, but I managed to squeeze through a narrow gap at the side and rode up the drive, which was surrounded on both sides by woodland. Before turning the last corner, instinct prompted me to leave my bicycle hidden in the foliage by the side of the road.

I set off on foot around the corner and the enormous hotel came into view. It seemed to be in total darkness, except for the lights of what looked to be a large suite on the top floor at the south-east corner of the building. The vestibule was in semi-darkness. The hotel was obviously closed, but there was still a man at the reception desk.

'Mr Faulkner?'

'Yes.'

'You're expected. I'll take you up.'

'What about the others?' I asked. 'Have they already arrived?'

He made no reply, but instead ushered me into the lift. At the seventh floor he stepped out with me and pointed down a long corridor. By now, I was feeling distinctly uneasy. As the man disappeared behind the lift's closing doors, I walked down the corridor and knocked on the designated door.

It was opened by a bald-headed man wearing a long tangerine dress and white shoes. On his wrists was a mass of gold bangles. Reaching forward, he took my hand.

'Trader,' he said, smiling. 'Welcome to our little fiesta. I'm Leslie Horniker, better known as Shirley.'

He drew me inside where, spread around the large sitting room, were twelve men in dresses of different pastel shades. They were all also wearing fashionable high heels, flashy rings, long exotic earrings, and necklaces.

Leslie began the introductions.

'Trader, this is Florence, Margaret, Hermione, Winifred ... '

I realised by now I was in a potentially awkward situation.

'Where are the other company members?' I asked.

'This is a celebration for you, Trader darling. You're the star, and we know you're going to perform marvellously for us.'

I have seldom felt so frightened, and so totally isolated.

I vaguely remembered that some three months before there had been what seemed a ritualistic murder on a lonely beach and the young man had been found mutilated. The police investigation was still ongoing, but seemed to be getting nowhere. I realised that I had to manage this situation very coolly while I planned my escape.

'Shirley' handed me a gin-and-tonic in a silver goblet. I toasted the group and started to sip the drink, which seemed too sweet to me.

I was then led to a sofa, with one of these bizarre characters seated either side of me.

'We're going to have a gorgeous evening,' said Hermione. 'You are going to perform for us, aren't you?'

'I'd be pleased to dance for you. But it's rather hot in here. Do you think we could go out onto the balcony for a minute? I'd like a breath of fresh air.'

I'd seen the balcony as I approached the hotel and wanted to check whether there was any means of escape from there. The 'girls' were delighted to accompany me outside, their arms curled round my waist like two hungry cobras.

The view from the balcony on that moonlit night was unforgettable. I could see the entire length of the island, from St George in the north right down to the naval dockyard at the southwestern end where HMS *Superb* still lay at anchor, her silhouette brilliantly outlined by the full moon. How I wished I was onboard that cruiser and not in this snakepit. I looked around me. What I had hoped and prayed for was there to my left — one of those American external fire escapes, and within easy jumping distance from a window. If that window was the bathroom I stood a chance. A feeling of absolute terror gripped me as I felt the gin-and-whatever taking effect. What in God's name had they given me? Pins and needles tingled in my legs.

I suggested I should dance for them straightaway, but first I needed to powder my nose. They were delighted, and showed me to the bathroom. Making sure the door was securely locked, I went to

the window. I was right; it was within easy reach of the fire escape. I
turned on both washbasin taps, then, flushing the lavatory, I squeezed
out through the window and onto the fire escape. Still feeling pins
and needles in my legs, I started downwards, hoping to jump to the
ground and creep across the lawn to the undergrowth and safety.
I was three floors down when two of the 'girls' appeared on the
veranda above me.

'Winifred!' shrieked Shirley. 'Our prize is escaping! You and the
others go down in the lift and head her off below. Florence and I will
follow her down the fire escape.'

I managed to reach the bottom platform, about fifteen feet from
the ground, swung myself downwards and dropped onto soft grass.
Half running, half crawling, I raced across the lawn as fast as I
could to what looked to me like a large pool across which I planned
to swim to safety. My pursuers had now emerged from the front
entrance and rounded the hotel corner, while the other two were still
laboriously descending the fire escape. I took a header into the pool
— which turned out to be an enormous pond of filthy, stinking water.
Nevermind. I swam as hard as I could through the quagmire of weeds
and slime.

When I reached the other side, I dived into the undergrowth and
glanced back. My pursuers had stopped at the edge of the cesspool.
Hurrying on towards my bicycle, I seized it and pedalled off down
the drive towards the locked gates as fast as I could, squeezing past
it, and coasting down the hill towards home. I wondered if they had
a car and would try to follow me. I looked back again. They had,
and were — a car was coming slowly down the drive towards me.
But they would have to unlock the gate to get through, which gave
me a bit of time.

By chance the road leading downhill towards the sea passed over
several dry rainwater runoff ditches, each with a deep culvert that
protruded on either side. My only chance was to jump into one of
those culverts and hope to God they would drive on by. I dragged the
bicycle down and thrust it and myself into the dark opening. Sure
enough, moments later I heard the car cruise down the hill past me.

Obviously they'd sooner or later realise that they'd missed me and would drive back. Just as I was thinking of clambering back up to the road, they reappeared, heading uphill.

What had previously been so beautiful — the bright moonlight — was now working against me. Everything around me was bathed in it, almost turning night into day. Slowly, the car crept back up the hill. Had they seen my hiding place? Would they get out and chase me again? Luckily they hadn't seen me, and the car proceeded back through the gates.

I raced back to the bungalow where I was staying, arriving just after 12.30am. The Broadway actor with whom I was sharing a room, John Malcolm, had not yet gone to bed. In I walked, looking as if I had just risen from the dead.

'Holy shit, man! Where have you been?'

'I'm going to immerse myself in a hot bath,' I told him. 'Then I'll explain everything.'

Minutes later, over a very welcome Cuba Libre, I told him my story.

'Wait a minute! That boy they found murdered on the beach …'

'Exactly,' I said. 'I could've been his successor if I hadn't managed to escape.'

'Right,' said John. 'Tomorrow morning we sort this out.'

At 10am the next day we entered the office of the organiser of the Bermuda Festival, Bruce York.

'Bruce,' I said dramatically, 'I think I bloody near lost my life last night.'

When I told him what had happened Bruce surprised me by declaring that I had been stupid to accept the invitation in the first place. I replied that we had often accepted after-show invitations without question, and asked how was I to know what this invitation implied.

'Remember what happened to that young lad on the beach only a few weeks ago, Bruce? What if I had turned up the same way this morning?'

'Trader, your acceptance of the invitation was naïve and unwise. What do you say we just leave it at that.'

I couldn't believe my ears.

'I want to go to the police,' I told him. 'It's quite possible this gang is behind that murder, and probably a lot more besides.'

Bruce sighed. 'I'll take you to the police if that's what you wish, and you can state your case. But if you do, I can assure you you'll be on the first plane out of Bermuda tomorrow morning. Why not simply forget the episode and continue playing those five wonderful parts. One way or another the matter will be closed without any investigation. These are very influential people you're threatening.'

'But can I go about Bermuda in safety? Surely, knowing what I know I'll be an embarrassment to them.'

'Provided that you say nothing you have nothing to worry about. From now on, don't go to lonely places, keep with the crowd, play your shows and enjoy yourself. You won't run into any more trouble, I promise you. You may well meet those characters again, but if you do behave as though nothing had happened. If you don't, you might well open a box of very nasty spiders.'

I realised then that Bruce was right: tact was my best means of survival.

At the end of November, the triumphant season finished and we all flew back to London via New York.

That was over half a century ago, but I still remain determined that nothing could induce me to spend time in Bermuda ever again.

In the winter of 1953, the lease of the flat at 32 Beauchamp Place was coming to an end. Where were my mother and I to go with our modest amount of capital?

Of course, I was still besotted with Dorothy Tutin, who had recently moved and was now living on a houseboat, the *Undine*, on the Chelsea embankment. One day I was painting *Undine* on the lifebuoy by her front door when I looked out over the water and saw a beautiful two-decker houseboat, the *Relax*, being towed in. I later discovered it had belonged to a businessman who'd kept his mistress on it up a creek at Wivenhoe in Essex. The boat had a large sitting room and quarterdeck. Below the sitting room by the front door was a small galley. At the other end of the sitting room a flight of steps led down to the bottom deck on which were two bedrooms and a

small bathroom. The neat little houseboat had been a landing craft
in the invasion of Normandy and was beautifully converted, with the
quarterdeck ideal for sunbathing — English summers permitting. The
Chelsea Yacht and Boat Company wanted £1,000; I negotiated and
bought her for £825. She ended up being moored five boats away
from Dorothy — ideal, I felt, for my love campaign.

My problem, of course, was that my mother had to share the boat
with me. I remember moving our belongings out of Beauchamp Place
on a stormy November evening in 1953, with the rain hosing down.
How would I survive in this damp boat lit by a few candles and
rocking manically at her moorings on the Thames a stone's throw
from Cheyne Walk? I needn't have worried. My years aboard that
houseboat turned out to be the most colourful period in my life.

It didn't take long to make the little craft comfortable and warm
with an Aladdin heater, and we decided to rename our new floating
home *Stella Maris* — Latin for 'Star of the Sea'. I believe that name
is also attributed to Our Lady the Virgin Mary. I would live there for
the next ten years until I married, and my mother too until she died
in 1969.

That first winter was certainly the worst I've ever spent. *Stella
Maris* rocked and creaked at her moorings like a writhing sea horse,
and when the tide went out — twice every twenty-four hours — we
lay on a sloping bank of Thames mud. Had I bought a hell ship?

Then spring and summer made us realise we lived in a London
paradise.

The Chelsea Yacht and Boat Company let us our moorings at £9
a month. We had electric light, Calor gas in cylinders delivered when
required, and a water tank on the roof — filled every day by a tall
Welshman called Taffy. The staff and our neighbours were a rich
Chelsea mix of that time. Charles Fleming, an ex-army officer and an
English gentleman of impeccable manners and style, was the owner
of the company, although it was Alec Osgood, who had been his
batman during the war, who ran it. The boatmen were a marvellous
collection: Alfie and Peter Allen (cockney boys), and Charlie, a wily,
Dickensian character who was, to quote Mum, as 'shrewd as a gelded
cat'. No flies on Charlie! He had to be treated with great charm and

deference if you wanted anything done — especially when *Stella Maris* had to be periodically towed round to the floating dry dock to have her bottom scraped and tarred.

As for the actual inhabitants, what a motley lot we were: Claire Bloom's brother John, soon to become a top international film editor; Mrs Murphy, an ebullient middle-aged charmer with more humour in her soul than anyone I've ever known; and a Swedish girl called Poopsie, a very sexy and most charming bundle of mischief. But the star of the moorings, of course — and very aloof — was Dorothy Tutin, the object of my unfortunately unrequited love.

The whole houseboat saga had actually started when we were on holiday together on the Scottish island of Arran the previous summer. Sitting by the water's edge, we were discussing how Dottie could get away from her possessive mother. Living at home, jealously guarded by both parents, she desperately craved her freedom. I equally desperately wanted sex with this irresistible virgin, or at least an unchaperoned opportunity to win my way into her graces.

Suddenly, I had a flash of inspiration.

'Why don't you live on a houseboat?'

'Darling!' she said. 'You're a genius! What a *divine* idea. Oh, if only it were possible!'

In her enthusiasm, Dorothy turned and gave me a strong hug — something I was rarely able to enjoy.

We were staying with Dorothy's close friends, Tom and Catherine Alexander, who in those days ran the store at Brodick-on-Arran. It was one of those marvellous stores where you could buy anything from a nail to the entire ingredients for your Sunday roast. Catherine and Tommy were very sympathetic about my passion for Dorothy.

One day during a heavy thunderstorm, and for no accountable reason, Dorothy suddenly said, 'Do you really want to make love to me?'

For the past eighteen months, every little virginal kiss had been granted only after I'd declaimed long reams of English verse, and always with 'Mama' in attendance. So this sudden *volte face* was totally unexpected. I quickly agreed and we went up to her bedroom.

As Dorothy started to undress, I went to lock the door. No key!

'What're you waiting for?' she asked.

Afraid that our wonderful hosts might unknowingly disturb us, I fought down my desires and called off the whole thing. Sadly, that opportunity never returned. We went back to London and Dorothy got her houseboat.

Her boat cost £750. Initially called the *Jane Muriel*, it was my suggestion to rename her the *Undine*. Dorothy was to live there until the mid-sixties. Robin Howard, who owned and ran the Gore Hotel in Kensington, was a close friend and offered to lend her the money to buy it.

Shortly after moving aboard the *Stella Maris* I met the sculptress Dora Gordine, who had studied with Aristide Maioll and was highly regarded in London. I took Dora to see Dorothy in Ibsen's *The Wild Duck*. The outcome was that Dora wanted to sculpt her as Hedvig, the character she played. But who would commission the sculpture? Robin Howard, like me bewitched by Dorothy, agreed to pay for the work. Four bronzes were cast. Dora kept one, one went to Dorothy, one to Robin and he gave me the fourth. Dorothy proudly presented hers to her mother, who apparently loathed it and wouldn't have it in the house. For me, looking as I have at my bronze over the past fifty-odd years, Dora certainly captured something elusive and tragic about Dorothy in that enigmatic green head.

Stella Maris was berthed at the far end of the front row of houseboats, which gave us a superb view looking upstream towards Lots Road power station. We were moored alongside the end houseboat *Esperance*, which meant you walked down a gangway onto *Esperance* and then across another gangway to our front door. One night soon after our arrival, I was dressed up in a dinner jacket and bowtie for a formal dinner. Leaving the *Stella Maris* in a hurry at low tide, I set off across our small gangway, which had come loose from its fixings. Capsizing, I was flung into thick, black Thames mud. Fortunately, it was a summer evening so many residents were on their verandas enjoying the sunset. It took three hefty neighbours to hoist me out of the ooze and back on deck. I had to strip to my underpants, have a bath, and ring my hosts to explain my delay.

Then there were the nights when storms raged and I felt certain the *Stella Maris* would snap her moorings and be smashed to matchwood on Battersea bridge. Yet in all those tempestuous storms *Stella Maris* held fast and our Chelsea boatmen kept us secure and watertight.

There were many friends who loved to visit us on the houseboat.

Probably long forgotten now was Bernard Shaw's admired leading lady, Lillah McCarthy, first wife of theatrical legend Harley Granville Barker. Lillah was very grand, very Victorian, and was of the generation that succeeded Henry Irving and Ellen Terry. All I remember of her now was that she was large, imposing, and a friend of my mother's (Lillah had known Diaghilev and Pavlova and was part of that glittering theatrical pre-First World War generation). It was always a treat to listen to and learn from Lillah.

One day we received word that Lillah wanted to visit the *Stella Maris* for afternoon tea — something extremely unwise at her age and with her degree of infirmity — but the request was tantamount to a Royal Command.

On the agreed day, tea was prepared and Lillah's faithful 'help' brought her by taxi to the moorings.

That afternoon the Thames was raging and the houseboats were creaking and wrenching at their moorings. With the assistance of two of the longshoremen we managed to get Lillah to the top of the narrow gangway leading down to the *Esperance*. Two more heftys were then summoned and the ancient Lillah, paralysed with terror, was laboriously hoisted down and across to the front door of the *Stella Maris*. Having finally got her inside, I suggested a cup of tea.

'Tea?' she bellowed, in true Shavian style. 'Not bloody likely. A large neat whisky, if you please!'

Amid what turned out to be a riotous afternoon party, we handed out whiskies to each of the four longshoremen who had helped to hoist our illustrious guest aboard, as Lillah continued to regale us with stories of her friendships with Bernard Shaw, Henry Irving, and other glittering luminaries of her day.

Of course, I'd never seen Lillah perform onstage, but her exit from the *Stella Maris* had a style and grandeur about it that I'll wager matched Sarah Bernhardt's. When the time came, the four hefty longshoremen eased her out the front door and onto our gangway. Manipulating her along the narrow gangplank, up onto the pontoon, and up to the waiting taxi in Cheyne Walk was a feat of muscular magic. By now a crowd had gathered. All it needed was for Bernard Shaw and her ex-husband Harley Granville Barker to suddenly appear to complete the scene.

'Goodbye, dear audience!' she boomed. 'I doubt this performance will be repeated, and it could well be my last.'

Indeed it was. She died a few weeks later. Thus ended George Bernard Shaw's leading lady, a true theatrical legend.

CHAPTER THIRTEEN

THE YEARS IN REPERTORY

ON MY RETURN from New York, I had told my agent Peter Eade that I felt I needed experience in the theatre, playing widely differing roles in repertory. In 1953 and 1954, I received my repertory grounding at Worthing, Windsor, and the Bristol Old Vic, where I was fortunate enough to play challenging parts and had one or two memorable encounters.

At the Connaught Theatre, Worthing, I appeared in *Anastasia* by Marcelle Maurette, and in *Silver and Gold* by Warren Chetham-Strode, both directed by Jack Williams.

My performance in *Anastasia*, playing the character Petrovsky, was one of those rare instances — every actor's dream — when every component suddenly harmonises and you hold an audience absolutely entranced. After the first performance, Williams came round to tell Rosemary Webster (who played Anastasia) and me that he had been held spellbound. Jack was not a man given to compliments.

I did one more play at Worthing.

Elsa Shelley had already written a highly successful play called *Pick-Up Girl*. We were mounting Miss Shelley's second play, *Tomorrow is a Secret*, which was supposedly going into the West End. My fellow actors were very distinguished, a selection that guaranteed box office drawing power — Rachel Roberts, Gordon Harker, Hartley Power (a well-known American actor who had starred in *Born Yesterday*), and D.A. Clarke-Smith.

The play was about a pigeon fancier, so the real stars in the company were an enormous flock of very noisy birds. We opened in Edinburgh, then played Aberdeen, Southport, and Blackpool, finishing our pre-London tour during Easter of 1953 in Cardiff.

One night during that last week prior to our scheduled West End opening, the pigeons escaped from their cages and crapped all over the audience — marking the end of our Cardiff run and the death of any idea of a West End premiere. This was no surprise to any of the cast, all of whom found the play laughably inept. The stage management retrieved only three pigeons from the vast auditorium — all the rest had escaped.

While we were in Cardiff, I decided to go to Pontrhydyfen and Port Talbot to see where Richard Burton was born and raised and, if possible, to speak to a member of his family.

I found the door of the cottage, where I was told his sister Cecilia still lived, and knocked on the door. It was opened by a buxom young woman who clearly resembled Richard in looks.

'Oh!' she said, obviously startled. 'I can't believe it. You're so like Richard! Not identical, but you have such a look of him.'

I explained who I was and why I'd come.

'Please come in,' she said. 'Any friend of my brother is welcome here.'

She sat me in a chair by the dining table.

'You're sitting in his chair. That's where he always sat. There are thirteen of us. Our mother died in her forties, and I brought Richard up.'

While she told me the family background, she insisted on cooking me breakfast, just as she had so often done for her brother — a large plate of bacon and eggs with toast and marmalade and beautiful coffee. It was the most extraordinary experience. She treated me exactly as if I were the young Richard she had nurtured. She obviously missed him terribly. What is so vivid in my memory now after all these years is the warmth of this woman who became the mother Burton never knew.

My friendship with the Oliviers began as a result of two performances I gave in 1953.

Dennis Carey, director at the Bristol Old Vic, offered me one of those thankless, one-speech noblemen parts in *Henry V* — the Earl of Westmoreland. For me, the bait was the opportunity to cover for John Neville — the handsome young star who was cast as Henry V. The play would run for three weeks at Bristol, tour briefly to Zurich, and then do a week at the Old Vic in London. I was out of work so why not take it on? There would be no understudy rehearsals, but for safety's sake I learnt the part in its entirety — a mental marathon. Then I had to decide where to work on my performance. I needed to find a secluded spot where I could declaim it with all the stops out.

'Try the Bristol Cemetery after midnight,' said my landlady. 'You can only disturb the dead there.'

So there I went every night for the three weeks the show played. After the performance and a good dinner I'd make my way to this deserted boneyard and give of my stentorian best. Thank God, neither the living nor the dead ever complained.

I remember little of the trip to Zurich, except that our hosts were very hospitable and I was once asked if I would like to go for what I understood to be 'a Rotunda Fart round the Zurich Horn'. Not having a clue what was being offered, I declined.

We opened at the 'Old Vic' in London about the time of the Coronation, *Henry V* being considered a suitable play for the occasion. There were extra matinees for the schools.

By Wednesday of that final week I saw my opportunity for playing Hal dwindling. Nevermind, I thought, the experience of learning the part was worth it. Then on the Thursday evening Dennis Carey arrived at my dressing room looking sheepish.

'Well, Bludge, John's voice has gone. Are you up to doing it, or do we cancel tomorrow's matinee?'

('Bludger' was Aussie slang for a no-hoper or lay-about. I had the entire company using it.)

'Try me!' I replied.

'Well, we'd better give you a rehearsal tomorrow morning.'

'Let's only rehearse my love scene with the princess, that long Harfleur harangue, and a few lines in the opening scene. That's all. I don't want to knacker my voice.'

We convened onstage at the Old Vic at 10am the following morning and I rehearsed what I wanted. The company was very friendly and supportive throughout.

Of course, the nerves were already starting. I couldn't eat, and decided to walk across Waterloo Bridge and along the Strand to steady my nerves. It was a beautiful June day, and just as I was passing the Savoy I heard a familiar voice behind me.

'Hello, Trader.'

I turned. It was Gielgud.

'John, of all people!'

'Dear Trader, how are you? And what are you doing these days?'

I told him, and added that I'd been given the star dressing room at the Old Vic that had been his over so many years, and asked, please, could he give me any tips? Yes, he could.

'Over the years I've seen many interpretations of Henry and one thing I can tell you is: be careful of Harfleur. Don't make it simply a copy of your heroic, *Once more unto the breach, dear friends, once more*. You have to find your individual way into that Harfleur speech. You saw Larry's film *Henry V*. Don't, whatever you do, try and copy him; the style must be yours and no one else's. Let your instincts have free rein, but keep him in check vocally and only give him his head when Shakespeare allows you to. Above all, be your own Henry. And God speed. I do wish I could be there.'

On the way back to the theatre I felt a surge of confidence.

I remember almost nothing of the performance, except that it seemed to be played through me and not by me. On that long marathon the oasis was taking Maureen Quinney's Princess Katherine in my arms and giving her a lingering, very warm kiss. In our clinch she whispered, 'Keep it up, Bludge. You're winning!'

On the first curtain call a packed audience gave us very warm applause. Down came the curtain and I was told to take the next call alone. As I walked forward the entire audience was on its feet. I was dumbfounded.

On the basis of that performance, I was allowed to do the extra matinee the following day, for which I received a special fee of £2.

★   ★   ★

Sometime in that period, Richard Burton visited the *Stella Maris*. He'd come to the houseboats to see Claire Bloom's brother John, who lived on the *Aku Aku* directly opposite. At that time, Richard met my colourful, devil-may-care mother and immediately fell in love with her, and the admiration was mutual. Over the following years he made several visits and we'd sit on the veranda as the conversation, and the wine brought by Richard, flowed. On these occasions he spoke at length of his boyhood as Richard Jenkins at Pontrhydyfen; of his indebtedness to his teacher Philip Burton, who gave him his early education and voice training (and whose surname he used as his professional name); and of his sister Cecilia, who had brought him up. He was amused that I had played two performances of '*Henry V*' at the Old Vic, where he had himself enjoyed such enormous success. He was also amused and touched that I had made the pilgrimage to visit his sister Cecilia in Wales the year before.

For a time then, we lost contact. Then one evening in 1957, in an alleyway by Wyndham's Theatre, I ran into him for the last time.

'Come and join me for a pint in the Salisbury,' he said.

I did. We spoke of Gielgud, whom we both admired as an actor and for his unpretentious attitude to what he regarded simply as his 'job'.

That was the last I saw of him.

After *Henry V*, I was out of theatre work for three months, and worked briefly as a house painter.

Then, in September, came a break that was to have a far-reaching effect. I was approached by Roger Winton, who was about to direct *Romeo and Juliet* at Guildford. He saw me as Romeo, but I saw myself as Mercutio, having been bowled over by my idol John Barrymore's film performance.

'No,' said Winton. 'I saw your Henry V. You can bring an Australian freshness and vitality to Romeo.'

A sucker for flattery, I accepted the challenge.

I remember little of that portrayal now. My mother at the time simply said: 'You were very good, but Geoffrey Taylor as Mercutio was outstanding.'

A fair comment. Geoffrey was a likeable, generous and very promising actor who, unfortunately, died young.

It was certainly an eventful production. One night when I came onstage a whole section of a rostrum was missing. This meant I had to jump down to the stage level where Paris, my rival for Juliet's love, was standing, engage him with my sword, and kill him. Unfortunately, however, I was without my sword, too, which had been laid out ready on the missing rostrum. Left with no alternative, I simply jumped down, rushed at Paris, and throttled him.

Dorothy Tutin's mother came to see the production — and to tell her daughter what she thought of it (Dorothy was busy as usual in the West End). On Dorothy's houseboat a few days later she delivered her *coup de grace*:

'Dear Trader, I kept waiting for the great moment in your performance, and it never came.'

Who knows? She may well have been right.

I've always believed that Adie Tutin was the driving force behind Dorothy's early theatrical career. Adie knew I was totally besotted with her daughter, and wanted to stop our relationship at any cost. Dorothy, after all, was at the pinnacle of her career, while I was frequently unemployed. Also, hard as I tried, I seemed to be a non-starter with her. One morning I met Adie on the moorings outside Dorothy's houseboat and in our casual conversation I suddenly felt the earth open beneath my feet.

'Trader,' she said, 'I know how fond you are of Dottie, but you must forget her.'

'Why?'

'Because, dear boy, she's very fond of you but she's not in love with you.'

'How do you know?'

'A mother knows these things. And ... oh, I mustn't be indiscreet, but you see ... '

'See what?'

'It's an absolute secret,' said Adie. 'No one must know. You see, Dorothy's madly in love with someone very important, and he's in love with her.'

'For God's sake, *who* Mrs Tutin?'

'I can't tell you. There'd be the most terrible scandal.'

'But I've a right to know. Tell me!'

'Well, on your honour, you mustn't speak of this to anyone!'

'I give you my word.'

'It's Sir Laurence Olivier. He's in love with her and she's crazy about him.'

In the spring of 1954, I appeared in Federico García Lorca's *Blood Wedding*, directed by Peter Hall for the Arts Theatre, London, and starring Beatrix Lehmann as The Mother and Rosalind Boxhall as The Bride. My part was The Moon. Learning of my flamenco studies, Peter asked if I would choreograph some dance movements for the wedding scene. *Blood Wedding* received good reviews — including favourable mentions of my 'unique contribution,' which gave me increased confidence.

Shortly after *Blood Wedding*, Peter Hall sent me Andrew Rosenthal's play *Third Person*. This play, with its then forbidden theme of homosexuality, had already been produced at the Arts Theatre in London, but still had to have permission granted by the Lord Chamberlain to be presented again — which it finally was for the Oxford Playhouse, to be directed by Peter. Peter wanted Derek Francis and me for the two leading men. Back in 1954 this was explosive stuff. In the play, Derek, unhappily married, is in love with my character, Kip Ames. At rehearsal, Hall was so nervous that we could hear him moving about the auditorium, flicking the clip of his fountain pen. It was exactly like playing to a mobile cricket. Unsatisfied with the scene as played he suddenly rushed onstage.

'Boys,' he said, 'this scene will only work if Trader slowly approaches you, Derek, and gives you a lingering kiss on the lips.'

Obedient pros that we both were, Derek and I prepared to try this piece of stage business. I remember my line was: 'Oh, Hank, I so love you!'

As I approached Derek to plant my kiss on his waiting lips, his moustache started to twitch and we both exploded with laughter.

At that time, Peter's idea seemed grotesque to us. As it turned out, however, his instinct was absolutely right.

On opening night the theatre was packed. When Derek and I managed to kiss quite unselfconsciously there was a silence in that theatre that I've never forgotten. The audience was absolutely spellbound.

After the performance, I remember a crowd of people at the stagedoor who were very complimentary. Of course, what made it especially poignant was the illegality of the play's theme.

Unfortunately, Peter Hall was only at Oxford for that one play and returned to London to run the Arts Theatre. I stayed on until October, appearing in some widely diverse plays, several of which we took for a short season to the Cambridge Arts Theatre.

The first play was Somerset Maugham's *The Letter*. I shared a dressing room (and never stopped laughing) with a young character actor — the incomparable Ronnie Barker. In spite of his wonderful sense of humour, I came to know Ronnie as a deeply complex and very serious man. We were cast as two Chinamen; he was Chung Hi and I was Ong Chi Seng. As a joke, we would improvise in our scene together several seconds of gabbled mock Chinese, whining Chinese style in different keys — none of which, of course, was in Maugham's script — and causing our colleagues no end of consternation. But the audience loved it and roared with laughter. The third member of our little group was a nameless servant girl whom we called 'Lum Pee Pooh'. On my old programme this actress is billed as 'Margaret Smith', but we called her Maggie, the name by which modern day theatre-goers know her so well. I remember that Maggie was also on the prompt book, which she loathed. She wanted to act. She subsequently went off to do a review in Edinburgh and from that point on never looked back.

Maggie was a lovely young lady and soon I had fallen very strongly for her and very nearly got us both into real trouble, only averted thanks to a bloody belt buckle — a brilliant piece of metal work by Derek Francis, who had made it for her. The thing was a work of art, but in its complicated fastening it amounted virtually to a chastity belt. Derek fancied Maggie too, and as he had designed the thing he had the 'key' to opening it (the bastard!) — but fortunately he never got the opportunity to use it. Neither, as it happened, did I — though I did have a go.

It happened after the first night. We had all had a lot to drink and I was about to go home when Maggie came over and whispered, 'Do you want me?'

'Like a good Aussie wants his roast dinner!' I eagerly replied.

'Come on then. But where?'

'Lets go back to my digs,' I said.

Back we went. After a good intake of alcohol neither of us had any inhibitions. We got horizontal and I set about trying to undo her belt buckle, but without a hope in hell. Derek's masterpiece turned what could have been high passionate drama into banal farce. There was no way I could undo the belt to get at her zip. Finally Maggie looked up at me.

'Well, Trader?'

I raised my voice in frustration.

'How the hell do I get this bloody thing undone?'

At that moment there was a knock on the door. It was my landlord. (Remember, this was 1954, when respectability and social propriety were the order of the day.)

'Is there anybody in there with you?' he sternly asked.

'No. I'm rehearsing,' I called out. 'I'm playing a girl with terrible problems in the next production.' Then I whispered to Maggie. 'For God's sake imitate me imitating you!'

She did so brilliantly.

'Can I come in?' said the landlord.

'No,' I said. 'I'm not feeling well.'

Muttering angrily, he went off to bed.

I had an old bike and I put Maggie on the bar and gave her a lift home. I always remember her words.

'For God's sake, Trade, don't take me to the front door. If my father sees us there will be hell to pay.'

Years later, I met her father and mother after one of her performances and remember him as a very charming old man who couldn't have been nicer to me.

'I've heard all about you,' he said, laughing.

I wondered what Maggie could have told him?

In early September of 1954 we assembled for our first reading of a very challenging play — Emlyn Williams's *The Corn is Green* — with a wonderful central role I was lucky enough to play. (Years later Emlyn became a close friend, and how I wish I'd known him then so that I could have learned about that autobiographical character from the playwright himself.) Into the rehearsal room swept a twenty-one-year-old blonde whom I can only describe as one of the most sexy, charming women I've ever been lucky enough to know, with a wonderful sense of humour to match. Billie Whitelaw had just come out of hospital.

'You'd never guess,' she said. 'I very nearly had an encounter with my maker. Didn't Strindberg write a play called *The Dance of Death*? Well, I was nearly a natural for the dancer.'

This infectiously happy girl gave us a graphic account of what her surgeon did with his sharp scalpels.

'From the base of my breast to the very summit of my nipple he opened me up and removed a large cancerous growth — without a trace of his knife's cut left behind! I still have a perfect boob!'

Believe me, she had. I was lucky enough to examine it closely later — together with the surgery. Truly a masterpiece!

The first reading of the play was an anti-climax after that. I don't remember the details now, but I do remember thinking — as I watched this fresh, vital girl reading Bessie Watty (which she later played brilliantly) — what a narrow escape she'd had.

Late in 1954, a call came from my agent.

'Sir Laurence Olivier wants you for a non-speaking part in his forthcoming film of *Richard III*. Apparently he's invented a character called the Duke of Northumberland, who simply stands there in the crowd looking splendid.'

Of course I accepted his offer. When I turned up at Shepperton Studios to have my fitting I was astonished at what had been prepared for me. Roger Furse had designed the most arresting and elegant

medieval costume in black velvet with scarlet facings. If you watch
the film very carefully you'll glimpse the costume, which is my most
memorable contribution to the production.

But I enjoyed watching Olivier's work as director. I had seen him
run through these very scenes in Sydney some years before, working
as one of six extras hired to fill out the stage picture for his Sydney
performances as *Richard III* with the London Old Vic Company. He
knew this play backwards, having been associated with it for years.

One day we noticed a beautifully dressed woman in dark glasses
watching the filming. It was winter, very cold, and she was well
muffled. There was a break in the filming and I was sitting dozing in
a corner during a lighting fit-up when there was a gentle tap on my
shoulder. I turned to stare up at Richard 'Crookback' himself.

'Where have I seen you before?'

'Tivoli Theatre, Sydney, in 1948, Sir Laurence. The play version of
this film. I was a walk-on in one of these very scenes.'

'Of course you were, Cully.' (He's the only person I've ever heard
use that very old-fashioned cockney expression.) 'You're Trader
Faulkner. You're going to play Vivien's twin next year. She's sitting
over there. Come and meet her. By the way, you must call me Larry.'

Olivier's charm was devastating. He took me across the floor to the
lady wearing dark glasses and the thick tweed overcoat. I could tell all
eyes were watching us.

'Puss,' he said, using his pet name for her, 'meet your long lost
brother-to-be, Sebastian, for next year at Stratford — Trader Faulkner.'

Vivien stood up, took off her dark glasses and grasped my hand
firmly in hers.

'Dear Trader. Peter Finch has spoken of you. I'm looking forward
to our working together. I think we'll make a credible pair of twins. I
look forward to our friendship, and I long to know how you got that
wonderful name!'

A bell rang. Everything was ready for the next take.

I realise now that I was being considered to play Sebastian to
Vivien's Viola in *Twelfth Night*, and Malcolm to Olivier's *Macbeth*
for the 1955 Stratford season. My being hired to appear in Olivier's
filmed *Richard III* was his opportunity to look me over. My agent

must have known about this, but the details of casting hadn't been finalised and the deal was being kept under wraps.

Understandably, I was devastated by that encounter and it took me several hours to recover.

Thinking back now, my first impression of Vivien was of a gaze absolutely direct and honest, disarming in its frankness, and her soft unforgettable smile. There was a great spiritual quality in Vivien that often brought her considerable suffering. Hers was a very delicate balance and therein, I believe, lay her tragedy.

Several years ago, I was driven back to Stratford for my first visit in twenty-five years. I walked to a tree on a bank of the Avon, very near the theatre, which had been planted in memory of Viv shortly after she died in 1967. The placard beside it quotes a line from *Twelfth Night*: 'A lass unparalleled.' Which indeed she was, as I was soon privileged to discover for myself as her friend.

There on the soundstage of *Richard III* that afternoon I suddenly felt a rare charge of self-confidence and jubilation. After my return from Broadway and the uncertain years between, I felt I was finally on track again for an interesting future. In the meantime, however, there were still several months before the Stratford season would commence.

One day my agent rang with an opportunity to meet an American actress whose work I admired tremendously.

'They're making a film of your girlfriend's current theatre success, *I Am a Camera*.'

'I know,' I said. 'I've heard. But Dorothy Tutin should be playing the part. She created it.'

'Well, they're making it here now, with Laurence Harvey as the Christopher Isherwood character and an import from America, Julie Harris, as Sally Bowles. They want to know if you could dance a Russian Gopak in a nightclub sequence. Berlin, 1930? It'd be worth a few quid.'

Nevermind the few quid, I thought. Here was a heaven-sent opportunity for me to meet Julie Harris! I had recently seen the film *East of Eden*, derived from Steinbeck's classic novel, in which she starred with James Dean, and had been very impressed by her truthful, understated portrayal. Of course, I accepted the job.

The film of *I Am a Camera* didn't make much of a stir when it came out, and Larry Harvey was miscast as Isherwood; but having seen Dorothy play Sally Bowles on stage and believing hers was the definitive portrayal, I was amazed to watch Julie at work on the set. She had a very cerebral Actors' Studio approach to her work. We'd be deep in serious conversation about García Lorca, whose poetry and plays she greatly admired, and suddenly she'd be called to do a shot — whereupon I saw her transformed in a trice into a giggly 1930s flapper that was spot-on for the character, utterly different from Dorothy's interpretation but just as convincing. After the film wrapped we corresponded for some years, but eventually our contact was lost.

As it happened, my tiny contribution as the Gopak dancer in the film was wisely cut, but for me that was no matter. The sole reason for accepting the job had been to meet Harris, and I had done that and had come to know her slightly — a treasured memory that I have never forgotten.

One day another call came from my agent.

'You're wanted for an interview with Orson Welles. He's filming a version of Herman Melville's great novel called *Moby Dick Rehearsed*, and he's looking for young men. I'm sending you and Kenneth Williams.'

The audition was held at the Adelphi Theatre in the Strand. After I had done my audition piece, Welles' famous voice boomed out from the darkness of the stalls.

'Mr Faulkner, do you have any other accomplishments besides acting? Do you sing, play a musical instrument, dance?'

'Well, I'm learning to dance flamenco.'

There was a long pause.

'Perhaps you'd oblige me with a short *zapateádo*?' he asked.

Welles knew Spain, and what flamenco was all about.

'I'm in flat-heeled shoes, Mr Welles. And actually I'm struggling to learn *farruca*.'

'Then show me a short sequence of that.'

I clapped and stamped a few steps.

'Thank you, Mr Faulkner. We'll be in touch if we need you.'

Sadly, I never heard another word. Later I heard that Kenneth Williams had got the part.

'Oh well,' I thought, brushing aside my disappointment. 'What does it matter? In a few weeks I'll be working with the Oliviers at Stratford. What more could any actor want?'

CHAPTER FOURTEEN

THE OLIVIERS AND STRATFORD-UPON-AVON

THE THEATRE'S GREATEST LESSON: if you want to succeed, keep your mouth shut and do as you're told. This I learnt from the directors who worked at Stratford in the two seasons I spent there. Are you a good company man and easy to handle? Fine. If not you are out. On the other hand, seen objectively, one dissenting voice — no matter how talented the actor — can be an element in the cast working against you and your concept of the production. The rehearsal process requires a delicate balance between frankness and constructive compromise. But that takes humility and sensitivity on both sides — from both director and actor.

The opening play of the 1955 Stratford-upon-Avon season was to be *Twelfth Night*, directed by John Gielgud. Our first company meeting to read through the play was held on a cold February morning, and was a gathering typical of that time.

Most of the people were new to me, but Gielgud, whom of course I already knew, was very cordial. As was Olivier. I knew one other actor in the company — Kevin Miles. We had both been in *Fly Away Peter* at the Comedy Theatre in Melbourne in 1949. There were several rows of chairs and you were expected to choose a place in accordance with your status and reputation. I chose to sit right at the back.

From the front row Vivien Leigh caught sight of me.

'Trader! Come and sit here, with me.'

This was the first of several such incidents that were to put me out of favour among the company, where I could ill afford to be at that time.

★   ★   ★

I remember this season primarily as a duel between the two leading men — the gladiators Laurence Olivier and Anthony Quayle — who were to play opposite one another in *Titus Andronicus*, the last play of the season. But there were other fine talents among the company that year, many of whom would soon become established stars: Ian Holm, Patrick Wymark, and Keith Michell, to name but three. Then there was the beautiful Maxine Audley, who would shine as Olivia in *Twelfth Night* and as Tamora, Queen of the Goths in *Titus Andronicus*.

I remember, during one rehearsal of *Twelfth Night*, Olivier giving a hilarious performance as Malvolio — clowning about outrageously. Suddenly, from the stalls, Gielgud shouted: 'Oh, Larry! It's all so vulgar! Please, no!'

Everyone froze. Olivier stood absolutely still for a moment.

'John,' he said then, very quietly. 'Have you any idea what it's like for me to create an extremely difficult character in front of a room full of young actors, all of them thinking how they might play it better?'

Gielgud was shattered by his *faux pas*. He apologised profusely, told Olivier to do whatever he liked. But something fragile had been smashed. Olivier's potentially brilliant comic Malvolio was stillborn from that moment on. His eventual performance was fine technically, of course, but was laboured and never really took flight. Such a shame. I could remember him as Sir Peter Teazel in *School for Scandal* back in Sydney, and was well aware of Olivier's genius for comic invention when he was on form.

I don't believe Gielgud and Olivier ever worked together as actor and director again.

The play opened on Shakespeare's birthday and was a damp squib, with mixed reviews. Kenneth Tynan wrote that Vivien's Viola looked like a principal boy in pantomime. Vivien was never happy under Gielgud's direction. My feeling, looking back, was that we all felt corseted. The one person who rose above it was Maxine Audley, playing Olivia. She just did her own thing, looked beautiful, and acted superbly.

I don't believe in retrospect that I was anything more than acceptable as Sebastian. You are simply there as part of the plot to resolve the mistaken identity of Viola by Olivia, and after all who the hell could truly look like Vivien Leigh? Certainly not me. But she was adorable to work with, and I was being paid £25 a week to kiss her every night. Could any man ask for more?

One Saturday I was approached by Vivien and invited to come back with her and Larry after the evening performance to spend that night and Sunday at their large estate in Buckinghamshire.

Notley Abbey, a vast property of some sixty-eight acres situated on the Thame near Oxford, had been founded in the twelfth century by Henry II, and had numbered Henry V among its distinguished visitors over the centuries — a fact which immediately endeared it to Larry. He and Vivien had bought it in 1945, and had spent their savings renovating the interior with the advice and help of the decorators Sibyl Colefax and John Fowler. With seven bedrooms, six baths, and an extensive and well-developed garden, it became the focus of frequent social gatherings hosted by the glamorous pair.

For that Sunday luncheon, the non-resident guests were invited for 1:00 p.m. Marlene Dietrich arrived at 2.30 p.m., and we were all summoned to gather round to admire photos of her grandchild. Vivien stood patiently, waiting to usher her guests in to lunch. We finally sat down at 2.50 p.m. I was placed between Dietrich and Lily Palmer, then divorced from Rex Harrison. Marlene started a conversation with Lily across me in German. I felt exactly like a tennis enthusiast at a Wimbledon final watching the ball, with this conversation in German volleying in front of me from one side to the other. Ronald Colman, sitting opposite, looked highly amused, while the rest of the table chatted away in their separate groups. Vivien, at the end of the table on my right, was deep in conversation with Mike Todd. Conversation was what Vivien excelled at; it stimulated her and kept her going — especially when, as she put it, 'the demons of black depression begin to hover'. Meanwhile, Olivier, at the top of the table on my left, was watching us all — looking as if he wished he were somewhere else. Possibly irritated by seeing Vivien in full flight with her neighbour, Olivier suddenly pinged his fork against his wineglass and announced to the table: 'Trader's in love, everyone! He's nursing a secret passion for Marlene.'

I was gobsmacked, for I entertained no such feelings for the German legend and was horrified that Olivier should announce such a lie for a joke.

'Who the hell's Twader?' asked Marlene in the silence that followed.

'On your immediate right,' replied Olivier.

I remember a pair of granite-hard blue eyes glaring at me.

'Oh? Well, I'm certainly not in love with him.'

'Ah, but Trader's crazy about you,' Olivier continued. 'And I know he aches to be alone with you. After lunch why don't you go for a walk together under the pergola? Go on Marlene, darling. Recapture a lost second of your romantic youth.'

At Larry's insistence, we did go for that amble under the pergola, but very little was said as I was paralysed with shy embarrassment. As we walked back to join the others she suddenly turned and, taking my chin between her thumb and forefinger, gave me a soft peck on the lips.

'That was mean of Larry, so there! Just to show you I'm not as cold as they say.'

I couldn't help thinking of that wonderful song sung by Dooley Wilson in the film *Casablanca*:

A kiss is just a kiss,
A sigh is just a sigh,
The fundamental things apply
As time goes by ...

Seeing it from Marlene's point of view, she was a sport to go along with Olivier's childish prank. And if only I'd been older and a little wiser, what fun it could have been!

That year at Stratford was a process of humiliating self-realisation. Charm and good looks were bringing me a certain degree of popularity among the company. But then an acutely embarrassing experience made me realise the hollow value of charm when it's allied to ambition and divorced from any thought for others.

As the season progressed, some of the older members of the cast were taking a liking to 'Trader's funny stories', one of whom was Michael Denison, who played Sir Andrew Aguecheek and who had become a friend. I felt flattered, having recently seen him give a definitive performance as Algie in Anthony Asquith's film of *The Importance of Being Earnest*, in which my paramour Dorothy Tutin played Cecily.

Eager to develop this friendship, I invited Michael and his wife Dulcie Grey to have lunch on my houseboat in Chelsea one Sunday when we were free. We made a date, but I then forgot to write it in my diary and thought no more about it.

Shortly after, Vivien invited me again to Notley to spend another weekend with the Oliviers and a clutch of their international celebrity friends.

'Part of your education, darling,' Vivien told me. 'Your opportunity to mix with the hierarchy of the artistic and literary world.'

How could I refuse?

That weekend was as memorable as its aftermath was a nightmare. Arriving back at Stratford on the Monday night for a performance of *Twelfth Night*, and half made-up, I went down to the canteen for a cup of coffee.

'Oh boy, Trade!' said an actor. 'Are you in deep trouble!'

'Why? What have I done?'

I was feeling very arrogant after that weekend.

'Didn't you have a date on your houseboat yesterday?' he asked.

There are very few moments when I wished I'd never existed. That was one.

I rushed immediately to Michael Denison's dressing room.

'Michael, I completely forgot! I have no excuse, and I'm deeply ashamed.'

'Yes,' he said. 'Your behaviour was in very bad taste. The Dulce and I drove all the way down to London to your houseboat, and you weren't there! We had to drive all the way back.'

Stratford to London at that time could be a full three-hour drive.

'I suppose you were with the Oliviers!' he said.

'Yes, I was.'

Quite possibly Michael and Dulcie were not invited to Notley that season. I don't remember. I do remember that very few members of the cast were, and this of course caused bad feeling within the company. Vivien was very social and needed people round her who would keep her buoyant and help hold at bay the depression that so often beset her. Happily married couples were not of great interest to Vivien. Young, unattached men who could amuse her were.

'Michael, I humbly apologise, and will make amends to you in any way I can.'

'Well, if you have any sense of decency, you should offer your apologies forthwith to the Dulce.'

'Fine. Where can I find her?'

'She's staying at the Arden Hotel opposite. I suggest you get yourself over there as soon as possible.'

'I'll do that.'

I rushed out of his dressing room and dashed across the road to the Arden Hotel — half-dressed in my Sebastian costume, which included a very tight corset, a suspender belt, thigh-high black stockings, and black slippers with pink pom-poms attached. I was also wearing thick make-up. This is the spectacle that rushed into the Arden, raced down the passage, and burst into a packed dining room of middle-aged wealthy gentry — most of whom would shortly be watching us in the theatre.

I saw Dulcie sitting in a corner, rushed across and went down on one knee. Most of the diners were instantly on their feet, one elderly gentleman's monocle dropping down onto his tartan waistcoat.

'Dulcie! How can I apologise? What can I say?'

She simply stared at me.

'My God, Trader! What are you doing here looking like that?'

I looked down. Shock must have given me the speed of light. In a flash I was back in the theatre, up two flights of stairs and into my dressing room. I don't believe even the stage doorman glimpsed me. At least nothing was ever said.

That evening, during the performance of *Twelfth Night*, when

Toby Belch eggs on Sir Andrew Aguecheek into fighting a duel with Sebastian, Aguecheek (Michael) departed from his usual effeminate mild slap on the face.

'Well, there's for you!' he said, giving me a much harder slap than usual. Instinctively I hit him back so hard that he collapsed, dazed, to the floor. Then, quite out of character, I helped him to his feet. I had committed a cardinal sin in the theatre, letting my emotions get the better of me.

When we came off he said, 'Well, now you've added injury to insult.'

'Dear Michael, please forgive me! It's simply not my night.'

The friendship then split apart completely with his final riposte.

'Well, of course, you're an Australian. You simply don't know any better.'

It was a great sadness to me that I subsequently failed to find any means of healing the rift.

After *Twelfth Night*, we rehearsed and opened *All's Well That Ends Well*. Meticulously directed by Noel Willman, and with beautiful Spanish Velazquez-style costumes by Mariano Andreu, the production was exquisite and lifeless. It was agony to be in, even if you were a gorgeously be-robed courtier (as I was) simply dressing the stage. It was a lavish, well-acted production that was, ultimately, eminently forgettable.

Once *All's Well* opened, rehearsals for *Macbeth* began, with Laurence Olivier and Vivien Leigh playing the thane and his lady. The last time they had acted on stage together was in a Shakespeare and Shaw double bill of *Antony and Cleopatra* with *Caesar and Cleopatra*, both productions of which I had been lucky enough to see. This was their 1951 Festival of Britain contribution in London, which they later took to Broadway. So the excitement among the company was almost tangible.

The part of Malcolm was my only potential winner that season, and I was determined to make good with it. Unfortunately, at the very first reading I fell foul of the director, Glen Byam Shaw (who was also Artistic Director of the Stratford Memorial Theatre at this point). I was the only member of the cast whom he told exactly how he felt the character should be played. Byam Shaw saw the character as effete and degenerate, a weakling. I saw Malcolm as someone worthy to succeed Macbeth as a leader. In other words, my interpretation was the very opposite of what Byam Shaw wanted. I told him I would have to play it as I saw it or he could give the part to someone else.

'Glen, you must let Trader play his own interpretation,' Olivier told him.

Glen's reply was, 'All right, then. I shan't argue.'

When we'd finished reading through the play, Byam Shaw made his comments to each actor, but said nothing to me. I realised then that I wasn't considered part of his team. My confrontation with Glen Byam Shaw proved to be my professional suicide at Stratford. He never spoke to me again, and I didn't return to Stratford until Trevor Nunn's tenure in 1970. But there was no way I could have played the character according to Byam Shaw's dictates.

In spite of his antipathy towards me, most of the company members were very friendly, and their respect for what I was trying to do gave me the confidence I badly needed. Most important of all, so were Olivier and Vivien, busy as they were with their own problems.

Those two international celebrities — appearing constantly as a team both in the media and out of it — were slowly splitting up, and sadly I was close at hand to observe it.

Fortunately, *Macbeth* was a success for Olivier, and equally for Vivien — her greatest challenge since *A Streetcar Named Desire*.

Throughout that season I was very grateful for Vivien's friendship. Ian Holm, playing Donalbain, and like me in his first season at Stratford, was also a good friend. Peter Hall saw the enormous potential that Ian had and would give it free rein when he took over from Byam Shaw towards the end of the 1950s. I remember going up to Stratford then to see Dorothy Tutin play Juliet. Ian was still in the company:

'Still playing small, thankless parts,' he said. 'God, I'm pissed off! I'm actually thinking of throwing it in and trying to get work in London. Should I?'

'No, Ian,' I told him. 'Peter knows what he's doing and I can't help feeling that he's biding his time with you. Stick it out. Give it one more season.'

Ian's subsequent rise to well-deserved fame in the sixties was no surprise to most of us who knew him — playing at Stratford, during Shakespeare's quatracentennial season in 1964, both Henry V and Richard III to great acclaim.

The afternoon before our opening of *Macbeth* at the Stratford Theatre I was in the actors' pub, the Dirty Duck. A man asked if he might join me. We began to chat. He said he was on his way to the stagedoor to drop a note for Sir Laurence Olivier.

I told him I was an actor in the company and could save him the trouble. He gave me the note. It was on a plain card. The handwriting was Dorothy's. The man had met her at the Edinburgh Festival and mentioned he was going to Stratford next day, and she'd asked him to deliver the note.

Saying I'd see Olivier got the card at once, I raced across the road to the comparative privacy of the Bancroft Gardens where I read it. It was a warm and loving message of good luck. No more. But, like Iago, I knew: *Trifles light as air are to the jealous confirmations strong as proof of holy writ.*

Inflamed by having had no word from Dorothy myself, my imagination ran riot. Olivier, my hero — to whom I'd once confided my love for Dorothy — was now my rival. You bastard, I thought. I ran to the theatre and up the stairs to the star dressing room.

Knock, knock ...

'Larry?'

'Yes?'

'Could I disturb you for a moment?'

'Baby! A moment and no more. We're on in forty minutes.'

'I've got a message for you,' I told him. 'A man in the Duck asked me to give you this.'

Olivier needed glasses to read. He put them on, glanced quickly at the card, then stared at me in the mirror.

There was a long pause.

'Little Tutin is a great actress,' he said finally, sitting back, 'but it's time you stopped waving a banner for her, Cully, and concentrated on your own career — because you *are* talented, and for those who procrastinate it's always later than you think. For a start, you're wasting your time with all this flamenco dancing. Believe me, baby, British actors don't dance.'

I bit my tongue. This was not the time for a confrontation about my dancing.

He took off his glasses and rubbed his eyes.

'Can I give you a piece of advice?'

I nodded.

'Malcolm. The way you're playing Malcolm.'

'What about it?'

'Having played it myself twenty-eight years ago, I know that it's one of Shakespeare's dreariest characters. But you do have a nice little speech at the end. And you're clowning it. Why, baby?'

'Clowning it?'

'Go on, say those last five lines.'

I did as he asked.

'*This and what needful else That calls upon us, by the grace of Grace, We will perform in measure, time, and place: So, thanks to all at once and to each one, whom we invite to see us crowned at Scooone!*'

My operatic 'scooone' was like Olivier's 'God for Harry, England and St Geeeoooorge!' in his film of *Henry V*.

'Baby,' he said, 'you sound exactly like an air-raid siren. If you do it that way tonight the customers will piss themselves laughing. Is that what you want?'

'How would you do it?'

'*To see us* crowned *at Scone*.'

He sat me down beside him and from his make-up tray scooped out a blob of undertaker's wax, a tiny ball of which he put on the tip of my nose and reshaped it.

'Now, baby, you begin to look like Vivien's twin.'

He had switched to another of my roles that season — Sebastian, twin-brother to Vivien's Viola in *Twelfth Night*. He'd moulded my nose with a little wooden spatula to make a perfect retroussé identical to hers.

'That's the spatula I used for the very first performance of *Richard III* at the New Theatre in London.' He handed it to me. 'Here, baby, keep it. And learn how to do a proper nose.' Then, 'Christ! Out, quick! We're on in five minutes!'

I was halfway to my dressing room clutching the historic spatula — treasured still, like a fragment of the True Cross — before I realised how brilliantly he'd switched my mind away from Dorothy.

But the potentially explosive situation between us was far from ending there.

One night we had all driven down to Notley after the evening performance of *Macbeth*. Noel Coward had attended the performance, and we'd all had dinner with several bottles of vintage wines from Larry's cellar. In spite of the wine, I was still feeling very uncomfortable at a table full of sparkling and witty guests. The wines elicited dazzling conversation and Coward juggled his notorious witticisms with consummate ease until finally we all reeled off to bed.

The following morning, all the other guests had their breakfast in their rooms. But I, very excited to be there, had chosen to come down for breakfast. I collected my bacon, eggs, sausage, and toast and was quietly enjoying them when down the stairs in an elegant dressing gown, smoking a de Reske cigarette in a long, silver cigarette holder and exhaling perfectly rounded smoke rings, glided England's 'Talent to Amuse'. He floated over and offered me a winning smile.

'Thought you were very good as Malcolm last night, dear boy. You have a promising future.'

'Thank you Mr Coward.'

He leaned towards me, exuding an overpowering odour of Mitsouko.

'Tell me dear boy,' he murmured, 'is your bum available this morning?'

'No, Mr Coward. Not this or any other morning. I'm a plunger, not a poofter.'

'What a tragedy! Ah well, life is full of disappointments. But we must soldier on, mustn't we? Would you be a darling and pass me the marmalade?'

I suppose I can boast: I've always been very lucky in that whenever I've been propositioned by men it's always been done with style.

CHAPTER FIFTEEN

END OF A DREAM

THE PENULTIMATE STRATFORD PRODUCTION, *The Merry Wives of Windsor*, also directed by Glen Byam Shaw, was pretty, eminently tasteful, and lifeless. I was cast as the juvenile lover Fenton, 'all merry May and sunshine'. Truly this season at Stratford was turning out for me to be a stiff prison sentence, with a Governor — Byam Shaw — who had condemned me to a grating solitary confinement.

The last production of the 1955 season was *Titus Andronicus* — rarely done because there is so much bloodshed in the play. I was hoping to be cast as one of the sons of Tamora, Queen of the Goths, and had heard I would be when I joined the company. But as a result of the altercation with Glen Byam Shaw over my interpretation of Malcolm I knew I was in trouble. The part he had promised me, Charon, went to the other Aussie, Kevin Miles. I was demoted to playing Third Goth, who only had two or three lines. It was a difficult snub for me to accept, but it did give my friend Kev a wonderful opportunity to shine.

The director was the greatly celebrated Peter Brook, whose production of *Ring Round the Moon* in London — the first play I had seen there after my arrival — made me realise we were in for a memorable production.

One afternoon Vivien and I were among the very few not called for rehearsal.

'Darling,' she said, 'would you punt me down the river?'

'Of course!' I said. 'I'll get a boat and pick you up on the riverbank.'

So I quickly dressed in my best white shirt, shorts, and white shoes, realising that if I was going to punt Vivien Leigh down the Avon I must look as stylish as possible. Racing over to the boat shed, I hired a punt and waited at the appointed spot. Across the lawn she came in a beautiful floral skirt, white blouse, and a wide-brimmed straw hat. She looked the personification of English summer beauty. I remember thinking, if only a master painter could have captured her at that precise moment.

She took my hand, stepped lightly into the boat, and away we glided.

Our course along the river passed directly opposite the canteen balcony of the theatre. Just as we came into view, everyone called for that rehearsal — including Olivier and Peter Brook — was on the balcony, as it was the tea break, and a few whistled and catcalled down to us. I felt like an Egyptian slave punting Cleopatra down the Nile, though I instantly felt the potential danger of this situation. Our little boat trip was nothing but a spontaneous gesture by Vivien to pass the time; but seen from the vantage point of later circumstances, it could not have been more ill-timed.

We virtually had the river to ourselves, floating along under Clopton Bridge and on through meadows, cow pastures, and past a small island. All the while, Vivien commented on everything around us. Her knowledge of nature seemed encyclopaedic — flowers, trees, birds, insects. We were in Warwickshire, Shakespeare's home county, and Vivien soon went on to ponder out loud what his life there must have been like. All that was required of me was to shut up and steer the punt.

Of course, I had no designs on Viv. She was Olivier's wife, and I was still besotted with Dorothy Tutin (who apparently was besotted with Olivier). My friendship with Vivien was entirely platonic — though she was certainly bewitching. Equally spellbinding for me, however, was her encyclopaedic mind, coupled with her charm and wit when she was on form. That afternoon she was radiant. I remember thinking what a contradiction she was as a human being: so in harmony with nature, and yet so entirely dysfunctional within her own psyche.

As we neared the theatre on our return, I impulsively said, 'You are such a kind friend, Viv. I wish I could be of some help to you.'

Everyone knew and spoke of the fact that the Oliviers' marriage was coming apart at the seams (her intermittent but ongoing affair with my old teacher and friend Peter Finch was by then a well-known fact). I knew immediately that I'd spoken unwisely. Nothing more was said until, as I helped her ashore, she turned, kissed me on the cheek, and said: 'Trader darling, a quote from the wisest among us: "Use all gently."'

Then she was gone.

Back in rehearsals once again, I felt that what had happened had put me in an intolerable situation. It was clear that I was tacitly seen now as Vivien's 'toyboy'. For me, the politics and jealousy within the company were coming into ever-sharper focus.

Like so many young actors on their own at Stratford, loneliness and a sense of rustic isolation were incessant. If you were on your own up there you became very introverted. If you were in all five plays you were on every night, but with no transport except a bicycle the days could seem eternal. Long rides in the local countryside soon lost their allure. Also, with the last play of the 1955 season about to open, I felt my chances of being invited back the next year dwindling.

But the *Titus* rehearsals continued to be wonderfully exciting to me. Brook had the whole thing worked out in his head — actors' moves, costumes and music — and slowly but surely he put it all together, like the pieces of a jigsaw puzzle. His concept was unforgettable. In the most violent and bloody of Shakespeare's plays, the audience was to see little violence and no blood, but imagine the opposite. This was the work of a consummate master.

Lavinia, Titus's daughter and played by Vivien Leigh, had to come on with both hands cut off, and her tongue cut out. Dressed in white and veiled, she came on with two red ribbons dangling from her empty sleeves and her head lying on her shoulder like a strangled bird. The sight was horrendous. As Titus, Olivier had the role with the greatest *gravitas*, but Anthony Quayle, as Aaron, had the edge of popular appeal because his character was flamboyant, wicked, and dazzling. It was a combat of two titans.

Maxine Audley as Queen of the Goths looked ravishing, and it was her moment to outshine Vivien — which, of course, she did because she had the greater dramatic weight of Shakespeare's writing.

As with his *A Midsummer Night's Dream'* fifteen years later, Peter Brook created a masterpiece, a production that is still remembered and spoken of to this day.

One night Vivien invited the cast to a midnight barbecue on the banks of the Avon. The picnic spot was less than a mile from the theatre. Everyone was to go down by punt after the evening performance. My landlady lent me her new rug on which to sit and spread my picnic. Vivien's chosen spot for our rustic celebration was a field full of fresh cow shit. Suffice it to say that when I returned Freda Elmore's rug next day it nearly ruptured our friendship, which was hardly surprising.

After feasting on barbecued steak, the best Warwickshire sausages, and copious helpings of vintage wine, the party got restive.

Then Vivien announced that she was going for a dip.

'Anyone coming with me?'

The ravishing Maxine Audley agreed to go in with her. To my amazement no one seemed to register what was about to happen. Most of the party seemed happy to just lie among the cowpats, chatting and imbibing. Not me; I simply couldn't allow such an opportunity to pass by and slunk away to take a surreptitious gander at Venus bathing with her handmaiden. What I saw caused me to wander back to the others on three legs. The vision of those two women splashing about naked — barely visible in the night — is something I will always treasure.

One afternoon, not many weeks after our midnight revels on the Avon, Vivien invited several of us to go for another picnic, somewhere out towards Evesham. I don't remember how, but I found myself sitting alone with her on a grassy knoll. We were talking of Peter Finch and his then wife Tamara, and I suddenly became aware that I was balancing on a very slippery slope. Peter's total, satyr-like freedom from all conventional mores had drawn her strongly to him, and through him to me. As we talked, Vivien was very close, her perfume intoxicating.

'Tell me Trader darling,' she said seductively, leaning even closer, 'do you have a girlfriend?'

'I do. But I don't see her much at the moment. She's in a play in London.'

'Would it be indiscreet to ask who it is?'

'Dorothy Tutin.'

If I'd fired a pistol she couldn't have reacted more physically.

'I'm so glad!' she said, jerking back.

The words came out in a rush. I knew at once that some kind of a marital hurricane regarding Olivier's association with Dorothy must have swept through their relationship, and I was right, as events later revealed.

One Saturday evening soon after, I was invited down for another Notley weekend. I was to be driven down by Vivien; Olivier and the rest would drive separately.

Arriving first, Vivien and I sat in the library sipping gin. I noticed that Vivien seemed very on edge. She spoke to me of Finchie and what fun he was to be with, 'like a wild, sensual Pan', and so full of wonderful Aussie anecdotes. Then she said:

'He's so different to Larry. Larry only thinks about his career. Peter in bed is like a very naughty faun, while Larry tends now to be rather like a sanctimonious parson. Did you know that Larry's father was a reverend?'

Sitting opposite the half-closed door, I suddenly became aware that Olivier was standing outside, listening. Immediately I wanted to be far away from this horribly awkward situation, for I was sure that he knew I'd spotted him. Vivien had a fondness for the theory of reincarnation, and I remember her then remarking that she, Peter Finch and I were 'old' souls in life's spiritual evolution, but that her life with Larry had led her to realise that he was a brand new soul, still with all its youthful rough edges that needed a lifetime's smoothing down.

'Well,' I replied, 'to use a cricketing metaphor, he certainly hasn't done too badly — scoring a century in his first innings!'

At that moment, Olivier made his entrance. Nervously, I sprang to my feet and offered him a drink.

'I'm perfectly capable of pouring my own drink,' he said. 'This is, after all, my own house. Meanwhile I suggest, baby, that you get yourself off to bed!'

Vivien frowned at him over her glass.

'Stay where you are, Trader, and finish your drink,' she said. 'If Larry wishes to behave like a boor then he's best ignored.'

'Go to bed,' said Olivier again, glaring at me.

'Stay put, Trader. Just ignore him.'

'Please!' I said in desperation. 'I'm your guest, and I feel very privileged to be here. But please, don't fight. And could I ask a favour? There's a full moon tonight, and from what I saw driving in the garden looks beautiful. Would you both walk with me once round Notley Abbey? Then I promise I'll go to bed.'

'Come on, Larry boy, be a sport.'

Off we went, accompanied by Vivien's cat. It seemed that an uneasy peace had been re-instated as I walked arm-in-arm between them through their moonlit garden.

How wrong I was. When we returned, I went off to bed and left the others to foregather for a nightcap.

At 6 a.m. I woke up, aware that someone was sitting beside me. I shot bolt upright to find myself face to face with Larry.

'Baby,' he said, 'I think you'd better go home.'

'What, now?'

'After breakfast. I've already spoken to Keith.' (He was referring to Keith Michell.) 'He'll drive you back.'

'What on earth can I say to Vivien?' I asked.

I told him she had arranged to take some of us for a picnic to Minster Lovell because of my desire to see the place where the little girl playing hide and seek had climbed into a trunk, inadvertently locked herself in, and lay there undiscovered for two hundred years. Vivien had been thrilled at the idea, but Olivier cut me dead.

'Baby, I shan't repeat myself. I want you gone from here after breakfast.' As he opened the door, he turned back to me. 'And not a word to Vivien. She mustn't know I've spoken to you.'

'But Larry, what possible excuse can I give her?'

'You're an actor, baby. Use your imagination.'

Then he was gone, quietly shutting my door behind him.

What was I going to say to Vivien?

I went down to breakfast. Vivien was in top form — or was she supercharged with an excessive energy?

I had worked out an excuse and simply took the plunge.

'Vivien, I must apologise. I clean forgot, I've got a driving lesson this morning.'

'Ring him, darling. I'm sure he'll understand.'

'They're not on the phone.'

'You could send him a telegram,' she persisted.

Suddenly, I flared.

'Larry, I have the address. Could you please send a wire?'

I'd had enough. I meant to make it clear to him: 'This is your doing, mate — you sort it out!'

Vivien saved the day. She had realised by then what the game was and turned to me with her typical charm:

'Dear Trader, if you must go, you must. I can see that it's out of your hands.'

I left with Keith, and if I remember correctly that was my last visit to Notley — until Vivien invited my mother and I for a very embarrassing weekend several years later.

The experience of the 1955 season at Stratford taught me so much — not only about my craft, but also human nature. It was a period of rich experience; the rivalries, friendships and humiliations. Vivien Leigh was a wonderful friend to me, as was Olivier at the beginning. After the incident at Notley Abbey, Olivier understandably began to dislike me and wanted me nowhere near him. He saw me as a threat to his relationship with Vivien after her affair with Peter Finch (who, of course, was my good friend). He never forgot. Even after his marriage with Vivien crashed and he married Joan Plowright, Trader Faulkner was to remain *persona non grata* in any future Olivier enterprise.

For me, Olivier was a ruthless, brilliant, and spectacular actor, but finally incapable of projecting genuine emotion. He may have moved millions, but I could always see the mechanical process by which he worked. Still, he was certainly one of the greatest twentieth-century actors and a consummate technician. Back in Sydney in 1948, when I first saw him onstage at close quarters as Richard III, I thought him the most exciting actor I'd ever seen — a dazzling firecracker, exploding spectacularly into myriad sparks and colours. And whatever his faults, he certainly influenced my development.

CHAPTER SIXTEEN

THE WALTZ OF THE TOREADORS

BACK IN MY houseboat again, the Stratford season having finished, I got to know the night watchman at the Chelsea boatyard, Ben Bowyang — a lizard-eyed mischief-maker who spied on everyone. He knew of my passion for Dorothy and confirmed my suspicions by telling me that she'd recently received a late night visit from Olivier. Crazed with jealousy, I was ready to deck him the moment he set foot again on Dorothy's boat.

I'd made no bones about this to Ben.

'Trader,' he said one evening, 'why don't ya clock 'im wiv a bottle? That'd be just the job.'

I was in such a state I took him seriously.

The moment to strike came at the end of a freezing January day when Ben told me Dorothy was expecting another visit from Olivier that night.

Now at the top of the gangway leading to the houseboats in those days was a dirty great garbage bin. One of its handles had been torn off, leaving two holes. Long after dark, I emptied the stinking contents into the river, climbed in, put the lid back on, and waited — using the holes to peep through.

Sure enough, after about half an hour the great man himself arrived and vanished down the hatch of Dorothy's boat.

I must have crouched in that bin for hours.

An icy wind whined in at me through my peepholes. My teeth were chattering with nerves and cold. Eventually, I had to get out to stretch my legs.

Presently, I saw a Bentley pull up on the opposite side of Cheyne Walk, and out of it stepped what looked like a very classy whore bundled up in a leopard-skin coat. Touting for customers, I thought. But after walking up and down for a bit, the leopard-skin beauty climbed into her Bentley again and drove off.

I returned to my vigil in the garbage bin, and pulled down the lid.

At last, sometime near dawn, I saw two figures emerge from Dorothy's boat.

'Goodnight, my darling,' I heard Dorothy whisper.

Up I rose. Dorothy, glimpsing this bin-lidded apparition across Olivier's shoulder, shot back down her hatch and slammed it shut.

Climbing out, I lumbered forward, one hand behind me clutching an empty wine bottle, as Olivier made his way up the gangplank. When he saw me he stopped dead. In the grey dawn he stood there, an exhausted man in a bowler hat, pinstriped suit and canary-yellow gloves, staring at me aghast.

I moved in to savage him. His response threw me. He opened his arms wide. He was Jesus, forgiving and loving.

'Baby ... baby ... ' he crooned, unshaven, haggard, vulnerable.

I was lost. I tossed the bottle behind me into the Thames and flung out both my arms.

'Larry! How lovely to see you!'

And there we swayed, clasped in a silent embrace on the rocking pontoon.

'Baby, what are you doing here?'

I lied desperately.

'I'm about to play a madman on TV and I'm getting into character.'

He took my face between his hands.

'Well, let me tell you you're a very convincing madman. You're going to be wonderful in the part. A definitive lunatic, baby.'

He kissed me on both cheeks and, looking beyond me, said, 'I've got to go. I see my car's waiting.'

And off he went, blowing me another kiss as he disappeared.

It was snowing. I just stood there.

Years later at a dinner party given by Vivien Leigh shortly before she died, I told this story. Vivien knew about Larry and Dorothy anyway. Her face was a study.

'Oh Trader, jealousy was crucifying *both of us*. The leopard-skin whore you saw on the embankment that night was me.'

Within weeks of the close of the 1955 Stratford season, I was contacted by Peter Hall and offered the role of Gaston in Jean Anouilh's *The Waltz of the Toreadors*, which was to be presented at the Criterion Theatre, Piccadilly.

'I know the part of Gaston is not a world-beater,' he told me, 'but if you'll sign this run of the play contract I shan't forget it. I can always get you out of it if you want.'

I took the job, and was then lumbered with a twenty-three-month marathon at the Criterion that left me depressed and dispirited, even though the distinguished cast included such names as Beatrix Lehmann and Hugh Griffith. The production had opened at the Arts Theatre for what was expected to be a short run, became a great hit, and transferred. Now at the Criterion, all the other principals but me had six-month contracts. Like it or not, I was in it for the count.

The things that kept me sane over those long months were the discipline of my continuing regular training as a flamenco dancer and the odd radio jobs I did for the BBC — the only other work my contract permitted.

At one point I was offered the lead in the play *Crime on Goat Island* by Ugo Betti for the BBC Third Programme, now Radio 3. The part was a marathon. The director, John Gibson, was also a personal friend — a chain-smoker with a perpetual thirst for alcohol. Needless to say, he died prematurely. Brilliant at his job, he decided simply that I was this dubious satyr-like character. The vocal qualities that sprang into my imagination were exactly those of the Welsh actor with whom I was playing in *The Waltz of the Toreadors*, Hugh Griffith. Put hooves and a faun's hindquarters on Hugh and there was the character. The challenge was that for the two-hour duration of the play I never stopped talking. All I remember now was that I got through the one-hundred-and-twenty-minute stint without a fluff.

The BBC recently found and sent me a recording of *Crime on Goat Island*. I think I'll have a strong whisky before listening to it.

During this period I was agonising over my frustrated and obviously one-sided love affair with Dorothy Tutin, and had not been able to extricate myself from my passion for her, despite the occasional sexual adventure that chance afforded me on the side.

Six months into the run of *Waltz*, there was a change of cast as it began to seem that the play would run indefinitely. An actress arrived for whom I felt an instant and very strong physical attraction — Renée Asherson. I had seen her as the Princess Katharine in Olivier's film *Henry V*, and as Stella in the stage production of *A Streetcar Named Desire* with Vivien Leigh in London. It seemed that we were mutually attracted to one another. In the play I had the good fortune of being able to kiss her at each performance — and, as with Vivien Leigh, I was paid to do so. But I wanted more than that, and soon was brave enough to make my move. One night I invited Renée to dinner and made my position clear.

'At the moment,' she said, shyly, 'I'm having an affair with Douglas Fairbanks Jr, but he's such a ram I suspect he's having affairs with everybody!'

'What about your husband?' I asked.

Renée had been married to the actor Robert Donat since 1953, though by the time I met her they had been separated for some time. She told me a lot about her relationship with Donat, and how they'd agreed to a divorce because, as she said, 'I'm just too neurotic to cope with dear Robert's asthma attacks. So often I've felt he was on the point of death. He's a brilliant actor — one of the country's finest. Robert is a true chameleon.'

'Like Peter Finch,' I said.

'Exactly,' she said. 'However, I just couldn't live with a man who threatens to die at any second. And what of my career as an actress? I admire Robert so much, and I truly adore him, but I couldn't stay with him.'

Not long after that first conversation she cornered me backstage.

'Well, Trader, I've dispatched Fairbanks. Now I can think about you.'

'What do you mean, *dispatched*?' I said. 'Is he floating in the Thames somewhere?'

'No,' she said. 'I simply told him it was time to hunt for another paramour!'

Renée and I became passionate lovers. But the relationship with this woman twelve years older than me was obviously a strain on her.

Renée was a lady in the very best sense of the word and insisted on being treated as such, and I did try. We had wonderful times together — she had a hilarious sense of humour. My mother was rabidly jealous, but could do nothing about it.

One morning in 1958, Renée rang me.

'Trader, I've got to say goodbye. I know Robert is with someone else, but he's in the clinic in Dean Street and he's dying and I've simply got to go to him.'

She hung up. As I remember, Robert Donat died a few hours later.

That evening, Renée rang me again.

'They wouldn't let me see him. I wanted so much to be near him, but I was prevented — *she* was there! I know I should never have left him, should never have let him down.'

After the close of *The Waltz of the Toreadors*, it was many years before I would see Renée again.

In 1999 I was sent an obituary from an Australian paper, for a very well-known ballerina who had just died. In the article, my mother was mentioned as the initial guiding force in her career. The obituary was honouring a Sydney-born girl who had enjoyed a huge success with the Sadler's Wells Ballet under Dame Ninette de Valois, with Frederick Ashton as principal choreographer. The article awoke emotions I've seldom felt so strongly.

My first memory regarding this girl was an account my mother gave me one afternoon back in 1939 when she had returned from her dance studio in Manly. Apparently, the child had been brought in by her mother to join Mum's ballet class. Mother got her accompanist to play a Chopin Nocturne and asked her to move to it. Watching her, my mother was transfixed.

'Well, Mrs Faulkner?' asked the mother. 'What do you think?'

'She's the only child I've ever seen who has something of the quality of Anna Pavlova,' she told the woman. 'I'll take her!'

The girl was Elaine Fifield.

A couple of years later, when I was fourteen and she was twelve, Mum invited 'Fifi' (as she called Elaine) to lunch at The Orchard, where we were then living. She was arriving from the Sydney side, and I was sent to Manly Wharf to meet her off the ferry. Down the gangway came this exquisite young girl with a pink flower in her hair. As I escorted her home, I thought she was absolutely gorgeous, and remember being struck by her innocent purity — she had been very strictly brought up as a Seventh Day Adventist — and her complete dedication to dance. I enjoyed Elaine's visit that day, but then thought no more about it.

Some years before me, in the 1940s, Elaine had come to London and soon found her niche with the Sadler's Wells Ballet Company.

One afternoon during my long stint in *The Waltz of the Toreadors* Elaine turned up in desperate straits at the *Stella Maris* to see my mother. By that time, Elaine was recognised as one of de Valois's best ballerinas, and according to some sources was being groomed by her to become her prima ballerina. A few years earlier Elaine had married John Lanchbury, the conductor of the ballet orchestra, and had had a baby daughter by him. Apparently, de Valois was so upset by Elaine's seeming lack of single-minded dedication to the company that she demoted her in rank, making her understudy the other ballerinas dancing the roles that should have been hers. Now she had come to my mother for advice. All of this is well-documented in Elaine's autobiography, *In My Shoes*.

When she arrived, Elaine was very disturbed — unsure whether to continue with de Valois and English ballet or return to Australia to take up a post she had been offered there. My mother told her that at all costs she must stick it out with de Valois. It would be foolish for her to throw in the sponge now, having worked so hard and been so successful. Drying her tears, Elaine decided to think it over.

I had come home halfway through all this, and — seeing how upset Elaine was — offered to take her out to dinner. When she was ready, we took our leave of Mum and went out to dine at Rules in the West End, both of us ending up well sated with food and drink. Before I paid the bill she reached across the table and laid her hand on my wrist.

'Trader,' she said, 'will you make love to me? My marriage to Jack is a cover. He's really AC/DC, and more on the *A* side than the *D*.'

Off we went for a night of unforgettable lovemaking at the Strand Palace Hotel — Elaine's frustrations fuelling her passionate intensity.

Elaine Fifield and I remained lovers for a time and my relationship with her was an unforgettable, deeply enriching experience. Having been privileged both to know her intimately and to watch her dance I can only say that she was truly a remarkable woman.

Some days after our night at the Strand she came again to the *Stella Maris* where my mother gave her a treasured copy of *Undine*, the classic fairytale by Friedrich de la Motte-Fouqué, with wonderfully ethereal illustrations by the great Arthur Rackham. She told Fifi to give the book to Frederick Ashton and to ask him to create a ballet from the *Undine* story for her. Apparently, Ashton took the book and said he would consider it. He finally did create the ballet, but not for Elaine. *Undine* was to be a renowned success for her friend and rival in Sadler's Wells — and Ashton's protégé — Margot Fonteyn.

Various other problems with Sadler's Wells — which was later to become the Royal Ballet — possibly related to the break-up of her marriage and a subsequent drink problem — finally sent Fifi back to Australia. There she remarried, lived for a while in New Guinea with her planter husband, and died prematurely.

Though at the end of her life she did make a late comeback and returned to dance roles on tour in London and elsewhere (Mum and I saw her and she was still truly beautiful to watch), she was never able to realise her full potential as a dancer. Elaine was a girl absolutely dedicated to her art, but unable finally to cope with the politics of the ballet world which, behind the scenes, was a seething cauldron of jealousy and intrigue.

Throughout the period of *Waltz* I was continuing my training as a flamenco dancer under the rigorous tutelage of Cora Martell. Finally, after fifteen months' hard slog, we formed a group, 'Trader Faulkner's

Quadro Flamenco', and decided to audition for Clement Freud at the then Royal Court Theatre Club (above the Royal Court Theatre) in Sloane Square. I feel compelled to mention here that it is to Clement Freud — who went on to have a highly successful career, including appearing on various very popular BBC programmes, a spell as a Liberal MP and a knighthood — that I owe my initial success with flamenco. If he hadn't employed me at his nightclub, so much of the subsequent creative work I was to do on Spain and its culture might never have happened.

I well remember auditioning the show in the empty nightclub above the Royal Court theatre with my ensemble: the thundering South African redhead Cora Martell (who could dance any flamenco *bailadora* clean off any stage in terms of power and sheer presence); a superb Spanish guitarist called Paco Juanas; a second guitarist, Ricky Lawrence; and a singer from Gibraltar known as Paco Victory. Señor Victory had the highest pitched voice I've ever heard in a male — very like Yma Sumac. *Mista Frrrood*, as the Spaniards could only ever manage to pronounce his name, gave us the nod to begin. We took our places on the small stage, to the accompaniment of Freud's secretary's tapping typewriter while she took his whispered dictation at his side. Then the typing stopped and we began. We gave him seven minutes of ear-splitting music, song, and dance, which must have been heard in the Peter Jones department store on the other side of Sloane Square.

'Thank you,' said Freud when we'd finished. 'Very impressive. I can offer you three weeks.'

For our opening night, I invited all the influential people I could muster. Most of them came, and the press with them. The first night was packed with supportive friends: Olivier, Vivien Leigh, Marguerite Steen (the author of *The Sun Is My Undoing* and a great Hispanophile), the critic Ken Tynan, John Gielgud, John Mills, and Anthony Kimmins. That was where the rot began.

'Trader no longer acts — he's become a flamenco dancer,' was the resultant rumour.

In 1957, that was considered a very unwise career move, despite the fact that I was still in a highly successful West End play.

Our flamenco career started to take off; we were invited to dance on television in a new programme for Granada TV, *Chelsea at 9*. Then came a phone call from the director Don Chaffey.

'Could you dance an orgasm in the film *Question of Adultery*?'

The film was to star Anthony Steel and the American torch singer Julie London. If the sequence worked, there would be quick cross-cutting between Anthony and Julie — showing the passion between the two of them building, while I matched them with a frenzied *zapateádo* that steadily grew in intensity and pace.

On filming day, when my guitarist (Paco Juanas) and I finally finished, there was a thunderous burst of applause from technicians and everyone watching on the set. I shall never forget the producer Raymond Stross's words.

'Trader, if you make love like that on your wedding night your marriage will last a lifetime!'

By now, work was pouring in for me as an actor, but the strain had begun to tell. I was cast in a play by Sacha Guitry, *Don't Listen, Ladies*, translated from the French for Granada Television. I had a leading role opposite the talented comedian Colin Gordon. The director was James Ormerod. It was a wonderfully light comic piece. I played an arachnologist called Blondinet, a rather effete character who knew everything there was to know about the copulating activities of lethal spiders. In the play I had a gargantuan speech of about two pages in which I had to explain to Colin exactly how the spider copulated — what she did, and her effect on her male partner. Guitry's French humour at its best was incomparable.

In rehearsals I was finding this speech impossible to memorise and was becoming neurotic about it. What's more, this hour-and-a-half-long play was going out live, with no chance of retakes. The day we were to go on air I felt absolutely terrified, with a sense of awful foreboding.

'Stand by everyone! We're on air in fifty seconds,' said the studio manager. Then he must have taken leave of his senses, for he added: 'Make it good, cast. Remember, there're hundreds of thousands of viewers watching you.'

He couldn't have said anything more guaranteed to mentally freeze the lot of us. A ninety-minute nightmare lay ahead.

All went smoothly to begin with. Then came the moment of truth: the long speech about the sex life of the female spider. James Ormerod put his number one camera practically up my nostril and Colin Gordon, off camera, asked me:

'So tell me, Blondinet, what exactly does this lady spider do during the act of copulation?'

I started to speak ... and immediately suffered a total mental blackout. The eye of number one camera glared at me like a raging Cyclops. Countless thousands of TV viewers waited for my answer.

'Speak, you dickhead!' I told myself. 'Say something ... anything — but speak!'

I could no longer see Colin Gordon. My eyes were full of salty sweat.

'Monsieur,' I said. 'What that spider does is so revolting that I cannot bring myself to speak of it.'

'But,' spluttered Colin, 'you must! Come on, man! For God's sake, you must!'

'Monsieur,' I smoothly replied, 'if I possibly could, believe me I would!'

Please, I thought, take the bloody camera off me. Move on to the next scene! But the red light on the camera indicated it was still on, gleaming in malicious defiance at my desperation.

'As I said, monsieur, I cannot speak of it. What that spider does is so repulsive ... '

Then the red light was off, the camera glided on to another set and the show moved smoothly on.

I played the rest of my scenes with no problems. When it was over, my first thought was: 'How do I face James Ormerod and the cast, having let everyone down and made a public fool of myself?'

The outcome was that everyone had assumed it was all part of the script.

'How did you manage to sweat like that on camera?' asked friends who had seen the show. 'It really didn't seem like acting!'

I learnt an extremely valuable lesson from that experience: if you dry, make it up and keep going. Your pro colleagues will always come in to save the sinking Titanic.

★   ★   ★

By 1958, the Olivier-Leigh marriage was well and truly on the skids. Larry had moved out, and Viv was not only depressed but desperate. To me it was patently clear how unsuited they were in the first place.

Vivien and my mother had instant rapport from the moment they met, and would often see one another without me being present. For instance, I remember coming home to the *Stella Maris* one afternoon to find a crowd of newspaper reporters outside the front door — Vivien was inside, having called round for a quick visit.

One day in 1958 my mother received a phone call from Vivien. We were invited to spend the weekend at Notley. Vivien would send a car to drive us there and back. It was the first time I'd been to Notley since my awkward morning departure three years before.

After a magnificent Sunday roast we retired for coffee to the library. I remember our fellow guests were Vivien's mother, Gertrude Hartley, and an elderly actress of whom Vivien was very fond, Ena Burrel. We had just been served when in walked Larry, who had driven up from London to collect some belongings for his new apartment.

'I shan't disturb you,' he purred, at his most charming. Then, 'Puss, can I see you for a moment?'

Vivien followed him into the hall. When she returned she seemed very upset, but with her consummate skill soon got the conversation up and running again.

Then came the moment that would spell disaster.

'Darling Sheila,' said Vivien suddenly. 'I've never asked you before but would you read my stars?'

Mum froze. I remembered back to that episode in my youth when she had tried to read the girl, Anna Philomena Morgan, who was subsequently found murdered.

'No, Vivien,' she told her. 'I've told you. I've put all that well behind me.'

'Please, Sheila,' our hostess continued, ignoring mother's reluctance. 'Haven't you enjoyed your weekend here?'

Vivien was relentless. But Sheila wouldn't budge, and was on the edge of losing her temper.

'Vivien, please drop it. I assure you, no good would come of it.'

It was useless. Vivien was determined. Finally she came up with a compromise.

'Suppose I give you three different birthdates but no names? Then you wouldn't know who the figures identify.'

Reluctantly Mum agreed, and Vivien then gave her three birthdates (the third was probably her mother's, I don't remember). The first, 5th November 1913, was Vivien's. The second, 22nd May 1907, was Larry's. Of course, mother had no idea whose the dates were.

She began, writing down Vivien's. There was a long pause as she became totally detached, almost in a kind of trance state.

'This is a woman ... ' she said at length. 'Very beautiful. She marries young ... has a child. She's not strong physically ... very troubled in her mind. Then she begins a very successful career, remarries ... becomes pregnant, and then...miscarries. The marriage is very successful at first ... then the ... illness ... grows worse. Her career aggravates the illness. She and her husband work together...then the marriage starts to falter ... then ... I'm sorry, this is too stressful. I can't do any more!'

She looked up, her face drained.

'I'm sorry, Vivien,' she said again. 'It takes too much out of me. I really can't do any more. I hope it was useful, I have no idea what I've said.'

Vivien seemed almost supercharged with energy.

'Sheila, darling, please! You must go on! Now do 22nd May 1907 ... '

'No — I'm exhausted,' my mother pleaded. 'Why for heaven's sake do you want to delve into this? Please leave it, Vivien!'

But Vivien would not relent. Finally, to keep the peace, Mother started on 22nd May 1907 — fleshing out Larry's character very accurately in her rambled descriptions, including his three marriages. But when Vivien asked about the second marriage, my mother simply flared up, and our stay at Notley unfortunately ended on a very sour note.

Nevertheless, my mother and Vivien remained good friends, and I remember Mum later telling me how moving she found Vivien's memorial service, at which John Gielgud had spoken so poignantly of his old friend.

CHAPTER SEVENTEEN

THE FIRST TRIP TO SPAIN

WITH *Don't Listen, Ladies* safely behind me, and the almost two-year sentence playing in *The Waltz of the Toreadors* at the Criterion now at an end, I felt it was time to leave London for some fresh air abroad.

Sometime in this period I had a call from Peter Hall.

'I'm considering doing a play called *Bullfight*, by Leslie Stevens. You'd be absolutely right for the lead — a young matador.'

Having nothing better to do, I decided to go to Spain to research the role, while at the same time learning to dance flamenco with some semblance of true Hispanic style.

My plan was to go direct to Seville to take lessons from a gypsy legend called *El Cojo* (the Lame One).

The journey there by train was long and eventful. I travelled third class, which involved sitting in a dog box for eight hours on a cracked wooden seat that pinched your bum every time the train rocked, which it did incessantly. The window ledges sported boxes that before the Spanish Civil War probably housed geraniums. Now, twenty-two years later, they were planted with what looked like blackened pipe cleaners.

The journey to Seville was my initiation into post Civil War conditions for the underprivileged masses. The carriage had no glass in the windows so the smoke from the ancient locomotive billowed straight into the dog box. The train stopped at every station. At Guadalajara, a peasant woman in an advanced stage of pregnancy clambered aboard with two goats and a sack containing two screeching fowls. After several hours the woman produced a long sausage, *una salchicha*. Pieces of this were broken off and eaten with chunks of bread. A slice was thrust at me. I took it and managed to swallow it all down. Several hours later, somewhere near Linares, my abdominal machinery went into open revolt. To add to my discomfort, the peasant woman started wailing with the breaking of her waters. At Cordoba what seemed like months later, the woman was taken from the carriage to what looked like an ambulance from the First World War. As she was being moved, I desperately rushed to find *el retrete* to be free of my sausage, but the shriek of the locomotive whistle found me racing in agony to reboard the now rapidly passing dog box.

I remember little of the last agonising hour from Cordoba to Seville. When we at last arrived I leapt from the carriage and raced wildly through the milling mass of people to find the lavatories. I saw a long queue. The ticket office? No, it was apparently a toilet. Unfortunately, it seemed the entire train had lined up to relieve themselves.

I joined the queue, the sausage doing pirouettes in my gut. Finally, arriving at the front, I found a woman who charged me one peseta. I paid her and she moved away from the door. I entered and set about my desperate business. When I had finished, I reached for the paper. There was none.

'Por favour,' I yelled, 'no hay papel.'

'Si señor,' she replied. 'Cuesta una peseta.'

I withdrew a peseta from my pocket and passed it round the door. To my horror I was handed a piece of cardboard. Having disposed of that, I found I needed more.

'Otra papel, por favor,' I moaned.

'Si señor. Cinco pesetas.'

I left that horrendous place having finally been relieved of fifteen pesetas — in those days, a small fortune. Spain in those early years after the Civil War was primitive beyond belief to someone coming from London.

In Seville I took lodgings with an elderly spinster who directed me to the dance studio of the legendary maestro, *El Cojo*. I found this character in one of Seville's back streets. He was an elderly gay man in a wheelchair (he had been crippled by polio in his youth). For twenty pesetas a lesson, I was taught effeminate Spanish arm movements and no footwork (obviously you were never meant to move).

In London I had been given an introduction to a well-to-do Seville widow who invited me to lunch. We sat together at a long table; she obviously had a large family, who I imagined were working or living elsewhere. After lunch, we had coffee in the sitting room. There were several pictures of her family. I asked her about these characters.

'My husband and sons,' she said. 'Yes, they are all dead. They fought on opposing sides in the war and all were killed.'

Seville still bore traces of the Civil War. But there was all the same a superficial gaiety everywhere that masked the terrible memories of what had taken place, and soothed the animosities that were still prevalent just beneath the surface.

My stay in Seville coincided with the famous *Féria*, the Easter Fair, where what seemed like the entire population of the city spread itself over a large fairground in different *casetas* (tented booths) drinking sherry, munching tapas, and dancing their national dance, *Sevillanas*.

At the *Féria* I ended up dancing in one of the booths with one of the most beautiful girls I have ever seen. I had wandered in and was handed a glass of sherry and asked if I could dance *Sevillanas*. Luckily, it was a dance I had worked on at the beginning of my flamenco studies with Elsa Brunelleschi. As the girl pulled me into the middle of the room there was general laughter; it was obvious I was going to make a fool of myself. We started and the girl so mesmerised me that I simply followed her and she carried me along. I remember little now of that afternoon except that the onlookers stared with disbelief as they watched me following her with my halting but accurate steps.

After my sessions with *El Cojo* had finished, I left Seville and went to Granada to observe the bullfighting world for the projected Peter Hall production. Once there, I was befriended by Paco Velez, habitué of Spanish café society, called a *tertulia*. He introduced me to his tertulian amigos, all stalwarts of the Granadine establishment.

Paco told them I'd come to Spain to be a *torero*. I thought he was having them on, and they seemed to believe him. But as they offered to put me in touch with a famous ex-matador, Rafael Fandila, I didn't disabuse them. Rafael had been badly gored, and was now giving lessons to aspiring *toreros*. Each morning this pitifully crippled man would charge at me with a bicycle front wheel yoked to a pole, the bicycle handlebars surmounted by a bull's head made of basketwork.

I became totally caught up in this. No longer interested in merely researching my role in *Bullfight*, I was now determined to try my hand as a matador. What the *tertulia* thought I was there for, I now decided I was there for.

Rafael showed me how to do some of the different passes with the *muleta* — that red cloth used to enrage the bull — including the most dangerous, the *veronica de rodillas*. In this dangerous move, in order to cape the bull as he charges, you swivel in a pirouette on both knees; then as he turns and charges back, your cape has to wipe his sweating snout — just as Veronica wiped the face of Christ.

After six weeks of this the *tertulia*, led by Paco, came along to see my progress. Their response was friendly mockery — they sent me up rotten, claiming I would cut a dash as a cabaret *torero*, leaping about in a sequined bullfighter's suit in some nightclub. Off they went into a huddle, which gave me time to nip off to get the box of Havana cigars I had bought as a gift for Rafael when he'd refused any payment. But when I presented them he wouldn't take them. I was non-plussed. Was there anything I could offer that would please him?

Paco took me aside.

'Rafael ees very offended.'

'Why? What have I done?'

'Th'only thanks he would rilly appreciate ees for you to show heem that he hasn' wasted hees time wit you.'

'Look,' I told him, 'I'll do anything he wants.'

'You min that?'

'Of course.'

'A man of hees word?' Paco solemnly put out his hand.

'Absolutely.' I shook it.

'What Rafael wants ees to see you in the ring confronting a live bull. He belivs you are riddi.'

God almighty! But to a Spaniard like Paco my word was sacrosanct.

For the next week I could think of nothing but fighting that live bull in some godforsaken village bullring on the outskirts of town.

The dreaded morning arrived. Dolores, the plum-ripe maid at my pension, brought me olives, sherry, and sausage called chorizo.

'Macho hombre, tienes que comer.' ('A macho lad like you must eat.')

Down went the olives with a gollop of sherry. Five minutes later up they came.

A knock at the door. The tailor with my made-to-measure bullfighter's suit. Behind him were three gorgeous Granadine girls who quickly began the ritual of dressing me, the *novillero*, in the traditional clothes: grey striped trousers, white frilled shirt, short tight-fitting grey jacket, champagne-coloured suede boots, and a wide dove-grey sombrero *Cordobés*. One of the girls spun me into an emerald-green cummerbund and fastened it tightly.

A 1930s Packard was waiting outside the pension where a small crowd had gathered (the word had got around). From under the lid of the boot protruded the handles of several swords, the weapons with which I was expected to despatch the bull. Someone handed me a bunch of red carnations — a symbol of Spanish machismo. Amid shouts of 'Olé torero! Coraje! Vaya con Dios.' I was driven off.

Paco met me at the bullring and took me into the bullring patio. Along one of its white walls were several red doors. I opened the first — a lavatory. The next room contained an operating table and a tray laid out with surgical instruments. Against the back wall, discreetly covered by a black cloth, I could see the outline of a coffin. In front of it, smiling pleasantly, was a white-coated surgeon.

'Hola, hombre. Ten suerte!' ('Hello, man. Be lucky!')

I opened the third door and saw a little chapel. Above the altar a painting of the Virgin, La Macarena, Our Lady of All Brave Toreros, gazed down at me compassionately. I mouthed a Hail Mary. Despite the heat of the day I was shivering.

'Are you riddi, Trahdare?' called Paco.

My *cuadrilla* (assistants), Manolo and Xavier, lined up on either side of me.

A band struck up a paso doble. We moved across the shadows of the patio, through an archway, and out into the blazing sunlight of the arena. The place was packed. Coloured shawls were draped along the *barrera* separating the ring from the spectators. Behind them, I caught a glimpse of the three Granadine beauties who had dressed me.

Rafael had said I was to go to the centre of the ring, look up to the President's box, raise my sombrero in salute and call 'Permiso?' ('Permission to fight?') I still remember my terror as I went through that ritual in a trance.

From the President's box the keys of the *toril*, where the bull waited penned up, were thrown down to me. I managed to catch them and threw them to one of my *cuadrilla*, who walked across the ring to the toril gate and unlocked it.

The trumpet blasted for the bull to come out. Nothing happened. Only a rattling noise as the gate started to lift. Then stuck. Then dropped.

By now I could hear the minotaur snorting, ready for the kill, viciously kicking his pen.

The trumpet blasted a second time. This time up clanked the gate like a guillotine right to the top. Nauseated, I closed my eyes, just conscious of the soft thud of hooves coming across the sand. Closer and closer they came. Then suddenly stopped.

I opened my eyes. There in front of me was a tiny bull-calf. Two large oranges were fixed on his nubby hornlets. He nuzzled my belly with his wet snout, blinked in the sun, and lay down at my feet. For the first time in the annals of bullfighting, Toro and Torero were evenly matched.

Spanish practical jokes can be very elaborate!

Sadly, all of my bullfighting training turned out to be a wasted effort as the production of *Bullfight* never happened. Peter Hall, at the point in his career when wonderful opportunities were being presented one after another, was simply too snowed under by his success to find

John Faulkner,
'Jack the Rattler', 1921

Sheila Whytock Faulkner

Ceramic Flats, Manly, 1941–42

The Orchard

Trade and Ganfi Whytock, 1935

Grannie Whytock, 1940

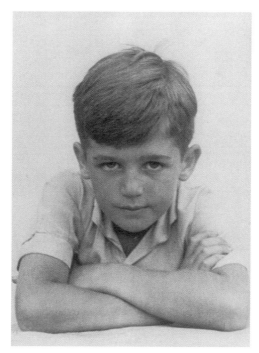

Trade, 'The Young Rebel', 1935

Trade, November, 1945
One year after the shark encounter

Lofty Sharp, 1944

Ah, Wilderness!,
with Elaine Montgomery

Back somersault on Queenscliff
Beach, taken by Peter Finch, 1947

Queenscliff Beach, 1950

The Lady's Not for Burning,
Richard Son of Nobody, 1950–51

Mr Denning Drives North,
with John Mills, 1951

A Killer Walks,
with Laurence Harvey and Susan Shaw, 1951

Dorothy Tutin, 1952–53

The Corn is Green,
with Billie Whitelaw, 1954

The Amazing Dr Clitterhouse,
with Ronnie Barker, 1954

1953-1969.   HOUSE BOAT   "Stella Maris"- at Chelsea Embankment.   Home for 16 years

Stella Maris

Vivien Leigh and Peter Finch, with Abraham Sofaer,
in *Elephant Walk*, 1954

Twelfth Night, as Sebastian, with
Vivien Leigh as Viola, Stratford,
1955

Trade and the Oliviers, 1955

Cast of *Our House* TV series, 1960–61

Promenade, with Tom Bell and Susannah York, 1959

Queen After Death
with Diane Cilento, 1961

Queen After Death
with Leo McKern

Antonio Gades in the 1960s

Happy times with Bobo,
December 1962

A High Wind in Jamaica,
with Quinn and Coburn, 1964

Bobo, 1967

Sheila Faulkner, 1968

'Foggles' (Patti Edwards), 1969

The Price, as Soloman

Los Rondeños, 1972

Chatting with Christine Keeler, 1973

Hattie ('Tumplemouse'), 1974

Spanish Order of Merit

Lorca, with Tito, 1986

Lorca, with Carmela Romero, 1994

Lorca

Trader and Kathryn, 2003

Trade

Jim and Sasha, and the grandchildren, 2010

time to put together a production of this modest play, and so far as I know it was never mounted.

A final word on bullfighting.

In 2008 an invitation came to stay with friends in Arles. I accepted, and during my stay we lunched at the Hotel Nord Pinus, a favourite haunt of Picasso, Cocteau, and many matador legends. That afternoon it was agreed that we would attend a bullfight in the famous Roman coliseum. 'Dead on five,' to quote García Lorca, I took my seat on the stone ledge of the vast Arles amphitheatre (very relieved this time not to be down in the ring), where in Caesar's time thousands had cheered on embattled gladiators. As I watched, a gargantuan bull unseated the *rejóneador* of the day, Pablo Mendoza, who — mounted on horseback — was engaging his adversary using a long thin lance. With mighty strength, the bull had flung horse and rider to the ground, but both got up unhurt. Remounting, Pablo received another lance, placed it in the bull's withers, then dismounted again and executed a series of masterful passes with the *muleta*.

When it came, the kill with the sword was clean and quick. I'd seen the best.

I never want to see another.

My next destination during that first visit to Spain was Madrid, where I took lodgings at 11 Abada Street.

Before I'd left London, my friend Tom Burns and his wife Mabél, who ran the Catholic bookshop Burns & Oates at Westminster, had invited me to lunch at their home in Toledo. Soon after my arrival in Madrid I took a train to Toledo, and remember standing in their garden and looking across the gorge towards the ancient city. I turned to my host.

'This spot must be very near the place where El Greco painted *Toledo in a Storm*.'

'It's thought to have actually been on this spot,' he said.

Tom's wife is the daughter of a famous Spanish medic, Don Gregorio Marañon. A Republican sympathiser at the time of the outbreak of the Spanish Civil War in 1936, he had to take his family to Paris to ensure their safety.

It was at lunch with Tom and Mabél that day that I met John Pilcher and his wife Delia. John was the number two at the British Embassy in Madrid, under Sir Jock Balfour. A brilliant scholar in Japanese, he was subsequently knighted and ended up as British Ambassador to Tokyo.

I vividly remember them driving me back to their Madrid apartment, where John immediately got on the telephone to line up all the contacts he could for me in Madrid's flamenco world.

'You must meet our daughter Julia,' Delia told me. 'She's just turned fifteen. Unfortunately she's staying with friends in the south just now, but when she returns she will escort you to see you aren't fleeced when you go for your flamenco lessons!'

Thus began a friendship with John and Delia, and with Julia (and Seymour Fortescue, whom she later married), that has lasted to this day. Indeed, Julia became godmother to my daughter Sasha, but all that was still a long way off.

When Julia returned from Andalucia, this very sophisticated youngster with plaits escorted me from the embassy in a chauffeur-driven Rolls to the studio of Antonio Marín, reputed to be the greatest flamenco teacher in Madrid at that time. In Plaza Vara del Rey, in the flea market district of Old Madrid, we descended a flight of stone steps to a basement that smelled of old socks and entered a small, cell-like room to find a one-legged man sitting majestically in a chair. I began my introduction. He cut me short.

'Show me what you can do.'

I danced a sequence of *zapateádo*.

'That's quite good, but you need to be lighter and faster.'

I thought, 'How is he going to demonstrate on one leg?'

'Mari Nievis!' he called, and a girl of about fourteen appeared in soft, ill-fitting shoes.

He spoke to her in Spanish, indicating the steps he wanted her to demonstrate. I was to watch and then repeat her steps. She flitted across the floor, dancing with amazing lightness, but with an absolute precision — and so began an extraordinary experience for me. Mari was totally helpful; when I needed her to repeat a sequence slowly, she did so. Then Marín would show me the arm movements to syncopate with the footwork. These arm movements were the very essence of the true Spanish style I was seeking. It was a unique series of lessons, which gave me a foundation in style that I badly needed.

In the years immediately following the Civil War, Marín, then in his twenties, had danced with a nail in the heel of his boot that pierced his skin. His foot became infected, but Spanish medical care at that time was primitive to say the least, and penicillin hadn't yet arrived as a treatment. In short his foot became septic, gangrene had set in, and finally they'd been forced to amputate his leg.

I shall always remember our last day, this sad fellow giving me a firm handshake of farewell and the little girl standing beside him as I said goodbye.

During the run of *The Waltz of the Toreadors* Pilar Lopez and her Spanish dance company were playing at the Palace Theatre in London. Unfortunately, I couldn't see the show because our matinees coincided. However, I went along to the stage door and left a letter for Pilar stating that if she had a male dancer in her company willing to teach me flamenco I would like to learn. Several days later I received a reply with a time to go to the theatre to meet her young flamenco soloist, who might consider giving me lessons. The twenty-two-year-old I met was Antonio Gades, who would succeed Antonio (*El Bailarín*) as the greatest of his day, leaving his legacy of flamenco films that included *Blood Wedding*, *Carmen*, and *El Amor Brujo* (all three directed by Carlos Saura). This very serious young man wanted to know why on earth *un Inglés* wanted to learn flamenco. Once he realised that I wanted to *use* flamenco and not to be a flamenco dancer, a *baila'or*, he was willing to take me on. Thus began another close friendship that lasted until he died of cancer in July 2004.

I started my classes with him onstage at the Palace Theatre. He was very strict, critical and terse at times, but what he was giving me was priceless. He refused any payment. In return I was to teach him English.

'To wee o noh to wee, thaes the kweshon.'

His English was more than unbelievable — it was grotesque! For years I'd tease him.

'How's your Hamlet progressing?'

'En Espanish berry goo. En Iglés, murió.'

Lazy bugger! In his dancing he was so disciplined. Why couldn't he apply the same concentration to learning English? Had he been able to speak good English, as a bilingual actor/dancer he would have been an even more unique contributor.

On our last day working at the Palace a small group had assembled at the back of the stage to use it when we finished. I had my back to them. Suddenly, Gades clutched my arm.

'Tradair, look behind you! It's Laurence Olivier.'

He was just about to open there in *The Entertainer*.

'Tradair, he's my idol,' Gades whispered.

'Do you want to meet him?'

He nodded vigorously and I took him over and introduced them. Thank God Larry was at his most charming.

Afterwards, as we left the theatre, Gades said, 'Tradair! Dios Mio! You actually *know* him!'

I had to laugh, knowing how low God rated in this idealistic young communist's estimation.

Gades had been so kind to me that my mother suggested he be invited to lunch on the *Stella Maris*. Fine, he said. Could he bring his girlfriend, who was his partner in the company? But her mother would have to come too, as chaperone. (This, remember, was 1957 and Spain was both heavily Catholic and thoroughly Francoist.) They came, none speaking a word of English. My mother had a smattering of Spanish and I knew a little more. The girlfriend, I remember, never stopped smiling. Then as the afternoon tide came in, *Stella Maris* rose from her muddy bed and started to rock. The chaperone indicated that she was about to be sick and the trio hurriedly departed.

Antonio later told me that the *novia* had broken his heart by jilting him for another famous flamenco dancer of that time, José Greco. But Antonio's broken heart mended in about a week, as he was always irresistible to his *aficionadas*.

A Spaniard with an impeccable sense of decorum, he had said to me over lunch:

'When you come to Madrid you must dine with my family. My father was an officer in the army of the Republic.'

Consequently, when I was finally staying in Madrid I looked forward to meeting this elderly plumpish Republican ex-army officer with a rabid hatred of Franco, under whom he and his family had suffered so much. They weren't on the phone, so I wrote to Antonio; he rang me, and a date was made. I was to catch the train to Pacifico (on the outskirts of Madrid), cross the road and I'd be in front of his building. I followed his instructions, but 154 turned out to be a gutted, bombed-out relic from the war. I saw chalked up on a door leading to the basement *portero*. 'How odd,' I thought, 'a porter in a virtually uninhabited building.'

I rang the bell and presently a wild-looking character with an eye patch thrust his head through a window.

'Si?'

'I'm looking for Señor Gades.'

'That's me. Soy Gades padre.'

'Ah. I'm your son's friend, Trader.'

The fellow gave me an explosive greeting.

'Tradair!'

He disappeared from the window, then soon reappeared beside me and clutched me to him in a vice-like hug.

'Welcome, Antonio's friend, welcome!'

I was led down a flight of stone stairs to a basement where in one room lived all the Gades family: mother, father, and a younger brother, Enrique. Antonio himself was away. Their home, as I remember, was impeccably clean, with a large double bed beautifully made up, and a round table with several chairs and a *brasero* beneath it to warm the family's feet in winter. I was given a sumptuous lunch: Spanish ham and eggs, bread and wine. I felt strange as I was the only one eating, but was told they had already eaten. I realised later that I had probably been given their rations. That lunch, and the hospitality the family showed me, left me with an enormous sense of respect for these people who shouldered their poverty with dignity and managed somehow to rise above it. It also showed me how the left wing losing side in the war was clearly still being punished and discriminated against by Franco's government long after the hostilities were over.

Still, there were benefits from Franco's rule. It is certainly true that during his tenure I always felt perfectly safe in the darkest lane or on the loneliest beach because nearby there was always a Civil Guard on patrol.

This was not the case, unfortunately, after Franco's death. Years after I had visited them, during the time of the liberal post-Franco regime, Antonio Gades's younger brother Enrique saved up and bought himself a very expensive leather coat. One evening he went out to celebrate in Madrid's Puerta del Sol area (the equivalent to London's Piccadilly Circus). There he was set on and stabbed to death for the coat, which he'd refused to part with. The Antonio I met again shortly afterwards in Madrid was even more taciturn than usual. I don't think he ever got over his brother's tragic death.

Years later, in 2004, I went to see Gades's company perform in London and as he hadn't led them onstage himself I left a message with the company manager. Later I'd heard that he had been to see his friend and fellow communist, Castro, in Cuba.

Six months after that my phone rang.

'Tradair? Gades. Thank you for your message. You're a good friend. Adios.'

He was certainly the most laconic friend I've ever had.

A few days after his call he was dead.

CHAPTER EIGHTEEN

ANTONIO 'EL BAILARÍN' AND TELEVISION SUCCESS

A FEW DAYS before I left Madrid, at a British Council lunch party thrown for Anthony Steel (who was filming there), he came over to me.

'I hear the Aussie flamenco dancer is making great progress,' he said. 'Look, I want you to meet a friend I've been working with. Come with me. It's your chance of a lifetime.'

He said no more but drove me across Madrid to a palatial building, led me inside, left me at the door, and disappeared down a hallway. Then he returned and took me into a large room of baroque splendour. At one side on a sofa, dressed from head to foot in scarlet, lounged a familiar-looking young man delicately fingering a long black cigarette holder.

I stared.

'You're Antonio! It was you I saw dancing like a god in London.'

'Yeth, darlinc. When I danth badly I danth better than anywan in the worl', and when I danth well, I danth like Jesuth Christ! I hear you, too, danth the flamehnco. Well, the actor who danth the flamehnco ith now going to danth for me.'

I protested that I was wearing a double-breasted suit and flat shoes — hardly suitable dancing attire. He merely shrugged. I pleaded that without a guitarist I hadn't Buckley's chance of putting on any kind of a show. Moraito Chico, a famous gypsy guitarist, suddenly materialised as if by magic.

There was nothing to be done. I struggled through my *farruca*.

173

When I finished there was silence. Then Spain's dancing idol covered his face with his hands and peeped at me through his fingers. All I could see was one gleaming eye.

'Darlinc! You danth like a horth!'

Humiliated, I made for the door. He said nothing until I opened it.

'But not a cart horth, darlinc. Come back. All ith forgiven.'

I returned to London. Six months went by. Antonio was in London for another dazzling season, this time at the Coliseum. I went round to the stage door to see him. There was a vast crowd of celebrities waiting to pay homage. I decided to see him later in the week. I went home and to bed. The phone rang.

'Darling Trader, it's Vivien. Come round to 54 Eaton Square at once. I'm giving a late supper party with lots of friends you know. Get a taxi.'

You didn't argue with Vivien Leigh.

There were lots of familiar faces: Gielgud, Paul and Joy Scofield, and Michael Redgrave and his wife Rachel Kempson (whom I'd met at Stratford through Vivien). Then suddenly a loud voice boomed from across the room.

'Tradair! You didn't come round to see me tonight!'

'Antonio! I got as far as the stage door, but the crowd of your admiring public made me decide to see you at a later date.'

He made time to talk to me and invited me to a party to be given the following weekend by a very hospitable Jewish friend, Moussia Soskin.

Antonio had brought his company with him to Vivien's flat that evening to dance, sing, and play their guitars for the guests. That was an unforgettable evening for everyone present. While we consumed copious glasses of wine Antonio taught us all a basic flamenco handclapping rhythm. We then clapped while he taught Vivien a few steps as the guitars played and the night rolled on.

The following Saturday after Antonio's performance I went with him to the Soskins' dinner party. After dinner there were party games.

'I *love* games,' said Antonio, 'if *I* can choose the game.'

Everybody was told to sit around wherever they could find a space.

'Now Tradair is going to danth *farruca* for os.'

As before, I was wearing a double breasted suit and flat shoes. But since my return to London I had really sweated on that dance to give it some semblance of style.

Moraito Chico started to play. By the end of my dance I knew I hadn't done too badly.

'Do you have a *traje de baile*?' asked Antonio.

A *traje de baile* is the tight, narrow-waisted, chest-high trousers, frilled shirt, short jacket and boots worn at that time by the *baila'or* — the male flamenco dancer.

'Yes.'

'Good. Then I invite you to danth your solo with my company on our latht night at the Colitheum.'

Was he throwing me to the lions for his own amusement? Did it matter?

'All right,' I said. 'I'll have a go.'

That last night I was to come on at the very end, so I had the whole evening to get the shakes. I'd be going on cold with no rehearsal in front of nearly three thousand people.

Mesmerised, I watched the finale from the wings. The entire company was involved in a steadily gathering crescendo of sound and movement. Suddenly, Antonio held up his hand and stopped the show. The audience waited, pin-still.

'Ladieth and gentlemen, tonigh' I harve wetting in thee weengs a green man. Green he ith with terror, green like you would be if I athk any one of you to come up here an danth weeth os. Thees poor man ith so frighten that two peoples is holding him op. Because he eesn't reeli a danther of flamenco. Hees an English actorr. But he loves thee danth, and he feels thee danth like I do. And so he weel danth *farruca*.'

I walked onto the stage. Spain's top guitarists, dancers, and singers were all lined up behind me, all hoping to God I wouldn't let them down, whispering:

'Que te coge El Duende! Hombre, suerte!' ('Feel the spirit, man. Good luck!')

Moraito Chico came up close.

'Tradair, don' worr'. We'll follow you with the music whatever you do.'

The company began to clap out the rhythm ... the *palmas*. The guitars started to play. And away I went.

Minutes later we were all — the entire company — bowing to the audience. The house was on its feet. Onto the stage flew red carnations, shoes, combs — even a suspender belt (which Antonio caught, kissed, clutched to his heart, rolled up, and threw back).

Finally the company exploded into a gypsy *bulerías* with me joining in. As it finished Antonio — a featherweight — leapt onto me piggyback and we all swept off into the wings.

As we passed offstage he whispered in my ear.

'Well, darlinc, like I thed before, you danth like a horth. But tonigh' you were a *rathe* horth.'

During the period from my return from Spain in 1958 until early in 1962, I was working regularly and being given wonderful opportunities. I remember this period as a frantic maelstrom of creative activity — all more or less successful.

Some time in 1958 I was cast in E.M. Forster's *A Room With A View*, playing the repressed Cecil Vyse. Never before or since have I felt so miscast. One critic wrote: 'Trader Faulkner looked so right as Cecil Vyse, and sounded so utterly wrong.'

All I remember feeling is that I should never have attempted this part because I had absolutely no affinity with the character. I should have remembered Gielgud's words to me: 'There are characters I simply couldn't begin to play, and Henry V is one of them, for *obvious* reasons.'

Three inspiring directors for whom I had the luck to work were Julian Aymes, Donald McWhinnie, and Joan Kemp Welch.

Early in 1959, Julian Aymes was looking for an actor to play Max in a television adaptation of Elizabeth Bowen's novel *The House in Paris* and apparently could think of no one ideal for the role. His wife had seen me the year before in *Don't Listen, Ladies* on Granada TV and — having liked my work — was convinced that I had exactly the qualities required for this new role.

I went to see Julian, who handed me the script. I read for him and he cast me. To his surprise and mine, when the show was broadcast I seemed to have turned in a good performance. Not long afterwards I received a telephone call from Julian saying that Elizabeth Bowen, on seeing the show, had said: 'Trader Faulkner played Max exactly as I'd pictured him when I wrote the novel back in 1935. I'd like to meet him.'

Julian arranged a meeting, and her appreciation of how I had interpreted her character gave me enormous confidence.

Shortly after that, Peter Nichols' play *Promenade*, made again for Granada TV, gave me an opportunity to play a crazy extrovert Jew who sported a baseball cap, outrageous women's sunglasses several sizes too large, a beard, and a pistol — which I pointed at every passer-by. I was part of a youthful trio along with Tom Bell and Susannah York, whooping it up in a sports car along the promenade at Brighton. This again was Julian Aymes, casting me this time as a character as different from Max in *The House in Paris* as Romeo is from Bottom.

In March 1960 I was playing farce again, in *Off a Duck's Back* by Robert Kemp, with Phyllis Neilson-Terry, Sophie Stewart, and Ellis Irving at the Lyceum Theatre, Edinburgh. That was at night. By day I was rehearsing a murder thriller, *The House of Lies*, for Associated Rediffusion. This meant that I would fly from London to Edinburgh at 4.30pm after rehearsal for the television play, do the stage show, and then fly back to London for the following morning's rehearsals at the television rehearsal rooms. People now probably do much more ambitious high-wire scheduling, but this was back in the early days when such a precarious shuttle offered huge challenges in terms of being 'dead on time'.

The House of Lies told the true story of Madeleine Hamilton Smith, who poisoned her young lover Emile L'Angelier (the character I played) by administering strong doses of arsenic in his coffee. He died in agony in his rooms at No. 11 Franklin Place, Glasgow, on the night of 23rd March 1857, after several cups of Madeleine's coffee. Apparently, Madeleine's papa had arranged a very advantageous marriage for her, but Emile was passionately in love and not to be easily shaken off. Being utterly ruthless, Madeleine effected her own fatal resolution to the problem.

Madeleine Smith was tried at the High Court in Edinburgh, where her scandalous love letters were read out in court to a shocked assembly. The jury, however, brought in a verdict of 'not proven' and she walked free.

Playing a character who actually once lived required research, but when the play was recorded I managed to 'live the part' to everyone's satisfaction — including mine.

At some point in 1960, I appeared in an American television version of '*Macbeth*' ('Hallmark Hall of Fame') starring Maurice Evans and Judith Anderson. I was cast as Seyton, one of Macbeth's henchmen.

Who could ever forget Judith Anderson as the sinister Mrs Danvers in Alfred Hitchcock's film *Rebecca* with Laurence Olivier and Joan Fontaine?

Judith, who had been made a Dame Commander of the British Empire, was a no-nonsense Aussie born in Adelaide in 1898. She came to dinner once on the *Stella Maris*, and we found we had much in common. She had played Gertrude to John Gielgud's celebrated 1936 Hamlet and told me that she admired Gielgud for his humility, and regarded him as one of the best in our profession.

'You could hear every word he spoke,' she said, 'from every seat in the theatre.'

She also admired Olivier — as a brilliant, dedicated technician — but agreed with me that he lacked the ability to truly move an audience.

'I was lucky to work with both,' she said, 'and so were you. You can learn so much working with such actors, as long as you never try to copy them!'

Judith then got to the nitty-gritty of our profession.

'How you look can be an enormous advantage for you, but it's what you project from within that makes its impact on your audience. In film it's your sincerity that the camera will pick up.'

I felt lucky to have known this kindred spirit, if only very briefly.

★   ★   ★

In February 1961, Leo McKern, Diane Cilento, and Trader Faulkner — three Aussies — were the unlikely stars in Minos Volanakis's production of *Queen After Death* (*La reine morte*) by Henri de Montherlant. We opened at the Oxford Playhouse, then played the Arts Theatre, Cambridge, then Streatham Hill, and were due to go into the West End when Diane received a film offer that she couldn't refuse and we finished at the Golders Green Hippodrome. A pity, as the play was superbly directed and costumed, and was based on an episode from the reign of the sixteenth-century Portuguese King Ferrante. For me the production is memorable for Diane's practical jokes onstage. She was fun to work with but wanted to change the moves every night.

'We must keep the show alive and us on our toes.'

I noticed she didn't apply her philosophy to her scenes with Leo McKern as the King. But I found, as a fellow Aussie, her 'larrikin' tricks both a challenge and good fun. In our love scene I was on a raised stage several inches above her. She — in a beautiful long, flowing white gown — stood below me. We played our love scene with Diane facing the audience, I immediately behind her with my arms resting on her shoulders. I would bend, kiss her on the neck, then she would turn to me and I'd kiss her on the lips — she had the most gorgeous mouth. All went beautifully for several performances. Then one night as I leant down to kiss her neck she sidled slowly forward and I was left teetering on my ledge like a balancing kangaroo. It got a ripple of laughter from the audience. 'Touché,' I thought, 'but I'll bet you won't try that tomorrow night.'

What luck! She did. Away she started to glide, but this time I was ready for her. My fingers were surreptitiously inside the top of her gown and as she moved forward, down it came, revealing the tops of two lovely nipples. She made a hasty retreat, and from then on we had no more unscripted stage moves.

Diane was a fun girl, soon to marry Sean Connery and later Anthony Shaffer. Diane, Leo, and I would occasionally have a drink together and the conversation was usually about Oz. Diane was the daughter of Sir Raphael and Lady Cilento, great Queensland medics. Sadly, I am told, she died only recently.

Leo, awarded the Order of Australia for his services to the performing arts, subsequently became identified as TV's *Rumpole Of The Bailey*. Back in Australia, apparently, working with an adze as a young man, a stone flew up and took out his eye. Whatever the cause it made no difference to his dimension as an actor. Though he was small, he had a monumental stillness onstage and compelled your attention. I found him challenging and mesmeric to work with. He dominated in our very dramatic scene together (I played Don Pedro, his son), and I had to fight him every syllable of the way to keep the balance of de Montherlant's superbly written text. Working with and knowing Leo was a demanding challenge. Unfortunately, we never met again.

The only record I've kept of my work is a notebook registering every payment I've ever received for my professional jobs. Looking at the endless list of radio plays and television features recorded there, I realise now that having the ability to be a chameleon when called on was a great advantage.

The proof of this came in 1961, when I was offered contracts for several jobs that were to spread my face over the nation's TV screens like 'hundreds and thousands' on a birthday cake.

The comedy series *Our House* was made under the guidance of the light entertainment director Ernest Maxin. His fiancée Leigh Madison and I provided the young love interest in a cast otherwise made up of wonderful comedians, including Hattie Jacques, Norman Rossington, Charles Hawtrey, and Joan Sims. Suddenly, I found myself working with, and learning from, many of the absolute masters of English comedy. *Our House* was a popular series for its time and proved a sheer delight to do.

Joan Kemp Welch was a perspicacious director who knew exactly what she wanted. She always respected you if you knew what you were doing, but God help you if you were groping for your part.

She cast me in the television adaptation of Somerset Maugham's short story *The Mother*, with my old friend Beatrix Lehmann in the title role. A young actress, Pip Hinton, and I were cast opposite one another. This play, a torrid romance and family tragedy set in Seville, was memorable for me because of the sultry Spanish dandy I was playing, Kemp Welch's direction, and the challenge of playing opposite Bea in the emotional scenes — which was like fencing with Goliath. Added to all this was the fact that my character had to dance flamenco with Pip in one scene! I also remember an ongoing argument I had with Joan throughout rehearsals about the pronunciation of my character's name. He was called Paco, pronounced by the Spanish as 'Pah-co'. Joan kept referring to him as 'Pay-co', as in sago.

'Joan, its Pah-co!'

She simply looked at me blankly and continued calling me 'Pay-co'.

Joan was a woman who knew her own mind and stuck to her guns, right or wrong.

In late 1961, through my flamenco dancing, I met a young lawyer from Seville, Ricardo Pachón, who was also a talented guitarist. He introduced me to a friend of his, Tatiana Reyna — a fiery, very attractive sixteen-year-old Venezuelan. Together with Tatiana, Ricardo and I formed a flamenco group, *Los Rondeños*, and managed to secure another booking with Clement Freud at the Royal Court Theatre Club. We packed it out for three weeks.

While we were rehearsing, Ricardo was staying with me on the *Stella Maris*. (During this period Mum was away for a time in Seville.) One day Ricardo and I decided to give a party on the *Stella Maris*.

There were about fifteen of us altogether, including Hattie Jacques (all twenty stone of her!) from the *Our House* cast.

The party was a riot, with lots to eat and unlimited booze. According to the account later given me by Ricardo, at some point he had gone below to relieve himself and, as he emerged, found himself face to face with an empassioned Hattie who embraced him feverishly, drawing him into her fulsome body with fierce sexual determination. Minutes later they ended up on my bed.

Upstairs the rest of us continued our revels, drinking and chatting, until suddenly the boat started to pitch markedly from stem to stern. We were so drunk that at first no one seemed to notice — until we heard from below Ricardo's strangled cries.

'Dios mio! Hattie, please!'

Discretion prevents my elaborating on the sexual collision between Tom Thumb and Pantagruel, but for the rest of us, transfixed by the groans and mutterings that rumbled from below, it was hilarious.

Eventually, both lovers ascended to rejoin us looking very exhausted and each demanding a drink. Later Ricardo told me: 'Ayee, Trader, what a woman! Her passion matched her size. I thought I was a man, but with her I felt like a child with its mother, not a man making love to a woman!'

'Ah,' I said in reply. 'And I've always understood that you Spaniards consider the English cold-blooded!'

In 1962 I was interviewed by the Danziger brothers, who were looking for an actor to play nine entirely different characters in their ITV series *Richard the Lionheart*, a historical-fiction romp for the younger generation to be directed by an 'old-stager' called Ernie Morris. It turned out to provide many months of laughter for me, and a continual challenge for my imagination to bring my nine different characters to life.

On filming days I'd arrive at the Elstree studios at 7.30 a.m., where the elderly make-up man would put me in the chair and begin his work. By 9 a.m. I would be transformed into Prince John (who would become King John) or Philippe Auguste (King Philippe II of France), my two principal characters. Or there might be guest appearances by my other regular roles as Ubaldo (a Saracen mercenary), Celestine (an effeminate tailor of Rheims), Marcel (a highwayman), Raphael (a young monk), plus a Cornish pirate, a wise old Jewish rabbi, and finally Vilanus of Rouen (a sorcerer and kidnapper). When the day's make-up was complete, one of these characters would be glaring back at me from the mirror. Given such a wide variety of characters to play, I relied on the writing and always played for comedy.

I never saw the series, now long forgotten, and thought it would probably remain so. How wrong I was. Some months ago, I received a letter from Derek Pykett, who was writing a book on the Danzigers and on the Elstree studios where *Richard the Lionheart* was filmed. To my amazement, through the post one day came a video from Derek containing several episodes from the series, featuring four of the characters I played — a fascinating way to revive forgotten memories!

Throughout the filming there were never any problems with the multiple casting, until an episode arrived when King Richard becomes involved with two very dubious Saracens — my character Ubaldo, and Zara, his younger sister, a princess of Granada. The problem was to find an English girl who could play my Moorish sister. Several hopefuls were unsuccessfully tested and Elstree Studios was becoming worried. Then I suddenly thought of Tatiana Reyna, the sixteen-year-old Venezuelan bombshell with whom I was then dancing flamenco cabaret. Tatiana was brought in and tested, and I was pleased to see that she acted as superbly as she danced. That young natural simply saved the day.

After *Richard the Lionheart*, Terence Williams cast me as Adrien Josset in the episode 'A Man Condemned' in the Rupert Davies *Maigret* series. Adrien Josset, a man wrongly condemned for the murder of his wife, is about to face execution. The audience witnesses his mental torture, and Inspector Maigret's belief in his innocence. I was surprised a few years ago to receive a National Film Theatre leaflet with details of that episode which had been chosen to be screened there. I wrote to the BBC and they very kindly sent me a copy. How styles and techniques have changed in forty-three years.

Looking back now to those years spent aboard the *Stella Maris*, was it cramped and confined living with my mother? Not really. I was free to come and go, to indulge my lusts ashore at my favourite haunt, the Strand Palace Hotel. 'You're young! Have fun!' Thus argued many close friends. I did, and don't regret it, except for the hurt I may have now and then inflicted. But at thirty-five I felt I needed to stabilise and mature emotionally.

My ten years aboard the *Stella Maris* were rich, colourful, utterly selfish and free. But all this was about to come to an abrupt end when one evening during my mother's absence a mutual friend stopped by for a visit with her attractive, twenty-year-old schoolmate, and changed my life.

CHAPTER NINETEEN

BOBO, MATERNAL RESISTANCE, AND WEDDING BELLS

VERONICA NICHOLSON HAD been a friend of my mother's during her Seville days. Arriving unexpectedly that evening in November 1961, Veronica was accompanied by a close friend from her school days, Ann Minchin. My mother, thank God, was still in Seville, or Ann would have been vetted on sight. We drank and chatted and I thought, 'What an attractive girl!' Ann listened with rapt attention while I reminisced incessantly about Seville and the world of flamenco.

I was still rehearsing my flamenco cabaret act *Los Rondeños* for Clement Freud at the Royal Court Theatre Club, and at the time Ann and Veronica appeared I was facing a small crisis. The mother of Tatiana, my sixteen-year-old flamenco dance partner, was threatening to leave and I had to find a dresser-cum-chaperone to take her place. When I mentioned my problem, Ann kindly offered to step in as Tatiana's dresser whenever the sixteen-year-old's mama or brother were unavailable. This she did, and it was Ann's working for us so unselfishly each night — after finishing work at her office — that made me realise what a friend I had made. I had found someone who was loyal, intelligent, and who sported a sense of humour that was both witty and bawdy — for me a quality that enhanced everything else about her. We soon became very close and all was going wonderfully.

One evening several of us were dining on the *Stella Maris* when quite unexpectedly the door flew open and there stood Mum, come to reclaim her domestic realm. Seeing Ann seated beside me, she froze, with a look on her face that reminded me of a ferocious animal when its young are being threatened.

'Mum,' I said, 'I want you to meet my friend Ann, who's been a great support with my flamenco show.'

'Hello,' was all my mother said, and from that moment on the evening went into deep freeze.

Nevertheless, my mother's attitude brought Ann and I even closer together. I had always enjoyed my relationship with Mum, but I had also resented her incessant maternal protection. And if it came to a question of choosing between her and Ann, I knew what the choice would be.

I often give close friends affectionate nicknames that represent the very opposite of what they are as people. In Ann's case, her warmth and my sincere affection for her inspired me with the nickname 'Bobo', which in Spanish means 'silly one'. Bobo is really the masculine form of the word (for Ann it should have been 'Boba'), but in spite of that, Bobo she remained, and as it happened that nickname was to prove as valuable professionally to Ann in her later career as 'Trader' has been for me.

The early months of 1962 were really stormy. Mother's jealousy was festering, and the explosion happened one afternoon when, just as I was about to leave the *Stella Maris* to do a job at the BBC, my nose started bleeding profusely.

One cardinal rule for anyone working at the BBC: be punctual. Being careless about leaving myself plenty of time for journeys had become an insidious habit, and now I ran the risk of being late. Just outside the bathroom door several newspapers were stacked in the passage for disposal. I grabbed a couple of pages to staunch the flow of blood, which I finally succeeded in doing. Then, crumpling up the paper and pushing it into a corner to be cleaned up later, I raced out to my car.

I made it on time, did the job, and arrived home later planning to dispose of the bunched up, bloody newspaper. However, stepping aboard the *Stella Maris* I was confronted by my mother, wearing a look of absolute rage.

'Come and look at the unspeakable mess your girlfriend has left in the bathroom!'

She drew me to the passage and pointed at the bloodied newspaper.

'Don't worry,' she told me, 'I've rung the disgusting bitch and told her never to set foot here again.'

'Mum,' I said, 'it was a nosebleed! It had nothing to do with Bobo.'

Luckily John Bloom, who owned the houseboat *Aku Aku* opposite, was in Hollywood editing a film at the time and had said I could use his boat if I needed. I decided a few days away from Mum would do us both good. In retrospect I am amazed by the way Bobo responded. She was outraged at first, but then said: 'There's no fury like a *mother* scorned.'

It was then that I became aware of how my mother's tenuous emotional stability was beginning to crumble. From that moment on she realised that if our relationship was to survive it would have to be with no maternal interference in any decisions I would make. I believe my mother's jealousy and resentment festered, hard as she tried to rise above it, until it finally dissolved some months later with the birth of our daughter, Sasha.

The next fifteen months seemed like a very unsteady walk along a circus high-wire. During our Royal Court flamenco cabaret season we played to packed and quite distinguished audiences. But after a two-month run, split between the Court and the little restaurant the Marengo, near the Old Brompton Road, *Los Rondeños* disappeared without a trace.

I had managed to save a little money from two years' consistent employment and, being financially stable, I felt by early 1962 that I was finally in a position to ask Bobo to marry me.

After I finished the flamenco cabaret season, Bobo and I planned to go for a month's holiday to Seville. Ricardo Pachón, who had been staying with me on the *Stella Maris*, offered to put us up. Bobo and I would drive my little Morris Minor there and back. We had it all planned when, choosing her moment very carefully, my mother said over dinner one evening: 'I'm sure it'll be a wonderful trip. Can I come?'

Caught off guard, I made one of the greatest mistakes of my life.

'Well ... yes, if you want to.'

It was really the last thing I wanted, plus I hadn't consulted Bobo. It's easy to be wise all these years afterwards, but clearly I had been maternally clean-bowled, middle stump. Bobo, good natured as always, went along with it.

We set off after Easter — Bobo and I in front, Mum in the back. (She should have been in the boot!) The car was a two-door mobile oven with no air conditioning. A driver only since 1960, I hogged the wheel while Bobo, who was an infinitely better driver, sat patiently waiting her turn. Our first stop was Poitiers, where we slept in a place that turned out to be a brothel, situated next door to a *pissoir* — so that all night we tried to sleep to the sound of French 'water music'.

Why hadn't we gone to a decent hotel? The reason was that we had arrived at 11.30 p.m., exhausted and in pitch darkness. (We'd left London at 8 a.m.)

The next day we stopped for a picnic lunch in a field near Bélin, south-west of Bordeaux. While Bobo and Mother prepared the food I went for a walk. I remember walking through undergrowth and coming out at a clearing — and there before me were ruins. I had a feeling that the ancient building had something to do with Eleanor of Aquitaine, wife of King Henry II. I'd been given Amy Kelly's book *Eleanor of Aquitaine and the Four Kings* as a first night present for *The Lady's Not for Burning* in 1950, and it had made a deep impression on me. I remembered a photo of the ruins of Saint Pierre de Mons near Bélin. Was I staring at that same relic, a place that Eleanor must have known well, and wherein she may have prayed? I wanted to explore further, but we were pressed for time. I raced back and asked both women to come with me to see my discovery. Neither was interested. So I decided I would go there on our way back. Sadly, I never returned, but have often looked at the photo in the book. It is definitely what I saw in that clearing.

I remember little now of the rest of the journey to Seville, except that in Cordoba we saw Antonio and his company dance de Falla's *El Amor Brujo* in the gardens of the Moorish Alcázar, with a massive orchestra and under a full Andalusian moon — for us a deeply-felt experience. Next morning, quite by chance, we met Antonio taking his morning constitutional in the gardens of the Alcázar, and he greeted us with his characteristic good nature and acerbic wit.

Driving into Seville itself we heard someone in the distance.

'Hey Trader!'

There at a window on the main street was an old friend from my St Ignatius school days, Chris Meagher, an Australian lawyer-turned-matador. During the time my mother was living in Seville in the 50s and 60s he had kept an eye on her.

My mother and Bobo were installed in comfortable beds in Ricardo Pachón's father's office beside Seville cathedral. I stayed with the Pachón family at their home. They invited us all to lunch the following day.

Later we joined Chris Meagher (now Cristóbal Morales) in the bullfighters' bar, *Bodega Morales* (from which Chris took his name as a matador), near the famous Maestranza bullring. We drank with Chris's matador mates, and got the full low-down on just what a dirty game bullfighting can sometimes be.

I remember one of that group was a rotund little Sevilliano named Carlos Cadezota, a well-known character. He ran a coffee bar in Mateos Gago, a famous street by the cathedral, where we'd meet for our morning coffee. We happened to be there when the conversation turned to the colourful spring fair, the *Féria*, and the bullfight with which it would open.

The Spanish bullfighting fraternity loathed Chris, and were out to queer his pitch. Though he wasn't Spanish, he'd secured a little financial backing in a city where poverty was rife, and most Spaniards — who are very proud and chauvinistic — were determined not to allow this foreigner to show his stuff. On many occasions they set him up against bulls that had already fought, or that had some defect and so were withdrawn before the kill. Chris told me: 'Also many times they gave me bulls that had already been caped and were lethal. Two of the matadors who fought with me in my last fight were killed two years later. When the game is clean and fair it's a sublime experience. But that is rare when so many people are involved, and with human nature being what it is.'

Bobo, who later saw Chris fight (after I had returned to London), told me he was incredibly brave, stood his ground and — unlike so many self-acclaimed bullfighters — killed his bull cleanly and quickly.

In 1965 Chris developed hepatitis, went back to Australia, returned to the law, and got married. Hepatitis may well have been a blessing in disguise. Now comfortably retired, his challenges are no longer his bulls, but his balls on the golf course.

'But my life was made richer by the experience,' he later told me, 'and I certainly have no regrets.'

Throughout our Spanish trip, Bobo — the little English girl — was being thrown in at the deep end but, being very adaptable, seemed to be enjoying it.

We were invited to the *Rocío*, an ostensibly religious pilgrimage where each year Andalusians, as well as thousands of hangers-on, process in a train of highly decorated wagons called *carretas* (two-wheeled, canvas-covered bullock carts) to pay homage to the Virgin Mary of Rocío at her shrine near Almonte, east of Huelva. This Virgin is said to have appeared in the middle ages to a hunter/horseman and performed a miracle, and a shrine was erected there. Now a large church marks the spot, visited each year by tens of thousands of devout pilgrims. But typical of the Andalusians, it is also an occasion for feasting, drinking, and what you will.

Years later I made a programme on the *Rocío* for BBC Radio, but for me this first experience of the *Rocío* was a nightmare. Mum came down with a bilious attack on arrival, after a drive of several hours from Seville, and needed to be driven straight back. Fortunately, our *Rocío* hosts looked after Bobo while I retraced our trip back to Seville, left Mum with our friends, and then made the return journey. Arriving exhausted, we still danced and feasted with the crowds, but by 2am, when festivities were in full swing, I felt like a spavined carthorse. In a word, knackered.

The next day, having driven up to collect Mum again from Seville, we drove down to Algeciras and gazed across the Strait of Gibraltar to North Africa. My little second-hand Morris Minor had carried us from London as far south in Europe as you could go. In those days many of the roads were very rough, and the tourist invasion hadn't gained its momentum, so the coast west to Portugal was full of wonderful places to explore, like Sanlúcar de Barrameda at the mouth of the Guadalquivir. Then, by a circuitous route, we drove to Huelva, Columbus's port of embarkation for the Americas. From there we took a ferry across to Punta Umbría, which seemed to us like a deserted beach resort, but was a summer paradise to those Spaniards who frequented it forty-six years ago.

I then had to fly back to London to do a television job, leaving Bobo and Mum to enjoy each other's company on the beach. Watching the Atlantic surf roll in at Punta they reached a temporary truce.

When we finally reconvened in Seville, Bobo was offered a job in advertising and decided to stay on for a while to perfect her Spanish. She had given up her London job, having saved some money, and at twenty-one wanted time and space to think ahead. She would share lodgings with the faithful Chris, so I knew she would be safe. I needed to get back to work, and so, after a tearful farewell, I started the marathon drive back to London.

Bobo returned to London in October. Realising that if we *were* to marry the ball was now in my court, I set about courting her for all I was worth with the only weapons I had at my disposal: my undoubted love for her, complete sincerity, and the determination to succeed. Finally Bobo agreed to marry me. We planned the wedding for February, but were persuaded to put off our nuptials owing to family opposition. Bobo's parents and my now desperate mum had joined forces, and, viewed in retrospect, parental reason wisely prevailed. The wedding would now take place on 31st May 1963. Bobo, out of loyalty to me, decided to convert to Catholicism.

Before the wedding, Bobo left her London flat to live for a time with her parents at Liss in Hampshire and to work locally. I was busy with two television episodes — one of *Moonstrike* and the episode of *Maigret*.

The wedding day arrived just after the completion of the latter.

On the wedding morning, Mum took to her bed and — unlike Lazarus — when summoned to rise, refused to do so in the face of all entreaties, and despite the persuasion of my buxom old Aunt Kate McKeown — a distant cousin once removed on the Whytock side who had come up specially from her home in Hythe for the event. It seemed it would take the divine touch of Jesus himself to get Mum vertical, so we left her to it.

Then, when the organ started playing and we all stood awaiting a radiant Bobo, suddenly there was Mum, looking smarter than I've ever seen her.

It was a superb day, so everyone walked from the Holy Redeemer Church in Chelsea to the reception at Crosby Hall.

One feature of that day seemed symbolic in light of subsequent events. Bobo and I were supposed to cut the cake together. Unaware of what I was doing, I gripped the handle with Bobo's hand over mine and plunged the knife in hard. Suddenly, blood gushed, spurting all over Bobo's white satin dress as the wedding guests gasped. Foolishly, I'd gripped the knife blade upwards and had gashed my index finger.

Robin Howard, who owned the Gore Hotel in Exhibition Road, hosted us there magnificently on our wedding night, and we honeymooned at Kruger Kavanagh's little hotel at Dunquin, way out on Ireland's Dingle Peninsula.

I suddenly realised the huge responsibility I had taken on. A very sweet young woman had promised to share her life with me, believing that life with Trader Faulkner would be exciting and at least reasonably comfortable. The truth of the matter was that work just now had become elusive. One of the problems was that for eleven years I had been working hard to be a top young establishment actor. But the new theatrical styles of the 60s — the bloodless revolution represented by Samuel Beckett's *Waiting for Godot* and John Osborne's *Look Back in Anger* — were turning everything I had strived to achieve against me.

Vivien Leigh told me at the time: 'We're in a time of cataclysmic social change. The West End of Noel Coward, Larry Olivier, and the H.M. Tennent elite is fading.' She was dead right, and sadly knew that she was to be no part of this new wave. It is significant that the break-up of her marriage happened to coincide with all that.

Shortly after we were married, discussing Vivien during dinner one evening, Bobo said how much she admired her because everything about her seemed to suggest elegance, style, and intelligence.

'Well, I haven't seen her for a while, but she's such a sport I'll give her a ring and ask if she'd slum it over to visit the Chateau Trade.'

I rang, and received a typically warm response.

'Darling Trader! Of course, I'd love to meet your new wife. Would it be a trouble if my friend and comfort John came with me? And my little cat?'

John Merrivale was her companion and support after the marriage break-up, and remained with her until she died three years later.

Vivien, John, and her little cat arrived in a Mini Minor. I'd invited two other close friends: Nigel Davenport and Eleanor Fazan. If anyone could make an evening go, it was that pair. They easily matched Vivien's sometimes wicked sense of humour.

Vivien was casually dressed and, for the first time I had noticed, looked her fifty years. She was animated and talked brilliantly, but her constant bad health, the loss of Larry, and the awareness of her fading stardom had taken their toll.

I shall never forget the utter charm and genuine warmth she showed Bobo. It was a relaxed evening spent with close friends that went very well. I'll always remember Viv's parting words:

'Congratulations, Trader darling. I've always known you have good taste, and your Bobo is truly lovely. She's one of those lucky ones.'

I wondered what she meant. Looking back now, I realise she was saying that few truly beautiful women are ultimately very lucky in their lives. Sadly, her own life was proof of that

CHAPTER TWENTY

MARRIED LIFE AND A HIGH WIND IN JAMAICA

FROM THE OUTSET, my marriage — which was the most precious gift I'd ever had — was cracking. Bobo had undertaken this commitment full of idealism and ready to make the partnership work. I believe the fault was unquestionably mine. Basically the realisation of my responsibility as a husband — without the financial stability to fulfil it — weighed heavily on my spirits. The reality was that I was a struggling actor approaching middle age. I can't think of anything worse for a newly married couple than a man losing his self-esteem. One of the most disturbing aspects of my angst was that I was unable to make love, which wasn't helped by the telephone ringing at 8 a.m. every morning with Mum asking, 'Aren't you two up yet?' The situation was becoming unreal. My health, my marriage, and my mother would soon be spiralling into freefall.

For the first month of our marriage, Mum had agreed to stay with Aunt Kate down in Hythe. So we had the *Stella Maris* on our own for a time, after which we found a very comfortable top-floor flat nearby at 34 Courtfield Gardens. I shall always remember our first dinner party there, about to start on the food and already high on wine, when Bobo's barrister brother-in-law Peter Down burst in.

'President Kennedy has just been assassinated!'

We sat stunned. Suddenly, no one wanted to talk.

Bobo had found administrative work with the PR firm Newslines. She worked very hard, while I sweated more from trying to get work than actually working. I did do a fair amount for BBC Radio, and also translating and doing occasional earphone commentary jobs for the National Film Theatre.

I was then cast in one of the most disastrous movies ever devised, *The Bay of St Michel*. It was directed by John Ainsworth, and starred Ronald Howard (Leslie Howard's son), Mai Zetterling, and me. I don't remember much of the filming except that three or four of us either endlessly stood at attention or marched about the precincts of St Michel. I remember seeing the rushes and cringeing, but Mai Zetterling was brilliant, conveying so much with so little apparent effort. I wouldn't have thought many films are actually so bad when completed that they are never released, but that certainly seems to have been the case with '*The Bay of St Michel*', of which, for a long time, I could find no trace. Then some years ago I rang my friend Waltraud Loges at the BFI's National Film Theatre.

'Trader,' she said, 'your film is in the vaults.'

I thought: dare I invite a few mates to come and have a look at a private view, or could it utterly destroy their respect? I decided to chance it and had several around to watch it. It was appalling, and though I certainly didn't lose their respect, my friends all agreed that whatever story might have existed in the film had been completely destroyed in the edit. Another project best forgotten.

While I was still struggling professionally, Bobo, at twenty-three — determined to keep the domestic boat stable financially — knew that she had the potential to be a top model. This was at a time when Jean Shrimpton and Twiggy were the fashion icons. Bobo's mother had refused to let her go to Lucy Clayton's fashion school, but Bobo believed she had more than a chance of succeeding. She asked if I'd mind if she had a try. I was only too glad to encourage her. To tell the truth, the Bobo I married was far from confident, despite having abundant reasons to be so. All my friends accepted and loved her at once. She had had the advantages of a very good and expensive education. What's more she was 'cool', had style, and what the Yanks call 'real class'.

In 1964, an offer arrived for me to join the BBC Radio repertory company on an eighteen-month contract. Finally I had the security of full-time employment.

Six weeks into my contract with the BBC came an urgent phone message: could I go for an interview that afternoon to the 20th Century Fox film office in Soho Square? Luckily, I was free.

Alexander 'Sandy' MacKendrick was about to direct Anthony Quinn and James Coburn in the film adaptation of Richard Hughes's novel *A High Wind in Jamaica*. He was offering me the part of the pirate Paco. I was to write any snatches of Spanish dialogue that might be required and arrange a dance sequence with Quinn and the crew for a fiesta scene. They would be shooting for several months at Rio Bueno on the north coast of Jamaica, with interiors done later at Pinewood studios in London. I explained my situation, and declared that I would immediately ask the BBC if they'd release me.

In writing an autobiography, it is imperative to acknowledge a good turn done or help given. The woman to whom I was answerable on that occasion was Anita Apel, head of BBC Artists' Contracts. I went straight round to Broadcasting House knowing that ethically and legally I had not a leg to stand on. 'Auntie' Anita gave me several very uncomfortable moments. After all, my request was tantamount to treason — breaking faith with the BBC, after they had been so good to me. Then she winked.

'I've read the book. It's a classic. You must accept the offer.'

I couldn't wait to tell Bobo. I'll always remember how she smiled.

'Jamaica rum. Lucky you!' she said. What she didn't say was, 'I wish I was coming too.' But there simply wasn't the money.

The day I left I realised Bobo loved me very much and was being very British in trying to hide her feelings. For the first time since we'd married she was going to be left on her own.

Hollywood had two schooners that had sailed out from San Pedro in California under the command of Captain Zender, a Hollywood skipper who put Bligh of the *Bounty* to shame when it came to being aloof and imperial. But he was experienced and very capable.

Shooting onboard off the coast of Jamaica was a paid luxury holiday. Sandy MacKendrick's credits already included *The Man in the White Suit* with Alec Guinness (which he'd also co-scripted),

The Ladykillers with Alec again (and Peter Sellers), and *The Sweet Smell of Success* with Burt Lancaster, to name but a few. Although he had also co-scripted several other films, he was constantly hounded and bullied by 20th Century Fox, who sent out a clipboard man to oversee every take Sandy shot. Fortunately, Sandy's wife Hilary was on hand to give him moral support off the set. I don't know how he kept his temper or his reason. He would tell us actors how he wanted a scene played and why. If the scene involved Anthony Quinn, Quinn would always question Sandy's concept, so that the shooting of the film became a continual battle of wills. I shall never know how Sandy managed to bring in the film he did. Quinn was playing a power game with a talented director who knew exactly what he wanted. Regularly Quinn didn't feel a scene favoured him enough as the star, but always getting his own way meant the film would run counter to MacKendrick's concept. Then the studio man would be consulted, and more often than not MacKendrick would be over-ruled. It was a horrible game to witness.

Years later, I reminded Sandy of that debacle when I stayed with the MacKendricks in Hollywood. Sandy told me that working with Quinn was a 'no win' situation because Quinn had a very agile intelligence and was accustomed to getting his own way. Coming up in the 1930s, once married to Cecil B. de Mille's stepdaughter, Quinn was a handful for any director to reckon with. Also, the year before *High Wind* he'd made *Zorba the Greek*. And for Fellini he'd won international repute as Zampanó in *La Strada*. So for Darryl Zanuck, head of 20th Century Fox, he was hot property. He was also a major film personality as a result of the films he had made much earlier, like *Viva Zapata* with Marlon Brando, and *Lust for Life* as Paul Gauguin, opposite Kirk Douglas as Van Gogh. For both films he won Oscars for Best Supporting Actor. So by the time 20th Century Fox employed him for *A High Wind in Jamaica* he was a formidable force to be reckoned with. He was also a physical force to avoid, as I would learn soon enough.

A quiet unassuming power behind the scenes on that film was the editor Elmo Williams. He had edited *High Noon* (with Gary Cooper), and been brought in because the Elizabeth Taylor film, *Cleopatra*, was a box office flop a year before and the studio needed to recoup their monumental loss.

Filming was well underway when extras were recruited from Jamaica for the brothel scene, wherein one of the children — watching a cock-fighting match — accidentally falls out of a window and is killed. Among the extras was a beautiful Jamaican girl, Beverly Anderson, who also had the responsibility for hiring the extras in Kingston. During the shooting of this long night sequence, we broke while they were setting up for a very difficult shot. Anthony Quinn suggested we go upstairs, where there was a room with a long table, and relax. About a dozen of us were sitting round this table when Quinn suggested we play the 'truth game'. Someone would be elected to ask a question and you had to honestly answer only 'yes' or 'no'. Quinn took charge and in typical macho style asked the leading question: 'Did X (a woman) find Y (a man) attractive?' I could see this was going to become tedious and it did, with extraordinary repercussions. As the game progressed Beverly was asked if she found Anthony Quinn attractive.

'No,' she replied.

Not liking her answer, Quinn then asked her if she found me attractive.

'Yes,' she answered.

The break ended when we were called back to the set. I went over to Beverly and apologised that she had been put in such an awkward situation on my account.

That night, when the shooting finished, we all drove back to the Runaway Bay Hotel, where we were based. A crowd of us went after dinner to the swimming pool with our Cuba Libres. Beverly was there and we got into conversation. I told her I was fascinated by Jamaica and that a great friend of mine, the authoress Marguerite Steen, had told me about its history. I said that while we were filming I hoped to discover as much as possible about the island. Beverly invited me to spend a weekend at her parents' home at Port Antonio, a good hour's drive south from where we were. Could I hire a car?

The idea appealed to me, so I hired the car and we drove down.

The Anderson family greeted me warmly. Beverly's father ran

Jamaican Railways in that southeastern part of the island. The train used to come direct from the banana and sugar plantations and pass literally under their front veranda, then wind down to the bay where a sugar boat, the *Camito*, was lying at anchor. I shall never forget the sight of the locomotive passing underneath us laden with bananas on their way to England.

I was introduced to the family, which included several brothers and sisters. Mrs Anderson had very kindly told Beverly that I should bring my laundry down and that she would do it, which she did. I remember having a dinner of local fish and vegetables, followed by a marvellous evening with a lot of Cuba Libres. Then came bedtime.

The house, old wooden colonial style, had one enormous central room with cubicles all along one wall. The parents were in the middle cubicle; we men in the cubicles to the left of Father; and the girls in the cubicles to the right of Mother. All the beds had mosquito nets. I got into my cubicle next to Mr Anderson's, so excited that I found it difficult to sleep. Within minutes of lights out there was a symphony of snoring. After some time I became aware that one of the girls was getting out of bed. Peering across the room, I saw Beverly crossing the floor towards the kitchen directly opposite us. From the ceiling in the kitchen hung one of those old-fashioned 1920s lights with a porcelain shade. As I watched, she took out the ironing board and a basket full of washing — which I saw was mine — and began to iron. Her white nightdress was almost transparent. Here was this beautiful girl ironing my clothes! Sensing that I was awake, she looked in my direction. I could see there was an invitation in her expression for me to join her. In one moment, all my Catholic resolutions simply evaporated. More to the point so did my marital loyalty to Bobo. Climbing cautiously out of bed, I started to make my way across the floor, forgetting that I was wearing only my pyjama shirt and briefs because of the heat. Slowly I approached her on tiptoe. Meanwhile, Beverly was smiling voluptuously and ironing away. Just as I was about to take her in my arms a floorboard creaked, very loudly. Mrs Anderson's voice came in a sharp whisper from behind me.

'Beverly! Come to bed at once!'

Ashamed, I retreated as inconspicuously as possible towards

my cubicle, hoping that I'd not land on the snoring Mr Anderson. Putting my hand out, I felt the end of my empty bed. I settled back and immediately sank into a deep slumber.

The next day — Sunday — the parson arrived and we all had sherry and biscuits. This was 1920s Kensington in 1960s Jamaica. Everything was very formal, very correct, and utterly unreal. I remember little else of the rest of my stay there.

We finished the Jamaican sequences of *High Wind* and flew back to London — Beverly as well. She had asked me if I could arrange hotel accommodation near Bobo and me in the Kensington area as her sister lived in East London, far from Pinewood Studios. If she lived near me, she could get a lift. So on our return I found a hotel and reserved a room for 'Miss Anderson'. I must have mentioned that she was from Jamaica. Immediately the clerk looked up.

'Is she black?' he asked.

'Yes.'

'Ah. We're very sorry, but we don't take coloured people.'

I couldn't believe it. From every hotel I tried I got the same response. Finally I made my apologies to Beverly, who realised it would be easier to stay with her sister after all.

On my return from Jamaica, I remember coming through the door to confront a horrified Bobo. The man who had left her three months previously had been clean-shaven. The man who returned was a wild, tropically tanned, unshaven pirate. But I had brought very nice presents for Bobo and her mother — of whom I was very fond — and life soon returned to normal, the marriage bus rattling more or less steadily along.

I was determined that Bobo would never suspect there had been the slightest spark between Beverly and myself. I never wanted to jeopardise my marriage. To this day, I don't know if Bobo ever suspected anything.

On one occasion we invited Beverly to lunch. Afterwards, Beverly and I had gone for a walk and I was showing her The Boltons — one of the most expensive streets in Kensington, with enormous houses for the mega rich. We were walking along when suddenly round the corner from the Old Brompton Road came Anthony Quinn.

'Aha!' he said. 'The two lovers, taking an afternoon stroll.'

'Tony,' I said, 'you have such an imagination. You should be a scriptwriter as well as a star. Why not write this, since you obviously believe in it?'

He gave me a look of intense dislike and moved on.

I knew that the rest of the filming was going to be a nightmare — especially the dance sequence in which he and I would both feature. It was. When we came to do the shot, Quinn had me dance opposite him and every time there was an opportunity he would try to smack my face. Not having seen the film for many years, I don't know how much of that scene was cut, but it was almost a free-for-all. Quinn had very long arms and a powerful punch, but I was agile and for the most part I kept out of his reach. But on one occasion he connected, striking me across the face. In retaliation I landed a hard punch in his soft gut. From that moment on he was my bitter enemy.

Among the children we 'kidnapped' in the film was Kingsley Amis's taciturn young son Martin. When the time came for the dance sequence, Sandy MacKendrick asked me to choreograph a Jamaican rumba featuring the four children, Jeffrey Chandler, Deborah Baxter, Roberta Tovey, and Martin Amis, with Quinn and myself. We were all excited and looking forward to having a bit of fun. Quinn, who when he chose could be very childlike, swept the kids along with his enthusiasm. But not young Martin. He stood at the side, immobile, clutching his mug of morning tea. Nothing would induce him to join in. He must have been about fourteen or fifteen, but looked much younger. I've often wondered if he had no sense of rhythm, or if he dreaded — being older than the others — making a fool of himself. Who knows? Suffice it to say nothing would persuade him to join us.

When the filming was finished, Beverly went back to Jamaica. Fourteen years would pass before I met her again, under extraordinary circumstances.

Martin Amis, whom I never subsequently met, surfaced again in my life when his novel *Night Train* was first published in 1997.

'I thought you'd died,' said my well-known Australian broadcaster friend, Phillip Adams, in a dawn phone call from Sydney. Later that morning came a call from a reporter on the *Guardian*.

'Is Trader Faulkner dead?'

By the time I'd put the reporter wise, I was ready to 'deck' the little nerd who had used my name for his chief murder suspect in *Night Train*. Apparently, Martin believed that I had passed on and decided to use my name as a stylish touch for his plot.

I've since come to wonder if this was a subconscious *riposte* for what he may well have felt was a humiliating situation for him all those years before. In any event, it's all history now.

My next and last film was *Murder Game* for 20th Century Fox, directed by an old stager from Hollywood, Sidney Salkow. I starred with Ken Scott and Marla Landi. My old flamenco cabaret employer Clement Freud played a nightclub croupier.

With my coffers filled again from all the film work, Bobo and I started house hunting, and were about to buy a top-floor flat in Wimbledon when a great friend, Paddy St Clair, found us a house down the road from it in Church Lane. It was called 'Pax'. We bought it and for a time enjoyed relative peace as a family, so the name suited.

Bobo by then was doing well as a model and found herself in demand. Mum, however, was not getting much attention, and would soon take her revenge.

One evening, Bobo and I were invited to a theatrical dinner on that restaurant-boat moored by Charing Cross Bridge. Mum came along. The place was packed with celebrities, some of whom were friends. We three were at a conspicuous table in the centre of the dining room. Somehow a row started about table manners and my mother — who knew the laws of etiquette very well — did something deliberately tasteless to provoke Bobo, who unfortunately rose to the bait.

'Sheila,' she begged, 'please, not here. People will start looking at us, and it will reflect badly on Trader.'

That was it. Now Mum saw her moment to really star — knowing it would humiliate us both. (I suppose her actions simply demonstrated the level of resentment that had built up within her at having been displaced in my life by Bobo.)

The dish was a large plate of sole *meunière* in a thick white sauce. Picking up her plate with two hands, Mother started slurping the sauce noisily. Soon her performance had the entire restaurant's attention. Fed up, I grabbed Bobo's wrist and pulled her away to the other end of the boat, leaving Mum to it.

In retrospect I realise that was a brutal over-reaction to what was only Mum's grotesque attempt at gaining my attention. Since Dad's sudden death in 1934, she had come to depend on me so deeply that she was probably not even aware of what she was doing. My mother was such a strong character, but she'd sacrificed so much, and Bobo was her Achilles heel.

One night, in torrential rain, we held a dinner party. The invitees were considering me for a very important TV job, so it was one of those ridiculous occasions when we were walking on egg shells. Halfway through Bobo's elaborate dinner there was a ring at the doorbell.

'Who on earth could that be, in this storm?'

I opened the door and in from the blast tottered Mum, barefoot, looking as if she might have come from a swim. In her arms was an elaborate wooden box with an oval lid — obviously a gift for us and the pretext for her visit.

'I'm wet through and frozen. Could I have a stiff toddy? Then I'll go.'

I could have taken her upstairs, told her what I thought of her desperate antics, put her to bed and sent her back to the *Stella* the following morning. Instead I excused myself from my guests, gave her a drink, and packed her straight into a taxi.

I realised then that there was no way I'd ever get the better of my incomparable mother, short of having her certified.

CHAPTER TWENTY-ONE

SASHA'S ARRIVAL, SURGERY, AND SEPARATION

OVER BREAKFAST ONE MORNING Bobo told me she was pregnant. So, we were to be granted a new life, and a real responsibility. Bobo at that time showed incredible resilience, working steadily until shortly before she was due.

In the last weeks of her ninth month, on the evening of 21st February 1966, we sat by an open fire at Pax, waiting. At 10.30pm Bobo turned to me.

'Come on, Trade. Get me there quickly! It's starting.'

St Theresa's hospital was just up Wimbledon Hill. I drove Bobo in. I wanted to be present for the birth. Shortly before 1am a young medical student and the midwife called me into the delivery room. Bobo was all ready in the delivery position.

'Where's Dr O'Leary?' I asked.

'I'm afraid he's indisposed,' said the midwife.

As it happened, he was drunk on his back in a nearby room. So we three proceeded. I was about to play a privileged and an unforgettable role in a theatre that was anything but make-believe. Soon this tiny head appeared, and we gently eased the curled up bundle of wet flesh into the light. The little thing was in such a hurry that she damaged her mother on her arrival. Bobo, whom I had completely forgotten as I ogled my tiny daughter, suddenly cried out. I remember saying to the midwife, 'Give her something to ease the pain.'

We had brought the child into the world, but now Bobo was bleeding and would need stitching.

'Mr Faulkner, will you cut the umbilical cord?'

I remember being handed a pair of surgical scissors and I did the job.

I believe all fathers should witness the birth of at least one of their children. It might help to save many marriages, sharing the painful nitty-gritty with your wife as well as the sensual delights.

It's all a long time ago now, but everything happened as it had to — and very quickly. Now that the job was done, I had no more to do for the time being with the little squirming bundle that would soon be called Sasha. By this time other nurses were arriving. I was told to go home and was gently ushered out. The waiting room was empty. I sat in a chair while the nurses did their work inside. As they stitched — with no anaesthetic available — I could hear Bobo gasping with pain.

Eventually, her cries stopped. I could hear the gentle drone of voices — the nurses were obviously trying to soothe her. The hospital seemed deserted. I drove home.

Next day I was back to see Bobo. She was all right, but exhausted and weak. Then she told me.

'Trade I converted to Catholicism to please you, but the encounter I've just had with the Mother Superior here makes me question aspects of your so-called faith.'

Apparently, the Mother Superior had come in early to visit Bobo and Bobo had told her that the pain of being stitched up without any anaesthetic had been absolute agony. The nun, she claimed, had looked at her with impatience.

'My child, you should consider yourself privileged,' she said. 'Think what Christ suffered, and how much worse your pains could have been than they actually were.'

I remember telling Bobo, 'I'll be back in a moment!'

As I was in a hospital I couldn't start shouting, but I did stride angrily through the corridors, asking any nurse I encountered where the Mother Superior was, or the senior resident doctor. But both had vanished. Right, I thought, I'll get you. Just give me time.

Bobo and Sasha were soon back at Pax. Mum came to visit and immediately ceased to cause any more trouble. She had found someone on whom she could lavish all her pent-up affection. Meanwhile, I sat down at the first available moment and wrote an acerbic letter to the *Times*. They published it and to our amazement St Theresa's was shortly thereafter threatened with closure. This was not solely because of my letter — apparently there had been many complaints — but my public criticism had finally lit the fuse. St Theresa's remained under threat for a while. I remember being approached by the hospital to ask what I wanted exactly. I responded that I simply wanted to prevent what happened to Bobo happening to anyone else, and that for me the threat of closure was enough. After all, there were wonderful people working there; we had simply been unlucky. But I know Bobo never forgot it.

The great blessing Sasha brought with her was the new love she awoke in my mother. All the possessive affection she had felt for me was now transferred to the child. For a time the domestic scene stabilised.

One morning in the sitting room I had been shaving with my electric razor on a plug and had taken the razor off, stupidly leaving the plug and coil in the socket. As I looked about for the razor case, I turned to see to my horror that Sasha had the coil and was just about to put the loose end into her mouth! I sprang across and wrenched the plug from the socket. Bobo and I went straight out and bought a 'bouncette' and for the next months Sasha bounced, safely and endlessly, to *The Nutcracker Suite*.

Another incident occurred, which I still think a great deal about now. One day, leaving my toddler daughter locked safely in my car, I had turned my back to run quickly to a shop twenty yards away to buy something — glancing back occasionally to catch her eye. As long as I could see the child I felt secure. I had to wait in the shop for my order. While I waited, I several times went back to the door to check on Sasha and I could see her small face looking for me. As soon as I could, I paid for the purchase and raced back. Sasha had seen me reappear and her gaze was fixed on me. When I got in to start the car a tiny hand reached out to clutch my index finger.

'Dad-Dad!'

Said with such relief and gratitude. How much can be conveyed with so little.

When I think of what goes on now with children left unattended — even for a moment — that experience still makes my flesh creep.

The relationship between Sasha and my mother blossomed. She would take Sasha for walks to a nearby park, make her touch the leaves and flowers and tell her what they were. As I remember from my own early childhood, walks with my mother were an encyclopaedic expedition into nature. I have always longed to know how much my mother truly influenced her. Mum had so much to give because at times she could be absolutely childlike and enter quite unselfconsciously into that magical realm of the child's mind.

Christmas of 1966 was the only time I would have my family together in my own home.

Bobo invited Mum to stay. She arrived with a toy sleigh drawn by mechanical horses with which she hoped to amuse Sasha for hours. It wasn't to be. A friend came bringing another present that completely mesmerised the tiny child — a toy television set that showed Snow White and the seven dwarfs moving to Tchaikovsky's waltz from *The Nutcracker Suite*. It played all day. My poor mother kept discreetly winding up her horse and miniature sleigh and setting it down to race away over the floor. Sasha took no notice. Watching my mother, I did feel for her. She showed no bitterness, but her toy was simply ignored. It must have hurt her enormously.

Nineteen sixty-seven was to be a year of constant work and a momentous series of events. Early in the year I was very lucky to be part of a handpicked cast in Donald McWhinnie's television production of Evelyn Waugh's *Sword of Honour*. Donald was a director who, having cast the ideal actor for each role, then left it to him or her to deliver the performance. Among his cast was Ronald Fraser, in the role of Apthorpe. Ronald was an excellent actor who later drank himself to death. The rest of the superb cast included Edward Woodward as Guy Crouchback and Freddie Jones as the mysterious Major Ludovic, with James Villiers, Vivien Pickles and Paul Hardwick supporting. I was cast as the upper-class, self-confident Colonel Tommy Backhouse, an establishment product of Sandhurst. Tommy Backhouse was a demanding challenge for an Australian actor, though admittedly by 1967 I had been working in England for seventeen years. Nevertheless, McWhinnie had a score of true English actors from whom he could have chosen. Fortunately, there were some excellent notices of the piece in the press when it was broadcast.

One bonus of my involvement with the production was my brief friendship with Edward Woodward and his then-wife Venetia. Bobo and I invited them to dinner. Our daughter was just over a year old. As I remember, Teddy and Venetia had two sons, Tim and Peter, both slightly older than Sasha, and a younger daughter, Sarah. Teddy became a close friend whom I admired enormously both as an actor and as a man of impeccable integrity. For a time thereafter we often re-connected in the BBC studios.

Both Donald McWhinnie and Edward Woodward had seen me dance flamenco at the Royal Court Theatre Club in 1962 and were fascinated as to why any actor in Britain would choose to learn such an unlikely dance form. Over dinner with the Woodwards I tried to explain to Ted that, to me, learning to dance flamenco was simply a means of improving my skills as an actor. He saw my point and respected it.

After a time we lost contact. The next I heard, Teddy was married to Michelle Dotrice, daughter of Roy Dotrice — an actor I knew, and of whom I was very fond, back in the 1950s. As I write this Edward Woodward has passed on, and our mutual friend the director Donald McWhinnie is also long gone. However, I'm told that Roy Dotrice, whom I last saw so many years ago in his one-man show masterpiece *Brief Lives*, is still very much alive and kicking in America.

After that job finished, I was kept busy with regular BBC Radio assignments, and frequent live commentaries for the National Film Theatre of their foreign film and documentary offerings. One of these, I remember, came from China, and in the shipment the cans of film had become mixed up. They arrived at the NFT with no time for us to rehearse — always a tricky situation, but in this case catastrophic. During a passionate love scene on screen, a Mongolian cavalry charge suddenly swept down a gorge. The reels were obviously out of sequence, and the film had to be stopped while the projectionists sorted them out. There was never a dull moment working for the NFT.

One morning I discovered a swelling beside my Adam's apple. Because I was so swamped with work I did nothing about it. Then, in July, Bobo took Sasha for a short holiday to Cyprus. Her sister Rosemary was married to the resident doctor on the air force base at Akrotiri. On her return Bobo insisted that I see our local GP. According to what she'd been told, my swelling was either cancer or a benign growth. My GP referred me to a top surgeon in the field at that time, Victor Riddle. This small, rather brusque medico with a twinkle in his eyes, said, 'I'll do what I can. We'll meet in my theatre, not yours. Don't be late!'

I'm sure my career was never meant to lie in films. The day before I was due for the operation I had an interview for a lead role in a film to be directed by John Frankenheimer, who had directed Laurence Harvey in *The Manchurian Candidate*. He had seen something I had done and felt I was right for the role. Unfortunately, on the day he wanted me to start I was scheduled for the operation. I remember a disappointed Frankenheimer saying, 'Well, good luck then!'

I don't remember being wheeled in for the big cut, but I do remember waking up three hours later with Victor Riddle smiling down at me. He had very kindly waited until I regained consciousness.

'You had an adenoma cyst the size of a golf ball on your thyroid gland. It was about the finest excision I've ever had to do to avoid cutting your vocal chords, but there's no damage there. From collarbone to collarbone I've left you a scar as fine as cotton thread. Come see me in ten days and I'll remove the stitches.'

Victor Riddle's surgical necklace is there to this day, barely visible.

Long after the operation I was told that that thyroid problem — latent since a year before my marriage — had been the cause of my disappointing sex life with my young and very beautiful wife.

★ ★ ★

It was at this time that Bobo received an offer from *Vogue* magazine to represent Britain at an international fashion model display in Sydney. It meant six weeks' work in Australia, a very good salary, and international recognition. We discussed this and agreed it was too good an offer to turn down.

I had three weeks to recover from my operation before she left. Sasha would stay with Bobo's sister, Audrey, who had two little daughters of her own. Also, she would visit Bobo's mother nearby at Liss, so we knew that 'Sam' (as we had nicknamed her) would be well looked after.

I had received an offer to direct a play at the Lyric Theatre in Belfast in October for the theatrical doyenne, Mary O'Malley, so I had work to look forward to.

Just before Bobo's departure for Oz, we drove Sasha down to Audrey's in Hampshire, where Sasha was lovingly taken in hand by Audrey's slightly older daughters, Siobhan and Claire. I remember hugging the little bundle with Bobo and slipping away unnoticed.

Bobo's Australian job seemed a heaven-sent gift as my BUPA medical insurance didn't cover the full amount owed for the operation. I was left with £800 to pay for Victor Riddle's work, which I didn't begrudge but could hardly afford.

Bobo was one of five international models selected by *Vogue* for the Australian assignment. The others were from France, Italy, the USA, and Scandinavia. There was also the possibility of extra modelling work for her out there. I would be working in Ireland, so the arrangement was ideal.

Before Bobo left, I went to see Mr Riddle with £800 in my pocket. He deftly took out my stitches, then I produced the notes, counted out the money and handed it to him. Riddle smiled, took a £10 note and handed me back the remaining £790. I had told him of Sasha and Bobo, whom I gathered he'd seen visiting me one day.

'Keep that for your little family,' he told me. 'They need it much more than I do at the moment.'

I burst into tears — one of the few occasions in my life when that has occurred. There was a lot more behind that outburst than I can explain. He escorted me gently to the door and that's the last I saw of him.

Some time later there was a phone message left for me by Mr Riddle.

'I'd like to invite you to dinner. Please come.'

At that time I was due to leave the UK on business and was unable to comply. Not having had the chance to see him again and thank him for what he had done is one of my greatest regrets.

The day came for me to drive a glamorous and very excited Bobo to Heathrow airport for her trip to Sydney. We said our goodbyes and I realised how lucky I was to have such a gorgeous partner, my darling daughter Sasha, and to have survived intact from the surgeon's knife. At last, I thought, we were secure and all was well.

How wrong I was. As a family we were about to descend into the maelstrom.

There seemed hardly any time after Bobo left for Australia on 12th September to think of anything but the play in Belfast. I remember little about it now except that the play — *Breakdown* by Eugene McCabe — was very well written. Mary's Lyric Theatre was a large upstairs room in a private house. The whole set up was utterly professional and absolutely unique. At the end of rehearsals Mary, an Irish Catholic, would serve us coffee laced with brandy, and I remember there was always lots of laughter.

At that time, the storm clouds of the Northern Ireland troubles were only just building and I was spared any exposure to violent incidents on that visit.

Back in London, at the conclusion of my Irish work, I received a phone call from Bobo. The fashion show had been a great success. She asked me if she could stay on till after Christmas, as she was in demand for other modelling work and earning good money. She would be back in early January, she told me. We agreed that I would go to Audrey's for Christmas to be with Sasha. Bobo, meanwhile, would stay with Chris Meagher's mother at Double Bay.

After finishing some BBC Radio work, I drove down at Christmas to see Sasha, whom I'd last seen in early September. I shall always remember stepping into the back garden, where she was engrossed in a ball game with Claire and Siobhan. I stood at a distance and called her name. Hearing my voice she looked up.

'Dad-Dad!' she shouted, and raced full tilt to clutch my leg.

Audrey had very kindly invited Mum as well and it turned out to be one of the happiest Christmases I can remember. Bobo's parents were also at that Christmas lunch. Her mother, who was devoted to Sasha, told me that on her visit with them our daughter had slept in an open bottom drawer in the chest of drawers near her bed.

'No trouble with that little one,' said Vivien. 'I gave her a cuddle and gently laid her in the open drawer, and there was not a sound till morning. She knew she was safe.'

The only other memory I have of that day is that after Christmas dinner, wrapped up against the snow, I took Sasha outside for a little walk. She immediately stretched out her arms, indicating that she wanted to be carried. I picked her up and she snuggled into my neck.

'Cooooold!' she said, shivering. 'Cooooold!'

That was all she said, but her eyes, and her need to be constantly cuddled by me, spoke volumes.

Before her departure, Bobo had several times threatened that she would leave me, since I seemed incapable of showing her any physical love. The marriage had suffered in that department from the outset — something that was bound to take its toll eventually.

Meeting Bobo off the plane in January, she had that detachment people who are very successful sometimes have. But I was enormously pleased to see her, and listened with rapt attention to her stories of Sydney, her work, and of the friends with whom I had put her in touch and hadn't seen for seventeen years.

Her first question was about Sasha. She wanted to drive down next day to collect her.

Then, in the car on the way into London, she said, 'Trade, I've found another man. I'm leaving you and I'm taking Sasha with me to Australia. You must understand, we'll both have a better life in Sydney. Let's be honest, you've had your chance as an actor, and at forty you still haven't made it. Now it's my turn. I'm doing really well. This man I've met is a very successful impresario. His name is Harry M. Miller. He can do a lot for me, in all ways. I'm sorry, Trade, but our marriage is finished.'

My immediate thought surprised me: 'Serves you bloody well right, Trade. If you marry a truly beautiful young woman and you starve her of physical love, then by God you deserve this.' (The sad irony was that Mr Riddle's successful surgery had restored me to my old sexually rampant self.)

How was I to answer such a devastating piece of news?

'But Bobo,' I bleated, 'what about our marriage? You're now a Catholic. What about Sasha, our little family, our home?'

But I knew it was a lost cause.

Over the next few weeks it all became like a horrendous game of poker, with Bobo holding every winning card. Her arguments were hard to face down. I had had my chance. Now it was her turn. Bobo's words cut me to the quick, because they were true. Within the profession I was known and established, but I was certainly no household name. Clearly, given the influential backing of Harry Miller, Bobo had a great chance to be one, having the enormous advantage of being beautiful and a London product — qualities very much respected and in demand in the Australian media at that time. Bobo's position was a strong one, but I was determined to fight my corner. I may have been an unsatisfactory husband, but I hadn't been cruel or violent. Still, no matter what I said, Bobo countered by telling me that 'come hell or high water' she *would* go back to Australia, and she'd take Sasha with her. Finally, realising that a fight over our daughter's custody would only damage Sasha — who not only loved her mother but depended on her — I agreed to her proposal.

The next day we went down to collect Sasha.

Sasha didn't run to Bobo as she had to me when we first arrived. Her mother picked her up and, as I remember, she was just a silent recumbent little bundle.

Back at home I pleaded with Bobo, hour after hour and day after day, not to break up our family, but she was adamant.

'Trade,' she told me, 'I'm in love with Harry, and he can support us. For you it's obviously an effort. Clearly you'd do much better on your own.'

We decided not to tell my mother until the day they were due to leave.

Bobo told me Harry had already paid for their flight back to Australia on 22nd February — Sasha's second birthday. That final humiliation I wouldn't accept. I made my terms clear to Bobo: she could go back to Sydney with Sasha, but only to break off with Miller and return to the UK to have a go at saving our marriage. On no condition would I agree to a divorce. Neither would Miller pay the fare. If I agreed to Bobo taking Sasha then the fare was my responsibility. I also bought Bobo some £700 worth of new clothes, which she felt she needed out there to hold her own professionally — all of which, of course, I thought was putting me in a stronger position with her.

Looking back now, I recognise all of this was simply the confused logic of a desperate man. In my heart of hearts I knew that Bobo's mind was made up and could not be changed. Still, I had to cling to the possibility of her coming back to keep my sanity.

One afternoon, Sasha's godmother Julia Fortescue invited us to lunch and pleaded with Bobo not to break the family apart. To no avail. Bobo was hell-bent on having her chance.

What about my poor mother? From the time of Sasha's birth Sheila had lived for the child. What a sadness to lose all that she could have handed on to her. True, she had behaved terribly to Bobo from the first moment. But this destruction of our marriage, and the taking of Sasha to the other side of the world, was payback of horrendous magnitude. Bobo's reaction to mother's suffering was indifference.

'When are you going to tell her, Trade?' she asked me.

As I said, it was decided I would tell Mother on the day Bobo was leaving. All I can remember now is that I told her in the car that morning as we were driving back to the houseboat. When we got to the King's Road she made me stop and got out. She crossed over the street and seemed suddenly to lose her strength, leaning against a shop window on the corner of Beaufort Street. My mother was very tough, but this was a body blow.

It was not that Bobo was vindictive; she was simply infatuated and determined to make her fortune in a new world — without me.

I drove back to Pax and collected the two of them for the trip to Heathrow. Luckily a great friend, Tia Pepa Richi — a Spanish woman close to both of us — insisted on coming with me to the airport to see them off. I really didn't fancy that excursion on my own. All went calmly until we reached the departure gate. I was carrying Sasha until it was time to say goodbye. She was very quiet and nestled into me. I sensed that all wasn't well.

'Come on, Sam Lamb,' I said, using my nickname for her. 'It's time to say goodbye to Daddy.'

The next minutes were an unforgettable nightmare. Sasha started to scream, and clung to me, gripping my shirt with all her strength. I remember Bobo saying:

'Come on, Sasha. Come on!'

With a wrench, Bobo pulled her from my arms and hurried through the entrance with the distraught child. The last I saw of Sasha was her red face and clenched fists, screaming at the top of her voice.

'Look, Trader,' Tia Pepa said to me when they had gone. 'Your shirt. Sasha has taken a little of you with her.'

I looked down. My two middle shirt buttons had been ripped off.

Anyone returning to a home when your family has gone (probably for good) will know the feeling of absolute despair and emptiness I felt that afternoon. What I remember now was carrying out the sad task of throwing away empty shoeboxes and tissue paper — all the stuff that had wrapped Bobo's newly acquired wardrobe for Australia. A forgotten suitcase filled with Sasha's clothes I would send on.

Over the next days, I disposed of Sasha's remaining toys and clothes quickly and ruthlessly, giving her things away to charity shops. I realised my only hope was to try to blot out the entire episode and to set myself new tasks — re-learn my acrobatics, dance flamenco, start a writing career, and continue to act whenever work came my way.

But living without Bobo and my tiny daughter was going to be hell.

CHAPTER TWENTY-TWO

LIFE WITHOUT A FAMILY

THE MORNING AFTER Bobo and Sasha's departure my good friend Rosemary Hawkins, married to the then well-known actor Peter Hawkins, arrived at the front door quite unexpectedly with a carload of cleaning materials. I had known Rosemary Miller (as she was then), another 'true blue' Aussie, since our early acting days on Sydney Radio playing very young lovers in the late 1940s. We had remained firm friends ever since, and had worked together for the BBC.

Rosemary heard of Bobo's hurried departure and rightly guessed there'd be some clearing up to do. Her helping hand in sorting out the chaos left by Bobo's leaving was invaluable — especially as I had arranged a dinner party for my old friend Julian Aymes (the television director) and his wife for that evening and needed to make the house presentable. In the past, Julian had given me some of my best television work and I wanted to offer them the finest meal I could prepare.

Unfortunately, their car broke down and they arrived an hour late by taxi. Suffering from a lot of strain, and having had little sleep the night before, I was exhausted and had a hell of a job keeping awake during dinner. At 1.30 a.m. they asked if I could drive them back to Colherne Court in the Old Brompton Road — a drive of a little over forty minutes there and back at that time of night. Instinct warned me that I shouldn't attempt such a journey in my state, but I agreed to take them anyway. On the way back I momentarily blacked out and came around to the sound of a loud bang and broken glass.

Looking up, I saw stars and a full moon through a window. The car was on its side and there was a strong smell of petrol. I seemed to be unhurt, so I climbed out onto the road. I had hit a parked van — apparently writing it off, as I subsequently found out in court — and I was bleeding badly under the chin. In a house nearby, a first-floor window opened and a woman poked her head out and stared at me.

'You look more than a bit dented,' she said kindly. 'I'm just dialling 999. Come on in and I'll make you a cup of tea.'

Halfway up her stairs was a mirror. I was covered in blood.

'I think I'd better get to a hospital,' I said. 'I don't think I'll have time for that tea.'

I heard the ambulance siren, and others approaching behind it. I thanked the woman and raced downstairs. A police car, an ambulance, and a fire engine had all arrived.

'You're bleeding badly,' the policeman said. 'You'd better get into the ambulance.'

I climbed aboard and he rode with me while his fellow officer followed in the police car. Luckily the fire engine wasn't needed.

At the hospital I was bustled onto a gurney and stitches were placed in my chin — without an anaesthetic. Suddenly, from the nextdoor cubicle came an Irishman's voice.

'Ahh! Mother! Holy Mary ... glug ... glug!'

Then there was silence.

'Thank God, he's gone!' said a second voice.

I couldn't resist asking my 'stitcher': 'Who has gone? And where?'

'An Irish drunk,' the nurse replied. 'He's been on his way for the past twelve hours.' She sat back. 'All right, Mr Faulkner, you can go home now. See your GP first thing tomorrow morning.'

'How do I get home?' I asked.

'We'll order you a taxi.'

Once safely inside my front door, I howled like a wolf in a blizzard. I couldn't take any more. Fate had dumped too much on my shoulders. Then immediately I started laughing. If there truly is a divine purpose behind our existence then the Almighty has one hell of a sense of humour. Divorce, a car smash with two cars written off, and — as I looked in the mirror — the face of Frankenstein after a punch-up. My jersey (I'd worn no coat) was soaked in blood. I had a hot bath and a triple whisky and slept like a drunk.

Next morning I saw why there were no bandages: the glass had peppered my face, but my eyes had been closed. The tiny surface cuts would heal very quickly, and although my eyelids had been punctured there was no serious damage.

The next event in this bizarre sequence was my appearance in court. I explained my case before a panel, describing in brief all the events that had led up to the crash. I was told I had to pay a fine. Then I was beckoned forward and a large, middle-aged lady leaned over to whisper in my ear.

'Loved your performance as Tommy Backhouse in *Sword of Honour* on TV recently, Mr Faulkner. Would a fine of ten pounds be all right?'

While I was recovering from the accident, Mum rang.

'That house is too big for you on your own,' she said. 'Why not let it and come back to live with me on the boat?'

'Mum,' I said, 'there can be no return to things as they were. Sorry. This is my problem, and I must go it alone.'

However, Mum's suggestion about letting Pax was worth considering. With very little work coming in, I needed the income. The neighbours next door kindly offered me a room and a bed and I rented it out. Living next door, looking out of my window straight into the home I'd just left, was bizarre. I felt I no longer had an identity or lived within my own body.

Letty Littlewood, a wonderful Dickensian character who ran a ballet school up on Wimbledon Hill, offered me some work teaching her girls the basics of flamenco. Then, an extraordinary telephone call came from my agent. An actor cast in a play had backed out in order to play the lead in a film. Would I go for an interview with the play's director at his house in Putney?

Why not?

The director turned out to be the Hungarian Janos Nyiri, recently arrived from Marseilles, where he'd been the resident theatre director there. Nyiri, a heavy smoker and drinker, was the most creative thinker I've ever known, and his crazy humour made him a truly lovable companion.

The play he was about to direct was Moliere's *The Imaginary Invalid*. I was to audition for the part of Beráld, brother to the hypochondriac Árgon. Nyiri handed me the script and asked me to read. What I didn't know was that his wife Jenny was hiding behind the door, listening to find out if I truly spoke the Queen's English (he'd heard that I was Australian). When I had finished, Mrs Nyiri stepped into the room.

'Yes, Janos. His English is fine.'

I was offered the role, and thus began a long and close friendship with Janos and Jenny. I was to go to Billingham in the north of England, where the play would rehearse and open before transferring to London. I would drive up to Billingham, leaving my room in Wimbledon at 4 a.m. to be in time for rehearsal at 10 a.m.

The night before my departure my landlady, a buxom woman with a husband and three children, said:

'I'll wake you at 4 a.m. with a cup of tea and some toast to set you on your journey.'

A few days before I had contracted a virulent case of conjunctivitis, so I needed to be up early in order to bathe my eyes. I had set my alarm clock, but was woken by my landlady with the tea and toast on a tray. She sat on the edge of my bed while I ate it, and I soon noticed that she was breathing rather heavily, and that her dressing gown was hanging open.

'Are you feeling all right?' I asked her. With my eye condition I couldn't see her properly, but I felt a distinct trembling coming from behind her heavy breathing that made me decidedly uncomfortable.

'You're a very attractive man,' she suddenly said. 'You know, we could really could get it on together, you and me.'

I was aghast. I thought I'd been living in the house of a happily married woman.

'But what about your husband? And your children?'

'Oh, Stanley wouldn't mind at all. And the children are all sound asleep.'

I suddenly felt a wave of appalling claustrophobia.

'No! Please! I've got to bathe my eyes. Anyway, if I don't go now, I'll never get to my rehearsal on time. Forgive me, but I've got to go!'

I threw myself out of the bed and made for the safety of the bathroom, determined that on my return from the north I would give my notice and seek other accommodation.

I found Janos Nyiri's ideas for the play inspiring. The central character, Árgon, is obsessed with the idea that he's extremely ill, whereas in reality he's a perfectly healthy hypochondriac. This French classic is an imaginative director's dream, and Nyiri was ideal to direct it. As a young man he had escaped from Budapest during the uprising of 1956 and, arriving in Paris, had studied at the Sorbonne, where he met Jenny, who soon became his wife. At some point Janos was offered a theatre director's scholarship by the iconic French director Jean-Louis Barrault.

In Nyiri's production the concept was changed so that in fact I would be the genuine invalid, a cripple in a wheelchair with paralysed legs. My character immediately became both sympathetic and comic as the brother trying to buoy up the spirits of the miserable, constantly complaining though completely healthy Árgon.

The leading man in this production was the actor Richard Wordsworth, a descendant of the English poet. Handsome and arrogant, he and Nyiri hated one another on sight. The problem was that, apart from myself, Nyiri had no say in the casting, which had all been done by George Roman, the then-resident director of the Billingham theatre. What transpired was a venomous and almost continual war of words. Wordsworth, with all the arrogance of the English upper class, would argue every line with his director, who, having lived and worked in France, knew exactly what he wanted. Wordsworth, who might have been ideal casting for Oscar Wilde or Noel Coward, was completely out of his depth with classical French farce.

When we opened, the play proved a great success in Billingham. After the run there, we transferred to the Vaudeville theatre in London's West End.

This theatre had a raked stage, which meant that it sloped down to the audience. At the dress rehearsal in London I managed to manoeuvre my wheelchair without any problem. But on the opening night, as I wheeled myself onto the stage the chair started to slew round; the brakes failed and I found myself sliding in the direction of the audience. Then the chair abruptly stopped, turned on its side and tipped me onto a kettle drum in the orchestra pit, luckily only a few feet below. There was a gasp from the audience until I bobbed up unhurt, then roars of laughter and applause as I regained the stage and the curtain came down. The play continued a few minutes later — this time with my chair and me firmly anchored.

Unfortunately, *The Imaginary Invalid* only lasted ten days. Nyiri's concept was obviously a little too unorthodox for conservative London audiences.

On my return to London, my rampant landlady saved me the trouble of giving her notice by immediately asking me to leave. Fortunately, I found another room with a neighbour, where I remained for the next six months.

Then, early in 1969, my mother had a stroke and was admitted to St Steven's Hospital, now the Chelsea and Westminster, in the Fulham Road. My great friend Seymour Fortescue rang and told me that she had collapsed. The following Sunday she was to give a big party on the houseboat. I went straight to the boat, leaving a note on the door saying the party had been cancelled. When I arrived at the hospital, I found Mother sitting in a wheelchair, bent over to one side. She seemed perfectly normal mentally, though she'd been severely debilitated physically by the stroke. I told her that I would return a couple of days later, on the Saturday, as I was working and had to try and organise what to do with her when she came out of hospital.

On the Saturday, the phone rang as I was cleaning my car. It was Mrs Murphy, a neighbour at Chelsea Reach.

'Trader,' she told me, 'your mother's gone. She died ten minutes ago. You'd better go straight to the hospital.'

I got there as soon as I could. As I climbed the stairs to the ward, a young doctor asked, 'Are you Trader Faulkner?'

'Yes.'

'Mr Faulkner, don't worry. Your mother had the most spectacular death. Several women in the ward were complaining about their ailments. "What on earth are you all complaining about?" your mother suddenly said. "Life is a wonderful gift! Shall I dance for you?" Apparently, she got up very gracefully, danced a few steps, did a slow pirouette, and slowly and gracefully sank down. She must have died before she even hit the floor.' He put a hand on my shoulder. 'You probably want to go and sit beside her for a while.'

I did, for quite a long time. I couldn't help thinking of Pavlova, the great influence in her life. Would those two souls meet again in the great beyond?

Finally I took her wedding ring, kissed her still-warm face, turned away, and left.

Her Requiem Mass funeral was held at the Holy Redeemer Church in Chelsea. My mother's old friend Canon Alfonso De Zulueta officiated. Mum was a well-known and popular figure and the church was packed with people who came to see their friend off in her shawls and flowing scarves — all the houseboat residents and staff from Chelsea Reach, as well as various shopkeepers from the King's Road, many of whom had never before been inside a Catholic church. I was sitting in the front pew with Janos Nyiri.

Outside a heavy storm was brewing, with deafening rumbles of thunder and flashes of forked lightning. The coffin had been wheeled up the aisle to the front of the altar. On the lid was a tiny silver cross. De Zulueta mounted the pulpit to face the mourners.

'Well,' he said some minutes later, bringing to a close his reminiscences about his old friend, 'we certainly shan't see her like again.'

At that moment there was a blinding flash of lightning, like an arrow, that shot down through a high rectangular window and reflected a tiny flash on the little crucifix, immediately followed by a deafening thunder crack.

'I see,' De Zulueta said to the congregation in the following silence. 'Sheila is not only starring at this afternoon's matinee performance; she's obviously doing the sound and the lighting as well!'

The entire church echoed with laughter and everybody applauded. True to form, Mum went out with a bang — in every sense.

At the end of the Mass many friends offered to come with me to Putney Vale Cemetery, but I simply wanted to be alone to see my mother buried. I was, however, relieved when old Zulu insisted he'd come with me.

On the way it started to hose down with rain. The coffin went down what seemed about fourteen feet. As I threw down a handful of soil I realised that one day what's left of me would lie in my own urn a few feet above her.

When I arrived home, there was a letter from Sydney lying on the mat. It was from Mallesons, Bobo's Sydney solicitors, requesting an amicable divorce. I felt like Sisyphus in Greek mythology, endlessly pushing an enormous boulder up a slope to the mountaintop, only to have it roll back down again.

Except that each time my boulder landed on top of me.

A few days after Mother's funeral I went down to sort things out on the *Stella Maris*. There was a strong wind and the rain was still hosing down. I went downstairs to the small front cabin to find that the houseboat had taken in water and that Mum's shoes, a handbag and a few other belongings were floating round in the ooze on the floor. It was late January. I would have to sort this horror out and put the boat on the market. I sat on the bed wondering how I could ever — with so little money — get out of this mess. I even sent a small plea into space. Silence. There was just the sound of the Thames lapping round the hull, the rain spattering on the roof, and the *Stella Maris* creaking and groaning as she tugged at her moorings.

I thought of the ten years I'd lived on her, such happy years. And now this. How on earth would I manage to get out of this noose?

Suddenly, there was a sharp *rat-a-tat-tat* at the back door. I went upstairs and opened it to find two men with felt hats pulled down over their faces.

'Trader, can we come in?'

'Of course, but who on earth are you?'

'Don't you remember me? I'm Harry Fine, casting director for MGM. This is my assistant.'

As they were soaked to the skin, I made them hot tea.

'Trader, I've a proposition to put to you,' said Harry. 'MGM are making a film called *Hushabye Murder*, with Orson Welles and Romy Schneider as the stars. There are some sequences to be shot on a houseboat and your *Stella Maris* is exactly what we're looking for. The deal would be that we pay you £150 per day for the days we film, and we do the *Stella Maris* up to your specifications. You'll have to put yourself up elsewhere while we film, but it would only be a few days.'

For a moment I had some misgivings. In 1966 film director Michael Winner — about to direct *I'll Never Forget What's 'is Name* (ironically another film starring Orson Welles, with Oliver Reed and Carol White in the other leading roles) — approached my mother to ask if he could shoot scenes from his film on the *Stella Maris*. Hard pressed for cash, this shrewd operator said that he would put Mum up in a modest hotel of her own choosing and paint the interior of one room — the downstairs main bedroom, which had been mine over the ten years I had lived there. I don't remember any mention of my mother receiving a fee.

She accepted his offer and chose a modest hotel in Bloomsbury, where she and her parents stayed the last night before leaving for Australia in 1917. Winner's crew did their filming and when Mum returned she rang me — furious. I came round to see her as soon as I could and found my old room had been given a single coat of off-white, very cheap, emulsion paint. I ran my nail along the wall and the paint just peeled off. My mother had been absolutely conned and there was nothing she could do. But that had been Michael Winner. This was MGM, and the deal seemed honest and most welcome.

I asked Harry when they intended to start filming.

'Mid June.'

Of course, I accepted his offer with alacrity.

Later on I looked up *Hushabye Murder*. No trace. Perhaps it was never released. Another mystery. But the Winner film still exists, and received reasonable reviews. It would be interesting to see it now, just to catch a glimpse of my old bedroom on the *Stella Maris* — complete with its tacky, off-white paintjob.

CHAPTER TWENTY-THREE

BELFAST, DUBLIN, AND PATTI EDWARDS

I WAS CONSIDERING where to go when I needed to vacate the boat for Orson Welles, when I received a call from my agent. Would I be interested in going back to Mary O'Malley's Lyric Theatre in Belfast to direct Alejandro Casona's one-act play *The Cudgelled Cuckold* in a double bill with Peter Shaffer's *Black Comedy*?

Since Bobo's departure with Sasha for Australia, needing a challenge and as a way of keeping my sanity, I had started to translate several plays from Spanish that I felt would appeal to English audiences. As it happened, Casona's was one of these, and I had been quite eager to see it produced. This was a golden opportunity to test my new translation and try out my dialogue with the actors in rehearsal. I would also have to train them to use their bodies in stylised *commedia* movement, as Casona had adapted this trifle from one of Boccaccio's *Tales from the Decameron*.

The other play I would direct was an English gem. Shaffer's inspired central idea for *Black Comedy* was that the play opened in pitch darkness and switched to full light only when the lights within the scene had fused. Thus Shaffer cleverly reversed reality for his theatrical purpose. In the darkness, we would hear the actors behaving normally. Then, when the electricity was lost, the stage lights came on and the actors played as if plunged in total darkness. A director's dream.

The cast were all young and inexperienced. When rehearsals began I found they were all capable of giving really good performances but totally unused to using their bodies and voices onstage. All that would very quickly change. We began rehearsals and as the days passed they all proved wonderfully inventive, giving *Cuckold* exactly the feeling and the style it needed. Strangely it was *Black Comedy* — the more straightforward play — that was the problem.

One of Mary O'Malley's protégés, a tall streak of an actor named Liam O'Callaghan, turned out to be my ninety miles of bad road. From the beginning he decided he knew all about his craft and needed no trumped-up director from London telling him anything. He was an uphill slog on a gearless pushbike at every rehearsal, and his attitude became contagious. Soon both my leads complained of fatigue. The pity of it was that in the other play they really were sweating, working hard to apply methods that were totally alien to them. By the dress rehearsal they were exhausted. I remember a phone call from the parents of my leading lady.

'Trader, do you know what you are doing? Roz is exhausted! She'll have nothing left to give if you drive her any harder.'

Another factor in the mix was that the leads fancied each other, and their rehearsal concentration was flagging. This, along with the recalcitrant Liam, was threatening all our work on Shaffer's play.

On the opening night, after the thunderous applause when the curtain fell, I felt vindicated. *Black Comedy* got us through with enthusiastic audiences and unanimous rave reviews. I felt safe — more fool me.

Northern Ireland was about to explode.

One evening, returning from a visit to west Belfast to the theatre in the east, and passing a house with a low hedge and a front lawn, an army vehicle pulled up and stopped beside me. Almost immediately someone fired at it from a second story window. The vehicle returned the fire — fortunately above my head. Still, I could clearly hear the whizzing bullets and took a header over the hedge onto the front lawn for safety, finding that the palm of my right hand had splayed a dog turd. Wiping it on the grass, I decided that Belfast was, at that point, not a city in which to spend any more time than necessary.

A week after we opened, Liam O'Callaghan announced that he had a television offer from London and would be leaving the show. I went to Mary O'Malley. Her response: 'Why don't you stand in for him, Trader? You take over and show us how that part should be played.'

Given no alternative, I learned the role and played it for the rest of the run. I received no complaints.

After our run in Belfast, the production transferred to the Gate Theatre in Dublin, run by Micheál MacLiammóir and Hilton Edwards, the now legendary pair of theatricals who gave Orson Welles his early break in the 30s. Again, Dublin gave us rave notices. I was lucky. The success of that production helped me to regain precious self-confidence.

I shall never forget returning to London and walking down the rickety gangway to the old *Stella Maris*, discovering her looking as I had never seen her — gleaming white in the afternoon sun, her windows and facings painted aquamarine blue, and with two white stars resplendent on her bow. Inside, the MGM art department had repainted my Seville flamenco chairs in cream and gold. She had never looked so beautiful as on that summer afternoon, as she gently rode the shifting tide on Chelsea Reach. With great regret I knew that now was the time to sell her, which I did that September. Bought in 1953 for £850, she was sold in 1969 for £4,000 — only to be destroyed by fire three years later.

At some point in this period, while staying with friends in the south of France, I experienced a chance but unforgettable encounter.

One afternoon, sitting alone on the beach at Golfe-Juan, my attention was riveted by a vaguely familiar figure doodling in the sand by the water's edge. Squatting on his haunches he looked exactly like a burnished brown satyr, 'well worn but worn well', to quote the old Kiwi boot polish advertisement.

His eyes shone like black opals. As he doodled, those black opals were fixed on a group of German oldies sunbathing nearby. They were lying in a row, all but naked — oiled flabby bellies sunny side up, like grounded white whales.

I started to laugh. The satyr caught my eye. He spoke in French.

'You wouldn't find them amusing if you'd lived in Paris during the Nazi occupation.'

His French bore unmistakable traces of his Andalusian origin. There was no mistaking Pablo Diego José Francisco de Paula Juan Nepomuceno Maria de los Remedios Crispin Crispiniano de la Santisima Trinidad Ruiz Picasso.

'My French is very rusty,' I told him in Spanish. 'I'm happier with Spanish, and I can *even* understand Andaluz.'

'How come?'

'I learnt to dance flamenco from the Sacromonte gypsies in Granada.'

'Why?'

I told him the story of my flamenco odyssey, of my lessons in Seville and Madrid with *El Cojo* and Antonio Marín — who had one leg. These two sedentary *maestros* had taught me 'style', the essence of flamenco. The rest I had learned from the greatest flamenco dancer of that era, Antonio Gades.

Picasso roared with laughter. He knew Gades, who had danced for him.

'Man! You are a clown! Only in Spain could a British actor learn to dance flamenco from a man with one leg!'

He knelt and drew in the sand two figures — a one-legged man and me dancing wildly together — working like lightning with a strong, stubby finger. Just a few strokes and there it was, conjured up in the sand, my likeness unmistakable. With a flourish he signed it: *Payaso y Baila'or con una pierna* [clown and one-legged flamenco dancer] — *Picasso*

Then he winked. At that moment a small wave broke across the sand — and washed the image away.

Without a word, he got up and walked me across the beach to a bar in a side street, where he ordered *dos copitas* — two small glasses of *vino*.

'What's your dance?'

'I've been working on *farruca* with Gades. He has modified his own version to suit my limitations.'

'Show me. I'll clap your rhythm.'

I was in soft shoes so the footwork went for nothing. Luckily I knew how to use my arms and wrists. When we'd finished — Picasso clapping the *palmas*, and I contorting — there was thunderous applause from the large crowd that had gathered to watch. Picasso said nothing. He simply raised his glass, and touched mine. I swallowed my red wine in a gulp, thanked Picasso, and raced out into the alleyway.

Was this a dream? No way. I had thumped my feet so hard on that stone floor in my rope-soled *alpagatas* that I was limping!

One day my friend Diana Richey rang.

'Trade, Paul and I want to introduce you to a girl I'm sure you'll be more than interested to meet. She's extremely pretty, very chic, and — most importantly — she's Bobo's predecessor with Harry Miller. Can we bring her to the boat to meet you? Her name is Patti Edwards. Her father is Sir Elton Griffin, the Australian oil magnate and managing director of BORAL.'

'A Sydney society beauty with a father in castor oil,' I couldn't resist saying. 'Diana, I can't wait to meet her.'

Paul and Diana arrived with the most elegant, doll-like creature I'd ever seen. Immediately I was out for the count. Patti oozed genuine charm and was obviously as pleased to meet me as I was her. This thirty-one-year-old Australian beauty was very widely read, sophisticated, thoroughly spoilt, and extremely generous — though I soon realised that she only ever did what she wanted.

The great surprise to me was that she found me attractive.

Apparently, Patti had married a Sydney 'society boy' called Edwards, who was the living image of the gorgeous Hollywood beefcake star of the 60s, Rock Hudson. Unfortunately, her marriage was a disaster, so Patti went her own way — eventually picking up with Harry Miller. She gave me a detailed account of her appearances with Miller at various social functions in Sydney, of how Harry was lionised socially and how the Sydney women in that circle had hated Bobo when she had appeared on the scene. Where was Sasha during all this? Bobo had told me that there was an elderly woman, a Mrs Eddings, who looked after Sasha — and that she was a devout

Catholic. So I knew, listening to Patti's nauseating descriptions of Sydney's social and media celebrities, that Bobo had conscientiously kept Sasha well clear of all that.

As I needed to blot out any thoughts of Sasha and Bobo, Patti Edwards was a welcome distraction. We went out to very expensive restaurants, nightclubs, the occasional theatre, and art gallery. Now in my forties — a dangerously vulnerable age for a man — I was reliving the nightlife of my youth on a much grander and more sophisticated scale. For me this adventure was a pleasant lunacy, as Patti was financially way above my league. In reality, I was simply her escort of the moment, but I was oblivious to that.

There was never a dull moment with 'Foggles' — which was what I called her because she always wore dark glasses that looked like an airman's goggles. Even though she would seldom allow me to pay, it was costing me an arm and a leg. What an indulgence. But the real downside to our hedonistic joyride was that I was becoming totally besotted with this enchanting butterfly, even though I knew it was madness.

Patti was what the Americans call a 'snowbird'. The moment the London days turned colder at the end of October, she would fly back to Sydney — returning in May, when the British weather was warm again.

Early in our relationship I received word that Julia Pilcher Fortescue (Sasha's godmother) and her husband Seymour were moving to an eighteenth-century house in Barnes. They had a large spare room downstairs. Would I like to live with them? I would. For the next five years I had the security of a home again.

That autumn Patti had routed her flight back to Australia via Hawaii (she was always a great one for lying in the sun), and I was missing her acutely. One night in Barnes the phone rang and Seymour answered.

'Trader, quick! It's Patti. From Honolulu.'

'Hello, darling!' she purred down the phone. 'It's your Foggles, missing you dreadfully.'

We chatted for a few moments, then:

'Darling, could you call me back? This line is phenomenally expensive.'

I did phone her back, and for some minutes we exchanged amorous platitudes.

Several weeks later, Seymour approached me, looking awkward.

'Trader, I feel embarrassed asking you but Julia and I have just received our phone bill. I hate to mention it but that call to Hawaii has cost £300!'

At my advanced age I was beginning to learn that for the illusion we believe to be love there's often a stiff price to pay.

During this period I arranged to go on a Mediterranean cruise with my uncle, Bill Tedcastle, to Dubrovnik, Greece, Turkey, and Venice.

Bill was the youngest brother of my Aunt Lily. I had met him when I first arrived in London from Australia. Uncle Bill was the essence of kindness. Lanky, and with protruding ears, he reminded me — as I often told him — of a benign bandicoot. He'd been a merchant seaman, knew the world, and was a true connoisseur of good living.

The Mediterranean cruise was a fascinating voyage of discovery. How wonderful to have seen those cities and ruins of the ancient world.

Our cruise ship was called the *Liburnia*. One night at sea, I was called to the wireless cabin.

'Mr Faulkner, a Mrs Edwards is calling you from Venice.'

'Hello, Trader,' a familiar voice said when I picked up the phone. 'Darling, I'm really missing you. I'll be waiting to greet you when you dock.'

Venice on our arrival was enjoyed with Patti, always impeccable in some elegant Dior or Balenciaga outfit, accompanied by the casually dressed bandicoot Bill, and me wearing shorts and a battered straw hat — provoking much amused laughter from the Venetians. Patti insisted on paying for all the Gondola trips and sightseeing excursions — including a visit to see Diaghilev's grave, which I wanted to do for Mum. (I felt 'Sheilova' would have wanted that.) Bill and I covered the rest.

One evening, on the way back to our separate hotels, Patti suddenly complained of feeling unwell. After Bill and I arrived at our hotel there came a phone call.

'I'm leaving for London, darling. It's my liver. See you soon. Bye!'
That was Patti, as unpredictable as a child's kite in the wind.

The end of the affair, to quote Graham Greene, was bizarre.

Back in London, after one of our nights together, we had bid one another our usual passionate farewells. But when I rang her hotel the next day she'd apparently gone and had left no forwarding address or contact number. I waited a day more to see if she'd contact me, but then — as we had arranged to meet the following day and there was still no sign of her — I decided to ring her father, the oil magnate Sir Elton Griffin, in Sydney. I dialled and eventually a curt, gruff voice answered.

'Griffin here. Yes?'

I told him I was a friend of Patti's in London and that I was very concerned as Patti seemed to have disappeared.

'What do you mean disappeared? She had dinner last night with my friend Sir Stanley Cock. What're you on about? And just who are you?'

I was out of my depth and hung up as politely as I could.

A week later came a phone call.

'Hello darling. I'm just back from Paris, and I'm dying to see you.'

'So how's Sir Stanley's Cock?' I couldn't resist.

'What're you talking about?'

'We had a date last week, Foggles, but you'd vanished. I was so worried that I rang your father.'

The voice that replied was a Patti I didn't recognise.

'How dare you pry into my private life!'

'We need to talk,' I said.

Over dinner she told me that, feeling unwell, she'd booked out of her hotel, gone to France, and had been back in London for two days. Sir Stanley was an old business friend of her father's who had invited her out. I accepted her story and life returned to its unreal normality. Or so I thought.

Soon after, on the eve of her next departure for Sydney, she was staying at The Ritz. I offered to drive her to Heathrow and suggested meeting for a coffee beforehand. No, she told me, it would be easier if she went to the airport alone. She was leaving the hotel at 11 a.m. I can't remember the exact details now, but we'd had a quarrel over something and I decided to drive to the hotel anyway. Something in her tone seemed far from right and I was determined to resolve this issue before she left, if at all possible.

I drove to the Ritz and, knowing her room number, went straight up and rang the bell.

She opened the door — stark naked. My mouth fell open.

'What the ... ?'

'I'm waiting for my driver, Trader. Now, please go!'

I never saw her again, though several times over the next few years I'd get calls out of the blue.

'Hello darling. It's Foggles. Have you got someone in your life yet?'

'No, Patti. I'm resting.'

'Was I awful to you? Am I impossible?'

'No, dear Patti. You're just not from this planet.'

'Oh darling, I still love you. Bye!'

Late one evening five years later, while on a visit to Sydney, I asked a friend to drive me to the house where Patti had lived in the wealthy Bellevue Hill area. We found it and slowed to a stop. A downstairs light was on and the curtains to the spacious living room were partially drawn. I peeped in. There was Patti, dancing alone. She moved very gracefully. I backed away so as not to frighten her. Then I called out, as gently as I could.

'Foggles! Come and say hello. It's Trader from your past come to visit.'

Suddenly, the lights went out in the room. I waited. Nothing more happened. She had decided obviously to remain in the darkness, excluding me from her fantasy world.

Apparently, Patti died in 2000, having divided the rest of her life between Paris and her Sydney house. I'm told that the Vintage Clothing Shop in Sydney displays a lifetime's collection of her exquisite gowns.

CHAPTER TWENTY-FOUR

TREVOR NUNN, THE RSC, AND FEDERICO GARCÍA LORCA

SOMEONE HAD APPARENTLY seen the double bill at the Gate Theatre in Dublin, as a result of which I was being considered for the RSC. But it hinged on whether I would give an audition for Trevor Nunn, John Barton, and Terry Hands, who would be directing the 1970 season. They wanted to see my range, as I hadn't played any Shakespeare since 1955. As a result of my audition I was hired for the season, though not with the casting I would have wished — Elbow in *Measure for Measure*, Catesby in *Richard III*, and Antonio in *The Two Gentlemen of Verona*.

Nevertheless, the 1970 season at the RSC promised to be a very stimulating one. Trevor Nunn had a team of challenging directors. The guest director for the final production, *A Midsummer Night's Dream*, would be Peter Brook. Also, there was fresh young blood among the acting company: Alan Howard, Helen Mirren (just back from Australia, having made her first film, *Age of Consent*, with director Michael Powell), Ben Kingsley, Patrick Stewart, and many others who would thereafter make their names. Added to this was a list of extremely talented designers and technicians, without whom no production could shine.

For the first read-through of the opening production, *Measure for Measure* (with the wonderful Ian Richardson as Angelo), we all assembled at an RSC rehearsal room in Covent Garden. Trevor Nunn, as artistic director, gave the introductory talk.

'I see this company,' he began, 'as a large Gothic stained glass window — from Chartres Cathedral, for instance, or any stained glass window of medieval genius that you care to name. Every individual piece is a vital component of the whole.'

Ah yes, I thought. I see where you're going with this — but some components of the window, vital as they may be to the creator, are scarcely ever noticed, and for the marginalised actors represented in the analogy such underuse could only mean a long season of unspeakable, soul-destroying boredom.

Nunn's eloquence and enthusiasm had everyone spellbound. Nunn was a product of Cambridge and, like his predecessor Peter Hall, had a good academic mind with the true creative imagination to be a really fine theatre director. But this new wave of university-trained directors needed to gain the practical experience of directing, and, above all, to learn the subtlest and most difficult challenge of all: how to handle actors, especially of the older generation. Insensitive, tyrannical directorial power causes so many problems, and during the 1970 season at the RSC it is fair to say that there was a great deal of bad feeling and unrest in the company.

Measure for Measure and *Richard III* (with Norman Rodway as Richard Crookback) we rehearsed in tandem, as the latter would open a week or so after the former. Both are very long plays, and when *Measure* played on a matinee day and *Richard III* in the evening, in the middle of summer, the hours spent in the hellishly warm theatre were extremely debilitating. More often than not, though, humour kept us sane.

The expected *pièce de resistance* of the season was Trevor Nunn's production of *Hamlet*, with Alan Howard cast as the melancholy Dane and a set designed by Christopher Morley. This consisted of a Venetian blind stretching right across the back of the stage. To underscore the subtext of a scene the blind would turn to represent either a white interior or a black one. However, keeping with the old adage 'whatever can go wrong, will go wrong', on the opening night the blind stuck halfway on its revolve, revealing everyone crossing backstage behind it. But that initial bad luck didn't mar Trevor's concept for a very original production with some wonderfully memorable scenes.

The next play scheduled to go into the repertoire was Robin

Phillips' production of *The Two Gentlemen of Verona* — an amazingly effective updating of the play to modern dress. The highly imaginative Phillips had cast me as Antonio, father to Proteus (one of the two gentlemen, and played by Ian Richardson). My one brief scene had me swimming the length of a luxurious pool. To create this, a module was removed from the stage and a tank filled with water set in its place. Daphne Dare designed a shoulder-to-below-the-thigh 1920s maroon bathing costume, and I decided to play Antonio as Aristotle Onassis. My outrageously wealthy appearance would be supplemented with various accoutrements: gold-rimmed sunglasses, a gold wrist watch, gold bracelet, a gold chain with gold medallion round my neck, and one gold finger ring. Thus attired, I would be divested of my ornate dressing gown and slippers at poolside by my servant Panthino (played by the actor Ted Valentine) and would smoke a cigar as I breaststroked up the pool, wearing a longish grey Onassis wig. The scene, thanks to all who created it, got a thunderous response from my colleagues during rehearsals.

By June, Trevor's 'stained glass window' had started to crack. Members of the cast with very little to do were becoming restless. Then we heard there was talk of dissatisfaction with Phillips' *Two Gents* and that those in control might take the production out of the repertoire before it opened for political reasons. One of the problems was that we never saw our leader, Trevor. To be fair, he had major domestic problems of his own (we had heard that his marriage to Janet Suzman was foundering). Also, he was running a second RSC company in London at the Aldwych. We were beginning to feel neglected, especially those of us with far too little to do. The threat of Robin's production being cancelled caused a great deal of hard feeling in the company and several members even discussed the idea of staging a public protest. As it happened, *The Two Gentlemen of Verona* did in fact open, and that calmed some of the company unrest — but not all of it. As for myself, I was so fed up with my poor casting and the simmering bad feeling in the company that I felt like making some kind of mild protest of my own.

In Nunn's *Hamlet*, I was cast as a sailor who brings letters from

Hamlet to Horatio, played by Terry Taplin (Act IV, Scene 6). I had two lines. To voice in a small way my general displeasure, and to relieve the excruciating boredom of hours spent in the dressing room waiting to go on, I decided to write my exchange with Terry in Spanish, translating Shakespeare's exact words.

First Sailor (me): God bless you, sir. (*Dios te bendiga, Gran Señor.*)

Horatio (Terry): Let him bless thee, too. (*Dios te bendiga tambien.*)

First Sailor: He shall, sir, an't please him. There's a letter for you, sir. It comes from the ambassador that was bound for England, if your name be Horatio, as I'm led to know it is. (*Me bendiga, señor, si le gusta. Hay una carta para usted, señor. Viene del embajador que fue destinado por Inglaterra — si usted se llama Horatio, como lo creo es su nombre.*)

I outlined the plan to Terry who, being a great practical joker, was all for the idea. We learned the lines and during one boiling summer matinee we played the short scene in Spanish. Immediately there was a disturbed ripple in the audience and the sound of students frantically leafing through their texts. As I was playing my Messenger as a captured Spaniard I had no bad conscience about what we were doing. We were, after all, using the bard's actual lines — only in a different language.

The stage manager came to my dressing room at the end of the performance.

'Trader, your scene with Terry ... it sounded different. I was fetching a glass of water and didn't hear it clearly.'

'Better check with Terry,' I said.

He did and we heard no more of it. But Trevor obviously had, and that was the beginning of the end for me with the RSC. Hearing about our tacit protest, and aware of the general unrest in the company, Trevor countered by pinning up a notice for actors on the company board: *Gripe Day: any actor wishing to air grievances is invited to discuss these with Trevor for ten minutes anytime between 10am and 10pm.*

The moment I saw the notice, I put my name at the end of the list. The time I chose was 9.50pm — the last interview slot.

Arriving right on time, in I went.

'Well, Trader,' said Trevor. 'What's your gripe?'

'I don't have a gripe,' I said. 'I have three suggestions.'

'What are they?'

'First, why not let your understudies have a few performances during the season? This company is supposed to be an ensemble, so why not give the understudies a chance to show their potential — if only on Thursday matinees. You told us, Trevor, that everybody in this company was equally important. Why not prove it?'

'Quite impractical,' said Trevor. 'You'd never persuade the stars to agree. What's your second suggestion?'

'Movement classes,' I said. 'At the moment, we all have to be here at ten in the morning to go through a dreary routine of ineffectual geriatric exercises. We need someone to teach us to move properly.'

'I suppose you'd like to see us all doing flamenco?'

'No, but I'd be happy to put you in touch with a friend of mine who could show the company a few of the basics that would help them to move better onstage.'

'Hmm. And your third gripe?'

'We're stuck here for ten months, rehearsing during the day and playing at night. Couldn't some space be provided where the actors could go read a newspaper and relax away from the melée? All we have is that canteen.'

'I'll think about it,' said Trevor.

A couple of days later another notice went up on the board:

'If any company member would care to try their hand directing an in-house production to be offered at the end of the season, please put your name down.'

I did so, immediately. Then thought: what in God's name am I going to do? It was very near the end of the season and I had a fortnight to think of something. That night I was dining with two friends — Welford-on-Avon residents who were interested in the arts, Edward and Pod Rutherford.

'Lorca!' Ed suddenly said. 'You know something about him. Why not put something together?'

It was an inspired idea.

The next day I approached Ben Kingsley, perfect casting for Lorca, to see if he'd be interested. Ben knew about Lorca, but as a leading player felt he'd be sticking his neck out. I got Ben and Mike Tubbs (one of the musical directors) round a piano and gave Mike my copy of Lorca's complete works, which had his songs and the music at the back. He started to play one of Lorca's lullabies, then went on to play several other pieces.

'Trader,' said Ben, 'this is fabulous stuff! I never knew Lorca was a musician.'

Ben also sang and played the guitar, which was another reason I wanted him as my Lorca. I remember Mike putting the song 'La Tarara' into Ben's key on the piano. The result was thrilling.

I wanted Alan Howard onboard to do all four parts of *Lament for the Death of a Matador*. Alan could project a cold metallic quality that would be ideal for the piece. Would he join us? He said he'd think about it.

Ben thought of Helen Mirren and said he'd have a word with her. She liked the idea, and agreed to be a part of it. Then two more mates in the company, Terry Taplin and Sheila Burrell, were approached.

'Yes, Trade, we'll back you. Just tell us what you want us to do.'

There was a young girl in the company, Celia Quick — a sensitive, very reserved girl of whom no one seemed to take much notice. I approached her and asked if she would sing a couple of the Lorca songs. Yes, she would. Her quality singing of Lorca's 'Popular Songs' held the audience spellbound on the night. (Sadly, after that season I never heard of Celia again.)

I now had the perfect cast. Jeremy Sinden (who died tragically very young just when he was making his name as an actor), an assistant stage manager in the company, volunteered to be my stage manager. I wish I could give credit to the other staff who volunteered to help but alas their names are lost to me and I cannot find them in the programmes. Needless to say, my sound engineer designed a superb 'Spanish' soundtrack that perfectly matched the visual effect that we were conveying. Next the wardrobe department got wind of it. They volunteered to get white waiters' jackets from the theatre restaurant, black tight-waisted trousers with scarlet cummerbunds, and black boots to give a final authentic touch. They also made us beautiful black *sombreros Cordobés*, those typical flat-brimmed Andalusian hats. They dressed Helen Mirren to resemble a girl from Seville. She looked so sexy we felt a black wig over her fair hair would add nothing and left her with her natural tresses.

We rehearsed in every spare moment, for the season was almost over and time was against us. At one point, I drove up to London and collected my Spanish chairs, flamenco posters, shawls, fans, and so on.

The performance was to be given in the tiny circular 'folly' in the Bancroft Gardens, between the theatre and the church where Shakespeare is buried. Alan Howard and Sheila Burrell danced a very sexy Cuban rumba; Ben did excerpts of Lorca. Helen acted a poem wherein a lover calls to her beloved who has died (with me playing the voice of the lover, calling back from the grave). Celia Quick sang some of the 'Popular Songs'; Terry Taplin recited some of the poems. Alan Howard was an Andalusian horseman who came into a bar to recount the death of the Matador, Ignacio Sanchez Mejias. My job was to present the entertainment, link it all together, do some of the prose and the poems — both in English and in Spanish — and, of course, to dance. The performance was timed for ninety minutes. The little circular folly was packed.

The ninety minutes went through non-stop like a Bondi tram down a steep incline. Throughout the audience sat pin-still. At the end they simply exploded. We had made it, and were accepted absolutely — thanks to the genius of García Lorca, and to the skills of a team of actors and technicians second to none. I will always remember Susan Fleetwood (Terry Hands' girlfriend at the time) rushing up and flinging her arms round me. She said nothing, but simply hugged me very tightly.

Where was Trevor Nunn? Predictably he didn't attend. But the other two in the triumvirate, John Barton and Terry Hands, did, and were extremely complimentary. Seizing the moment, I suggested to Barton that the RSC might consider this Lorca for its 'Theatre Go Round' to go out on the road to schools and young audiences.

'Oh,' he said evasively, 'it would need a lot of work.'

'Of course,' I replied. 'What initial concept doesn't?'

I heard no more about it.

A few days later when I received my weekly salary packet the payment had been reduced to £5 — I'd been charged for the costumes!

Not long after, I received a letter informing me I would not be required for next year's company.

I didn't see Trevor again until some years later. Seymour Fortescue had invited me to a preview of a new RSC production at the Barbican. During the interval I was on my own at the bar when suddenly an affectionate arm slid round my shoulder. Turning, I found myself nose to nose with Trevor. I can't imagine what subconscious impulse prompted my response. I knew that he and Janet Suzman had a son, Joshua. I simply said. 'Hello, Trevor. How's Joshua?'

I was so surprised by his show of affection that asking about his son was simply an instinctive response. This intimacy caused him to shoot back across the room as though a Florida hurricane had driven him away. I suppose he felt my mentioning of his son was somehow an invasion of his privacy.

That was the last I ever saw of him. I regret still that we never really worked together. I admire his work as a theatre and opera director. He and Peter Hall have followed similar career paths, and when you're in those powerful positions no consideration can be given to secondary issues like friendship or loyalty.

One night, just before the end of the 1970 RSC season, I was walking late down the Stratford high street when a voice called my name. It was John Goodwin, who had been head of press and publicity at Stratford since 1948, and who would continue in that position into the 1970s with the RSC, after which he left to run the publicity department of the National Theatre in London (for Peter Hall). As we stood chatting in the street, he said:

'We both work here, but I hardly ever see you. Nor did I fifteen years ago during the 1955 season. I tell you what, come and have supper!'

I did, and from that point on both he and his wife (the author Suzanne Ebel) became very close friends. Much later, in the 90s, John would become a collaborator on the project with which my life's work as a performer would end — a story that will be told in its proper place.

CHAPTER TWENTY-FIVE

DEBUSSY, DERVISHES, AND A DAUGHTER REGAINED

Two Gents AT Stratford had been such a popular production that it transferred to the Aldwych in the West End, which gave me several more months of employment.

On the London opening night it was snowing outside, and when I dipped into the pool for Antonio's nightly lap the water was icy and for a moment quite took my breath away. I managed to breaststroke across to the other end with my cigar as the audience roared with laughter at my obvious discomfort. In a pique, as Ted Valentine helped me out at the other end, I gave the water an almighty kick, spraying the front rows of the stalls and prompting shrieks from the startled public. Once offstage I complained to the stage management and was promised that steps would be taken to warm the pool water for the following evening.

The next night as my robe was removed I could see steam rising from my pool. In I went — but, dear God! This time it was too hot! Ted Valentine later said that I instantly turned the colour of a beetroot. The audience went wild again over my discomfort, and again I gave them an angry splash as I emerged.

The stage management was informed once more of the problem, and on the third night — finally — all was well. At last I had a pool wherein I could comfortably swim.

That engagement was followed with an appearance in a tour of Arthur Miller's *The Price*, playing the old Jew Gregory Solomon.

The other cast members were Marika Mann playing Esther, Dermot Tuohy as Victor, and Ed Bishop as Walter. The production played at the Northcott Theatre, Exeter, the Nuffield Theatre, Southampton, the Old Market Playhouse in Shaftesbury (Dorset), and the Ashcroft Theatre, Croydon.

In 1972, I appeared onstage only once, in a limited run of *The Aspern Papers* (adapted from the Henry James novel by Michael Redgrave) at the Theatre Royal, Windsor, playing the role of Pasquale. Apart from that, regular sessions teaching flamenco, movement and acting at Letty Littlewood's dance school in Wimbledon, and sporadic appearances in television dramas and on BBC Radio, filled out my employment schedule for the year. There were, however, long periods when there was no work, and my soul was filled with despair and a sense of failure.

To add fuel to my depression the only other great event of 1972 was the finalising of the divorce petition in the courts, so that my marriage with Bobo was finally and legally terminated. Of course, I had never got over the loss of my daughter, and of the opportunity to watch her grow and to be a part of her life. For five long years I was granted only occasional opportunities to share tentative and ultimately unsatisfactory conversations with her via long distance, and to pore over the photographs that Bobo would periodically send. In her little girl's voice I could sense her unwillingness to talk to me over the phone. Who was this man, after all, that she could now hardly even remember?

One summer Sunday in the early 1970s, while I was living with Seymour and Julia Fortescue in Barnes, they hosted an elaborate picnic lunch in the garden. Next door to the Fortescues at that time lived Robert Andrew Carnegie, 13th Earl of Northesk. I remember that on that afternoon the Earl's daughter arrived with a woman friend in her thirties who immediately took my fancy. That feeling might have been mutual, for she soon sat beside me and we started to chat. She seemed a sensitive, intelligent girl, and I instinctively liked her. What attracted me to her most was her vulnerability and her natural charm. She was interested in the fact that my mother had danced with Pavlova but also in what Pavlova had taught her. She was self-effacing, but asked very intelligent questions, such as where does an actor draw the line between technique and genuine emotion? My lasting impression of her was of a woman whose beauty might be fading, but who still had a girlish quality about her, with a genuine interest in *you* and an obvious thirst for knowledge of all kinds. Discussing my friendship with Vivien Leigh, she wanted to know if I thought Vivien was a woman who might have taken on challenges beyond her strength?

'Yes, certainly she did,' I replied. 'And paid a heavy price for doing so.'

'You mean her playing Blanche in *A Streetcar Named Desire?*'

'Exactly,' I said, impressed by her instinctive understanding.

While we chatted, I noticed that Seymour was moving around the garden taking photos of the two of us. When I caught his eye, he smiled and winked at me. I hadn't a clue what he was on about.

Later, when the Earl's daughter and her friend had gone, Seymour, in the midst of several amused guests, asked me:

'Do you know who it was that was so engrossing you in conversation?'

'I've no idea,' I told him.

'It was Christine Keeler, of the Profumo scandal.'

I was stunned.

Regardless of her sensational past, the Christine Keeler I met so briefly that afternoon has left a positive and lasting impression with me. Her interest in the people about whom we spoke was genuine and, more important, searching. There was obviously so much more to this girl than the scandal that had made her infamous. Truly, I was glad to have had the chance to know her, even so slightly, and have never forgotten our conversation.

One day I found myself being squeezed together with a very attractive young lady in a turnstile at Green Park tube station. The girl was in a hurry so, as I put my ticket into the slot, we both went through sandwiched as one. The girl was puce with embarrassment and profuse with French apologies.

'Where are you from?' I asked, somewhat breathless.

'Brussels.'

'After such an ordeal I could do with a coffee,' I told her. 'Will you join me?'

'Thank you, I will.'

Over cappuccinos at Fortnum and Mason we exchanged identities and discovered a mutual admiration for French music.

'Do you know Fauré's *The Dolly Suite*?' she asked me.

I told her I did, and that I liked it because I felt it had been written for children without being in any way sentimental. The girl, whose name was Ariane Dandoy, told me that as it happened she was going that evening to a lecture at the French Institute given by the very old lady for whom Fauré had written the piece, Hélène 'Dolly' Bardac.

This was in the days before mobile phones. Ariane asked to be excused for a moment, returning shortly after to ask if I'd like to attend Dolly Bardac's talk with her.

Thus began two long and very close friendships.

The couple who invited me to the talk — thanks to Ariane's phone call — was a young newly married pair from Paris, Michel and Brigitte Murat. They were then living in London, both teaching French (as I remember, Michel was on the staff of the French Lycée here). My own French schooling in Sydney had been limited to basic grammar and literature so when I met the Murats they immediately offered to give me conversation lessons. As they only lived round the corner from me, we met frequently thereafter and our friendship grew.

But to return to the night of the turnstile collision.

Apparently, there was a close connection between Brigitte Murat's family and her Aunt Dolly, the lecturer at the French Insititute whom I had the great good fortune to meet afterwards.

Aunt Dolly turned out to be the daughter of Emma Bardac, a singer and the attractive young wife of a wealthy Jewish financier. Emma's composer lover Gabriel Fauré had written *The Dolly Suite* for her daughter Dolly. At some point thereafter Fauré had introduced Emma to his friend Claude Achille Debussy. Their mutual attraction was so immediate and so stong, apparently, that in 1904 Emma Bardac cast off both her husband and Fauré and eloped with the already married

Debussy — becoming his second wife after a scandalous divorce. They had one daughter, Chou Chou, who died very young.

The lecture that Aunt Dolly gave that night at *L'Institute Française* was riveting. She spoke of the hours she and her stepsister Chou Chou had spent playing together, and of her kindly step-papa Debussy, as though he and his beloved daughter had died just a few years previously.

Meeting and talking with this old lady was one of the truly remarkable experiences of my life. Her stories of Paris during the *belle époque* fascinated me. But one story I found particularly intriguing.

When Debussy died in 1918 he was buried at Père Lachaise — the legendary cemetery in north-east Paris where so many great French artists lie entombed in glory. But Emma Bardac then decided she wanted her beloved Claude Achille closer to her previous composer lover, Fauré, who was buried in the tiny cemetery at Passy. Was this, I wonder, a touching romantic gesture? Or was it simply to make it easier for her to visit them both on the same day? Aunt Dolly never said, or didn't know, the reason for Emma's bizarre idea. Whatever it was, Debussy's body was indeed exhumed and transported across Paris to join his old rival in love in Passy.

Now, I've always admired Debussy's music so some years later, in 1990, when I was in Paris to visit the Murats, I went to Passy to look Debussy's grave up. Fauré's tomb was easily located, but there was no sign of Debussy. I went to the gatehouse and spoke to the porter.

'Monsieur, please, I'm looking for the grave of Debussy and can't find it.'

He told me where it was, but added, 'You won't see much. Just a mound covered by corrugated iron.'

Back I went and what I found was hard to credit. No cross — not even his name marked his grave.

At supper that night with the Murats, I told them of what I had seen.

'Why don't you have a bit of fun?' they responded. 'When you're back in London, get hold of some impressive official notepaper and write to Chirac. He'd flip his lid if he knew Debussy was so neglected.'

At that time Jacques Chirac was Mayor of Paris and not yet President of France.

Back in London I did exactly what Brigitte and Michel had suggested. Soon a beautifully typed letter on handsomely-headed National Theatre notepaper — kindly supplied by John Goodwin — was winging its way to *Le Maire*.

A week or so later I received acknowledgement from a Jean-Paul Bolufer in *Le Cabinet du Maire*. Along with some elegant Gallic compliments he wrote: *You have done well to call the attention of the Mayor of Paris to the abandoned state of the Sepulchre of Claude Achille Debussy. Your comments have been relayed to the relevant service in the Mairie.*

I heard nothing more for a year. Then Brigitte Murat called from Paris.

'You won't believe this,' she said. 'Our plan has paid off. Chirac has finally done something about Debussy. His face is on the new twenty-franc note!'

I doubted this was due to my letter.

'We'd only know for certain if something has also been done about the grave,' I said. 'Do go to Passy and take a gander.'

A few days later I received another call.

'Trader, it's amazing! A simple tomb of jade-coloured marble. Claude Achille must be wearing a celestial grin. It's the classiest grave in Passy!'

To return to 1973, I had fallen very much in love with Ariane — the girl from the turnstile sandwich. But Ariane lived and worked in Brussels. I was welcome to go and stay with her anytime I wanted. However, demoralised by my divorce, the loss of my daughter, and with my career at its lowest ebb, I felt I daren't leave London to share the intimate weekends with Ariane I so longed for. What's more, I had auditioned for a part in a play due to be presented in Sydney. If this materialised, I'd be able to see Sasha regularly and build a proper paternal relationship with her. Unfortunately, though, the chance to play in Sydney fell through and I remained stuck in London.

During this time, Ariane — fed up with my vacillations — had fallen in love with a British concert pianist and shortly afterwards married him. Now she lives happily in the Midlands with her family. For many years we remained in friendly contact, but, alas, the demands of family, work and life eventually drew us apart.

Nevertheless, it is to her that I owe my valued friendship with the Murats, which continues to this very day.

Also in 1973, while I was still living with Julia and Seymour Fortescue in Barnes, my daughter came for a short visit from Sydney. Bobo allowed her to spend the night in Barnes and I remember Sasha slept in my bed and I on the floor. It was absolute magic to be near her again, if only for a few hours. Bobo and Ralph Rosenblum (her new husband) were staying in a hotel in Knightsbridge.

I had two unforgettable days with my 'Sam Lamb', teaching her to swim in Seymour's new pool. We laughed together as I coached her — the last few moments I was able to share with Sasha as a child.

Bobo and Ralph came to lunch at Julia and Seymour's to collect her. When it was time to go I accompanied them out to the street. Stopping on the footpath, I gave Sasha a big hug and kiss as Bobo and Ralph walked slowly to the car. Then, as Sasha joined her mother, Ralph ambled back to me.

'Trader,' he said in a low voice, 'from now on you can forget about Sasha. I'm her father now.'

I've never known what supernatural force it was that stopped me from striking him down, right there on that pathway.

1973 was the seven-hundredth anniversary of the Whirling Dervishes of Konya, in southern Turkey. Remembering my mother's love of Arabic dance and her own study of the *Ouled Nails* in Tunisia, it occurred to me that I might undertake a similar trip, to research and to write an article about this ancient Islamic cult.

I bought my ticket and made my way to Konya via Istanbul, arriving there on the day of the ceremony, which was held in an enormous Islamic auditorium with one very tiny entrance. We were packed tightly into a vast hall, hung all round with draperies.

The music started and what followed was an amazing display.

Since then (now forty years ago) the dervishes have often been filmed and televised, but I was privileged to see them performing in their original environment, and I've often thought it's a pity we don't use dance in our own religious rituals.

Through their sustained whirling the Dervishes relinquish the earthly life, to be reborn in mystical union with God. The ceremony closes with a prayer for the peace of the souls of all the Prophets and of all believers. All is silent save the solo voice, vibrant and passionate, of the *hafiz* as he intones verses from the Koran.

I feel it is very important to know something about — and to feel tolerance for — all the spiritual beliefs of our world, whatever they may be. As a Christian observing this ancient Sufi ritual I was very impressed by this celebration of Islamic faith. Having spent much of my professional life studying complex flamenco dance rhythms, I was fascinated not only by the dancing itself, but also with the combined use of dance and music and spoken word in the symbolic representation of life, death, and rebirth.

Watching the Dervishes performing their mystic ritual markedly influenced my later work as an actor and director. This was especially true when putting together my one-man evocation of the Spanish poet-dramatist Federico García Lorca a few years later.

One sad postscript to that experience, which was in all other ways a pure Turkish delight. Returning on a crowded bus to Istanbul I allowed myself to doze off in the heat, only to awaken suddenly to find myself being scowled at by the young Muslim in the seat in front of me who had swivelled round to face me.

'Bloody Chreestian?'

I nodded, wondering where this was leading. His face darkened even further. I have never seen such venomous hatred. His eyes shone like black seeds.

'I hate you, bastard English. Christian pig!'

I bit my tongue and held his gaze until, at last, he shook his head and turned to the front again.

I know now, and knew then, that this was simply an unlucky encounter with a kind of blinkered religious fanaticism that fortunately few people of any religion embrace. I have a great fondness for Turkey, many delightful Turkish friends, and a great respect for their revered faith of Islam. What shook me about that experience was seeing at such close range the darkly malevolent power that had been unleashed within that poor boy through blind hatred and misguided fanaticism — a phenomenon that was sadly to become increasingly more common and widespread round the world over the coming years.

Once back in London, I wrote my article on the Dervishes and, using my mother's dancing connections, managed to get it published by *The Dancing Times* (December, 1973) and later by *Europa* magazine — a modest start in journalism, but a start nonetheless. Over the years I was to use this new means of self-employment often when nothing else was happening.

Not long after my return from Turkey, while I was living temporarily at Pax between tenants, Bobo rang to say she was coming to afternoon tea with Ralph the following afternoon.

The next day they arrived in a white Rolls Royce. From Bobo's slender wrist dangled a collection of expensive gold bracelets.

I have never in all my years felt quite so disorientated. The last time we had been together in that house was the day she flew off to Australia with Sasha.

My memories of Sasha during that period are fragmentary but vivid. I realised very quickly on seeing her again how vital it was not to rock the boat. Sasha had a stepbrother and sister now, whom I later met — Philip and Nicky — and to both of whom she is devoted.

Sometime in the early 70s I had had occasion to work with Dame Judi Dench when the two of us did a joint reading for BBC Radio of Jean Rhys's postcolonial novel, *The Wide Sargasso Sea*, which has parallel first-person male and female narrators. It was a pleasant job, and during the work Judi and I became friends.

After the recording we didn't see one another for a time until — on one of the few occasions Sasha was over from Australia — I rang her, as she had always expressed an interest in meeting my daughter if that were ever possible. Judi immediately invited us to go boating in Regent's Park, and brought with her her own daughter Finti, who was a year or so younger than Sasha. It turned out to be ice creams all round and an afternoon never to be forgotten. As a keepsake, Judi gave Sasha a glass bottle filled with different layers of blue sand on a piece of blue cord, which I know she still treasures.

Judi had told me she believed that a child should have unforgettable happy memories. She certainly went out of her way that day to gift Sasha with one, and to unite us unforgettably as father and daughter — if only for an afternoon.

Many years later, when Sasha herself was a mother, she sent me her baby daughter Eliza's copy of an Angelina Ballerina book, asking if I could possibly beg Judi's autograph for it. I sent it to her. Back it came beautifully inscribed, and is still treasured by nine-year-old Eliza.

The next time I saw Sasha, Bobo and Ralph had brought her to London to arrange for her schooling in England, as they were leaving Australia. I was to pick Sasha up at their hotel and take her to lunch. In this period I had started to sport a ridiculous hairpiece that made me look like a poor man's Melvin Bragg. Wanting to look my best, I checked myself carefully in the mirror before I left.

'Yes, Dad,' I thought. 'I'm sure you'll impress.'

We met in Sloane Street and off we sauntered arm-in-arm. There was a vicious wind blowing. I was deep in conversation with Sasha when a sudden, violent gust blew the toupé clean off my head, over a tall iron railing fence and into a secluded garden.

'Oh, Daddy! No!'

Needless to say, I was distraught. Meanwhile the hairpiece, like some furry animal freed from its cage, was flitting over the tops of various shrubs and bushes until a gardener thought to prong it quickly with his fork. As he examined it, mystified, I yelled: 'Please, it's mine. Can I have it back?'

'No, Daddy. Please,' said Sasha. 'Leave it. It looks awful.'

The gardener handed me the hairpiece with great dignity over the railings. I quickly put it on and clipped it tight.

Sasha turned to examine me.

'Daddy, it's back to front!'

Fortunately, I was quickly forgiven. Thank God, Sasha's sense of humour prevailed.

The tragedy of our relationship is that all through her life I have only seen her for stretches of a few hours at a time, and almost always with others present. In the brief period she was at boarding school in England, I seldom saw her. Once, when the school holidays started, I bought her a new bicycle. I painted her name on it, left it at her front door, rang the bell and hid nearby. She opened the door, saw the bicycle and ran her fingers lovingly over the frame, gazing at it. Then she saw me and threw her arms round me. But she said very little.

'Maybe we could ride together?' I suggested. 'There's so much to show you round here.'

Sadly, that never happened.

PART
THREE

THE
LATER YEARS

CHAPTER TWENTY-SIX

TRANSLATIONS, TORRID ROMANCE, AND TRAVEL

APART FROM BRIEF APPEARANCES in various television series and mini-series, and sporadic jobs with BBC Radio, between 1973 and 1975 my days were mostly taken up with writing translations of various Spanish plays into English, starting with Lorca's 1933 play *Bodas de Sangre* (*Blood Wedding*), then moving on to a second Lorca play, *Asi Que Pasen Cinco Años* (which I translated as *In Five Years' Time*), and then to Antonio Buero Vallejo's *En El Ardiente Oscuridad* (*In the Burning Darkness*). These translations were undertaken on spec, simply because I believed in the plays and felt that they should be presented in English. Having found no suitable translations already made, I decided to undertake them myself, thereby learning an enormous amount about the process of finding the right words and images in English to exactly mirror the author's original intentions. Apart from my translation of the Alejandro Casona play *The Cudgelled Cuckold* (which I had directed at the Lyric in Belfast), and of Lorca's *Blood Wedding*, none of my other translations ever saw production. But at least I had learned a lot in writing them — lessons that would prove useful to me when I was creating my Lorca evocation in the early eighties.

In 1974, I finally left the comfortable life I had enjoyed for several years with the Fortescues (Julia and Seymour) and moved back into Pax. My intention was to eventually sell it, but the actual sale was not to come about for two years. In the meantime I settled myself there, tended the back garden, carried on with my translation work, and did my odd jobs in radio and television. In 1974, the BBC again offered me a place with their Radio Rep company that guaranteed me a regular income, so life was not as precarious as it had been over the previous few years.

Julia Stonor, a very generous friend of this period who used to give hilarious dinner parties, invited me to one one evening at which she sat me beside a young buxom blonde who simply bubbled over with natural charm. Her name was Harriet Bligh. Harriet was a descendant of the famous Captain Bligh of HMS *Bounty*, but as I was soon to learn there was much more to 'Hattie', as I called her, than just her famous antecedent. Shortly after we met I invented a nickname for her, 'Tumplemouse', because she seemed to exemplify for me an adorably cuddly creature of that nomination. Among her many charms was a richly ribald sense of humour. For the brief time we were lovers we always made merry. She came to Pax and ran my house beautifully. Our life together was filled with lovemaking, laughter, and a shared interest in the Arts. Hattie worked in an art shop, and there was something elusively aristocratic about this girl, who could match any Aussie for vulgarity and bad language and yet deliver it all with such style. She must have been about twenty-five. I was forty-seven, and she made me feel twenty years younger.

One day a letter arrived addressed to 'Lady Harriet Darnley'.

Hattie was in the kitchen cooking breakfast when I brought it in.

'Don't tell me you're Lady Darnley.'

'Yes,' said Hattie, 'I think we inherited it sometime around 1700.'

I was gobsmacked.

'Well, if ever I had to define an aristocratic manner, Tump, it would be yours.'

'Yes, and so what? It's no big deal — someone's got to be a bloody aristo. It was an accident of birth. It's nothing to do with me.'

What an unpretentious girl she was — fun, and young, and completely sympathetic to my flamenco dancing and my interest in Lorca.

'You'll have to meet my mother,' she said one day. 'I'm sure she'll loathe you. She's a terrible snob, but she is my mother and I love her.'

'Mother' lived at Meadow House in Kent. Down we drove. On our introduction, one glance at me from Lady Darnley and it was hate at first sight. I have seldom felt on the receiving end of such intense loathing. But I felt secure all the same, knowing our love was unshakeable.

After dinner Hattie insisted I dance flamenco to entertain them. I knew this was the final coffin nail, but I couldn't have cared less. I pounded away on Lady Darnley's wooden floor with all the passion I felt for Hattie. Hattie's applause was thunderous. Lady Darnley's and her male friend's was polite and muted.

We arrived back at Pax with Hattie in tears.

'Oh, darling Trader, Mum loathes you! "Common spittle" she called you! How could she?'

'Because like all loving parents she wants you to make a good marriage, and I'm clearly a very nasty threat.'

Despite her mother's rancour, we continued our passionate, hilarious love affair. I knew that our relationship was to my advantage, not Hattie's, but I selfishly decided to let it drift on — and it did for several more months.

Then one afternoon Hattie arrived with sixteen large hatboxes.

'I'm leaving you, darling Caliban. My mother has won. She's just too strong.'

Sobbing, Hattie packed, and was gone.

Some years later I passed her on the pavement in Soho with a man I took to be her husband and two small children. I think she saw me, but she gave no sign of recognition. Then I had news of her through a mutual friend who confirmed for me that she had two children. I would have loved to renew our friendship, but she obviously felt otherwise, and I decided that now it was better to simply put Hattie right out of my mind.

1975 and 1976 were years of travel. Trafford Whitelock, a close friend of my mother's in the 1930s and 40s and a well-known producer for BBC Radio in the 1950s and 60s, invited me to go with him to Moscow and Leningrad. This was in the period before there was any let-up from Stalin's baleful influence.

In July 1975 we flew to Moscow, which was just as I had imagined — imposing and sinister. From the moment we arrived I sensed we were being watched. I was surprised by how little traffic there was, and how few people there were on the pavements compared with London. Everything was sombre and silent — the church of St Basil, the Kremlin behind its long forbidding wall. Then a walk to see Stalin's tomb. We lined up in an endless queue. An official inspected us, reaching out to tighten my tie as he mumbled something in Russian. (Probably, 'To pay proper respect to Comrade Stalin you must be dressed absolutely correctly!')

Moscow filled me with depression. It seemed a godless place. We went to Moscow's department store, Gum. I suddenly felt so lucky to be living in the West. We caught the night train to Leningrad (now St Petersburg again).

What a beautiful city. We stayed in a hotel directly opposite the famous Russian cruiser *Aurora*, which fired the first shots in the Bolshevik Revolution.

Was Leningrad now a better, happier, more prosperous city than before the revolution? Possibly, for a select few party members. But for me, I simply felt a sense of stagnant decay and repression. I never heard the laughter of children or saw any playing. There was such a feeling of invisible control that it stifled my appreciation of the superb treasures of Peter the Great and the Empress Catherine.

Still, the Hermitage Museum had paintings and an art collection that would take an eternity to digest. Leningrad/St Petersburg symbolises the very soul and spirit of the Russian people. The place echoes with all the stories one has heard of the Tsars and the boyars, of Rasputin and his demise in the freezing Neva, of the finest composers and literary figures that Russia has produced. Everywhere in the city, I sensed its history being kept alive through its art and its artists.

Trafford and I went to the Mariinsky Theatre to see *The Nutcracker*. It was interesting to see this ballet in the very theatre in which so much of what we know of classical ballet began — thanks to Sergei Diaghilev. Both at the ballet, and in the Hermitage museum, I knew I was wallowing in the very best of Russia, something that politics couldn't tarnish.

One evening while in St Petersburg Trafford and I were invited to a reception for a film company shooting *The Blue Bird*, a US/USSR co-production. We rode up in a lift, the doors opened and we were ushered into a crowded ballroom where there was a milling mass of people, some talking English, some Russian. Trafford set off towards the refreshments table. I saw a chair and sat down. A beautiful woman was sitting beside me. It was Elizabeth Taylor. I introduced myself and told her of my brief friendship with Richard Burton. She told me that her life with Richard could best be described as 'the agony and the ecstasy … but in reverse, of course'. I shall always remember her words: 'What a wonderful gift, free will, but what a price we pay for it!'

I remember little else, except that she seemed completely unaffected and very warm. When Trafford appeared with our drinks, he asked if I'd introduce him, but by this time she was surrounded by people and it was impossible.

Watching her chatting amiably with her friends, I remembered that when my old sparring partner Laurence Harvey was dying of cancer two years before she had not only visited him in hospital but had got into bed beside him and cradled him in her arms to comfort him.

Later in the summer of 1975, after a brief trip to Rome, I was pleased to be able to offer my assistance to my friends Julia and Seymour Fortescue. They had bought a house in Barjémon in the south of France and were moving a vanload of furniture down there.

Then, in 1976, I went off to the English Theatre in Vienna for a few weeks to play Bernard Kersal in Somerset Maugham's *The Constant Wife* — thereby experiencing at first hand the special Viennese ambiance that had been so vividly described to me by the Nossal family in wartime Sydney all those years before.

Back home again, it was time to put my plan to move into action. I spent the next few months readying the house for its sale, and looking around in various corners of west London for a smaller and more suitable residence for myself. Finally I was called to look at a flat on the top floor of a wonderful run of Victorian terraced houses in Lexham Gardens, off the Cromwell Road and not far from Earl's Court tube station. I went along, climbed the ninety-eight stairs to the top floor (there was, and still is, no lift), and was let into a marvellous, well-lit flat with two bedrooms, a reasonably sized sitting room, and an adequate kitchen and bath — with the added bonus of access to a roof for sunbathing, and narrow balconies looking east and west over the city at the front and back of the flat. I was entranced and made an offer immediately, which was soon accepted. Fortunately, a buyer for Pax was already waiting in the wings and in December 1976 I finally found myself settled in my new flat, where I have been ever since.

I immediately launched into two other translations of Spanish plays into English: *El Sueño De La Razón* (*While Reason Sleeps*) by Antonio Buero Vallejo, and Ramón Maria del Valle Inclán's *Divinas Palabras* (*Divine Words*) — the latter done on behalf of the National Theatre for Victor García's 1977 Spanish language production there (as a translation available via earpieces during the performances). The reviews of the production, which starred Nuria Espert, were not as I remember unanimously favourable and for the most part the audiences were mystified. Nevertheless, my translation was published later that year by Heinemann and the entire edition sold out.

One day I received a phone call from Dame Margot Fonteyn, inviting me to dinner. I had no idea she knew of me and felt very flattered to be invited to her flat in Knightsbridge. Apparently, she knew of my mother and of my reputation as a flamenco dancer, and was curious why a 'British' actor would want to attempt it. Over dinner I told her why, pointing out that how an actor moves is as important as his voice in establishing a character. She asked if I would show her a few steps of flamenco and teach her one *copla* (verse) of *Sevillianas*. The latter is danced with both partners (either of mixed sexes or the same) exactly mirroring one another's moves. Showing Margot the basics of flamenco and of Seville's national dance was a delight for me. This superb ballerina was so intuitive. I would do a step, she would follow, then I would partner her and hum the music. It was an extraordinary experience. She let me lead, and followed me instinctively. Margot's discipline and her life dedicated to dance helped her to absorb the Spanish footwork rapidly. Watching her perform the steps and body movements that I showed her made me realise why she was such a superb artist. It wasn't so much what she was doing, but the way that she was transforming it into her own unique style. It was a meeting that I would never forget.

Also in 1977 I struck up a close friendship with a very generous couple, Juan and Lolo de Lara. Juan was from a rich family in Santo Domingo, and Lolo was an American from Boston. Juan taught Spanish at Columbia University in New York. Lolo was a devotee of the Jewish philosopher Martin Buber and was into Theism. This leisured couple seemed to divide each year between New York, Santo Domingo, and London, where they rented a flat in Chelsea and gave delightful, intimate dinner parties.

One night Juan told us that they had decided to take a trip through Spain by car, but as neither drove they needed to find someone to be their chauffeur. Lolo suggested that I might undertake the job. All expenses would be paid, and we'd be staying in luxury hotels. The journey was to last a month. I was booked to do a television play that would finish just before they planned to set off. The offer seemed somehow preordained. I told them I would be happy to be their companion and chauffeur. When my television work was done I met them in Barcelona, we hired a car and away we went.

Juan's planned itinerary was impressive: Lérida, Sarragosa, Burgos, then Santander, Oviedo, La Coruña, Santiago de Compostela, León, Zamora, and Salamanca. Madrid was to be our last stop. As I knew only the southern half of Spain at that point, this was to fulfil for me a long-held desire.

I found the driving not too strenuous, though it had been a while since I had spent much time behind the wheel. (Several years before, in a desperate hurry to get to the BBC one morning, I had jumped into my old Morris 1100 and fallen straight through its rusted floor onto the road, after which we had parted company. Ever since then I have relied on my trusty 1968 pushbike.) Fortunately, even driving through Spain on the unfamiliar right-hand side of the road, my instincts didn't let me down.

The first stage of our trip was from Barcelona to Lérida (the birthplace of the composer Enrique Granados). However, we sped right on through Lérida, so I neither learnt nor saw anything. This, I soon discovered, was to be the pattern for the trip.

On we drove to Saragossa, where the film director Luis Buñuel had been educated by the Jesuits — an education he later savagely parodied in his film *Viridiana*. I asked my hosts if we could stop off in the nearby town of Callanda, where Buñuel was born. I was interested in Buñuel's life, as I had translated the dialogue of six of Buñuel's films that had been shown with my earphone commentary at the National Film Theatre in London in the 1960s. I wanted to talk to someone there who might be able to offer me an insight into what influenced Buñuel's work.

'No, no,' I was told again. 'We must press on.'

Our destination that day was a luxury hotel in Burgos. What could be the attraction there, I wondered, that required such haste? I never found out. Nevertheless, the chance to dine and sleep in luxury hotels made the trip bearable for me — except that Lolo was a terrible back-seat driver.

'Trader, you're driving too fast! Be careful! You're driving very close to the curb! We'll have an accident!'

At one point I stopped the car and invited her to drive. Tactfully, I tried to make her realise that you don't tell a driver how to drive, and that if she wanted to hire a proper chauffeur she could do so when we reached Burgos and I would make my own way back to London. No more was said. I drove in peace for the rest of the trip.

That drive through northern Spain was a revelation to me. Every region of the Iberian Peninsula is like a different country, with its own unique folk traditions, customs and way of life.

The jewel in the crown of our tour was Santiago de Compostela, with its Romanesque/Baroque cathedral where the body of St James was laid to rest in the ninth century. My interest in Santiago was intensified because the playwright Ramón Maria del Valle Inclán is buried in the Boysaca cemetery there. I wanted to pay that old literary eccentric my respects.

Why on earth, Lolo wanted to know, did I want to do that? I explained to them that it was Valle Inclan's play *Divinas Palabras* that I had just translated, and which had been published by Heinemann. Impressed, they allowed my visit.

Our journey across the Iberian peninsula brought us first to León, where we arrived in early morning sunlight to see its dazzling reflection on the stained glass windows of León's Gothic cathedral, and then enjoyed the awesome grandeur of its historic interior.

Then came a long and tiring drive to the frontier town of Zamora, not far from Portugal, on the Duero. Here I felt far removed from the Spain with which I was familiar. As we stopped for coffee, its unique Iberian identity made me want to linger. But that was not on the cards.

'Come on,' said Juan. 'We must reach Salamanca before dark.'

So off we sped.

We arrived in Salamanca just as a vibrant orange sun was setting. The lasting memory for me was of the famous university (shades of Oxford), at which the great Spanish intellectual Miguel de Unamuno taught for many years.

After three weeks driving solidly across northern Spain from east to west, then from Santiago de Compostela diagonally south-east, we arrived in Madrid on my fiftieth birthday and booked into the Ritz, where I was treated to a luxury balcony suite. That night Juan and Lolo de Lara wined and dined me in regal style and then announced: 'This voyage of discovery isn't over yet.'

First we drove south to Aranjuez. Situated on the banks of the Tagus, it features a royal eighteenth-century summer spa with its *fêtes galantes* — classical statuary that transport you in an instant to the long-vanished age of its construction.

Then to Toledo, with its rock-built fortress, the Alcázar. Toledo had been the most beloved city of the once inseparable three: Dalí, Buñuel, and Lorca. As I walked through its narrow streets with Juan and Lolo, looking up at the sombre citadel, I was reminded of the story of the Fascist leader, Colonel Juan Moscardó, whose forces were under siege in the Alcázar at the outbreak of the Spanish Civil War.

Apparently, the Republicans — having gained control of Toledo

— were trying to take the fortress, which Moscardó and his handful of soldiers were very successfully defending. However, the Republicans held an ace up their sleeve: they had taken Moscardó's son hostage. After the Republicans had tried every possible tactic to take the Alcázar without success, they finally gave their ultimatum: either Moscardó surrendered the fortress or his son would be shot. In the telephone exchange that was allowed between father and son, Moscardó told the boy he was sorry but that his duty as a loyal soldier gave him no option. The boy was shot, but the Nationalists held out until Franco arrived with his army and relieved the Alcázar on 26th September 1936.

Our final excursion took us north of Madrid to visit the Valley of the Fallen, the vast mausoleum and shrine that Franco had built in his own honour, surmounted by a gigantic cross that can be seen for miles. Within this cavernous mausoleum, close to the altar, lie Franco's remains. Beside him lie the remains of 'The Civil War Fallen', hundreds of bodies of Nationalists and Republicans. Now, I'm told, there is a fierce debate about what should be done with the Franco shrine. Apparently, there is a plan to persuade the family to remove Franco's remains to a private cemetery. *Sic transit gloria mundi.*

The same Latin quote could certainly apply to the last site we viewed of historical Spain — Phillip the Second's palatial mausoleum, 'The Escorial', a fitting ending to a remarkable journey. From this awesome monastery, Phillip ruled the Spanish world. Walking through its towering, sombre rooms, I suddenly felt I was a dwarf — surely exactly the effect Don Felipe wanted everyone he ruled to feel.

Our last few days in Madrid were spent viewing again those incomparable paintings in the Prado, and wandering through my old flamenco haunts.

While there, I took Juan and Lolo to meet Antonio Ruiz Soler (*El Bailarín*), my teacher and old friend. I hadn't seen him since I had danced with him and his company that memorable evening nineteen years before, and it was very moving for us to reminisce about those early years in London.

That was the last time I saw Antonio. (Nineteen years later, I answered the phone one morning to the *Guardian* arts editor.

'Trader, you knew the flamenco dancer Antonio? Well, he died yesterday. Would you be kind enough to do us a piece on his life? We'll run it as an obit.')

That night spent with Antonio in Madrid marked the end of my trip with Juan and Lolo. The next day I flew back to London.

CHAPTER TWENTY-SEVEN

THE PETER FINCH BIOGRAPHY

IN 1978 I WAS unemployed again and wondering how to move my career forward. One morning, I received a call from Jesse Lasky Jnr, who, with his wife Pat, had been a close friend for many years. Jesse's father had been one of the founders of the Hollywood film industry, together with Sam Goldwyn and Louis B. Mayer. Pat and Jesse had just finished *Love Scene*, a biography of Laurence Olivier and Vivien Leigh, which Angus & Robertson had published. Jesse's opening gambit was: 'Hello, Trader. How'd ya like to be a biographer?'

By that time I had done a bit of freelance journalism and several translations of Spanish plays into English, but I'd never thought seriously about attempting to write anything of any length. Jesse and Pat had just been offered the biography of my old mentor, Peter Finch, who had died eighteen months previously.

'You knew Peter well. You were trained by him, you were a close friend. You are going to write this biography. There's no one else better suited. Angus & Robertson approached us, but we've decided that you are the ideal biographer. So here's what you do. Over this coming weekend you write a synopsis of your book. You state the number of chapters and you send this synopsis to Ian Dear at A & R and he will come back to you. Get on with it, Trader! And good luck!'

Then he put down the receiver.

I sat for a minute, stunned. Could I write a book about my old friend?

After our shared years in Australia, Peter had come to England two years ahead of me. I remember going to see Finchie and his wife Tamara before their departure at their small flat near King's Cross in Sydney. I gave him Walt Whitman's *Leaves of Grass* as a farewell gift. He seemed very moved.

I next saw him in London when I went backstage to his dressing room at the St James Theatre. He was playing Iago to Orson Welles's *Othello*, presented by Laurence Olivier. Finchie told me he hated the experience.

'Welles has me well and truly underlit, farting about in the shadows like a fucking mosquito while he ambles about in a follow spot.'

Later, while I was living on the *Stella Maris*, the phone would ring. One day such a call came that was to be more than usually memorable.

'G'day, mate. It's Finchie. I'm just across the river from you at that little pub next to the church. See you in ten minutes.'

He'd been filming and I hadn't seen him in a while. Over I went and there he was with two schooners drawn and waiting on the table.

'Pete,' I said, some minutes later, 'I'm busting for a leak. Where's the dunny?'

'Go through that door and along the passage. It's the last door on the left. It sticks a bit, so give it a good hard shove and you'll be in there.'

I did as he suggested, shoving at the sticking door, and suddenly found myself floundering in the Thames at high tide. Fortunately, it was mid-summer and I was wearing shorts and a T-shirt. Also the tide had just turned, so if I headed diagonally north-east I'd end up by the *Stella Maris*. As I floated quickly away, I looked back. There was 'Finch, Bloody Finch' waving me farewell with a white handkerchief.

The strong downstream current was with me and in no time I was approaching the *Stella Maris*. As luck would have it Mum was on the veranda hanging out washing.

'Mum! Hey, Mum!' I yelled. 'I'll need a hand up. You can hang on to the railing to steady me and I can get up on the side where the tide isn't strong.'

She did as I asked.

'Trader, you stupid boy!' she berated. 'What on earth are you doing in there? You know that water's filthy.'

As I dried myself off, I told her what had happened. She had never liked or trusted Peter, and this certainly didn't help.

The next time I saw Peter, my mother, Bobo and I were dining in the West End at the White Elephant Club. Who should come ambling over to our table but Finchie.

'Come and join us,' I said.

This would be an ideal opportunity to confront him over my dunking in the river. He had obviously already had a few and was very mellow.

'I'll be back shortly,' he said. 'I'm the guest of friends over there, but I'll join you for coffee if I may?'

He left and we had our dinner. During the dessert, over he ambled again — none too secure on his feet. I pulled out a chair and he slumped into it — shortly afterwards sliding out of it and onto the floor, passed out. I can't remember which of us put him into a taxi and sent him home.

I didn't see him again until my old friend Robert Rietti called me to Rome in 1968 to dub one of the characters in Mikhail Kalatozov's film *The Red Tent*, which starred Peter Finch as General Umberto Nobile, who had unsuccessfully tried to cross the North Pole in an airship in 1928.

To be fair to him, Finchie was quick off the mark when he came into the studio.

'I owe you a good dinner, sport. No hard feelings?'

'You're lucky it was high tide and not thick Thames mud,' I replied.

The proferred dinner was of the best. And what a great performance Finchie gave as Nobile.

The very last time I had seen Finchie was in 1972. He had just finished playing Erich Krogh in the film of Graham Greene's *England Made Me*, directed by Peter Duffel. I remember Finchie was brilliant as a hard, metallic, German industrialist. As usual, he rang me out of the blue.

'I'm at de Vere Mews in Canning Place, just off Gloucester Road.

Come over and meet the love of my life, Eletha.'

Finchie had by then moved to Jamaica, where he had met and married a young islander (his marriage to Tamara had ended some years before).

I went along and found de Vere Mews, with what had once been a stables on the ground floor.

'Finchie!' I yelled. 'Where are you? It's pitch bloody dark!'

The door on the first floor opened. Then came Finchie's voice.

'Come on up, mate, and meet Eletha.'

I was introduced to a pretty but rather formidable Jamaican, very protective of Peter.

'Who *is* this man?' she asked him.

'Don't worry,' he reassured her. 'He's an old friend from the Aussie days.'

I remember so well Eletha's defensive hostility — she was afraid I'd try to persuade him to return to London to stay.

That was the last I saw of Finchie.

Who could say they really knew him? I doubt anyone could — even Finchie himself. And now I was being asked to write his biography. What a challenge!

'But ... why not?' I thought. 'What do I have to lose?'

So I started work, sketching out the man I knew. By Sunday night, I had the outline of what I would write about Peter. I posted it off on the Monday morning and on Tuesday I had a call from Ian Dear.

'Can you meet me today for lunch at the Ivy?'

We met.

'The assignment's yours if you feel up to it,' he said.

Yes, I told him. I'd give it a go.

Once the contract was signed, he delivered his first salvo.

'You must deliver your manuscript by the end of May because Ken Tynan's ex-wife, Elaine Dundy, is also writing a biography and she has an eleven-month headstart on you. We want the book out by the middle of next year.'

This was in late November 1977.

At the time, I didn't realise what he was demanding — otherwise I probably wouldn't have undertaken it. However, I agreed to his terms and started immediately. I was given an advance of £500. That would get me to America, where Peter had died. I realised that for any chapters on Australia and Jamaica I would have to rely on contacts living there.

One of my first moves was to ring Tamara Tchinarova, Peter's first wife, to tell her what I had undertaken.

'But Trader,' she replied, 'Kenneth Tynan's wife is already working on a biography and I've sent her all of the material I have.'

I realised that a nightmare period was about to begin.

During December and January I started my manuscript, and telephoned and sent out letters to Australia. Friends and contacts of Finch responded enthusiastically because of Peter's popularity, and the desire to see something authentic written about him. Having written over one hundred closely-typed pages, I re-read them — and was appalled. It was rubbish!

I started again, and this time as I wrote I felt that someone was writing through me. As I assembled the rough material a friend of mine, Anna Romani, a commercial lawyer, would take my hand-written material to be typed by her secretary. At 7 a.m. every morning I would cycle round to Anna's, who lived ten minutes away, hand her the new pages, then get back to my flat and write all the rest of the day. When I wasn't writing, I would travel to see various people here in the UK who could give me the material I needed about Finchie in taped interviews. It was a period of frantic desperation — but there were good moments, too. One day I received a phone call from Tamara. She had just got back the material she had lent to Elaine Dundy and I was invited to use whatever I needed. Progress!

I decided to leave for Hollywood in February and, once there, to contact all the people who had known Peter — in particular, those who had been with him at the time of his death. I bought my plane ticket and on the morning I was to leave the telephone rang. It was Peter's widow's lawyer.

'Mr Faulkner,' said the voice from Hollywood, 'you mustn't come here. Mrs Finch does not approve of your book. You will get no assistance from his friends here, as they have all been warned about you.'

He hung up. In a second, I decided to go anyway. Luckily, Jesse Lasky's sister Betty in LA had offered to drive me everywhere I needed to go, and to be my guide for a small fee. Alexander 'Sandy' MacKendrick and his wife Hilary offered to put me up. Sandy, who had directed me in *A High Wind in Jamaica*, knew Peter well. They had known each other from their time at Ealing studios, when Peter was making his first English film, *Train of Events*. Any material I got from Sandy about Finch would be invaluable. Also, staying with Sandy and Hilary, I had a base from which I could operate all over Hollywood — and a driver, Betty Lasky.

The first person I tried to contact after my arrival was Sidney Lumet, who had directed Peter in *Network* (for which Peter had received a posthumous Oscar). Whenever I spoke to him on the phone, he very politely prevaricated. I couldn't think why, until I was told that he was a friend of Elaine Dundy. Call after call I made, always to receive a similar reply.

'Mrs Finch has not authorised us to talk with you. She does not approve of your writing about her husband.'

I then rang Robert Aldrich, who had directed Peter in *The Flight of the Phoenix* and *The Legend of Lylah Clare*. He was very affable and said that Finchie had played Errol Flynn in a film that Aldrich put together about the actor, *The Greatest Mother of Them All*. Apparently, this had never been finished, but Aldrich still had the two reels he had shot, and said he would be delighted to show them to me. I was over the moon. The aborted film had starred Finch as Flynn, with Shelley Winters and Alexandra Hay as co-stars. When I arrived at Aldrich's house, he tersely told me that he had just received a call from Mrs Finch, who had heard I was in Hollywood and told him that on no account was he to show me the film. So many well-known Hollywood stars whom I visited were to give me the same response.

'Peter was my friend. I don't want you to write anything nasty about him.'

The Hollywood tribe had taken possession of Peter and were very protective of their hero, seeing me as a threat. I was beginning to realise that my Hollywood trip was becoming abortive. Then I rang and got an interview with Irving Kershner, who had directed Peter in *Raid on Entebbe* (his last film). Kershner told me that Finch's portrayal of the Israeli Prime Minister Yitzhak Rabin had been brilliantly intuitive.

'Though he was a through and through Gentile, Peter's performance on the screen was completely Jewish,' he told me. 'It was an amazing achievement.'

The most interesting Hollywood experience for me was meeting the man who had been the Vice President of three US television networks (ABC, CBS and NBC), David Tebet. I cannot remember who gave me this contact, but it was one of the most valuable in the whole of my research on Finchie. I rang him at his Beverly Hills hotel and he told me to come round at once.

'Do you want me to show you the exact spot where Peter collapsed?' he asked me.

He took me along the passage outside his hotel room and said, 'Peter had come to see me because he was going to play George Washington — with the famous wooden teeth! Coming towards us down the hall in the opposite direction was the theatre producer Cy Feuer. Seeing him, I said, "Cy, I want you to meet..." But Peter had suddenly collapsed on the floor.'

He told me they had then called the ambulance. Peter had had a massive heart attack. Sadly, he died on his way to the hospital.

My other invaluable contacts were the Doheny Drive paramedics. They allowed me to drive with them in an ambulance along the route where Peter had died. I went to the place where the stretcher had been sent down a draughty passage to the morgue. I was beginning to feel that I did have enough material to put together a book about Finchie.

Then I had a phone call from Murray Matheson — an extraordinary stroke of luck. Murray had been with Finchie in the pre-war days in Sydney, and had an album with photographs of Peter and the drama group that had toured the Australian outback around 1935 with George Sorlie and his circus entourage, playing light comedy under the canvas between animal shows. Murray filled me in on Finchie's life at the very beginning of his career. I had what I needed and felt it was time to go.

On my way back I stopped off in New York, where I met up with my old friend, the brilliant character actor George Rose. During our meeting, George related to me a string of colourful anecdotes on Peter and took me to a shop where I was able to buy wonderful film stills, subsequently used in the biography.

While in New York I introduced George to my cousin Kay Swift, who held us spellbound with her stories of Gershwin — both as a lover and as musical legend. Her description of Gershwin and herself in bed making love to 'Fascinating Rhythm' had us both prostrate with laughter. Never has the reckless abandon of the 1920s been brought more vividly to life than it was by dear cousin Kay — a 20s legend herself. Kay playing Gershwin songs on her piano, together with some of her own, was one of the unforgettable highlights of that visit.

Some years later, George Rose was to be murdered for his money by his adopted son's family in Santa Domingo, but that's another story.

Back in London, in March 1978, I was still not certain whether I had a book. One thing I realised was that I needed a chapter on Jamaica — his final home. Peter, at heart a true primitive, had visited Jamaica back in the early 1960s and had felt at once an affinity with the island and its people. Thereafter he had lived in three properties and had left the last one, Cardiff Hall, to make *Network*.

There was no money for me to fly there, so I would write to my one contact on the island who could get me all the information I needed — my old friend from *High Wind* days, Beverly Anderson. I sent her a letter asking if she could help me to get the interviews that would give me a chapter on Finch's life in Jamaica. Ten days later, the phone rang at 4 a.m.

'Trader? Bev.'

'Dear Bev,' I said. 'Can you help me?'

'Trader, you're coming to Jamaica.'

'Impossible, darling. I haven't the money.'

'You're coming. We are paying.'

'Who's we?'

'Don't you know who I am now?'

'Of course I do. You're Beverly Anderson.'

'No, man! I'm Beverly Manly, Jamaica's First Lady. I'm married to the Prime Minister, Michael Manly. So you're coming and we're paying. Your tickets will be awaiting you at the Jamaica Airlines office in London.'

I flew to Jamaica first class. At Kingston airport, a car and a driver were waiting to take me to the Ocho Rios Beach Hyatt luxury hotel. I was given a suite. There were flowers and a huge basket of fruit in my room. A few minutes later, the telephone rang.

'Trader, welcome to Jamaica!' Beverly's warm, Jamaican voice.

She told me to simply tell the driver where I needed to go and he would take me there. But would I come to Kingston to see her, and to meet Michael? Of course, I told her.

Over the next couple of days I visited Peter's three plantations and saw the various contacts I needed to interview — including his architect Ernesto Maffessanti, with whom I dined together with his family. Before I went south to Kingston for my reunion with Beverly I went to Cardiff Hall, the last plantation house that Peter had owned.

When my young driver arrived at the gates, they were bolted and chained. Official entry was thus closed to us, but we decided to chance it, as I wanted to get a photograph of Peter's last home. We were creeping along through a banana plantation when I suddenly came face-to-face with a young Jamaican who asked me what I was doing in his garden. I told him. It turned out he was Eletha's brother (Peter's brother-in-law). We chatted for a moment or two, and I think he realised I was genuinely fond of Peter. He asked if I would like to meet his mother.

We made our way up to a beautiful, colonial-style house where I met Miss Bertha, Peter's Jamaican mother-in-law. A small, very dark Jamaican lady of indeterminate age, she was hospitable and offered me the run of the house. On the mantelpiece in the large dining room was an elegant brown trilby. I picked it up and found the lining had come out with much use and tropical sweat. Miss Bertha said, 'Peter was wearing that hat when the telephone rang from Hollywood. He put it down where you picked it up, and there it has remained ever since.' I felt it was a symbol of Peter's hurried farewell from his last Jamaican home.

Now it was time to head off to Kingston to see Beverly again after fourteen years. Arriving at the hotel in Kingston, again I received VIP treatment. I was given a balcony room, more flowers, and a telephone call.

'Trader, it's Bev. A car will pick you up at two o'clock tomorrow afternoon. Michael is looking forward to meeting you.'

I replied that the feeling was mutual.

All through the morning of the next day, to keep myself calm, I worked feverishly on my book. At 1.50 p.m. I heard sirens and thought there must be a fire. I went out onto my balcony to see a large blue saloon with two motorcycle outriders pull up outside the hotel entrance. Then the telephone rang.

'Mr Faulkner, your car is here.'

I went down to find the vestibule packed with excited, inquisitive Jamaicans. Who was the VIP that was being collected? Luckily, I had worn an elegant blue suit and tie — what I had considered would be suitable clothing in which to meet the Prime Minister. I decided, once inside the limousine, to play the part of the mysterious VIP to the hilt, so as the car glided out of the hotel entrance to the screech of motorcycle sirens, I took out my white pocket handkerchief and did a Queen Mother wave to the mob of screaming fans.

We drove what seemed to be an interminable distance. I knew that Government House was not in the direction we were heading. Remembering my Bermuda experience, I thought: dear God, was I being kidnapped? But that was impossible. What was *I* worth to anybody?

'Driver,' I said, 'are we heading towards Government House?'

'No, sir,' he said. 'They're not workin' there. These Manlys are hard workin' socialists; they're out at the TV transmitters.'

And that was where I ended up. I went into a small room and waited. Presently, the door opened and a beautifully dressed, slim, elegant Jamaican woman with very short, tightly curled hair appeared, wearing a simple pink dress and white court shoes. Was this Beverly, the girl I had worked with filming up the coast at Rio Bueno? Then she had been dressed as a sexy prostitute, with long, black hair.

'Bev?' I ventured.

She obviously felt the same confusion.

'Yes. Can it be you, Trader?'

'The last time I saw you,' I reminded her, 'you were dressed as a West Indian lady of convenience.'

She was quick to reply.

'And I remember you as a dishevelled pirate, in buckled blue shoes with red heels!'

We reminisced, and presently a tall, smartly dressed man entered the room and I was introduced to her husband, the Prime Minister.

I remembered that I had seen this man three weeks before in an interview on BBC television and had not been very impressed. However, the man before me was quietly spoken and obviously highly intelligent. I told him of my first impression, and was at a loss to understand how I could have been so wrong. He told me that as a Socialist he was not popular with the better-off factions of Jamaican society, and that relations with the US were currently at a low ebb because of his premiership. America had apparently placed an embargo on their sugar and molasses exports as a punishment for his election. He asked if I had noticed an elegant new building as we drove through the old Spanish Town. I said yes, I had. The town itself had seemed poor and run down, but I had noticed that one very modern brick building.

'That's a present from Castro,' he said. 'Because of America's embargo, we are forced to do business with Russia and Cuba and, of course, it's in Russia's interest to look after us. So do you begin to get the picture as regards my standing in Great Britain?'

Our interview was very brief. I thanked them both for their hospitality, which had enabled me to give an account of Peter Finch's life in Jamaica, and took my leave.

Once I had a Jamaican chapter on Finchie — thanks to Beverly Manly — I realised that I had a book. From my return to London to the day I handed in the typescript of my book it was a steady routine of recording interviews, collating written recollections, and putting it all together into biographical form. By early May, thanks to Anna Romani and her team of typists, I had a manuscript. But I had no idea where I stood vis-à-vis my rival, Elaine Dundy.

After last minute corrections, at the beginning of June I handed in the finished manuscript to Ian Dear. It had been seven months of incessant work.

The book came out early in 1979, published in hardback by Angus & Robertson in the UK and by Taplinger in the USA. Pan Books then published a paperback edition. I was very angry about the Angus & Robertson edition because there were omissions and mistakes that should never have been allowed to happen. However, the book did well and, in July of 1979, Angus & Robertson sent me to Australia to promote it.

During my trips to Sydney for the publicising of my book I of course met up with several old friends, and was fêted, wined, and dined. My return to Australia was after an absence of twenty-eight years. Having left by ship, which took five weeks to reach London, I now arrived by plane in just under twenty-four hours. The Sydney I had left had rattled noisily with old trams that retired for the night in a large shed situated beside the harbour. That shed had now been replaced by the new Sydney Opera House.

I was lucky to be invited to stay with an old school friend from the Jesuit days, Bill Wootten, and his mother Muriel. It was strange to be back talking about the Peter Finch with whom I had acted on Sydney Radio, where I had started my career. Being Australian, and discussing Finch with several clever interviewers, the book's sales were boosted. Returning to London, I was able for a few months to forget about Finchie and continue with my career as a freelance writer and actor.

The following year, however, Leslie Norman's son Barry — who was hosting a popular film programme on television — offered me a trip back to Australia to do an interview on Finchie with him in the Sydney Botanical Gardens. We had looked at various places for the best location to conjure up the ghost of Finchie in his Sydney days.

Barry rightly believed the Botanical Gardens as a background gave Peter Finch the dignity he deserved.

Elaine Dundy's book, *Finch, Bloody Finch*, wasn't published until the following year, so it may well contain important factual material I either missed or hadn't time to ferret out. What is great is the fact that there now exist two separate biographies of Peter for future generations who might wish to know about this truly unique actor and personality.

To launch my biography, the British Film Institute asked me to give a lecture using excerpts from several of Finchie's films. I chose some from among his best as well as his lesser-known performances — a selection that included his portrayal of Bill Ryan in *Dad and Dave Come to Town* (1938); Jim Macauley in *The Shiralee* (1957); Erick Krogh (the German Industrialist) in *England Made Me* (1973); and finally, in total contrast, his performance as Yitzhak Rabin in *Raid on Entebbe* (1976). In that lecture I had intended to give a greater understanding of Peter's range and quality. I hope I succeeded.

The saga of the Peter Finch biography did not end with the book's London distribution. I received a call from a friend in America to tell me that Elaine Dundy's book was out there — but where was mine? I rang Angus & Robertson; they were profuse with apologies. Unfortunately, the employee responsible for foreign distribution had a drink problem. The entire consignment of book copies earmarked for America lay in a London warehouse. The alcoholic employee had forgotten to send them! So I lost the financial potential of the American market, and received very little money from US sales. Still, I could afford to be philosophical about it. I'm sure Elaine Dundy had worked just as hard if not as frantically as I did and, as it happened, in terms of sales I won in the UK; she in America.

Today the two books sit side-by-side collecting dust on a top shelf in my study.

CHAPTER TWENTY-EIGHT

THE BIRTH OF LORCA, AN EVOCATION

After trying to ensure that Peter Finch and his artistic legacy would not be forgotten, my next problem was finding a new work challenge. My experience with the RSC had made me realise I was not a 'company man', so I began to cast about for something I could do on my own.

Then a call came from my literary agent Andrew Mann. Would I care to write the biography of Stewart Grainger?

'No!' was my instinctive response. I was no admirer of his work, but I had nothing else to do, and the advance that was offered was very appealing, so I agreed to 'ghost' his story. I met Grainger and began. With Grainger, a bullish arrogance belied a deep sense of inadequacy. To me his acting skill ranked a poor second to his rugged good looks. In short, I soon realised that no level of payment would justify my taking on a job that was tantamount to munching chalk. I had to tell him that what I would write would not be very flattering to him.

'What would you call the book?' he asked.

'*Memoirs of an Arrogant Bastard*,' I replied.

'What?' he roared.

Fortunately, I was rescued by Kitty Black, a formidable literary and administrative brain.

'You, Trader, couldn't possibly write a book on my favourite pin-up boy,' she told me. 'Leave it to me.'

I was paid £1,000 for the work I'd done, and Kitty very successfully wrote the book with Grainger — the perfect solution.

Then came another call from Andrew Mann.

'Would you consider doing a biog on your old colleague of yesteryear, Beatrix Lehmann?'

'Of course!' I yelled. 'It'd be an honour, and a challenge to try to make my readers laugh as much as Bea did me.'

Besides being a superb actress, Bea Lehmann was a daunting intellectual, so I was hardly the ideal biographer. But her humour? There I could score, I was sure. Here was a book I really wanted to write. I went to see Bea's brother, John Lehmann, and told him I was immensely flattered to have been offered the chance to write about his sister.

'You're actually my sister Rosamund's choice,' he told me. 'We all think it's a good idea because Bea used to say you made her laugh. But you will have to go and see Ros.'

Invited to tea at her house in Chelsea, I was greeted by the elderly but still beautiful Rosamund. She was gracious and confirmed that she felt I would be the ideal choice to write about Bea. I said that the two qualities of Bea's character that were paramount to me were her sense of humour and her magnetic power as an actress. I mentioned that Peter Hall had described Bea as 'formidable' onstage. Rosamund promised that I would be given all the family background material I would need. I could feel myself growing more and more excited by the idea, and could foresee the possibility of a very amusing and original book. Also Bea had been in Berlin in the early 1930s and was a close friend of Christopher Isherwood and the Kurt Weill-Lotte Lenya set, so I knew I had a potentially very readable book if I could do it justice. Then Rosamund dropped her bombshell.

'There's one aspect of Bea's life, however, that you mustn't on any account allude to. There must be no hint of her being a lesbian.'

I was absolutely flabbergasted. My immediate thought was: 'There's no book!'

'Rosamund, Bea's sexual orientation was well-known in the business, and besides, what does it matter whom she loved? Bea was a completely unique person. It would be dishonest to omit such an important part of her life and character.'

But Rosamund was adamant.

'I'm sorry, but absolutely not — not even a suggestion!'

'Then I can't take on the book. I can't write a bowdlerised account of Bea's life. It would not be fair to her or to her memory.'

So the idea died, which was a great sadness for me, as I was sure I could have done her justice.

Bea Lehmann and I shared a love of bawdy humour — it had been Bea who had introduced me to Rabelais' *Gargantua and Pantagruel*, a work which I'm sure would have offended her sister Rosamund.

Years earlier, during my run in *The Waltz of the Toreadors*, after Renée Asherson had taken over the role of Mlle de Ste-Euverte from Brenda Bruce, Bea, Renée and I saw a lot of one another. On our first invitiation to dine with Bea at her house, I was given a glimpse of the raunchy humour, typical of Berlin in the 1930s, that Bea had described with such fondness.

Bea had a wildly affectionate Gordon Setter called 'Liquor'. She always warned her friends to be sure to restain him when they were introduced. On our arrival, Liquor had been temporarily shut away in another room. We were given a drink, then Bea released Liquor to introduce him to us. In he bounded, pawed me enthusiastically, then noticed Renée, who greeted him with polite affection. In one bound, Liquor had thrust his wet nose right up her skirt — causing Renée to shriek, and Bea to roar with raucous laughter.

I left Rosamund's flat that afternoon with a great sense of disappointment. I had worked with Bea in three separate productions — onstage in Lorca's *Blood Wedding* and Anouilh's *The Waltz of the Toreadors* and on television in Somerset Maugham's *The Mother* — and had learned an enormous amount from her professionalism and exceptional talent. It was a shame that I was denied the opportunity to repay at least a part of the debt I owed her by writing a tribute to her exceptional life and work.

In 1982 I was to embark on yet another false start when an offer came from the editor of a glossy magazine to write the text for a coffee table book on 'The Beauty of Australia'.

'But I left Australia in 1950,' I told her. 'How can I possibly write anything authoritative on the subject after a thirty-year absence?'

'Yes, but I liked so much what you wrote on Peter Finch.'

There was no point in arguing. She told me to research the subject and to keep my coverage general and factual.

'We'll supply lovely glossy pictures.'

She was very persuasive and I needed the money, so I decided I'd give it a go.

For several months I researched every Australian state, writing and editing my material before I sent it off. Weeks later I received a phone call from the editor.

'Trader, I've sent your typescript to Australia and they say there are errors.'

Of course there were! Trying to write about Australia while sitting in England was a crazy idea. But I had done my best. I suggested that they should pay me off and set the whole enterprise up again down under. They did.

One afternoon I was mending a puncture on my bicycle tyre when I received a phone call. My lodger raced down the ninety-eight stairs from my flat to tell me.

'Quickly, Trader! The Spanish embassy's on the phone for you!'

I raced up, and lifted the receiver.

'Yes?'

'Señor Fuckner, you have to be at the Inn on thee Par' at seben o'clor tonigh'. Hees Majestee Keeng Juan Carlos has a decoration for jou.'

I had no idea what he was talking about. Why was I being given a decoration? True, over the years the BBC had commissioned me to write and present radio programmes on Manuel de Falla and Isaac Albeniz, and I had done various programmes on Lorca and the Andalusian festival of *El Rocío*. I had also got a reputation through my flamenco dancing as a Hispanophile, but surely my contribution to spreading Spanish culture was too minimal to warrant such recognition? Then the voice continued.

'Jew mos be at Inn on thee Par' promptly at seben o'clor. An' jew mos wear a smockin'.'

Luckily I had a presentable dinner suit.

I got on my old bike and peddled off down the Cromwell Road. By then, at 6.15pm, it had started to drizzle. Walking up Cromwell Road towards me from the Exhibition Road intersection was a beautiful girl on the arms of two men. For a moment I was transfixed, and didn't see the large pothole in front of me. Down went the wheel and over it I went. Somehow the front wheel became disengaged from the fork and kept rolling on by itself. The traffic policeman at the intersection ahead put up his hand, but the wheel kept going. It was all pure Buster Keaton! He watched the wheel come to a stop just past him, then beckoned me over.

'You realise you're breaking the law, sir?'

'Not so, officer. My front wheel is breaking the law, not me.'

I explained as briefly as I could where I was going and why. Fortunately, the policeman had a sense of humour.

'Go on, sir. Off you go, and good luck.'

Hauling the bike in one hand and the wheel in the other, I got to the Inn on the Park at 6.50pm. Cars were pulling into the forecourt. Luckily I'd put a fiver in my pocket, which I handed to a concierge (together with the bicycle bits). Then I raced to the bathroom and cleaned up as best I could.

The reception room was packed and I was presented to the Marquis of Santa Cruz, the former Spanish Ambassador to London, a small impeccably dressed Spaniard who had come from Madrid for this special occasion.

'Señor Faulkner, how do you come to be receiving this decoration from His Majesty?'

'I was hoping you could tell me. But I have a great friend in your embassy here — the Cultural Attaché Jose Antonio Varela and his wife Sarah. He must have spoken to His Majesty on my behalf.'

'You will have to say a few words. Please be brief.'

At the presentation, he pinned on my chest an impressive gold medal with a blue and white ribbon, and handed me a small box (which I later discovered contained a miniature copy of the medal to wear in my buttonhole). Then he turned to address the audience of several hundred people, praising my contribution to the spreading of Spanish culture through my work in broadcasting, as a translator of classic Spanish plays, and as a student and performer of Spanish flamenco dancing.

My own speech was brief.

'With deep gratitude, I as an Australian can only say that His Majesty, King Juan Carlos, has clean-bowled me middle stump! *Gracias!*'

Collecting my bicycle remains from the amused concierge, I walked home in the rain.

We all like to be rewarded, but my Spanish Order of Merit has never ceased to amaze me. In Spain I am officially 'Your Excellency' — as I was once addressed in Madrid! This morning I was listening on the BBC to the British royal awards. Bruce Forsyth — hoofer, comedian, and light entertainment presenter extraordinaire — is now Sir Bruce. These encouraging symbols of royal approval for achievement are a tonic for one's self-confidence. I certainly was proud to receive my award from the Spanish king, but I always think of the thousands whose achievements have gone unrecognised.

During these years, it was Peter and Molly Daubeny whom I have to thank for introducing me to many fascinating people.

Peter Daubeny had been a young actor before the war and had lost his arm fighting on the beaches at Solerno. I shall always remember Noel Coward telling us one night over dinner at Notley Abbey how, while visiting the troops at Anzio and Solerno, he had suddenly come face to face with this young actor from his past, Peter Daubeny, now an invalid minus his left arm. Daubeny, not the least sorry for himself, was delighted to see his pre-war colleague.

'I simply burst into tears,' said Coward.

Invalided out of the war, with his acting career finished, Peter immediately set himself up in management. When I met them Peter and Molly were running London's annual World Theatre Season at the Aldwych Theatre, which they did from 1964 to 1975 — Peter arranging the logistics for the visits of leading companies from all over the world, and Molly running the social and domestic side. Peter had been given a knighthood by the UK, and a similar ranking honour by every other country he served in this international enterprise.

This is all simply a prelude to an unforgettable evening I enjoyed at one of the many Daubeny dinners I was privileged to attend — both before and after Peter's untimely death in 1975 in his early fifties. Across the table from me on this occasion were Peter Ustinov and a well-known English actress whose films I'd seen in my teens and I had longed to meet — Valerie Hobson.

I had spent some time in conversation with the woman on my left. Then I turned to address my other neighbour — a small, quiet man in a Savile Row suit.

'I'm Trader, and I know you are John,' I said. 'When and how did you meet Molly and Peter?'

The man explained that he'd known Peter through his theatre connections, and had admired and loved him as a friend for many years. This was a shy and reticent man I instinctively warmed to. He was a wonderful converstionalist — and as good a listener — and, intrigued by the man, I eventually asked:

'May I know your surname?'

'Profumo,' he replied.

I remember giving him a firm handshake.

'Sir,' I told him, 'you've got what it takes.'

'I do the best I can to repair the damage,' he said, 'working to help young people.'

Profumo was obviously a man of principle and courage who had momentarily weakened and taken a bite of the forbidden apple, for which he was made to pay a terrible price. Having myself met the extraordinary lady who had been his partner in scandal, I knew the calibre of the temptation he had been exposed to, and could both admire his good taste and sympathise with him for dropping his guard. Truly, I felt privileged to have had the opportunity to meet Profumo and his lovely wife Valerie, who had loyally stuck by him throughout his troubles.

Over coffee after that dinner I got into conversation with Peter Ustinov about marriage. He had recently split from Suzanne Cloutier, who had gone to Africa to work with Albert Schweitzer. Peter and

Suzanne had been married for fifteen years and Peter was very cut up about what he described as 'my severe emotional rupture'.

'My acting and my writing are my mental salvation,' he told me. 'The only things that give me any relief.'

I was fascinated that a man with such a fruitful, creative mind could also be savaged by 'the black dog' of depression.

'You forget, I'm Russian!' he said when I mentioned it. 'Depression is part of our national character.'

I learnt so much from that chat with Ustinov. Another brilliant conversationalist, he stimulated you to excel — a unique gift in the entertainment industry.

He took me to dinner at Rules one evening and we talked about García Lorca, and discussed the problems that Peter shared with him as a playwright. We also spoke of Peter Finch and his unique chameleon gift as an actor. But it was the bond Peter and I shared as shelved husbands that made such a deep and lasting impression on me.

Early in 1983 I was thinking, 'Where should I go now? I've written a biography, and as a journalist. I can act, direct, dance flamenco, and translate Spanish. But how on earth can I fuse all of these disparate abilities into a work for the English theatre?'

Someone at some point had made a suggestion that I never forgot: 'That Lorca show you did up at Stratford, why don't you develop it into a solo performance? You could play it anywhere — tour it internationally, if you wished.' It was a brilliant idea, and the answer to how all of my different skills could be used in one go. The result would be a show that only I could do, a totally unique piece of theatre. That creative challenge was to occupy me for the next ten years, and resulted in my theatrical tribute to Federico García Lorca: *Lorca, An Evocation*.

The production I had devised for the RSC had proved that a show about the life and work of Lorca could work well with English audiences, and possibly also for audiences abroad. But at Stratford I had a superb cast, plus a captive audience of artists and intellectuals. To transform that material into a solo performance that would hold an ordinary audience's attention would require careful planning and a well-written script. It would also have to be academically accurate. With three aborted projects behind me, and funds running low, I decided to go for it. Luckily acting jobs and journalism paid my bills while I researched and wrote.

As I saw it, my show would require me to dance flamenco, sing (thank God very little), and even be acrobatic in one sequence. By the end of 1983 I had recorded the music I intended to use and had written a first draft of the script. I had also been working with professional acrobats to put myself in shape for the performance and to relearn the backflip, which I hoped to use in one scene. With the extracts from Lorca's works, I would often do the first two or three lines in the original Spanish, then my own translation in English. It took me over a year to plan, write, and rehearse the piece before I felt ready to try it out on an audience.

The first run-through was given at the British Ballet Organisation (the BBO) at Lonsdale Road, Barnes. Edouard Espinosa, who founded the BBO, had taught my mother in the years before she joined Diaghilev's *Ballets Russes* in 1911. So John Travis, who administered the organisation at that point, very kindly allowed me to rehearse my show there. It was an absolute godsend, for I couldn't have afforded rehearsal space. As it was, I was there day and night, often seven days a week, whenever the studio was free.

Four friends were invaluable to me in this period: Liz Drown, who typed my scripts; Barbara Revill, who enabled me to get the show on (she had been Barbara Brunton Gibb when I'd worked with her in Sydney Radio but was now married to Stuart Revill, who was running the Australian Broadcasting Commission office in London); the actor Lewis Fiander, who stage-managed for me; and Janos Nyiri (who had directed me in *The Imaginary Invalid*) as director. Without the generous contribution of time and effort by these friends and several others, *Lorca, An Evocation* would never have lifted into orbit as it did.

One detail of that rehearsal period remains an indelible memory. The actor Julian Glover had turned up to watch. I knew him well by repute and respected him greatly. Apparently, he lived nearby and someone must have told him what was afoot. I was sitting absolutely drained, relieved to have lumbered through the ninety-minute stint without too many fluffs and blanks.

'That was really something!' he said, approaching me. 'It's so original. You absolutely held my attention. You must do this in the West End and tour it. It's so unique as a piece of theatre, and you obviously have the skills to make a great success of it. Good luck to you.'

I cannot say how much his encouragement meant to me. Sadly, I never saw him again.

Just before Christmas I received a message from Ognisko, the Polish club in Exhibition Road: would I like to try *Lorca* out in their small ballroom-cum-theatre upstairs — the proceeds to go to an orphans' fund in Warsaw? I leapt at the chance.

Another piece of luck: staying with me at the time was my friend Stephen Nossal. He volunteered to do my sound cues.

The first performance of *Lorca* at Ognisko — almost inevitably — turned out to be an evocation of mayhem. The Polish audience sat eating and drinking at tables and a quarter of the way through the performance I could see that they were becoming restless. After all, they were Poles. What interest could they have in a poet and playwright from Spain?

One man sitting with several mates started singing a Polish folk song. It was at a moment when I had to dance a rather spectacular *zapateádo*. Luckily, quick-witted Stephen raised the music volume and we blasted him out. When I finished dancing there was applause. This infuriated the group at the singer's table — all of whom started shouting comments about the performance. The rest of the room, however, was with me and told the hectoring drunks to shut up. There was so much noise that I simply stopped and watched as the two sides became more and more heated in their exchanges. Finally the police arrived, the troublemakers were removed, and I finished a slightly shortened version of the show with no one any the wiser.

But I wasn't too disheartened by the experience. If the show could survive such a baptism of fire, then I knew I was ready to offer it to a wider public. The next task was to find venues and managements that would take me on. Initially, I felt my best potential audiences would be found in the universities.

David Rees, who had worked for Sir Peter Daubeny when he launched and presented his successful World Theatre Season at the Aldwych Theatre, agreed to take on the managerial side and arrange the bookings. Professor Nick Round agreed to present the show at Glasgow University. St Andrews followed. Nick had contacted his colleague, David Howitt, who ran the Hispanic studies at Hull University, and I was booked there as well. Then I went on to Oxford, where I received a wonderful tribute from Sir Richard Doll, the famous physiologist and epidemiologist who had proved the link between smoking and lung cancer.

'From what I've read of Lorca,' he told me, 'you seem to reflect the very soul of the man.'

Coming from such an eminent figure, this encouragement meant an enormous amount to me.

In Cambridge, *Lorca* was presented before the sharpest audience the one-man version of the show ever played to. Then came bookings in Liverpool and Bristol and touring dates at Bournemouth, Exeter, the Chichester Festival, Windsor, Bracknell, and the Everyman Theatre in Cheltenham. All this time I was re-writing and polishing, adding and subtracting material, and tightening the show.

Bobo's sister Audrey, headmistress of Queenswood School in Hertfordshire, asked me to play it to the school. Next came an invitation for a performance at Roedean Ladies' College in Brighton. Facing the Roedean audience was a tremendously stimulating challenge — not least because of the tender age of my audience and the adult nature of some of Lorca's verse. In Lorca's poem 'Preciosa and the Wind', he depicts the wind as a sexy satyr who says: 'Open to my ancient fingers the black rose 'neath your belly here...' As you can imagine, it got more than a titter from my audience of schoolgirls. The occasion was to be remembered for one other reason, as well — and not a pleasant one. While I was performing onstage, the door of my dressing room had been left unlocked. A gang of youths on the prowl entered and stole my briefcase, which contained my wallet and other indispensable items. The school very generously compensated me for my loss, but that was the first of several occasions when I felt acutely vulnerable playing the show entirely on my own.

Throughout this period, thanks to David Rees, booking offers were plentiful. Interest in Lorca and his work was steadily increasing with a public who hitherto had known virtually nothing about him. My obvious success was a tremendous incentive to bring the show to an even wider audience, but how was I to do that with no money and no Arts Council backing?

'Lorca is not English,' they told me smugly. 'I'm sorry, Mr Faulkner. Why not get Spain to fund you?'

I tried. They didn't want to know either.

'You're English — playing our national poet in English.'

'And in Spanish,' I countered. 'So why not support me as an Anglo-Spanish cultural enterprise, since we're both part of the Common Market?'

I tried endlessly to get funding from both sides, without success. Finally I had to accept that I was on my own. Meanwhile, other support (though not financial) came unexpectedly from other sources. Thérèse Clancy, a close family friend from Sydney, was my houseguest for several weeks. This was in 1985, during the second year of *Lorca*, when I was incorporating new material using quite a few snatches of Lorca's original Spanish so the audience could hear the rhythm of the original and contrast that with the sound of the verse in English. These passages were obviously tricky to learn as the English and Spanish had to go quickly. Thérèse's patient help, however, enabled me to master the new material in a relatively short period of time.

About eighteen months after I had begun *Lorca*, I was asked to give two charity performances at the Mary Wallace Theatre in Twickenham. Thérèse came along to assist backstage. Paul Scofield and his wife Joy were in the audience. After the show they came backstage and Paul's comments told me I was on course with *Lorca* to achieve something truly worthwhile. Thérèse was so impressed at meeting Paul that she jotted down what he said, and I've kept it because, as with Julian Glover, this was an actor whose opinion I totally respected.

'You have brought in a foreign culture and made it work. This is Spanish, not a non-Spaniard trying to be Spanish. You managed to project for me the fundamental, spiritual essence of a universal, poetic voice. Someone will back you, Trader. It is simply a question of your knocking at every door.'

Meanwhile, television and BBC Radio jobs were continuing to provide the wherewithal with which to pay the bills. Then an offer came to play *Lorca* at the Bretforton Theatre Room in Worcestershire before a fashionable crowd at a sumptuous 'stately home' dinner — *Lorca* swanning with the elite.

Next, Lady Pen Zetland invited me to give a performance in the oldest and most uncomfortable theatre in Great Britain, the Richmond Theatre in Yorkshire. My introduction to her was made through Wing Commander Paul Richey, DFC, a close and generous friend, who had written the best seller *Fighter Pilot* about his air exploits in World War Two.

Early in that second year, Peter Wilson invited me to put the show into the Latchmere Theatre in Battersea — the nearest I'd come so far to playing a London venue. I was amazed to find myself playing to full houses every night, thanks to Peter's enterprising publicity. During that three-week run, I had one memorable confrontation. At the end of the show I was left in a circle of light. Now the proprietors of the Latchmere — which is an upstairs room in a pub — had promised me that the door on the left-hand side of the stage that led down to the bar would be securely locked. One evening, early in the run, the show had been running for nearly an hour and a half and I was approaching the dramatic moment at the show's end when Lorca was shot. As the lights dimmed I knew I had the audience in the palm of my hand, and was able to lower my voice almost to a whisper. Suddenly, I became aware that the door to the downstairs bar was slowly opening. Towards me crept a figure — obviously very drunk. Realising his mistake, he started to retreat, then bowed suddenly and vomited at my feet. Luckily the general lighting was dimmed so that most of what had happened was lost in darkness. Then, as quietly as he'd approached me, he drifted back and the door silently closed behind him. I now had to dance a very fast *zapateádo* — being careful not to slip on what had been left behind by the intruder.

'Well,' I thought, 'that performance was certainly ruined.'

I went to the dressing room ready to take on the staff of the Latchmere. But before I could several friends came round to see me, as well as a couple I didn't know.

'I thought that touch towards the end was absolutely inspired!' the man said.

'What touch?' I asked.

'The moment Lorca's ghost came up to you and bowed and then drifted back into the next world. The effect was superb! It was a truly eerie moment!'

'Yes,' I said, 'wasn't it!'

I decided not to confront the bartenders after all. I was just thankful that my 'ghost' got his timing so absolutely right. Perhaps the spirit of Federico García Lorca had guided him.

Next came an offer from Simon and Jackie Barnes, who ran the theatre in Llandovery, so *Lorca* was going to Wales. Again — so important to me — Lorca was hugely appreciated there. This led to a performance in Swansea, so the show had played all parts of Britain now except for Northern Ireland.

In 1986 came an offer to take *Lorca* to the Denmark Festival at Arhüs, where the audiences seemed either asleep or frozen stiff, as there was absolute silence for the entire performance. But talking to various individuals after the show told me that they had missed nothing. They were not only an appreciative but also a highly focused audience. What was thrilling to me was that obviously *Lorca* seemed to work so well internationally. Altogether, I was touched and surprised at the warmth and hospitality of these people living in such a forbiddingly cold climate.

A few weeks later, after a matinee performance of *Lorca* at the Mitchell Theatre in Glasgow, a man hobbled into my dressing room on crutches with a bottle of white wine under his arm.

'I've broken my bloody leg. I need to sit down. Can I offer you a glass of wine? I'm putting on a production of Lorca's *The House of Bernarda Alba* at the Lyric Theatre, Hammersmith, in a few months time. I'm bringing over Nuria Espert from Spain to direct it. Joan Plowright and Glenda Jackson are my leads. I've been looking for months for a show to go into the studio theatre to complement it. I've had dozens of scripts sent to me and none of them are right. Would you do your *Lorca* to run in tandem with *Bernarda*? Oh, I'm Peter James by the way. I run the Lyric.'

That engagement was to be the first taste of the West End for *Lorca*. It looked as though Paul Scofield and Julian Glover were right.

But Peter James did request changes.

'You can't possibly do for me the version of the show you're doing here. You must have a guitarist onstage with you, and you need a musician with a name. I would suggest Paco Peña — do you know him?'

I did indeed. Paco had recorded all my guitar accompaniments for the dancing sequences when I was putting the show together. I approached Paco, who unfortunately declined as he was booked to do a series of solo recital performances.

'But I can suggest someone who would be ideal for you,' he told me. 'He's a gypsy named Tito Herédia.'

'No thanks, Paco,' I said. 'My experience with gypsies has always been negative. I need someone I can trust.'

Paco was insistant.

'Meet Tito and you'll see I've done you a favour.'

I arranged a meeting with Tito and Peter James at the Lyric. This tall, handsome fellow from Algeciras spoke perfect English, but could he play? He strummed away superbly, but I asked him: 'Do you know Debussy's *Golliwogs' Cake Walk*?' which was a piece I wanted to use. He immediately played it — with style.

'Can you make the guitar sound like a Yankee banjo?'

Again he was spot on.

Tito turned out not only to be an asset but at the close of the sequences in which he played the audience always broke into spontaneous applause.

Peter James directed the show for me, and gave it a shape that was tight — making the cuts that I couldn't objectively see.

From the very beginning there had been problems obtaining the legal rights to do the show because *Lorca, An Evocation* was not a published Lorca work as such but my adaptation of his poems, prose, dialogue, and songs. I wanted to reveal García Lorca as the superb all-round artist that he was.

On the morning we were due to open, Peter suddenly appeared.

'We won't be opening tonight,' he announced. 'The Lorca family have refused us the right to perform the show. Legally we'd be in dead trouble if we opened without their consent. I've put call after call through to Madrid, and just now finally reached his nephew, Manuel Montesinos, who told me: "We know nothing of this man, Trader Faulkner. We need to see a copy of his playing script." I'm sorry, boys. I can't let you go on without proper legal authority.'

We sat stunned and speechless for several minutes, until Tito suddenly said, 'Hey! You spoke to him in English. Why don't I have a go at him in Spanish?'

Tito did. In the course of his conversation with Manuel he mentioned that I had received from King Juan Carlos the Spanish Order of Merit. As a fellow Andalusian speaking to him in his own tongue, Tito soon won Manuel over. This was to be the first of several occasions when Tito's spontaneous efforts absolutely saved the show.

Our first night at Hammersmith coincided with Nuria Espert's opening night of *The House of Bernarda Alba* — a glittering occasion attended by the queens of Spain, Greece and Jordan, and the Labour Leader Neil Kinnock.

As far as *Lorca* was concerned, we managed to draw in a full house, but unfortunately no press attended. They were all hobnobbing with the royalty and V.I.P.s in the main house. I knew that without reviews we couldn't survive. Then the *Guardian* sent a girl to review us who gave the show a damning notice — so awful and insulting that she could have shut us down. Her words, as I remember, were: 'If you want a good night's sleep Trader Faulkner's *Lorca* at the Lyric will certainly send you off.'

'You bitch!' I ranted. 'We may be wide of the mark in some areas, but soporific we certainly are not!'

How could I possibly counter this lethal press notice? Fortunately, my friend Diana Richey knew a top London critic, *The Evening Standard*'s Milton Shulman. Being very highly respected, he could repair the damage and save the production if he genuinely thought it merited a good review.

Diana rang Milton.

'Go and crucify Trader if he deserves it,' she told him, 'or resurrect him and his show if he's any good.'

Shulman came that very night and I caught a glimpse of him in a back row, scribbling away. It took all my powers of concentration to block him out of my awareness. From the following Monday, when his glowing review came out, the theatre was packed for the rest of our run. Being so highly respected, Shulman had obliterated the opposition. Further favourable reviews helped to create the public interest we needed to make *Lorca, An Evocation* an undeniable success.

CHAPTER TWENTY-NINE

LORCA *TRAVELS TO POLAND AND NEW YORK*

ONE EVENING, A GROUP of young Poles arrived in my dressing room and asked if I would like to take *Lorca* to Poland, all expenses paid. I enquired whether the audiences would understand it in English? That would be no problem as, apparently, Lorca's work was well enough known there. I approached Tito. Yes, he would come, as long as he could bring his wife and five-week-old baby. I made enquiries and was told it would be dangerous to tour with a baby in Soviet-dominated Poland at that time. So I went alone.

Arriving in a foreign country with no knowledge whatsoever of the language, carrying a huge suitcase that contained my entire wardrobe for the show, was a daunting experience. The Poles were extremely hospitable, but the country was still very much under the thumb of the Soviet Union so everywhere I went I sensed I was being watched.

In Wroclaw I was lucky enough to meet a Polish girl, Katazhena Swiecka (Kati), a theatre costume and set designer, who befriended me and for the rest of the tour I had a guide and protector.

The whole experience was totally bizarre. I have never felt so physically cold, yet the audiences were always warm and even vociferously enthusiastic. Gdansk was exactly like playing inside a refrigerator. How these people could sit through two hours in sub-zero temperatures and still be enthusiastic about the show says a lot about Polish stamina and intellectual curiosity.

By far the most beautiful city was Krakow, which seemed to have escaped any severe war damage. It was the cultural centre, where one felt a true sense of the artistic soul of the country. There was so much to take in, but I was working in two very different theatres and I found that doing the show alone again, without Tito's superb musical input, was a tremendous strain. Most of my time was taken up rehearsing with the technicians — a difficult job when they spoke no English. If my interpreter was absent it was a case of using sign language and hoping that they understood what I wanted. In one very small theatre in Krakow (part of the Stary Theatre complex), the sound and lighting was operated by one man from a cellar beneath the stage. There was no visual contact. This fellow, Wishek Dorota, had to work everything out by listening to my speeches on his earphones. His English was tolerable, but how he ever managed to bring our show through successfully I shall never know. When not working, he told me much about Polish resilience and their determination to survive no matter what. No wonder they survived the Second World War as they did. Their ingenuity, courage, and dedication were obviously indomitable. I left Poland having formed many warm friendships with a promise to return. And that I did with *Lorca* the following year, but this time to Torun, north-west of Warsaw.

My contacts and friends in Warsaw wanted Torun to see exactly the same *Lorca* that had been offered the year before. I met Kati in Warsaw, who kindly agreed to stage manage the show for me in Torun. The Alana Theatre was a medieval relic. On our arrival we rehearsed all day, but the rehearsal was chaotic because of the antiquated sound and lighting equipment. Fortunately, Kati mastered it, so that between us that thirteenth performance in Poland played smoothly to an enthusiastic audience. Afterwards I was invited to 'a feast' at the Alana Club, to be followed by an informal talk with the audience. I did not anticipate that this was a set-up to test where I stood politically, and to determine from what political angle I was interpreting Lorca. Very hungry — having had nothing to eat all day — Kati and I sat down to a plate of cold pig's trotters. The dessert was black (and undrinkable) coffee. When it was time to speak, I stood up and my stomach actually rumbled in a protest that could be heard even at the back of the room. It got a round of applause. I talked generally of Lorca being a Republican sympathiser in 1936,

and that along with Luis Buñuel and many other young intellectuals
at Madrid's Oxbridge at that time — the Residencia de Estudiantes —
he was rabidly anti-Fascist. His other close friend in that student trio,
on the other hand, Salvador Dalí, very much espoused the Franco
cause. Then, without thinking, I set off blithely and quite unwittingly
into a political minefield, stupidly forgetting where I was. I suddenly
found myself preaching anti-Communist dogma in a Soviet hotbed.
I remember saying that Lorca was far too idealistic and politically
naïve to suspect that the subversive spine propping up the Spanish
Republican government was the Communist Cheka, who had so
much political control in Madrid and who, like the Fascists, were
responsible for a great deal of indiscriminate repression and murder.
Typical vain actor that I am, I was in full flight, thinking my audience
was quiet because of its rapt attention. As I reached the climax of
my argument — saying what I had always said when talking about
Lorca, that he detested physical violence and that the Cheka to him
were probably as odious as the dreaded Fascists — I heard a low
murmur coming from the audience. Then I felt Kati's knuckles touch
the small of my back.

'Trader,' she whispered, 'we've got to get out of here now. You
have made a terrible mistake.'

'What mistake? Why?'

From her grim expression I suddenly realised the seriousness of
my gaffe. In desperation, I pretended to be sick and on the verge
of vomiting. Bent over in my feigned nausea, we hurried from the
hall amid a chorus of bewildered and unfriendly grumbling. Kati
insisted that we run like hell. We did. She knew which direction to
go so I blindly followed her through the pitch darkness. We must
have sprinted four hundred yards when a car suddenly swept past
and swerved across the pavement immediately in front of us. Out
leapt three men, one of whom addressed me very abruptly. I speak
no Polish, but I knew he was ordering me into the car. Gulag time,
I instantly thought. It was then that I saw true Polish spirit and
courage, a clear demonstration of the reason Poland has survived as
she has. Squaring her shoulders, Kati hurled a volley of abuse at the
three government stooges. I've seen many furious, vociferous women,

but nothing to compare with this Polish Amazon. She tore into the three hefties with such fury that they simply retreated, muttering, got into their car, and drove off.

'What on earth did you say to them?' I asked her.

'I told them that you were a British cultural representative here, and that if they tangled with you they'd be answerable to the government for their rashness. They may have known that I was there officially and realised that they could be getting out of their depth.' She smiled. 'Did you like my performance? Do I impress you?'

'Kati,' I said, 'I'm gobsmacked! You more than impress me. But I'll be even more impressed if you can get us back to the hotel in one piece!'

She did, and in the warmth of the hotel, with vodka and a large bowl of borscht, we celebrated our survival.

The time spent in Poland with Kati made me aware of what it meant to live in a Soviet-occupied country. The next day we decided to see the sights of Torun. On our way I became aware of a brown car following us — the same car we had encountered the previous evening. For the rest of our stay wherever we went they would be waiting for us, our stalkers, just a little way behind.

I left Poland after fifteen successful performances, thankful to be back on the right side of the Iron Curtain and resolved never to return again.

In March 1987, John Norton, an artist friend with a house in Fulham, invited us to perform *Lorca* in Spanish. Thus began a taxing but fascinating challenge. A number of Spaniards were invited to vet my authenticity. Tito and I did a reduced version, but it was so well received that I decided to do a full-length performance in Spanish as soon as opportunity allowed. That opportunity arose much quicker than I expected.

Later that month, Tito and I were invited to give two performances at Kean College, New Jersey. Peggy Dunne, Head of Drama, had seen *Lorca* at the Lyric and persuaded her faculty to invite me to do the show in two languages. I decided to take the plunge and do the complete two-hour version in Spanish. This turned out to be a terrifying experience. Throughout the performance I kept a copy of the script in my hand in case I 'dried'. With the faithful Tito ready to cover me musically if I did, I went through the show at a canter. I was well in my stride when the brain began to revolt. Panicking, I started throwing pages in all directions, desperately searching for the lines I needed. I must pay tribute to Tito's inventiveness. With a fearless ability to handle any crisis, he would improvise short musical comments to cover the seconds when I felt on the verge of drying — which made the audience laugh, gave me time to collect myself, and absolutely saved the day. I don't know how I ever managed to get through the performance. At its close the stage looked like the aftermath of a giant's wedding — confetti everywhere! Fortunately, the students loved it.

The next night I played *Lorca* in English, which was a doddle in comparison, and we left New Jersey with a feeling of having explored totally unknown theatrical territory.

I went back via New York to survey the possibility of giving *Lorca* a bite of the Big Apple. I remember trudging the sidewalks of Manhattan, talking to endless agents, climbing decrepit stairways to actors' studios, only to be told, 'Lorca is our preserve; don't trespass.' I certainly discovered interest in the show there, but the time wasn't right. Two years later, however, *Lorca* would bear fruit there in a most rewarding way.

Back home again there came a string of bookings, which included King's Lynn and Kidderminster. Ten days later came an offer to play *Lorca* in the Purcell Room on the South Bank. Luckily, that intimate venue was filled with a wonderfully responsive audience. One member of that audience, Marty Kaufman, had come over from New York to see the show with a view to putting it on in his theatre on 42nd Street. After the performance we were all invited to a dinner party given by my friend Beatrice Toruka Wagner, who had been married to Wagner's great grandson. Kaufman spent so much time talking to me in the dressing room that when he went to fetch his coat the cloakroom was closed and the staff had departed.

'Where's my goddamn coat?' he yelled.

Racing about the theatre, he became hysterical. Finally, a staff member was found and his coat returned to him. But he used such foul language that Liz Drown, my faithful friend — who was driving us to the dinner party — refused to have him in her car. Tito and I did our best to diffuse things. He could, after all, be a very useful contact. In the interests of the show, could she possibly be swayed to take him? Eventually, she agreed. All the way to Beatrice's house in Fulham Kaufman kept moaning on about 'my goddamn coat'. We arrived to be greeted by our elegant hostess. Beatrice managed to calm Kaufman down, but at the dinner table he started up again, offending the lady seated next to him with his gutter vocabulary.

'The theatre stole my fucking coat!' he ranted.

The woman rose from the table, outraged, after which Tito took Marty by the seat of his pants and hurled him out the front door. So *Lorca* never made it to the Marty Kaufman Theatre in New York.

But no matter. After his summary departure, Beatrice, blessed with an inspired sense of humour, hosted a sumptuous and most memorable Wagnerian dinner for the rest of us.

CHAPTER THIRTY

LORCA'S FURTHER TRAVELS

During the many years I had worked for the National Film Theatre doing earphone commentaries and translations of foreign films, I had become good friends with Faisal Kasim, who was house manager there. Early in 1989, he contacted me and told me he was interested in presenting the Lorca evocation as a West End theatre production, as he now had the funds to launch it.

Faisal wanted to increase the cast to four performers: the guitarist Tito, a female dancer, a singer, and myself. But what would be the ideal West End venue? I decided to go for the Donmar Warehouse. We approached Nica Burns, the artistic director, who agreed to take *Lorca* for a four-week run in April.

Now began several nightmare weeks of rehearsing the show with an enlarged cast. Carmela Romero, a beautiful flamenco dancer from Argentina, and the singer Rosa Calle from Seville (with a voice like a Spanish Edith Piaf) were both working in London with Tito at the Costa Dorada Restaurant, off Tottenham Court Road. Once I saw them I knew they would fit wonderfully into the show. Because of the exceptional quality of Rosa's voice I decided to bill her as *La Golondrina*: 'The Swallow'.

Rehearsals were a nightmare because the girls weren't used to the disciplined way of working in the English theatre. In spite of that, what they ultimately contributed to the show was superb.

Lorca had written some beautiful lullabies. I wanted to feature this, and so devised a touching moment when the two girls came onstage, knelt, took off their shawls and folded them up to give the impression of a baby bundle. Then they cradled their bundles and sang the lullaby together. It was a moment of quiet magic before the high drama and violence that was to follow.

As the show began to take shape I realised I needed to incorporate into the script a sequence of which I was physically afraid but nevertheless felt compelled to attempt: the acrobatic backflip, something I had been considering adding since I began the show.

On 11th August 1934, in a historic corrida held in a second-class bullring at Manzanares south of Madrid, Lorca's great friend, the matador Ignacio Sanchez Mejias, was gored in the groin by a bull called 'Granadino'. With no penicillin available in those days, the wound immediately became infected with gangrene. Two days later he was dead.

How was I to interpret this chilling account in the theatre?

There was only one way: to physically hurl myself into the air as the poor man himself had been thrown by the horns of that terrifying bull. That meant the dreaded backflip, which had been a challenge that had terrified me when I had first tried it back in 1947. I had finally learned to do it, but I had been twenty then. To introduce the move into the show I would have to again undergo a long period of hard physical training.

It took ages to get to the point where I felt I was ready, but after working for some weeks with Barry Martin, Philippa Musikant, and Claire Downie, three very talented acrobat trainers at the Hendon Sports Centre, I was determined to finally incorporate the acrobatic backflip into the show. Tito had the strength to support me in that dangerous moment when I would somersault backwards like a banana through the air — at sixty-one I knew that my body no longer had the strength it once had to gain the necessary height to land back on my feet and not on my head or my spine. I needed his touch to get me through it. I also realised that at my advanced age the only way to make the moment theatrically effective would be to use strobe lighting at the moment the bull struck me — in other words, while I was springing up and backwards. That, hopefully, would make me believable as the much younger matador.

By the first night at the Donmar I had put together a show on García Lorca that I felt would hold an English audience for two hours, plus a twenty-minute interval. The advance booking was good — for the premiere the theatre was packed. Then half an hour before the show started there was no sign of Tito. He was working in the little restaurant opposite the Costa Dorada called Sevilla Mia. I was about to announce to the audience that there would be no show when Tito suddenly arrived, fully dressed and ready to start.

'Were you worried?' he asked. 'I'm ready when you are.'

We started and all went beautifully until the moment came for the backflip. Addressing the audience as Lorca, describing Ignacio's death at Manzanares, I did two fast cartwheels before Tito, as the bull 'Granadino', tossed me over backwards onto my feet. Fortunately — thanks to Tito's technical skill — the move worked as I hoped it would, and surprised the audience, who had held their breath in silence throughout the sequence.

That first night in the West End was a complete success and we ran for four weeks to packed houses.

Later that year, the one hundred and third performance of *Lorca* was given at a theatre on Jersey, in the Channel Islands.

One morning in July, I bumped into a neighbour near my Lexham Gardens flat, Olivier's eldest son Tarquin (born of his first marriage to Jill Esmond). I hadn't seen him in quite a while.

'Daddy died this morning,' he told me.

I was stunned. When I got home I noted his death in my diary: 11th July 1989. Like the death of President Kennedy, and of my father, it's a date I shan't forget.

In 1991, at dinner with David and Caroline Hooper (Caroline being Peter and Molly Daubeny's daughter), I met an attractive young lady named Clare Ford Wille. Educated at the Frances Holland School, she graduated from Birkbeck College and began her career in 1973, lecturing at Birkbeck and Morley Colleges on European art, architecture, and sculpture.

As she was petite and cherubic, I fell for her instantly. Luckily, the attraction was mutual, though I was a good twenty years older. Apart from the physical attraction, I was fascinated by her broad general knowledge. Clare's lovemaking matched her intellect. I had been alone for several years and suddenly once again I was enjoying a veritable sensual banquet.

On 4th August 1991, an offer came to take the show to the Swan Theatre, Stratford-upon-Avon. Of course, I accepted. The stagehands there built me a superb wooden floor, their wig department serviced my wig, and altogether we were really well looked after. I had been told that Stratford on a Sunday night was death at the box office and we would play to a virtually empty house. However, on the night the Swan Theatre was completely booked out. All I remember now of the show is the video made by two friends, which is the only record of *Lorca* on film. The audience's reaction showed that we were a smash hit, and at the close people threw red roses onto the stage. We hadn't done the show since Jersey, so I was surprised that it went as well as it did. Among other friends who attended that night were Clare and her sister Vanessa.

A few weeks later, Clare came to dinner *à deux*. We feasted, we drank copiously, we philosophised. Then Clare went home — she had an early lecture the following morning. I remember walking part of the way with her. We kissed goodnight and she was gone.

Two days afterwards, I was told by a mutual friend that she was seeing someone else and intended to marry him. Clare may well have been wanting to tell me that on our last meeting, but had not been able to bring herself to do so. I was neither surprised nor hurt. With our age difference, I intuitively knew that our days together were numbered.

For years I didn't hear from her. Then, recently, she invited John Goodwin and me to a Christmas party where I met the new man in her life, Peter, with whom she seemed very happy.

In 1992, *Lorca* went to the Lincoln Centre in New York. My cousin, Valerie Nield, who was working there at the time, had organised two performances: one in the Clark Theatre (where the show was to play in Spanish), and one (in English) at the Bruno Walter Auditorium.

What we didn't find out until we started to rehearse the show was
that no technicians would be provided to do the sound. Val was
expected to do that herself, but she had no technical knowledge. In
spite of her good intentions, this spelled disaster. In the final seven
minutes of the show I had to cross-examine myself as Valdes Guzman,
the fascist who interrogated Lorca prior to his execution. This was
normally achieved through pre-recorded taping: Guzman would pose
his question on tape, then there would be a space of silence wherein I
would answer live onstage as Lorca. This was nerve-racking enough
under normal conditions, but how could poor non-technical Val
cope with such a complicated sound sequence? I decided to cut the
interrogation sequence altogether, to ad-lib a few lines and segue to
the final moment of the show. Having played *Lorca* by then over
an eight-year period, I was confident that I could simply narrate the
important bits of what had happened in the cut sequences.

In the course of the show, however, as the dreaded moment
approached Tito suddenly rose from his chair and walked off the
stage. I thought, 'You copper-bottomed bastard! The rat is deserting
the ship as he thinks I shall sink without trace!' I should have known
better. Seconds before I was about to plunge into the unknown with
the interrogation scene, Tito re-appeared with a script in his hand, sat
down and proceeded to interrogate me as Valdes Guzman — with a
perfect Spanish accent. His acting brilliance nearly left me speechless.
Tito did not seem to be reading Guzman's lines. As my interrogator,
he simply appeared to be referring to notes he'd previously made to
frame his questions. It was an inspired piece of improvisation.

It was in New York that I realised the limitations of my work
on *Lorca*. I knew it would never go much further or ever reach its
potential unless I had professional management behind me. Also, by
now I was beginning to wonder how much longer this still-mobile bag
of incipient decrepitude could induce audiences to believe I was the
handsome García Lorca in his thirties. Luckily, so far neither critics
nor anyone I spoke to had ever commented on the age discrepancy.

In the spring of 1994, I was invited to present *Lorca, An Evocation* for
the Spanish Arts Festival at the Sadler's Wells Lilian Baylis Theatre.

Richard Fletcher, whom I had met when he presented the flamenco dancer Mariano Torres at the Barbican, offered to be my producer and handle the business side. For what would turn out to be the last *Lorca* production, I was very lucky to have a superb team. An Australian, Liana Vargas, would replace Carmela Romero in the second week. Both dancers were excellent, but Liana was professional — unlike Carmela who by then was suffering from a 'star' complex. With Liana, the irreplaceable Tito, a new soprano (Luz Elena Caicedo), and the rock-solid Clare Scherer to handle our lighting, we had a tight, very buoyant ship. I would love to mention by name all of the artists and technicians who made the ten years' work on *Lorca* such a stimulating challenge, but sadly it's simply not possible. But I must mention our general manager for that show, Michael Jackson. His discipline, both front and backstage, was draconian.

For instance: The Spanish Ambassador attended our last night. At the interval, apparently, he was making his way backstage to greet me when Michael intercepted him and his retinue at the backstage pass door.

'Where do you think you're going?' asked Michael.

'To see Señor Faulkner.'

'You must go back to your seat. No one is allowed backstage during the performance.'

'With respect, I am the Spanish Ambassador.'

'I don't care if you're King Juan Carlos,' said Michael. 'No one visits the cast till the end of the show. Then it will be my pleasure to take you to him.'

I had met the Spanish Ambassador on several occasions, and knew that he had a great sense of humour — which was just as well on this occasion.

Sadly, that was the last performance we ever gave of *Lorca, An Evocation.*

So many people have asked, 'Why didn't you try *Lorca* in Australia?'

I certainly did my best to tempt producers and entrepreneurs, and came close to raising sufficient interest. One person of note who seriously considered backing the show was Rupert Murdoch, who agreed to see me, kept me waiting for twenty minutes and then apologised profusely for doing so. In spite of his reputation, I found him kind and considerate back in 1986. He listened to my presentation, then said he might well be interested in financing me and would consider the pros and cons. I left feeling elated that at last *Lorca* might be seen by audiences in my home country. Unfortunately, it was not to be. A fortnight later I received a phone call from his office to say that they had considered the project carefully, but had decided that financially it wouldn't yield them enough to justify the investment.

That was the outcome of every attempt I made to bring *Lorca* to Australia. There was just too much expense involved in transporting the show and its cast so far away.

I am convinced, however, that if I had been given the opportunity to do so, I could have sold the show in Australia. Sadly, I've come to believe it simply wasn't meant to be seen there.

CHAPTER THIRTY-ONE

THE FINAL CHALLENGE

THROUGHOUT THE TEN YEARS' intermittent work on *Lorca* I was still writing and broadcasting for the BBC, working as an actor for television and keeping my hand in as a journalist.

In 1996, I was asked to direct a production of Lorca's *Blood Wedding* with the students of ALRA, the Academy of Live and Recorded Arts, in South London. This was a challenge I relished. What I had seen of English translations of Lorca were often accomplished plays in English, but the true Spanish atmosphere — what the Spanish call *el ambiente* — was always absent.

As it happened, I was given a free hand in choosing the translation I would use (my own). My cast, however, were picked for me. Fortunately, when we began rehearsals I found myself surrounded with the most eager group of youngsters that it has ever been my luck to work with. Everyone seemed fascinated by the challenge of Lorca, who even for the finest professional English cast is an extremely difficult playwright to interpret. As we rehearsed the play simply came together magically. The actors worked instinctively; they were neither frightened of the play, inhibited by it, nor lacking in self-confidence. The Andalusian music, the dance and movement I choreographed for them, all helped them to feel their way into Lorca's world with total freedom. Certainly everyone involved with the production thoroughly enjoyed it.

I learnt so much from working with that young cast, and the warm response from the audiences told me once again that Lorca's plays really can work for the English.

As I left on the last night, the student cast rushed up with a gift — two green wine glasses and a matching jug — a gesture of thanks that I still cherish.

Not long after my directing experience at ALRA, I noticed in the press that the Poet Laureate Ted Hughes had just paid tribute to García Lorca by doing his own translation of *Blood Wedding*. I wrote to him to congratulate him on his successful effort, and shortly afterwards he rang me and we enjoyed an interesting conversation. Some years before I had taken part in a BBC Radio recording and broadcast of one of his plays, '*Dogs*', and during a break in the recording had enjoyed a spirited conversation with him and others in the cast about bullfighting. Ted loathed the very idea of the terrible game but agreed with me that in the fatal contest between matador and bull is the very essence of pure, intense theatre. He did admit, however, to a certain English hypocritical squeamishness — avowing that, like the rest of his countrymen, he wouldn't be at all happy to witness the slaughter of the animals we rely on for our daily food.

I found Hughes to be an amiable, very modest man, with a dark sense of humour. I also remember him joking that a symbiosis between a Yorkshireman and a Spaniard from Granada was as potentially viable as one between an Australian Aboriginal and a family member of the House of Windsor.

I remember little else of our telephone conversation — except that he spoke of the solitude he needed as a poet. For my part, I mentioned how difficult it was as an actor to maintain one's creative integrity in such a collaborative art.

I closed our conversation by telling him how much I wished that he had seen my *Lorca, An Evocation*, as his assessment of the piece would have meant so much to me. In retrospect, it is one of my greatest regrets that I never followed up his suggestion for us to meet for a drink sometime.

Back in the 80s, I met a young American actor/writer named Bill Roberts, another Hispanophile who was to become a firm friend over the next decades.

Sometime in the mid 90s, knowing my interest in things Spanish and having seen *Lorca, An Evocation*, Bill invited me to Spain to stay with him at a friend's primitive *cortijo* (farmhouse) perched on a rocky promontory near the village of La Mamola, on the coast south of Granada. I was fascinated to be in this area because Lorca's *Blood Wedding* had been based on an incident that had occurred not far from there — near the village of Nijar, in the Province of Almería — back in 1928. Having played The Moon in Peter Hall's 1954 production of the play, and subsequently translated and directed it, I was intrigued to see where the event had happened.

Lorca took the theme of his play from a newspaper report of this incident — the story of a young girl who had been promised by her father in marriage, but who had a secret lover (her cousin). The night before the wedding, they eloped. However, the bridegroom's brother saw them slip away from the farmhouse, followed them and, in a confrontation, shot the cousin dead. (In Lorca's play, it is the fiancé who follows them and kills the lover.)

During my stay with Bill he drove me down to Nijar and together we visited the large, abandoned farmhouse in the desolate fields outside the town and wandered through its rooms — some of which were open to the sky. Knowing the events that had taken place in these rooms, and in the environs — and that they had been the insrpiration for Lorca's finest play — gave us both unmistakeable ripples of frisson. The entire visit was an emotional and unforgettable experience.

The last few days of my stay with Bill in southern Spain took us on an overnight visit to my old friends Ian and Carol Gibson, who lived in the village of Restabal, just off the road north to Granada from the coast. Ian is the acknowledged biographer of Lorca, and at that time he was working on a new biography of Lorca's friend Salvador Dalí. As I write, this book has long since been published, and Ian is currently in the final stages of writing his biography of the film director Luis Buñuel, the third member of the trilogy of young friends at the students' residence in Madrid who were later to achieve such prominence in their professions.

As usual, Ian was full of fascinating information about all three, and we spent a memorable evening eating, carousing, and conversing on their terrace overlooking the foothills of the Sierra Nevada under a sky ablaze with stars. The following day I was able to guide Bill as he drove our hired car along the narrow roads some way to the north to the tiny village of Viznar, near to which very early on the morning of 19th August, 1936, Federico García Lorca — along with a group of others — had been taken out and shot. Though the exact spot where it happened is unknown, a small park has been created to honour his memory, and that of the others who died there during the war.

As a result of my directing experience at ALRA, I realised that I was perfectly capable of directing a production of a Lorca play — even with professionals, should such an opportunity arise. I found working as a director very stimulating, but one important element was missing: the threat of danger that I craved that would focus my energies and give me the thrill of successfully overcoming it. Whatever it was had to be something within the range of my capabilities (by this time I was in my late sixties and sensed that my powers were declining).

For quite some time I couldn't think what to do that would offer me a formidable enough challenge. I considered creating a one-man show on the life of Samuel Pepys, but my research soon convinced me that his story would send an audience to sleep. What about Nelson, then? Or Byron? Or Ataturk? The latter fascinated me, but I knew he was quite beyond my reach because of the research that would be required.

The answer to my quest came from a close friend of many years, John Goodwin, who offered a very simple answer to my dilemma.

'Why not do a one-man show on your own life, recounting the humorous and ridiculous experiences of your past? I'm sure you'll be able to give the audience plenty to laugh about, and humour must be the principal ingredient.'

It seemed a good idea. So I began work, setting down on paper all the most interesting characters and experiences that I could remember from my life — all of which would then have to be reduced to a theatrical form to hold an audience's interest. As I laboured away, my close friend Liz Drown took home my scribbled pages and typed them up. Finally she handed over the pages to John Goodwin, who carted it off to edit down into a playable format of eighty minutes. This he did brilliantly, and finally — after a year's work — we had a completed performance script.

John Goodwin, with his fifty years' experience as head of publicity at the RSC and then at the National Theatre, suggested several brilliant ideas for my project. One of these was to illustrate each story/episode with a large blown-up photograph of the principal character featured therein. Most of the people included in my stories were certainly well-known — Peter Finch, John Gielgud, Vivien Leigh, Laurence Olivier, Dorothy Tutin, and Picasso. John's idea was that I should come onstage with a large portfolio of the photos mounted on stiff cardboard, which I would take out and place in a row back to front across the rear wall of the stage. As I mentioned each character in the course of the performance, I would turn the portrait round to face the audience.

The key to John's direction always was simplicity.

'Trader,' he told me, 'there's no need for any décor other than the pictures. But you can have a stool if you like.'

There would be only five music cues, during one of which I would dance sixty seconds of very fast flamenco. John's ideas were inspired, and the show could never have happened without him.

We'd given the title a great deal of thought, and John had suggested *Chance'd be a Fine Thing*, but we both felt that that was too tame. Then Rex Berry, an old friend of John's and a theatrical enterpreneur, said: 'The obvious title is *Losing My Marbles*, the name of one of your show's first episodes.'

We all agreed to his suggestion.

The British Ballet Organisation in Barnes again granted me the use of their studio as a rehearsal space. Then, with the commencement of rehearsals came the greatest challenge of all.

The second episode in the show, *Finchie's Trick*, involved my telling the story of how Peter Finch had persuaded me as a young man to learn from his old circus colleague Ted Ardini how to do the acrobatic backflip. At the time I began rehearsing the new piece, I had been working steadily for thirteen years to master again that suicidal leap, and could at that point only manage to do it with somebody helping to throw me — just as Tito had done in *Lorca*. In the Lorca show the backflip had been executed in a flashing strobe light as I flipped myself backwards and upside down in mid-air. But I knew Tito well, and trusted that I could count on him always to throw me safely back onto my feet, and this he never failed to do.

In the new show — telling the story of my early backflip experience, and how I had finally mastered it — I felt that I had no choice but to perform that daunting manoeuvre just as I had done it in my youth: unassisted and in full light. When I mentioned this idea to John Goodwin, he liked it, and urged me to press my acrobatic coaches at Hendon to help me master the unassisted backflip once and for all. It was a challenge that terrified me, because I knew that in my late sixties I was well past it in terms of strength and suppleness. But pride and vanity won the day, so back I went to the gym month after month — right up until the year 2000, into my seventies — struggling to master an acrobatic trick that had for years been impossible to do alone, and in the attempt of which on two occasions I had nearly broken my neck.

Meanwhile, I was fortunately earning good money writing articles for the *Telegraph*, *Independent*, and *Guardian*, which paid the bills.

For several months, John and I worked to put the one-man show together, having agreed to give it its first tryout in the BBO's studio on 19th July 1998. Week after week I worked with my Hendon coaches, but I was getting no closer to mastering the backflip. At my age, in physical decline and without the necessary elasticity, I found it quite impossible to get sufficient lift-off so as to fly backwards through the air and come cleanly down onto the palms of my hands, and then to spring upwards onto my feet.

As the date for the tryout performance crept closer, I began to be quite concerned. Finally Barry Martin, my acrobatic coach, came up with a brilliant compromise solution. When in the course of the show I described to the audience doing the scary backflip as a young man, Barry, who was a plant, would shout from the house:

'Let's see you do one now, Trade!'

To this I would reply, 'At seventy-one? Are you kidding?'

Barry would then return, 'Come on, Trader, have a go. I'll spot you.'

He would come onstage and stand behind me, placing his hand in the small of my back. I would then begin the move — and lose my nerve. Feigning exasperation, Barry would slap me on the back and say, 'Come on, Trader, you can do it! Just go for it!'

Summoning all my strength, I would then fling myself into the air — and over I would go!

On the day of the tryout performance, the British Ballet Organisation's studio was packed with friends and supporters. John Travis, the BBO's administrator, had provided drinks and food for one hundred and sixty people. When the time came I simply went for it, and when I achieved the backflip — with Barry's help — the applause was deafening. It brought the house down to see this decrepit ancient dare to attempt a piece of certain acrobatic suicide and manage to survive. Thanks to Barry, and to that very warm audience, *Marbles* got away to a literally flying start.

I should also like to say that, in all my fifty-five years as an actor, never have I felt such an immediate rapport with an audience as I did the instant I came down cleanly that afternoon on the soles of my feet. I felt they had identified with my fear. For a second after I landed we were one. Of course, their response was relief, and a strong burst of applause was its reaction. In all of the performances I was to give of *Marbles* that enthusiastic applause always gave me confidence that I could hold my audience from that point on to the end of the show, as the backflip came very soon after curtain up.

After the successful tryout of the piece, Rex Berry contacted his ex-wife Penny Horner, who ran the Jermyn Street Theatre, and *Marbles* was booked into that venue for Sunday 31st January 1999. But for some reason Rex reneged on his earlier agreement to take on the publicity. No reason was given. I then went to Penny, who said, 'Right, get your stuff from the printers and I'll do your publicity myself.' Penny was as good as her word and saved the day.

Marbles got off to an unsteady start but made a profit — thanks to John Goodwin and Penny Horner. We were booked for several more performances. I'm sure the improbability of this old man daring to attempt a backflip helped to draw in audiences who are always looking for a cheap thrill.

I had it in mind to tour the show and to try for Australia, but before anything could be done on either front an offer arrived inviting us to do *Marbles* at the Canal Café Theatre in Little Venice, near Warwick Avenue tube station. However, the booking seemed somehow to be jinxed from the beginning, and serious problems arose when a disagreement with John Goodwin led to a temporary rupture in our friendship.

From the start, the understanding between us had always been that this whole production was to be a combined effort, and that included the writing. But in the last days John was absolutely adamant that nothing he had written should be altered. It was a question of the language for me: I wasn't prepared to use English idiomatic expressions in place of Australian ones, or to say lines that I felt were wrong for me. Johnnie had penned lines that only a 'Pom' would say, and that were completely unsuited in an Aussie anecdote. This problem had arisen from time to time during rehearsals and had led to tensions between us that we both worked to suppress.

To be fair, John probably felt that if he didn't object to piecemeal alterations the script changes would go on *ad infinitum* during the run, ultimately destroying his carefully structured language — which, I must say, was for the most part a joy to play.

The conflict finally came to a head at the Canal Café Theatre when John suddenly walked out just as *Marbles* was about to open.

The buzz of a good audience, mostly friends, was audible from out front. I was just about to get my call for curtain up when John and I had some silly disagreement and John, seemingly at the end of his tether (and probably with good reason), said, 'You're impossible to work with, so just get on with it!' and walked out.

I went on and did the show without him being present, and fortunately the audience liked it. In spite of John's angry departure, all seemed promising.

The following night I arrived early and sat quietly in my dressing room waiting to begin. At 8.05 p.m. the stage manager came to see me.

'Trader, there isn't a soul in the theatre. Sorry mate, you'd better go home. Ring me tomorrow and tell me what you plan to do.'

I can't remember when I've ever felt so humiliated — or so ready to give a close friend a mega kick in the arse. During rehearsals, whenever I had brought up the question of publicity, John Goodwin (the retired professional publicist) had shied away from any involvement with it, saying simply, 'I'm out of all that now.' And now John had gone and I was on my own. I knew that if there was to be an audience for the next night's performance it was bloody well up to me to find one. *And* I had to get at least one critic in if this show wasn't to sink without trace.

When I got home that evening I rang my good friend Elena Sherstnyova, a Muscovite with an iron will, and explained my predicament.

'Nevermind, Trader,' she told me. 'We'll get you an audience. Meet me at Warwick Avenue station tomorrow and we'll take it from there.'

Now, I had some days before scribbled a few lines that would serve as a promotional sheet for the show and had five hundred copies printed. Elena collected them from the printers, and when we met at Warwick Avenue the next day she handed me the two printed bundles.

'We'll simply thrust them at everybody,' she told me, grabbing a fistful of pages. 'Come on, Trader. Show me what you can do!'

Off we went together down the street, pushing copies of the printout into the hands of any willing takers. Meanwhile, I had also phoned two other friends who lived in the area — the author and journalist Alix Kirsta and the lawyer John Zieger — and arranged for them to meet us to help distribute the leaflets.

The last-minute efforts of my three close friends saved the day, and that night I played to a reasonably-sized house. We were even able to entice two reviewers to the next performance, and the encouraging notices that appeared as a result in the *Evening Standard* and *The Stage* saved my bacon.

After the audience's warm applause, I asked them to pass the word of my show around. Their word-of-mouth efforts — together with the glowing press notices — brought a succession of ever-increasing audience numbers, thereby ensuring that *Marbles* would carry on to the end of its run.

Sitting here now typing this, I realise what a bizarre and desperate measure that was, handing out flyers to strangers on the street for a show about an actor they probably had never even heard of. What we were trying to do was tantamount to trying to flog Chekhov on Manly beach. Never before or since have I had to sing for my supper on the streets in such a manner. A wonderful experience to be forced on you at seventy-one years of age? I don't think!

Nonetheless, in spite of my relative success at the Canal Café, with John Goodwin gone and no financial backing I sensed that the end for *Marbles* was fast approaching. (As it happened, it was not only the play but my entire acting career that was soon to be suddenly and brutally brought to a close.)

Looking back now, I think I felt intuitively that *Marbles* was never meant to have a long run, though the material subsequently did very well as a publication. This was thanks to John Goodwin, and to my close friend Mike Shaw, one of the seniors at Curtis Brown literary agency, who used his good graces to find a publisher — James Hogan of Oberon Books, also now a close friend. (I should point out that John Goodwin and I soon thereafter resurrected our friendship, and have remained close ever since.)

After the Canal Café, I was invited to give a performance of *Marbles* at the Southwold Theatre in Suffolk by Jill Freud, the wife of my friend and employer in the early flamenco days, Clement Freud. Though I didn't know it, this was to be my last performance in the theatre.

On the Friday following that engagement, I had attended my regular practice session with my acrobatic trainers in Hendon — still determined to master the backflip — and managed to do thirty-five perfect ones one after the other with Barry Martin's support. My confidence restored, I was certain that I would surely be able to master the totally unassisted backflip within the month. This was important to me because I was determined to do that acrobatic move in *Marbles* one day in Sydney — the city in which I had successfully executed it for the first time fifty years earlier in front of Ted Ardini and Peter Finch.

Two days later, on Sunday, I went out for a big lunch with my close friends Peter and Christine Sullivan. I was well away with the champagne, and I remember we drank our last toasts to my finally mastering the backflip. I went home afterwards feeling merry and exceedingly tired and fell into a deep sleep. I awoke the following morning determined to write a letter of thanks to my generous hosts. But when I put pen to paper, I found I was writing gobbledegook. I tried to read what I had written, but the letters started to move around and around and loop the loop.

Alarmed, I went straight to the doctor, who turned out to be not my own GP, with whom I had always felt a complete rapport, but his partner in the practice. I'll never forget his words.

'There's nothing wrong, Mr Faulkner. You just need to take it easy. Go home and rest. Come back again on Wednesday.'

As per his instructions, I went home and rested.

That evening, I gave a dinner party for eight people. As I rose to pour the wine, my hand simply flew into the air. I remember a stream of wine spattering the white wall and several pictures — as well as several of my guests.

A friend, Pamela Taylor, immediately said, 'Trader, I'm going to drive you to the Chelsea and Westminster Hospital.'

'No, I feel fine,' I insisted. 'Really. We'll go tomorrow.'

The following afternoon, convinced that there was something radically wrong with me, Pamela drove me to the hospital, determined that the doctors should examine me closely.

Ironically, I actually felt fine. The doctors asked how old I was; I told them seventy-two.

'You look sixty!' they said. 'Go home and take it easy.'

Just to be safe, they had booked me in for a scan two days later. On that day, I was placed on my back in a cylinder that rattled for half an hour. I came out of it feeling like a sheet that had been spun round in an electric drier — absolutely limp. The man who had supervised my half-hour nightmare was from Sri Lanka.

'Goh hom,' he gabbled in broken English when we had finished. 'You had a mild strok. Just goh hom.'

'But I feel peculiar,' I told him, which was the truth.

'Goh hom,' he repeated.

I started to get angry.

'Look, I need to see somebody. I feel a little giddy.'

'Mild strok,' came the reply. 'Goh hom!'

Deciding that he might be right and that it was probably just a slight dizzy turn, I headed for home.

On my way back to Lexham Gardens, I felt exactly like someone suffering from the effects of drink. Then, in my slightly dizzy state, I collided with a telegraph pole and began to feel very queasy. I managed to get home and staggered up my ninety-eight stairs, where I crashed onto the bed. Luckily, half an hour later, Pamela, who had copies of my front door keys, came in.

'Trader,' she said, after taking one look at me, 'what's your doctor's number?'

I went to get the number and, suddenly overcome by dizziness, fell down into the narrow space between my bed and the wall and couldn't move. Pamela rang the surgery — this time managing to speak to my own doctor.

'Get him to the hospital now!' he told her. 'He's obviously had a stroke!'

I remember little of what happened next except that two men arrived at my flat with a bosun's chair. They then tried to manhandle me down those ninety-eight stairs, but it was a farce. I ended up walking down under my own steam. Then I was taken to the Chelsea and Westminster Hospital and put straight to bed, where I immediately fell sound asleep.

When I awoke the next morning, the world had gone dark. I was partially blind, and in that state I have remained to this day.

When a stroke hits, its effect — like a venomous snakebite — can be lethal. It must be diagnosed and treated immediately in order to avoid the worst consequences. Even though my stroke had not been diagnosed immediately — or even diagnosed correctly when I was finally seen by specialists — I managed to get off lightly on 'the stroke slope'. The doctors told me later that it was probably my years of regular physical exercise — dancing flamenco and practising acrobatics — that had spared me a more serious disability and left me so lightly affected.

One mustn't complain. Isn't any such handicap — just like the backflip — simply another life challenge that must be faced and overcome?

Not long after my stroke my good friend Jean Nysen, from the Queenscliff days back in the 30s, arrived to stay for a time in my flat. Seeing my predicament, she gave me exercises to help me to read again, and to get my body back in shape. Seeing the value of this, I started a rigid daily routine of physical exercises every morning, followed by plunging myself into a cold bath — a hard discipline, but the only way I believed I would get my mind and body back on course. The results have been far from wonderful, but at least I seem to have helped prevent a more rapid physical and mental decline and can still lead a more or less normal life — with help.

CHAPTER THIRTY-TWO

RECENT YEARS, BITS AND PIECES - AND SUMMING UP

AT SEVENTY-SIX I certainly wasn't expecting to fall in love again, and with a much younger woman. But that is exactly what happened, and in so doing I found a companion with whom I could share the joys of laughter and good conversation, as well as travel — visiting with her my old haunts in Madrid and Sydney, and renewing old friendships.

Kathryn Park, a therapist, had been given my address through mutual friends. She came to live with me on and off for two years and we simply harmonised. I had two bicycles. She rode one and I rode the other. Though I was still in the early stages of recovering from my stroke, she made me completely forget about it, and together we enjoyed life and each other's company. Like me, she had converted to Catholicism and was staunchly independent, with delightful parents in Melton Mowbray who kindly invited me to spend Christmas with them in 2003 and 2004. Kathryn finished one job in a nursing home near Croydon, was then taken on as a therapist at Kingston and moved out of my flat after a year to live in her own space nearby at Shepherds Bush.

A couple of our shared adventures remain particularly vivid to me.

I had worked with Ronnie Barker at the Oxford Playhouse back in 1954 and had seen him occasionally over the years while working in BBC Radio at Broadcasting House. In 2003, I got a call from Ronnie inviting Kathryn and I to a party at his home near Oxford. He told me he had invited many of his old workmates, among them Maggie Smith. The last time I had seen Maggie was many years before, when

I had taken a very young Sasha backstage after a performance of *Peter Pan* to meet her. I remember Maggie's warm welcome, and the way she spoke to Sasha as an adult and equal, and not as a child — thereby giving Sasha another unforgettable memory, for which I was enormously grateful.

As it happened Maggie was ill and didn't attend Ronnie's event, but Kathryn and I did, and I was able to sit alone for a while with Ronnie, talking of old times and of the plays we'd done together. Those shared days had been filled with moments of such rich hilarity. But Ronnie was not only a brilliant comedian, he also had a magnificent brain. I remember that afternoon meeting his lovely wife Joy, and the rest of his family.

As we shook hands to say *au revoir* I sensed a deep sadness within Ronnie. Was he ill then? If so, he never showed it.

When I later heard that he had died I thought of the wonderful Latin military phrase of farewell I'd learned at school: '*Vale*, old friend and colleague.'

(Three years later I lost another dear friend when, listening to BBC Radio 4, I heard that Paul Scofield had died of leukaemia. I had first seen Paul playing the identical twins Hugo and Frederick in Peter Brook's matchless production of Jean Anouilh's *Ring Round the Moon* back in 1950, and I had never seen an actor with such style and charisma. In 1952, I had the great good fortune to watch him at close quarters onstage playing Don Pedro in Gielgud's production of *Much Ado About Nothing* at the Phoenix Theatre. He and his wife Joy became close friends of mine, but I have never known a more private man. As described earlier, Paul's enthusiastic support for *Lorca* was invaluable to me. Ours was a friendship without demands. I last saw him when I rang and asked the pair of them to dinner and we spent a quiet but memorable evening catching up with each other's news. I saw many of Paul's performances, and for me he was one of the greatest and most unforgettable actors of the twentieth century. I count myself lucky and truly honoured to have known him.)

Who would turn down a Royal invitation? In 2003, through Roz Fuller at the Royal Theatrical Fund, I received an invitation for two to attend a Royal Garden Party at Buckingham Palace. Of course, I took Kathryn. When she appeared that day all in white, with a broad-brimmed soft white hat to match, she personified to me the English woman of good taste, modesty, and elegance. Being able to accompany her filled me with pride, though — somewhat shorter than Kathryn — I must have looked like an elderly, doting uncle.

We entered the palace through that almost hidden gate at Hyde Park Corner among about seven hundred other guests and were let loose in a large area of the garden. In an enclosure set apart from the hoi polloi, Her Majesty circulated with diplomats, high-ranking officers of the armed forces, and other dignitaries. Jamie Craithorne (Lord Lieutenant of Yorkshire and an old friend of mine from my days living with Julia and Seymour Fortescue), a young naval Lieutenant Commander RN, and several gorgeously attired ladies joined our circle — an affable crowd of people who mixed and chatted in true British style. The whole afternoon was superbly organised, very easy and informal.

Afternoon tea was served in several long, rectangular tents: a pot of tea for each party, sandwiches, scones, and cakes for all guests. Very impressively, the whole enterprise ticked along like a Swiss clock.

At the end of the afternoon, we left by entering the palace from the garden. There was a flight of stairs to our right. How I longed to walk up to that first landing. But I thought better of it and out we emerged into the crowds through those familiar front gates accompanied by the young Lieutenant Commander.

One evening in 2004, due for dinner at seven, Kathryn arrived at six with my front door keys (she had always had a set), handed them to me on the verge of tears, and was gone. Apparently, she had found someone else — hopefully someone nearer her own age who would be kind to her, and with her capacity for loving and giving. Devastated as I was, I could certainly understand her position — a woman in her forties who had become too close to a friend in his late seventies. I have missed her companionship terribly ever since, but every woman needs her own space and has a right to make her own life decisions. That was a hard but necessary lesson for me, to love with open hands and to let go when the time comes and there is no alternative — just as had been the case with Bobo.

In my last years, I have come to realise the importance of valuing the positive rather than dwelling on the negative — as the old adage advises, leave the thorns and pick the roses instead.

Thrown once again back on my own resources, I had to work at something that would provide a challenge and keep the depression at bay.

Richard Ingrams, one of the founders of *Private Eye* and an old friend of mine from the houseboat days, was editing his monthly magazine, *The Oldie*. I sent him an article on my relationship with Dorothy Tutin and her affair with Laurence Olivier. Richard published it in the May 2004 edition. Since then, Richard has published around a dozen different articles I've sent him on the various personalities I've worked with and known over the years.

The Oldie has kept my hand in as a writer, and given me the confidence to write this autobiography.

I have spoken before of my friend, the American Bill Roberts, with whom I shared the memorable trip to Spain in the mid-nineties. As it happens, this versatile fellow also holds a pilot's licence and owns a light aircraft. Not long after Kathryn said her goodbyes and disappeared from my life, he invited me to come along for a flight — in an effort, I trust, to pick up my spirits. I had not been in a light aircraft since 1938, when as a schoolboy I had flown in a DeHaviland twin-engined plane from Sydney airport to Barrenjoey Lighthouse at Palm Beach and back.

Bill drove me to Biggin Hill Aerodrome, redolent for me of all those fighter pilots of the 1940s, where his plane was hangared. I immediately thought of my late friend, Wing Commander Paul Richey DFC, who had been a Spitfire pilot stationed there.

I squeezed myself into the right hand seat of the two-seater and was belted up by Bill, given a headset, and off we flew, heading south towards Kent. For the next three hours we flew east along the coast, over the cliffs of Dover, then westward towards Portsmouth and around the Isle of Wight, where we witnessed an unforgettable fiery red sunset that silhouetted the island against a dazzling luminous sky.

When we arrived at his home later Bill's better half, Carolanne, welcomed us both with large glasses of red wine and served us a beautifully cooked roast dinner. After a relaxed evening, Bill put me on the train back to London and I went to bed thrilled and immensely grateful for the whole adventure — which had, indeed, helped to uplift my spirits.

Over the last seven years, and owing to the fact that my sight and memory are fast deteriorating due to the stroke, I have been able to get this book written only due to the help and support of the organisation Sixty Plus, with girls like Haya Al-Yawar sent to work with me, as she did for six long years.

In the summer of 2006, I received a phone call from Ben Long at Sixty Plus.

'The politician Ed Miliband would like to talk to you about your autobiography, and the work Haya is doing on it with you.'

I thought why not, if it will help the people at Sixty Plus who have done so much for me.

After climbing my ninety-eight steps to the flat Mr Miliband looked winded. I asked him if he would like a cup of tea.

'No time,' he said.

He wanted to know why and how the working relationship between the young Iraqi Haya and an ancient Australian was so successful. I remember answering him in two words: intuition and rhythm. As a working team we harmonised completely, mentally.

He wanted to know how Haya and I planned our method of working together. (Obviously Mr Miliband had done his homework.) Was she typing as I dictated? And would she make suggestions on where to 'simplify'? Was her input constructive? Was her perspective as a woman useful? I remember a great deal of laughter when I told him that quite often Haya would tactfully point out that my raunchy Aussie metaphors might offend some readers.

Through his questioning, Ed Miliband made me aware of what a superb sense of humour my Iraqi literary muse had — and has still.

He left soon after. I have no idea what resulted from this interview, whether Labour gave Sixty Plus any financial support. Suffice it to say that what is now Kensington and Chelsea Age Concern UK's unswerving support has been of inestimable value to me — with or without government assistance. May it long serve the same purpose for others in similar circumstances.

One last salient memory.

Not long before my stroke, I was lucky enough to meet the writer Frances Partridge, widow of Ralph Partridge (who had been formerly married to the artist Dora Carrington) and the last surviving member of the famous 'Bloomsbury Set' that included Virginia and Leonard Woolf, Vanessa Bell, Lytton Strachey, and E.M. Forster. We met very near the end of her life and I was able to call several times at her West Halkin Street apartment in Belgravia for tea and conversation, and was continually fascinated by her crisp mind and sharp memory and the many stories of her life and friends. I used also, on occasion, to take her for walks in that tiny strip of park between Cadogan Place and Sloane Street, near her home. She was a fund of amazing recollections of the Set, and of the London and Spain of her early years (she had been born in 1900, and had been a close friend of the hispanophile Englishman Gerald Brenan). She was amused by, and charmingly dismissive of, my conversion to 'Roman Catholicism', as she liked to call it, and the influence of the Jesuits on my early life. 'Intelligent but naïve' was her probable assessment of me. Still, the hours I was privileged to spend with Frances were some of my most stimulating and educative. She had known so many of the literary giants whose books I had read and revered as a young man.

Then one day in February 2004 the phone rang. It was Elisabeth, the Portuguese carer who looked after her.

'Frances is dying. Please, Trader, can you find a priest and come quickly?'

Some years before, after celebrating Mass with Kathryn Park at the Holy Redeemer Church in Chelsea, I was walking away when Kathryn called me back to meet the priest who had said Mass, Monsignor John Arnold, with whom afterwards we were to form a firm friendship. Instinct had made me warm to this brilliant man of deep humility and kindness, who later became a Bishop.

I rang Westminster Cathedral and asked John if he'd give Frances a blessing.

'But isn't she one of the Bloomsbury Set and a rabid atheist?'

I pleaded with him.

'All right. I'll say a few words, give her a blessing, and try to comfort her. Where does she live?'

We were to meet in Ebury Street, only yards from my first ever lodgings in London in 1950. As I waited, suddenly I perceived a figure in black running towards me.

'Where is she?' asked this prince of priests, wrenching off his starched dog collar. 'Come on, let's run!'

Arriving at Frances's flat, John went straight through into the bedroom and sat down beside the dying lady. As he leant over the bed to comfort her, I left the room.

Moments later, he came out.

'I hope I've given her peace of mind.'

Elisabeth gave us tea, and then we left. All I can remember is her parting words: 'Thank you so much, Monsignor Arnold. Nobody could have been more surprised than I was when Mrs Partridge suddenly asked for a blessing!'

In 2007 I turned eighty, an event that was celebrated in a very special manner.

Back in 1950 John Gielgud had given all the male members of *The Lady's Not for Burning* company — apart from myself — the novelty gift of a fur-lined jockstrap. When I took over from Richard Burton in Fry's play in New York, Richard had given me his, which I then wore for many winters for its warmth and fur-lined comfort — until it moulted and had to be thrown away.

Burton's bequest to me had become a lifelong joke among my friends. He had left me a good luck note for my first performance saying that the developing quality of my acting over the years might yet one day earn me my own diamond-studded, fur-lined jockstrap, far more original as an achievement award than an Oscar.

Having repeatedly heard that story, at my well-attended eightieth birthday party my two close, very creative friends Silvia Napier and Radcliffe McCormick presented me with a specially-made, fur-lined and diamante-studded jockstrap/codpiece, which I ceremoniously wore that evening, and which I long to have occasion to wear again. The gift was a raunchy masterpiece, but I'm reluctant to offend. Where does one draw the line between rich Rabelaisian humour and simple bad taste?

A few nights ago I saw for the first time a film that featured my father, *Far Paradise*, made in 1928. It was so ironic, watching Dad silently miming his role on the screen (unlike his contemporary Aussies, he had a beautiful English speaking voice). I was riveted by his performance as Howard Lawton, advising his twenty-five-year-old son against becoming involved with a woman whose own father was on the wrong side of the law. It is easy to imagine the emotions I felt seeing Dad again, suddenly alive on the screen and at his most paternal. As I watched, I felt I was viewing a scene that might have been played out in reality between us, had he lived to see me as a mature young man. His performance was beautifully underplayed, and it hurt me deeply to watch him portray a father-son relationship that we were never allowed to share.

The impact on me of my father's death just after my seventh birthday has been momentous throughout my life. He seemed at the time, and for many years after, the chief influence, guide, and protector in my life, of which I was suddenly and brutally deprived. I had to find my own strength, and that has been a lifelong challenge. Now I'm almost thankful that I was left alone to fight my own battles and to learn how to survive with a sense of humour and a sense of purpose. I managed thanks to my mother, on whom I became dependent in my formative years, and against whose loving possessiveness I fought for the rest of her life. Still, no matter how bad things have been at times over the years, I've always managed to balance luck and disaster, laughter and tears. In spite of everything, I've always come out on top because of the precious gift of good health.

But my greatest gift has been my daughter, Sasha, who has made for herself a good life — thanks to Bobo, who was a superb mother. Our divorce was due to errors on both sides, but Sasha has done very well — completing a degree in America and earning her living at first in New York and then in San Francisco, where she married and is now the mother of three happy children, Quinn, Eliza, and Jamie. Jim Boyle, Sasha's husband, is a gift of a man — a wonderful father and a hard worker in the banking world — and I couldn't be happier about their union. It troubles me that I'm so far away from my daughter and my grandchildren, but luckily they are a united, happy family, and what more than that could I wish for them? Over the years there was, of course, a lot of heartache for me in being denied regular contact with my growing daughter, and there are scars that will never fade. But none of that really matters. What matters now are Jim, Sasha, and my grandchildren, and what they will give to one another and to life, and what life will give to them. Out of the pain and solitude has come for me a wealth of treasured memories and an acute awareness of the value of every living moment.

I have also been very lucky in my work. Looking back now to 1946, when I began as an actor — learning mostly by doing it as there was no established drama academy in Sydney at that time — I was extremely lucky to work in theatre and radio in tandem, and to begin in film and television some five years later. Of all the work I've done, I'm the least able to judge it. Suffice it to say, my profession certainly has taught me about people and about myself. I believe that what determines the quality of the work is its truth, and I have always strived towards that. Only others can tell me to what degree I have succeeded.

I don't believe I have ever realised anything like my real potential as an actor, because I lacked the singleness of mind of a Laurence Olivier, with his unswerving dedication to reach the very top of his profession. Instead I broke from the mainstream and used my study of flamenco to take me into areas no other actor had explored. With my dancing, and the ability to speak Spanish — as well as to translate and direct — I was able to bring the inspirational poetry and prose of Federico García Lorca to theatre audiences on two continents, an endeavour for which over the years I have received enormous support and some degree of recognition.

What, after all, could have been a more unlikely scenario than an Australian actor, transplanted to London, who ends up being decorated by the King of Spain?

What priceless wealth I possess — a wonderful daughter, grandchildren, reasonable health, and the unaccountable riches of numerous and incomparable friends. Looking back now over my eighty-five years, I have been the luckiest of men. Being raised in Sydney in the 1930s and 40s was to draw a winning ticket in life's lottery, and I came of age just three weeks too late to be called up for the Second World War. All in all, it's been a good ride, even if there have been a few bumps at the road's end. I still possess good health, faithful friends, and an insatiable appetite for laughter. And truly what a gift life is, if only one has the capacity — and the determination — to go for it.

ACKNOWLEDGEMENTS

WHEN A FRIEND FIRST suggested that I should write my autobiography, I thought, 'What would be the point? Who would be interested in an ageing actor from the past, long forgotten by the people who had once seen him act or dance?'

But my friend wouldn't back down.

'It's the people you have known, the crazy things you've done and the adventures you've been lucky enough to have experienced, that would interest the reading public. At seventy-five you're half blind but still *compos mentis*, and whether or not you publish the book the effort of doing it will stave off the lunacy of indolence and the depression it breeds. Don't forget, your life reflects eight decades of a world going through momentous changes.'

So I thought, 'What have I to lose?' — never dreaming how the priceless gift of friendship would yield an army of willing assistants who would help to make *Inside Trader* a reality in spite of my handicap.

To begin with, my stroke resulted in Eileen Gunn, Chief Executive of the Royal Literary Fund, offering me as an established writer financial backing to ensure my survival, thereby giving me the peace of mind to write this autobiography. Without that support, for which I am eternally indebted, the book could never have been written.

In 2004, Francesca Raphaely at Sixty Plus sent me a girl called Gery — alas! her surname has been shredded — the first of many who came regularly to help me type out and correct my autobiographical material. Over the years, this organisation has sent me a string of girls who have helped to make my autobiography a readable reality — the chief of whom was Haya Al-Yawar, who is now a close friend.

Ben Long succeeded Francesca Raphaely, and since then his belief in the book has sent me the following 'angels' to help it along: Kelly Fung, Olivia Hillgarth, Emily Reid, Deborah Korstad, Chandana

Shakar, Saria Safford, Emily Warren, Zoë Welden, Sara Edwards, Jessie Lethaby, Rachel Rayoudhi, Olivia Curtis Westerberg, and Lamorna Ash. These girls — all fast typists — read aloud and corrected the work that I had laboriously typed with one finger.

Then there were my wonderful friends who typed as I dictated or read, and who helped me to correct the mass of memories and misdemeanours that have formed the pattern of my life: Katrina Ashe, Alix Kirster, Maja Banenberg, Vivien Whitney, Philip and Christine Meagher, Libby Escolme Schmidt, Nick and Nina Daubeny, Jean Nysen, Joan Davis, Thérèse Clancy, and Diana Richey.

Mention must also be made of my dear and faithful friend Annie Waters of the RNIB, whose hilarious fortnightly visits helped me to organise my chaotic life and correspondence.

My deepest thanks go to Bill Roberts, who has worked tirelessly over the past eighteen months to edit the manuscript, and to suggest improvements and point out omissions, and to his partner Carolanne Lyme for correcting my appalling punctuation (and for letting me know when my crude Aussie humour has gone too far).

Finally, I offer my thanks to Kenneth Ross, whose editorial suggestions and advice was most appreciated.

I am eternally grateful for the encouraging response of Tina Betts at Andrew Mann literary agency, who read an early draft of the script and, though she felt she herself could not help it into print, urged me to keep looking for a publisher. And to my old friend Jane Conway-Gordon, the agent who did agree to take it on, and who found a most enthusiastic publisher in Naim Attallah at Quartet. To all three of them I owe an immense debt of gratitude for their belief in the book and for its initial appearance in print.

Finally, to all those friends and well-wishers — too many to include in this comprehensive list — who have given me encouragement over the years, and reminded me of incidents from the past that I had forgotten.

To you all, ever, thanks.

Y un abrazo MUY fuerte …

El Trade, June 2012

CHRONOLOGY

Year	Role	Production	Venue
1946	Irving Pincus	*The Front Page*	Independent Theatre, Sydney Director: Jerome Levy
	A Messenger	*Hamlet*	Independent Theatre, Sydney Director: Doris Fitton
	Fabian	*Twelfth Night*	Independent Theatre, Sydney / tour Director: Doris Fitton
1947	Kenneth Lake	*French Without Tears*	Mercury Theatre Club, Sydney Director: Peter Finch
1948	Read	*The Guinea Pig*	Minerva Theatre, Sydney Director: John Sykes
	Larry Tallent	*They Walk Alone*	Independent Theatre, Sydney Director: Harvey Adams
	Richard	*Ah, Wilderness!*	Minerva Theatre, Sydney Director: Fifi Banvard
	Michael Brown	*O, Mistress Mine*	Majestic Theatre, Adelaide Director: Richard Parry
	Claudio	*The Merry Wives of Windsor*	Independent Theatre, Sydney Director: John Alden
1949	Sebastian	*Twelfth Night*	Theatre Royal, Sydney Director: Mayne Lynton
	Doctor Caius	*The Merry Wives of Windsor*	Independent Theatre, Sydney Director: John Alden
	Ted Hapgood	*Fly Away Peter*	Comedy Theatre, Melbourne / Theatre Royal, Sydney Director: J H Roberts
	The Kangaroo	*The Enchanted Tree*	Theatre Royal, Sydney Director: Heather Gell

1950	Richard (Son of Nobody)	*The Lady's Not for Burning*	Royale Theatre, New York, and tour Director: John Gielgud
1950	Richard (Son of Nobody)	*The Lady's Not for Burning*	Royale Theatre, New York, and tour Director: John Gielgud
1952	Messenger	*Much Ado About Nothing*	Phoenix Theatre, London Director: John Gielgud
	Juvenile Lead	*Traveller's Joy*	Bermuda Festival Director: Hal Burton
	Hugo / Fred	*Ring Round the Moon*	Bermuda Festival Director: Hal Burton
	Downing	*The Family Reunion*	Bermuda Festival Director: Hal Burton
	Cis Farringdon	*The Magistrate*	Bermuda Festival Director: Hal Burton
	The Juvenile	*Miranda*	Bermuda Festival Director: Hal Burton
	Frankie	*A Killer Walks (original title: Gathering Storm)*	Film Director: Richard Vernon, under the name Ronald Drake
	Ted Smith	*Mr Denning Drives North*	Film Director: Anthony Kimmins
	Mr Barry	*Twenty-four Hours in a Woman's Life*	Film Director: Victor Saville
	Will Breague	*A Cradle of Willow*	Television film
1953	Bob Kemp	*Tomorrow is a Secret*	UK Tour Director: Wallace Douglas
	Earl of Westmoreland (covered John Neville as Henry V and played two performances at the Old Vic, London)	*King Henry V*	Bristol Old Vic Theatre / The Schauspielhaus, Zurich / Old Vic Theatre, London Director: Dennis Carey
	Romeo	*Romeo and Juliet*	Guildford Theatre Director: Roger Winton

Pied Piper	*The Pied Piper*	Adelphi Theatre, London Director: Heather Gell
Stephen Firbanks	*A Party for Christmas*	Connaught Theatre, Worthing Director: Jack Williams
Ruprecht	*The Broken Jug*	Television film Director: Hal Burton

1954	Petrovsky	*Anastasia*	Connaught Theatre, Worthing Director: Jack Williams
	Bill Braham	*Silver and Gold*	Connaught Theatre, Worthing Director: Jack Williams
	Michael Pritchard	*The Orchard Walls*	Connaught Theatre, Worthing Director: Jack Williams
	Second Young Man / The Moon / Third Cutter	*Blood Wedding*	Arts Theatre, London Director: Peter Hall
	Kit Ames	*Third Person*	Playhouse Theatre, Oxford / Cambridge Arts Theatre Director: Peter Hall
	Ong Chi Seng	*The Letter*	Playhouse Theatre, Oxford / Cambridge Arts Theatre Director: Hugh Goldie
	Mortimer Brewster	*Arsenic and Old Lace*	PlayhouseTheatre, Oxford / Cambridge Arts Theatre Director: Hugh Goldie
	Nicholson	*Youth At The Helm*	Playhouse Theatre, Oxford Director: Hubert Griffiths
	Aussie Oakes	*The Amazing Dr Clitterhouse*	Playhouse Theatre, Oxford Director: Hubert Griffiths
	Morgan Evans	*The Corn is Green*	Playhouse Theatre, Oxford Director: Lionel Harris
	Jim	*Saloon Bar*	Playhouse Theatre, Oxford Director: Gabriel Toyne
	Duke of Northumberland	*Richard III*	Film Director: Laurence Olivier
	Lory	*The Relapse or Virtue in Danger*	Television film

1955	Sebastian	*Twelfth Night*	Shakespeare Memorial Theatre, Stratford-upon-Avon Director: John Gielgud
	Courtier	*All's Well That Ends Well*	Shakespeare Memorial Theatre, Stratford-upon-Avon Director: Noel Willman
	Malcolm	*Macbeth*	Shakespeare Memorial Theatre, Stratford-upon-Avon Director: Glen Byam Shaw
	Fenton	*Merry Wives of Windsor*	Shakespeare Memorial Theatre, Stratford-upon-Avon Director: Glen Byam Shaw
	Third Goth	*Titus Andronicus*	Shakespeare Memorial Theatre, Stratford-upon-Avon Director: Peter Brook
	Fenton	*Merry Wives of Windsor*	Television film
	David Garrick	*Away in a Manger*	Television film
1956	Colonel	*March of Scotland Yard*	Television series
1956/ 1957	Gaston	*The Waltz of the Toreadors*	Criterion Theatre, London Director: Peter Hall
	Angelo	*Crime on Goat Island*	BBC Radio 3rd Programme (live)
	Director/ Performer	*Flamenco Group*	Royal Court Theatre Club
	Jack Warren	*Web*	Television series
1958	Guest Appearance	*Antonio's Flamenco*	Coliseum Theatre, London
	Flamenco Dancer	*A Question of Adultery*	Film Director: Don Chaffey
	Cecil Vyse	*A Room With A View*	Television play
1959	David Stevenson	*The Rain It Raineth*	Hampstead Theatre Club Director: James Roose Evans

	Max	*The House in Paris*	Television film Director: Julian Aymes
	Maurice	*Promenade*	Television (Peter Shaffer's play) Director: Julian Aymes
1960	Goronwy Price	*Off a Duck's Back*	Theatre Royal, Windsor / Lyceum Theatre, Edinburgh Director: Joan Riley
	Blondinet	*Don't Listen,* *Ladies*	Television play Director: James Ormerod
	Emile d'Angelier	*The House of Lies*	Television play Director: Cyril Coke
	Anatol	*The Lotus Eaters*	Pembroke Theatre, Croydon Directors: Derek Martinus and Clement Scott-Gilbert
	Guy de Seiberd	*The Four Just Men*	Television series Director: Don Chaffey
	Seyton	*Macbeth*	Hallmark Hall of Fame (TV) Director: George Schaefer
	Stephen Hatton	*Our House*	Television series Director: Ernest Maxin
1961	Don Pedro	*Queen After Death*	Oxford Playhouse / Cambridge Arts Theatre / Golders Green Hippodrome / Streatham Hill Theatre Director: Minos Volanakis
	Guest	*Antonio's Flamenco*	Royalty Theatre, London Appearance
1962	Philip the Mercenary	*The Spanish Sword*	Film Director: Ernest Morris
	Jacques Tissot	*The Avengers*	Television series Director: Jonathon Alwyn
1962– **1963**	King Philip of France / Prince John / Elias / Jacques / Marcel	*Richard the* *Lionheart*	Television series Director: Ernest Morris
	Adrien Josset	*Maigret*	Television series
1963	Dave Newton	*The Bay of St Michel*	Film Director: John Ainsworth

1964	Gino Carella	*Where Angels Fear to Tread*	Theatre Royal, Windsor Director: Mary Kerridge
1965	Paco the Pirate	*A High Wind in Jamaica*	Film Director: Alexander Mackendrick
	Chris Aldrich	*The Murder Game*	Film Director: Sidney Salkow
1967	Ned Holloway	*Breakdown*	Lyric Theatre, Belfast Director: Sam Macready
	Tommy Backhouse	*Sword of Honour*	Television mini-series Director: Donald McWhinnie
1968	Beralf	*The Imaginary Invalid*	Forum Theatre, Billingham / Vaudeville Theatre, London Director: Janos Nyiri
1969	Translator and Director	*The Cudgelled Cuckold*	Lyric Theatre, Belfast / Gate Theatre, Dublin
	Director	*Black Comedy*	Lyric Theatre, Belfast / Gate Theatre, Dublin
1970	Elbow	*Measure for Measure*	Royal Shakespeare Company, Stratford-upon-Avon Director: John Barton
	Sir William Catesby	*Richard III*	Royal Shakespeare Company, Stratford-upon-Avon Director: Terry Hands
	Bernardo / A Sailor	*Hamlet*	Royal Shakespeare Company, Stratford-upon-Avon Director: Trevor Nunn
	Antonio, Father to Proteus	*The Two Gentlemen of Verona*	Royal Shakespeare Company, Stratford-upon-Avon Director: Robin Phillips
	Deviser, writer, director	*An Evening with Federico Garcia Lorca*	The Roundhouse, Stratford-upon-Avon (for the Royal Shakespeare Company)
	Solomon	*The Price*	Northcott Theatre, Exeter and tour Director: Roger Williams
1971	Pasquale	*The Aspern Papers*	Theatre Royal, Windsor Director: Joan Riley

	Gerry Watchett	*Eyeless In Gaza*	Television series
1973	Arthur Du Cross	*The Edwardians*	Television mini-series
	Father Dixon	*Love Story*	Television series
1975	Sir Peter Malory	*Churchill's People*	Television series
	Gerry Jackson	*Public Eye*	Television series
1976	Bernard Kersal	*The Constant Wife*	English Theatre of Vienna Director: Jeremy Young
1977	Gregory Black	*The Late Edwina Black*	Ashcroft Theatre, Croydon Director: Peter Clapham
	Cmdr Hanley	*Warship*	Television series
1983	Deviser, writer, performer	*Lorca, An Evocation*	First performance The British Ballet Organisation, Barnes
1984	Deviser, writer, performer	*Lorca, An Evocation*	The Polish Club, London, and tour
	Customs Officer	*Duty Free*	Television series
1985	Deviser, writer, performer	*Lorca, An Evocation*	Tour
1986	Deviser, writer, performer	*Lorca, An Evocation*	Tour followed by run at The Lyric Theatre, Hammersmith and tour of Poland
	Matilda	*Call Me Mister*	Television series
1987	Deviser, writer, performer	*Lorca, An Evocation*	Alana Theatre Torun (Poland), Kean College University (New Jersey), Cheltenham Festival, Kidderminster, Purcell Room, London
1988	Deviser, writer, performer	*Lorca, An Evocation*	Taliesen Theatre, University College, Swansea, Greenwich Theatre

	Lucas	*The Return Of Sherlock Holmes*	Television series
1989	Deviser, writer, performer	*Lorca, An Evocation*	Donmar Theatre, London, Arts Centre, Jersey
	Manolette	*About Face*	Television series
1991	Deviser, writer, performer	*Lorca, An Evocation*	Swan Theatre, Stratford-upon-Avon
1992	Deviser, writer, performer	*Lorca, An Evocation*	Lincoln Center, New York, Tour of UK
1994	Deviser, writer, performer	*Lorca, An Evocation*	Lilian Baylis Theatre, Sadlers Wells, London
1996	Bishop de Quadra	*In Suspicious Circumstances*	Television series
1999	Deviser, writer, performer	*Losing My Marbles*	British Ballet Organisation, Barnes Jermyn Street Theatre, London Canal Cafe Theatre, London Southwold Summer Theatre

INDEX